THREE SOUTH SEAS NOVELS

by J. Allan Dunn

Off-Trail Publications
Elkhorn, California

Front cover artwork from
Short Stories, May 10, 1936

THREE SOUTH SEAS NOVELS
By J. Allan Dunn
Copyright © 2012, Off-Trail Publications
ISBN: 978-1-935031-20-8

OFF-TRAIL PUBLICATIONS
Elkhorn, California

Printed in the United States of America
First printing: December 2012

CONTENTS

— — § — —

THREE SOUTH SEAS NOVELS
by J. Allan Dunn

Dunn and the South Seas
By John Locke

J. ALLAN DUNN WAS A PROLIFIC PULP AUTHOR from 1914 until his death in 1941. He early on established himself as an adventure specialist, and is remembered as such, although the growing public appetite for westerns forced him to gradually shift focus. By the end of the career he was almost exclusively a western writer.

Dunn's adventure stories reflect a wide variety of exotic locales, spread across the Pacific Ocean, to the Far East. Only a small quantity take place in Africa, South America, or the bulk of Asia. His signature setting was the South Seas. About a third of his adventure stories have explicit South Seas settings, with a number of others taking place in Australia, New Zealand, or New Guinea. Eighteen of his South Seas stories were novels, many published complete in a single pulp, a few serialized; another twenty-six were novelettes, and thirty-four were short stories.

An Englishman, Dunn's westerns were inspired by his extensive travels in the western United States between his arrival in 1893 and his relocation to New England in 1914. The South Seas stories came out of a five-year interregnum, spanning 1899 to 1904, that he spent in Honolulu, when he learned to enjoy tropical island and boating life.

His professional writing career started with some humorous South Seas stories he sold to the *Saturday Evening Post*. The first, "Tamatau of Totulu," appeared in the January 3, 1914 issue. Dunn had appeared in print numerous times before this during his two decades in America, in newspapers and magazines, but "Tamatau" marks the beginning of his dedicated commercial fiction-writing career. The *Post* was a prestigious start, but the burgeoning pulp fiction magazines proved to be his true calling. When *Adventure* published his novelette of New Zealand, "The Greenstone Mask,"* in the October 1914 issue, the career that Dunn is remembered for began in earnest, and *Adventure* became one of his best markets. His second story for the magazine was a boxing short, which he then followed up with a South Seas story, his first novel—and our first selection here—*The Island of the Dead*, printed in full in the April 1915 issue as the lead story. He then turned to a short-lived series of western shorts featuring cowboy Sandy Bourke. His second novel, also set in the South Seas, and included here, was *The Gold Lust* (November 1915). In late 1915, Dunn started splitting his prodigious output with Street & Smith's *People's*, which published his third novel, *Boru*, a dog story, as a serial starting in December 1915. Dunn's fourth novel, the South Seas saga, *Beyond the Rim*, appeared in the July

* "The Greenstone Mask" is reprinted in *The Best of Adventure: Volume 2: 1913-1914* (Black Dog Books, 2012).

1916 *Adventure. Beyond the Rim* is a sequel, of sorts, to *The Gold Lust*, since it returns the same villain.

This, therefore, is a collection of Dunn's first three South Seas novels. All are smoothly-plotted, with plenty of high adventure, exotic locations, perilous predicaments, motley collections of characters, understated violence and heavy romance—very much the epitome of pulp adventure of the era. As evidence of Dunn's rapidly growing popularity, *Adventure's* 1917 poll, which ranked readers' favorite stories of 1916, placed *Beyond the Rim* in third, of all the many stories published that year.

In 2011, we reprinted Dunn's *The Peril of the Pacific*, a 1916 *People's* serial. An Asian invasion story which plays out primarily through various California locations, it's littered with references to Dunn's time out west, the places, many of which would be obscure to easterners, that he was personally acquainted with, and his experiences. Likewise, these three South Seas novels contain many references to his years in Honolulu. These early works are key connections to his pre-writer years. As his career progressed, and the number of his authored stories rose into triple digits, his past melted away. His stories were either based on research, or took on the generic quality of most middle-of-the-road pulp work. It's easy to understand the transition. His memories faded. It became harder for him to be fresh when the work turned into routine. And when rates plummeted in the Depression, he was less motivated to do quality work.

The most obvious connections are to Honolulu itself. Hawaii was in the midst of momentous changes when Dunn lived there. On February 15, 1898, the U.S.S. *Maine* was sunk in Havana Harbor, Cuba, leading to the Spanish-American War, with a short-term front against Spain in Cuba and a long-term front in the Philippines, the start of an era of American expansionism. The Philippines conflict elevated the importance of Hawaii, which became a way station for American forces. Accordingly, on July 7, 1898, the Republic of Hawaii was annexed as a United Sates territory, which it remained until statehood in 1959. Dunn arrived less than a year after the annexation into an environment seething with change, political, financial and cultural, a place of many opportunities and inducements. Even though Dunn doesn't date these three South Seas novels, he tips off the time-frame in references like this one from *The Gold Lust*: "their tactics had led to many a broad hint from the Territorial police that things could no longer be run as they used to be under the monarchy." Dunn's Hawaii, then, is the Hawaii of his memory, and not the Hawaii of 1915-16.

All three novels use the port city as a point of departure to the South Seas. References to hotels, waterfront bars, etc., are probably based on actual places although that can be difficult to crosscheck today.

There are references to places other than Hawaii. *Island of the Dead* mentions the Berkeley hills. Few outside of his close friends would have known it, but there was a house in the Berkeley hills, near the University of California campus, where Dunn holed up in late 1913 to produce the stories that launched his fiction career. *The Gold Lust* contains references to San Francisco, where he lived for about a decade, and other parts of California; references to Manhattan—Battery Park, Washington Square, Union Square, and the Mews—date from Dunn's first landing after he left California in 1914; the Berkshire Hills refers to the place where Dunn settled after it became clear he was going to make a sizeable income from writing. The Berkshires is an attractive area in Massachusetts where a number of famous writers settled, including Edith Wharton, Henry James, Longfellow, and another author of South Seas stories, Herman Melville. Earthquakes figure into the plot of *Beyond the Rim*. Dunn was in San Francisco during the Great Earthquake of 1906 and remembered its terrors well.

All three novels make numerous references to newspapers and newsmen. Dunn had worked in the business sporadically, and thought of himself as a newsman. He was like many other pulp writers who started out in the world of newsprint and deadlines. Honolulu's *Commercial Advertiser*, referred to in *The Gold Lust*, is a paper Dunn worked for. Among Dunn's many talents was the ability to draw, which occasionally turned into illustration work for newspapers; in the 1890s, the printing of photographs was prohibitively expensive, thus newspapers were illustrated with line-art, and staffed with artists. In *The Gold Lust*, when Dunn refers to Winton's "birthgift of the ability to draw and design," he's no doubt engaging in a bit of autobiography. Of note, *Island of the Dead* features Dunn's illustrations, an unusual contribution for a writer. These are not to be found in the latter two novels, which suggests that Dunn's workload inhibited such luxuries.

Speaking of talents, Dunn had a love of acting, and indulged himself whenever possible. He is one the few pulp authors—perhaps the only pulp author—who sprinkled his stories with references to Shakespeare. Literary allusions were foreign to the pulps, and would not have been valued by most readers. When Dunn writes in *Island of the Dead*, "Like Orlando, he felt the spirit of his fathers strong within him," he's referring to a role in *As You Like It* that he had played on stage.

Since these novels are all stories of modern-day buccaneers (who behave a lot like their olden-day counterparts), Dunn's references to Robert Louis Stevenson, the Scottish author of *Treasure Island* and South Seas voyager, have a greater relevance. The chorus of "Dead Man's Chest," which originates from *Treasure Island*, are recited, and enjoyed, by good and bad alike in *The Gold Lust*. In *Beyond the Rim*, the Chinese scoundrel Tuan Yuck cites from Stevenson's poem "Requiem": "Under the wide and starry sky / Dig the grave and let me lie." We have further reason to assume that Dunn was an admirer of Stevenson. In his early days in Hawaii, he lived in a little house on the outskirts of Honolulu that he claimed had been occupied by the great author.

A common theme in these novels, which may have been inspired by *Treasure Island*, is the use of rare valuables to motivate the characters. Whether pearls or gold, the quest for treasure sets the stories in motion, and fuels the conflicts between warring parties. Dunn would fall back on this device throughout his career. Sometimes it was diamonds, rubies or jade, but if the setting was the South Seas, pearls came up repeatedly. It clearly was a subject he knew something about. In the May 1916 *Camp-Fire—Adventure's* letters feature—Dunn provides a 700-word mini-treatise on pearl diving in response to a query from the editor.

The theme in these three novels that comes through loudest is Dunn's love of the sea and sailing. He was an experienced yachtsman, gained from his five years in Honolulu. His employment of nautical ideas and terminology is rich, detailed and thoroughly convincing. He seems to understand all the many variables involved in making a successful voyage, from navigation and weather, to fuel and supplies, to life aboard the boat, to the functions of each individual sail.

In conclusion, we might say that Dunn, the person, inhabits these stories to the extent that they reflect his knowledge and interests, his experiences and memories, and his dreams. We see facets of him in his fictional characters. In Chalmers, for example, the protagonist of *Beyond the Rim*, we find a newspaperman, whose favorite recreation is yachting, who loves and respects women, whose father told him to do things rather than write about others. Perhaps Dunn is also reflected in Chalmers' nemesis, Sayers, "a newspaper man of shady character who covered sports for the *Times*," whose articles "had all the distinctions of an educated man," whose "love of music coupled to an intimate knowledge of the art . . . had seen him detailed as critic to whatever musical affairs were given." How much any of this was based on Dunn's past acquaintances, how much was Dunn himself, how much a fantasy of himself, or even a joke about himself, who can say?

THREE SOUTH SEAS NOVELS

April
1915
Vol. IX
No. VI

The Island of the Dead
By J. Allan Dunn

I

LEVUKA LOUIS'

"THE PRETTIEST GIRL I'VE SEEN SINCE I WAS ON THE COAST," declared Captain Adams of the schooner *Lady Mine*. "She made me homesick. We passed her this afternoon early in a canoe with four paddlers doing their hardest. They was inside the reef or I'd have asked her if I could give her a lift. White she was, and plumb worried, driving on her paddlemen. Course we couldn't get nigh her account of the reef, but I got a good look at her through the glasses.

"I sent her a hail, but she didn't notice it, just kept on wigging to Kanakas. Never saw her before, but there's something stirring or my brain needs calking. Not many white girls this side of Suva. Mystery to me. Twice over. Who she is and what she was after."

There was a crowd at Levuka Louis', on Viti Levu in the Fijis. The "Snuggery" of the little Frenchman—trader, storekeeper, dabbler in a hundred enterprises—was filled with the captains, mates and supercargoes of the little fleet of trading-vessels that, the season being practically over, rode to their moorings in the tiny harbor. Louis knew every white man and

all the natives of importance in eastern Melanesia, and his place was the
clearing-house of the gossip of the southwestern Pacific.

It had been man-talk all evening. The price of trade—so many yards of
cloth, sticks of tobacco, tins of salmon or bottles of squareface, for so much
copra, hawk-bill turtle or *bêche-de-mer*; so much paid for pearl-concessions,
so much for plantation-land or trading-stations. It was the "gamming" of
men engaged in a common traffic, meeting after the interval of a year.

Saxons and Celts they were, with hardly an exception. Americans, British,
Germans, Scandinavians; rovers all, with the glamour of the South Seas in
their cosmos, loving their life in the belt that lies between Capricorn and
Cancer as much for the adventure it held as for the profits.

As the evening wore on, the games of pinochle and coon-can broke up
and the players joined the main group, listening to the tales of risks about the
reef-haunted, current-swept atolls and islands.

"The bottom's out of everything," growled Captain Adams of the *Lady
Mine*, a hard-bitten Yankee skipper of the old school. "The Kanakas want a
fathom of dress-goods where they used to be glad of a yard. A master-trader
ain't got no more show these days than a broken-legged jack-rabbit in a dog-
house.

"Maybe you don't go far enough afield, Captain," said Dick Boone,
youngest of all the skippers present but not the least successful. "There's
plenty of lagoons off the beaten track that hold good shell and haven't been
scratched yet. That's the way dad made his pile, and it's the way I hope to
make mine."

"When you're as old as I am, son," rejoined Adams, "you'll stick to
known cruising grounds. Your dad was lucky. 'Boone's Luck'! Mebbe it'll
hold for you. Ef it don't, you'll be changin' the name of your schooner from
the *Roamer* to the *Homer*, an' playin' safe. Wait till you've been scarred up
with *ngari-ngari* an' get the chills an' fever reg'lar every three weeks."

Boone laughed. Young as he was, just over his quarter-century mark, he
was not without experience as chief officer for his father in the *Roamer*, now
his own command. Over six feet, lean, dark naturally, and tanned by sun and
wind almost to the color of a native, the languor of the tropics passed him by
unscathed. Deep of chest, quick and supple as a cat, he was the equal of any
man in the room for strength and endurance. The heritage of ancestors from
America's early frontier days was an asset within him for courage, quick
thinking and dexterity.

"I'm going to make my pile and quit before that happens," he said. "Dad's
back there in the Berkeley hills, across the bay from San Francisco, taking
life easy and trying to grow roses; and I'm going to follow his example by a
short cut, if I can."

"Thet sounds fine, son, but I'll bet thet every time your dad sees a ship goin' out the Gate, topsails ready to break out, nosin' through to blue water behind the tug, he wishes he was aft in command, south'ard bound. Wait till you get the tropics workin' in your blood after a few years more of it. Ain't thet right, Louis?"

"*Vraiment*," assented Louis, cool and dapper in linen trousers and silk shirt. "*Moi*, v'en I come here, I mean soon to return to *La Belle France*, to the Valley of Loire. Now"—he shrugged his voluble shoulders—"I know I should not sleep not to hear the sound of the reef, the vind in the palms, the perfume of the flowers."

"An' the gen'ral excitement, eh Louis?"

There was a universal laugh. The ventures of Louis, often hidden, were known or guessed at by most of them. Some had shared in the profits that usually accrued. Established in British territory, doing business with Germans, his national enemies, Louis himself was, on the surface, placidly international. All present were his friends. His enemies generally gave him a wide berth.

"Ye're richt, Adams, aboot the condeetion o' affairs," said Menzies of the schooner *Cutty Sark*. "The corporations ha' cornered the pick o' the trade. And something's happened to the turtle. The beasties ha' clean left the seas. I believe it's the wireless they've got snappin' an' crackin' everywhere wi' their high-powered stations, fillin' the void wi' voltage an' *amperes* an' the like, roamin' wild. I'm readin' that not a millionth part o' the eelectreecity they discharge is used i' the message, but goes careerin' here an' yon, like the wind. 'Tis dangerous, mind ye, an' no canny."

"They tell me," said Adams, "that the Von der Mehden Company has put wireless at all their stations an' installed it in their ships. It's a cold day when ye'll find me clutterin' up my top-hamper with a mess of wires. An' their supercargoes," he went on indignantly. "By thunder, they *ain't* supercargoes. They're a half-breed between drummers an' counter-jumpers. Carryin' sample strips of muslin an' percale in leather cases, showin' fashion-plates an' takin' measures. Skippers turned engineers an' wearin' overalls over messy little putterin' engines. Shucks!"

There was no laugh this time, and the skipper glowered about him for the cause.

"You hav' not met Mr. Von der Mehden?" asked Louis. "I shall introduce heem."

A young man who had been sitting, quietly listening, came forward with extended hand.

"I am glad to meet you, Captain," he said with but the slightest trace of accent. "I haf often heard of you. I am Otto Von der Mehden, und I haf come from Hamburg to make the round of our stations and learn something of the trade at first hand. A vacation trip, with business on the side."

Captain Adams growled a somewhat embarrassed greeting, but shook hands cordially. The representative of the big trading-corporation was round-faced, flaxen-haired, inclined to general chubbiness. Blue eyes twinkled behind glasses, the scar of a college duel puckered his left cheek.

"The wireless has its uses, Captain," he said. "It was wireless that brought help to one of our schooners wrecked on the Guadalancar Coast, was it not?"

"You're right there," said Boone. "I was at Port Adams when they got the call. I went with the *Berthe*. The canoes were 'round the schooner thick as mosquitoes. They couldn't have held them off much longer. And power's a mighty good thing, too, in a calm or making a lagoon at nightfall on the ebb."

There was a murmur of assent from the crowd.

"We may use big gasoline launches altogether by and by, Captain," said the young German. "You saw the new double-ender in the harbor, Captain Adams. I brought her down with me on the *Louise*. Makes fourteen knots. We're going to try her out in the Fiji trade. Modern methods, Captain. Save time, cover distance, increase profits."

Adams grunted.

"If you will, I should like to drink everybody's health now."

There was a general shifting of chairs and loin-clad native boys busied themselves with the orders. Another suddenly projected himself through the open door.

"*Akami* comealong harbor," he said excitedly.

"The *Acme!*" said Boone. "Captain Thurlowe. I thought I heard a chain go a little while ago."

"Coming in after dark?" queried Von der Mehden.

"He can smell his way into any lagoon in Melanesia," said Boone. "Besides, there are the range lights. Here he is."

A big man blocked out the stars that shone through the door with his massive shoulders. A breath of colder climes seemed to creep in with him through the tropic night. Bearded like a Viking, his pale blue eyes shone with the true deep-sea gleam that comes from long gazing at wide horizons. Once a whaler, he had followed the game when profits took it northward, but he had given up the chilly Arctic for his first love and was now a freetrader of the southern archipelagoes, bound by the spell of the tropics, forsaking Polaris for the Southern Cross.

Nodding greetings to the crowd and introduced to Von der Mehden, he drained his glass with a good-will "Luck!"

"What's the news from the Tongas, Thurlowe?" asked Boone.

Thurlowe's face grew grave.

"There's news of Huddy," he said.

Exclamations broke from his listeners.

"I put into Viletu for repairs," said Thurlowe. "We ran into some driftage, broke the martingale and whisker-booms and messed up the stays. Hung up on the outer reef was what was left of Huddy's schooner, the *Number Four*. She'd been set fire to and burned close to the water-line aft. For'ard the seas had saved her and the figurehead, Kalua over at Tahiti carved for Huddy, was untouched."

"Natives?" asked Boone. "But they don't burn unless by accident."

"No. She'd been drifting a long while. Weed and shells over the scorched timbers showed, where she'd been driven high on the reef. I reckon you can put it down to the account of Sleeth."

"Sleeth?" asked Boone amid the general excitement. "Is he alive? Dad believes it, but no one seems to know for certain."

"Plenty of evidence, to my mind," said Thurlowe. "Figure up the missing men and ships. Backus of the *Ada*, Wahlgren of the *Lehua*, Gregg of the *Uau*, Barkhausen of the *Tropic Bird*, Jim Renton of the *Petrel*, Kennedy of the *Comber*—half a dozen more. All master-owners! None of 'em the kind of men to pile up on a reef and get wiped out by the natives. Good seamen too. They didn't all go down in a monsoon! And, what's to the point to my mind, every man jack of 'em cleanin' up big in pearls. Don't forget that. It's Sandalwood Sleeth, His Mark, take it from me."

"Who's Sandalwood Sleeth?" asked Von der Mehden.

Thurlowe looked at him as he stroked his beard.

"It's a bit of a yarn," he said, "but it needs airing, I think. Some of you men knew Sleeth. Your father did"—he turned to Boone—"all of you have heard of him. Sleeth harks back to the old blackbirding days. He and Slugger Reid, and Red Branscombe, combed the groups and supplied labor to the Hawaiian plantations. They were a tough crowd, Sleeth the worst of 'em, I guess. It's a wonder they weren't baked for long pig in the ovens long ago.

"But Reid's a pillar of the Central Union Church in Honolulu now. Red Branscombe ran afoul of French Frigate Shoals one night and made Honolulu in an open boat after eighteen days, and disappeared. They say he tried to blackmail Reid an' that Reid and his old Chinese cook, who was one of the original crowd, got rid of him. Some say they murdered Red and buried him in Reid's garden. That's another man's yarn.

"But Sleeth—he got his nickname from plundering sandalwood schooners—started out as a plain pirate after the blackbirding game broke up. He's been chased by cruisers, reported murdered, hanged and drowned a dozen times, but the rumor always came back from some out-of-the-way group that he was alive and robbing wholesale. He collected a tough gang of men who stay away from known ports for good reasons, ex-convicts, crooks, deserters, and cruised the lower seas in his schooner—the *Ghost* he calls her, I suppose he's rebuilt her more'n once by this time—like an eagle after fish-hawks.

"He'd pick the small fry, Chinese, Japs and natives who were getting out sandalwood, wait till they were loaded and swoop down on them with his gang, armed from toes to eyebrows. All kinds of complaints, but the chaps he robbed didn't count for much, and they never cornered Sleeth and that slippery schooner of his. She could sail like a witch and the islands weren't patrolled much those days.

"Sleeth grew bolder as he grew older—he must be close to seventy—a whale of a man, built out of teak an' whalebone at that, an' he kept gatherin' in the bad eggs. Presently the schooners began to drop out of sight. Backus of the *Ada*, who'd found a regular pearl-mine somewhere an' was bringin' in black pearls worth thousands, was the first. Sam Cree, a Portygee who murdered his captain an' put the hands who wouldn't join him in a leaky whaleboat, was supposed to have gone down to join Sleeth somewhere near the Kermadecs, an' more skippers failed to make port. All of 'em successful pearlers, mind you.

"Captain Boone, Dick's father, tried to organize to round him up, but we couldn't get any definite clue, and it was hard to get together. None of the gang dares to come back to civilization, an' they've got a big hang-out somewhere, women with them, natives an' white women too. A bad lot. Some say Sleeth's headquarters are over New Caledonia way. It's known he had a hide-out on Matemotu, but no one has the exact position of that."

"Matemotu?" said Boone. "The Island of the Dead! That was a holding of King Te Rakau's, wasn't it?"

"Yes. It's a barren crater. High cliffs out of deep water. No reef. Te Rakau used to send all his prisoners there—those he didn't eat. Took the group from his brother and stowed him on Matemotu. Had to haul them up on a rope and left 'em there to live off eggs an' sea-birds. There's a brackish spring too. Sleeth and Te Rakau were in cahoots till the chief died. It's somewhere northeast of the Kermadecs, sheer out of everywhere. The Directory don't give it. Wherever his main hang-out is, I believe Sleeth and his gang of cutthroats to be alive and responsible for those missing ships. What do you think, Louis?"

Louis, the living encyclopedia of the southwestern Pacific, nodded.

"Some say he is myth," he answered. "*Mais ma foi*, I have a doubt."

"He don't interfere with the big traders, you see," said Thurlowe to Von der Mehden. "Just the men who own their own ships and go scouting for new pearl-patches. Your father had a run-in with him once, Boone."

"A run-out, rather. Dad was coming from Noumea, full of shell, with some good pearls. Sleeth, if all's true, has spies everywhere, natives and beach-trash whites, and gets news of any likely hauls. The *Ghost*, she's painted gray and her canvas dulled, came up in the night. Got within half a mile of them before they sighted her. She was faster than the *Roamer* closehauled, and dad ran wing and wing down wind. Sleeth trailed him to Riviki shoals, where dad, who used to go there for turtle, crosscut. Sleeth didn't know the channels and they got clear."

"Then," said Von der Mehden, "the man is no myth."

That was twenty years ago, said Boone. "Huddy has been missing three years. Sleeth's been quiet lately."

"There is Newell," said Louis. "He's missing."

"Ned Newell, of the *Pleiades*?" exclaimed Boone. "He's Dad's best friend. One of mine too, for that, and most of us. You were partners with him, Thurlowe?"

The giant nodded.

"How missing?" he asked.

"Sailed from Sydney in April," said Louis. "Vent to his pearl-patch that he always keep so quiet, somewhere Norfolk vay. He vas to meet his daughter at Apia early last month. *Sacre!* There is no word! She is in Suva looking for heem, or vas last week. He is not likely to be forty day overdue. Maybe it is monsoon? Maybe reef, maybe Kanakas? Maybe Sleeth! Vat is eet, Tomi?"

He went out to the *lanai* in response to the signal of a native and quickly returned, beckoning Boone to join him.

"What is it, Louis?"

"Lady to see you, Deeck."

"White Mary stopalong Queen Hoteli," said the native, "she speakalong she want see Kapitani Booni."

"I theenk it is M'mselle Newell, Deeck," said Louis. "I heard she was to come to Levuka."

"It's ten o'clock," said Boone. "She want see me right away?" he asked the Fijian.

"She speak she like talkalong you plenty quick. She in plenty a damhurri. She give me *kala*." He grinningly displayed a dollar.

"Better go, Deeck," said Louis. "She is *belle*, Miss Newell. *Belle comme—la lune!*" He pointed to the garden where the great tropic moon was rising behind the breadfruits like a silver shield. "Go out thees vay, eef you like."

Dick hastened through the garden, fragrant with frangipanni and gardenia, crossed its bordering coco palms and strode down the coral-dust road, wondering at this sudden *rendezvous* with a girl he had never seen, of whom he knew nothing, save that she was the daughter of his father's good friend and his own acquaintance, Captain Ned Newell of the schooner *Pleiades*, forty days overdue, held somewhere in the sea-wastes under the hint of menace, in the person of Sandalwood Sleeth, latter-day pirate.

II

Sandalwood Sleeth, His Mark

There is nothing pretentious about the queen hotel at levuka, but the low building of coral blocks, set in a garden of tropical luxuriance, is cool and not without its comforts. The hostess, the much-relieved relict of a drunken trader, met Boone as he entered.

"The young lydy's hanxious to see you, Captun," she said. "She just got hin from Suva. Hif you'll go hon the *lanai* she'll be with you has soon has she chynges 'er dress."

"All right, Mrs. Johnstone. Thank you."

The broad veranda gave on to the garden, raised from it by half a dozen low steps. The grass thatch of the roof shut off the crests of the dense verdure, through tiny crevices of which the rising moon sent silver tentacles. The garden lay in a purple half-light beneath the stars, and the faint land-wind blended the odors of the blossoms into a mysterious incense of the night, the breath of the spirit of the tropics.

He heard a light footstep and turned, tossing his cigarette to the grass beneath. A slight figure, gowned in white that showed gray in the shadow of the *lanai*, came quickly toward him with both hands outstretched.

"Oh, Captain Boone!" cried the girl in a voice that slightly faltered. "I'm so glad to find you. I came by canoe from Suva when I heard you were in."

"Miss Newell?"

The girl stopped, drawing back her hands.

"Who are you?" she asked, looking intently at him through the dusk.

In the shadow Boone looked down into two eyes steadily meeting his own. They were wide apart and very widely open. There was a crown of hair of pale gold, with little gleams here and there where the straying moonbeams caught the strands, darker brows curving finely; a straight, short nose, a mouth firmly set but adorable, with a tiny pendule drooping from the bow of the upper lip; and a chin, upraised, cleft with a dimple that held a little pool of shadow.

Beyond that he was barely conscious of a figure, straight and slim, of a vague fragrance foreign to the perfume of the garden, and, within, a little shock, a vibration like the tinkling of a bell ringing deep within his consciousness, as if in answer to some message.

"I am Captain Boone," he said. "I think you expected to see my father. He is in California, retired."

"Oh!" she said, drawing back a little.

Boone sensed the note of disappointment in her voice.

"I am trying to fill his shoes," he said. "If it is anything to do with your father, Miss Newell, you can trust me to do my best to aid you."

He held out his hand. Her eyes searched his face as her cool palm slid automatically into his.

"Thank you," she said. "I am sure I can."

The moon broke through a tangle of the boughs and threw its calcium on the pair. Boone checked his first appraisal of the girl. He could tell the color of her eyes now. They were gray, clear and dark, and as their glances mingled he felt the little thrill deep within him once again.

"I have heard he is overdue," said Boone. "Let us sit down."

He drew up two lounging-chairs.

"Captain Boone," said the girl earnestly, "my father and yours were close friends. You knew him perhaps?"

"Quite well."

"I sent for your father, as I thought, late as it is, because the matter is urgent—terribly urgent! I need assistance badly. My father is in danger"—her voice shook, and she steadied it in a lower key—"and if you can help me I shall be glad."

"My time is at your service, Miss Newell. I am my own master."

"You have heard of a man called Sleeth?" she asked.

Boone nodded. There was a sudden, swift rustle in the crotons by the steps. The girl leaned forward tensely, grasping the arm of Boone's chair, the moon full on her eager face.

"There's some one there!" she whispered.

Boone sprang to the rail and vaulted over, crashing through the brittle leaves. The girl leaned down above him.

"I thought I saw a shadow crossing the lawn by the palms," she said. "It disappeared in the hibiscus. They've gone now, whoever they were. Can't we go where we can't be overheard? Not inside, the walls are too thin. I have felt for days as if I was being followed, even in the canoe coming from Suva."

"The open beach is the best place," said Boone. "Will you come?"

"Surely. Wait just a moment, please."

She left him, to return swiftly and press something hard and cold into his palm.

"It's an automatic pistol," she said. "You can probably use it better than I can."

They rapidly passed down the straggling street in silence and came out upon the crescent beach beyond the harbor. The moon flooded it with light beyond the slow-moving shadows of the coco palms, massed along the curve of the land. The land-breeze pressed the soft folds of her gown against her rounded limbs as she walked springily by his side. They kept close to the edge of the lagoon, its waves, their force broken by the reef, sending a lace of phosphorescent foam to their feet.

"About Sleeth," said Boone at last. "I know all that is current concerning him. In fact we were talking about him tonight. What makes you think that he has anything to do with your father's delay?"

"Captain Boone," she answered, "I was my father's chum. His little pal, he called me." Her voice choked for a second. "I think he wishes that I had been a boy, though he has never said so. I have wished so too, sometimes, but never more than now. After my mother died—I was sixteen then—I left school, and we have been together since then every moment that was possible. I have sailed with him several times, twice on the full trip.

"Last year, on the voyage back, Breggs, our first-mate, broke his arm ashore at Noumea. They said he had been on a drunken spree, but he had never done such a thing before in the fifteen years he had been with my father, and I believe now there was foul-play somewhere. We had no efficient second, and father gladly took a man who offered himself.

"He was Spanish or Portuguese, a good navigator, but to me horrible. He was a big, burly fellow. One side of his face was handsome, in a coarse way. On the other he had been scarred by a cut that had nearly lost him his eyesight, and the wound, in healing, had distorted his eye into a malignant squint. On that side, too, beneath his long mustache, was the scar of a harelip. The hair did not cover the seam, and sometimes when the wind was blowing it would expose this hidden, sneering grin. Those were accidents of course, but the two sides of his face seemed to typify the man—a rough show of good-nature and then the leer of a devil."

"Sam Cree! Sleeth's right-hand man!" cried Boone.

"So we found out, from description, after we reached Wellington. He disappeared the night before we got in, during his watch. I used to take a pride in keeping father's log. I had given it to him. It was bound in stiff leather with a brass lock that had taken my fancy. Several times Cree asked to look in it, for comparison, but father did not care for any one who was a stranger to read it and get the bearings of his island where our pearls have come from.

"Then father caught him forward, chatting with the men, and spoke to him sharply about it. The same night he disappeared I found him tampering with the lock. He made some excuse, but the brass was all scratched. Then he went overboard. None of the sailors saw him jump. We think a canoe must have come alongside for him on some signal, as we were sailing not far from the coast.

"Father was going to make only two more trips, this and one more. The two lagoons were nearly worked out, though the patches that were left were proving the richest of all in pearls. He would not take me, though I begged, because—I am sure of it now, though he made light of it—he was afraid of the risks. He was to meet me at Apia about the first of last month and we were going up to San Francisco and take a long trip together. And now"— she caught her lower lip between her teeth and Boone saw the film of tears in her eyes—"I am trying to be brave about it, but I am only a girl."

"Brave!" said Boone. "You're wonderful. Look here, Miss Newell, I'm with you in this. It's just the same as if it were my dad. We'll find him all right."

He spoke in comforting fashion, but the thought of the burned hulk of Huddy's schooner stranded on the lonely reef came to him, and he remembered the long list of missing men.

They had come to the horn of the bight and stood clear of the shadow of the rocky promontory, where the straggling pandanus grew thickly.

"I waited at Apia till the fifteenth without feeling worried very much," said the girl. "Then, one night—I slept with the windows open—I awoke suddenly. It was dark, but I felt sure some one was in the room. I pressed a little electric-torch I keep under my pillow and flashed it through the mosquito netting. I saw no one, but on the floor was this."

She took a little package from the bosom of her gown, unfolded it, and gave it to Boone. The full moon furnished ample light to read it. The girl stood by as he perused it, her eyes searching the shore and the promontory above them. The letter was written on fine, stout paper fiber, with dense black ink in an uneducated, scrawling hand.

MISS MARION NEWELL:
Not later than August twenty place in waterproof contaner fixed to buoy the exakt latitood and longitood of your father's pearl island. Anker on Reva Shole twenty mile east of Vaenga south of Viti Levu. Then yore father will get back to port. Otherways he will last as long as his grubb. Don't let ennyone kno yore bizness or he wont come back. We wont pick up the buoy unlest all is clear. Keep a quite tung in yore hed or yore father wont use his agane.
SANDALWOOD SLEETH.
[HIS MARK]

Below the signature was a crude sketch of a skull with a bone held between the teeth. Boone turned the paper over at the girl's gesture. On the other side were a few words in a bold handwriting.

DEAR MARION:
Don't tell. I am safe. Don't tell and don't worry. I—

The last few words were smeared so as to be indistinguishable. The ink had sunk into the layers of the fiber, and it was impossible to guess at the meaning. It was signed "Edward M. Newell."

"That is father's handwriting," she said.

"He says not to tell. I don't know what to do. If we could make out the last of the—"

She clutched at his arm, pointing upward.

In the deep shadows of the *pandanus* Boone thought he could make out a movement. Something flashed brilliantly in a sudden spark, and he fancied he could distinguish a hand grasping a bough. Whipping the pistol from his pocket he fired as swiftly as he could press, twice at the hand, six times slightly to the right. There was the sound of a slight scuffle, lost in the cries of alarmed birds that went whirring seaward.

"I fired at the sparkle," he said. "Stone in a ring, I fancy. And I shifted to the right. Think I may have got him. We'd better get back. We've got to get things in action."

They ran side by side for a while across the strand, the girl keeping easy pace with the man in a free, boyish stride. Then they slowed to a swift walk.

"There is plenty of money," she said a trifle breathlessly. "We are quite rich, you know, from the pearls. And I have my own share and account. I brought some with me and I got more by cable at Apia. If that isn't enough—"

"That'll be all right," said Boone. "I've got some, and I can raise all I want. We've got to start things quickly. You'll have to set the buoy, I think. Better let me do it. I'll try and track them. I've got some idea of where your father may be."

"Where?"

"On Matemotu."

"Where's that? Can't we go to him right away?"

"Well, that's to find out. Matemotu is not on the map. But we'll do it. Maybe I can get some idea of the latitude and we can run that down. The surest way will be to trail Sleeth or whoever he sends after the buoy. If we can get the location of his hang-out, we'll clear out the whole gang. Thurlowe'll join in. It's the end of the season. Maybe some of the others. We'll see. But the only real clue we have at present is the buoy."

"Do you mean to give them the position?"

"No. We'll play for time. If we gave them a false one they'd likely go there first, and, though I don't imagine your father is in immediate danger of starvation, especially if he's on Matemotu, we'll waste no time in getting him.

"Write a note saying that you do not remember the exact position, but have cabled home to get it. That will give us a few days leeway. Any longer would make them suspicious. This way they'll either go straight to where your father is to try and get it out of him again, though I imagine that's a useless job, or sail direct for their headquarters. If I trail them, we'll organize and soon get you in touch with your father."

"But they say they won't come for the buoy unless the coast is clear."

"We can get around that. I'll have to get a launch, mask it somehow, and hang off and on after I've set the buoy."

"Can I go with you?"

"Better not, Miss Marion. It won't do for both of us to take all the chances. There'll be a risk. You stay with Mrs. Johnstone. You'll come with us on the real trip to Matemotu or wherever we go, of course. I'll take a room at the Queen tonight, next to yours, and I'll send a message to Thurlowe. He can sleep on the other side. Then you'll feel safe. Thurlowe was a partner of your father's, you know."

"I don't know how to thank you."

"Don't. It's all going to come out all right."

They passed quickly to the Queen without incident, Boone keeping the automatic handy. He saw the girl to her room on her promise to try and sleep, returning her the pistol.

After arranging for his own quarters he wrote a note to Thurlowe while the widow's son waited to take it.

"I'll have to get a launch," he thought. "By George, there's the Dutchman's! We'll have to let him in on it. I'll wager he's game. I like his looks, scar and all."

Fifteen minutes later Thurlowe and Von der Mehden were closeted with Boone, talking in eager whispers.

"*Ach himmel!*" said the German, his glasses off, his eyes sparkling. "Sure can you haf de launch. This is what you call a spree. I go with you."

"Some one's got to stand by Miss Newell," said Boone. "That chap's skulking about somewhere. He may be just a spy or he may be up to something more desperate, especially now he knows she has told me everything."

"Wore a ring, did he?" asked Thurlowe. "I don't know who it could be. Several of them left the room soon after you did. Most of them I knew, though."

"He's nursing a bullet, I think—or two, I hope," said Boone.

"Hope so. How'll you mask the launch?" asked Thurlowe.

"Fell a palm or two and lash them alongside. Then lay off with a good pair of glasses. They said the twentieth in the note. Today's the eighteenth. If all's clear, they may come in earlier. If they put off in a canoe, I can catch them before they reach land. If it's the *Ghost*, I'll make shift to keep them in sight somehow. I wish we could get the position of Matemotu. Then you could go straight there."

"Goin' to be hard to get that," said Thurlowe. "Any native would be scared of Sleeth if they had the dope. And some white men. If any one knows it, it would be Louis, but I doubt if he would tell either. While you are gone, Boone, I'll try my best to find out and I'll have a talk with Adams and one or two of the rest we can trust. We'll have to go strong and armed to tackle that outfit."

"Why not get the British government?" asked Von der Mehden. "After we haf found where to go. Of course now Sleeth would be watching to see if we got in touch with them."

"British government—!" said Thurlowe. "They're sure, I grant you that, but they're all-fired slow. Sleeth'd get wind of it some way while they were getting a requisition through for coal. We'll tackle this ourselves."

"*Ach himmel*, I haf it!" exclaimed the German. "Listen. Captain Thurlowe, he watches Miss Newell. I shall go to our station here. I shall install a receiving apparatus in the launch and keep in touch with you. You can't send though, but it will do some good. We may get in touch with that chap you fired at. Some communications are better than none."

"How about the mast for the aerials?" asked Boone. "I can't hide that very well. I might scrape it dull, but it would stick out of the sea like a sore thumb."

"It is not necessary. I haf a degree of engineer, at Heidelberg. It is easy. A few wires grounded on iron and a good receiving-helmet, and you can get anything within five hundred miles. It is simble."

He glowed with the ardor of a boy over his first chemistry experiment, his dialect thickening with his excitement.

"All right," said Boone. "How about an engineer? I'll take my mate, Joe Stevens, but neither of us can handle that engine expertly."

"I'll lend you one," said Von der Mehden. "*Gott!* Der beer iss warm. Let's haf some fresh."

"Better be turning in," said Boone. "Miss Newell will feel safer when she hears some one either side of her. About Reva Shoals? I suppose I can get hold of a native pilot from Louis?"

"I wouldn't trust Louis with too much of your business, Boone," said Thurlowe. "He's all right, but his affairs spin a big web and he's not goin' to break any of his own threads if he can help it."

"I'll be careful. Early tomorrow then. Goodnight."

III

THE GRAY SCHOONER

WITH THE CREST OF VITI LEVU'S CENTRAL PEAK in a dim cloud on the horizon behind them, the launch cut its way cleanly through the glassy, deep-blue, almost purple sea. Vaenga, a lonely, low-lying islet, lay forty miles to the south and east, with Reva Shoals about thirty miles straight ahead.

The afternoon was breathless. The wrinkled waves seemed molded in blue glaze, as if the launch supplied all the motion, rising and falling on a rigid sea. Yet the depths were alive. Everywhere the grim chase for existence was on. The harassed flying-fish, between their bony-jawed pursuers of the deep and the wide-winged birds that made the waves their feeding-range, skimmed the air frantically on finny planes that dried rapidly in the sunshine. Turtles basked and bat-winged monsters flopped on the surface, the giant rays of those waters.

In the launch Boone sat aft, close to the wires that Von der Mehden had improvised, strung cross-thwarts in the cockpit. The microphonic receiving-helmet was on his head. Two or three messages, unintelligible to his untrained ear, had clicked through the sensitive diaphragm, weighty with national import perhaps, sent over the vibrant bridge established across the Pacific archipelagoes by Great Britain and Germany, part of a magic girdle around the world.

He had made up a hasty code with Von der Mehden, in case of need, though he had consented to the installation rather to please the enthusiastic lender of the launch than from any hope of its practical use. The German engineer, his cylinders purring evenly, registering fourteen knots for every hour of progress, mechanically watched his bearings and oil-cups. Forward, Boone's mate Haley held the course in the little wheel-house. Torua, the Fijian pilot recommended by Louis, asleep in the bows, lay asprawl in the hot sun that beat upon his bronze nakedness, one arm across his eyes.

The buoy that was to bear the message for Sleeth lay in the cockpit. Boone had taken an empty gasoline drum, ballasted it, made it conspicuous with red lead and attached to it half-a-dozen fathoms of light cable with a discarded mushroom-anchor for a weight. The note, with its play for delay, was in a baking-powder tin, secured to the drum with marlin and tagged with a label addressed to Sleeth.

It was very still in the waterwaste. The cry of a bird, the splash of a fish, were the only sounds that broke in upon Boone's reverie. Self-reliant by nature and training, the adventure on which he was embarked filled him with quiet satisfaction. Here was the very pith of life. Romance! Though as yet he was barely conscious of that phase. Danger! Which his spirit rose to meet. Mystery! Treasure! What more could a modern knight-errant demand?

Like Orlando, he felt the spirit of his fathers strong within him. They had braved the perils of unknown trails, beset with lurking enemies, had conquered the wilderness, proving their manhood, as he was proving his. They won their spurs by land, he was gaining the epaulets of seahood. That was the only difference.

He had not been without experiences and risks in his eight years of cruising, but this was the first time sex had entered into the adventure. With his level-thinking, clean-living father; from his mother, happy now with a stay-at-home mate in the Berkeley hills; he had ever thought of womanhood too seriously to care for its lighter daughters, the sensuous, laughter-loving children of the South Seas, and his hours ashore had ever been busy ones, fitting him for the relief of his father's command.

Apart from the mysterious thrill that beset him in the presence of Marion Newell, that haunted him even now, as a spur to prove himself worthy of her quest, he thought of her with admiration blended with pity for her plucky loneliness. She had bid him godspeed that morning with a quiet bravery of chin, steady lips and resolute gray eyes that had affected him as an accolade bestowed upon his errantry. There had been no disturbance through the night, and the watchfulness of Thurlowe's steady, stalwart manhood assured him of her present safety.

It was evident from the persistency of the spy on Viti Levu, from the open daring of the communication with the girl, that the treasure of pearls still left on the island by Captain Newell must be no ordinary one.

He had heard many tales of the marvelous treasure-trove in the lagoons that Captain Newell held the key to, of the size and purity of the gems brought to the market by the owner-master of the *Pleiades*; but all the rumors of Sleeth's cupidity and cruelty had been coupled with the caution that had kept him so long immune from capture and punishment. The hazard of the present attempt seemed to smack more of the ill-judged rapacity of Sam Cree.

It was possible, Boone mused as the launch sped on, leaving a long wake of sparkling foam behind its whirling propeller, that Sleeth was sick or growing too old for mastery. Another thought came that sent the hot blood tingling to his finger-tips. Cree had been on the *Pleiades* with Marion. Her beauty, her dainty femininity, unshadowed by the quaint boyishness she had adopted as her father's chum, that gave her such piquancy, was just the sort to have inflamed the coarse voluptuousness of the renegade Portuguese.

Marion—Boone thought of her as that with the mental intimacy of impending lovers—had said nothing of any attempts at familiarity, but the emphasis with which she had described the man as "horrible" aroused a host of sinister suggestions within the young skipper that made him resolute to pay especial attention to Sam Cree when it came to a time of reckoning. His own heart recoiled, in the shyness of young, clean manhood, at thoughts of personal intimacy with the girl's maiden daintiness, and the idea of Cree's crude desires set the muscles bossing in his lean, well-chiseled jaws. And somewhere in the void, Cupid laughed. The leaven of love works swiftest in absences.

It was two o'clock. By Boone's reckoning Reva Shoals were not far ahead. He stood up, unclamped the helmet and adjusted the focus of his powerful marine-glasses, sweeping the waste for some discoloration of the water. A mile ahead a flock of sea-birds hovered, a sure sign of shallows where they are to be expected. Going forward, he aroused the slumbering native.

The man started, alert at the touch. He was powerfully built, though the corded muscles and gray, crisp hair showed the marks of age. His eyes looked surlily at Boone, with bloodshot whites and inflamed lids, proclaiming the diver and fisherman who sought his catch beneath the surface, sweeping the reef-fish into a net while he clung to the coral.

"Reva Reef?" asked the skipper.

"*Ai*," grunted the native.

"How much water stopalong?"

"Two fathom belong along this side—top water. *Lele* water sou'side."

"Two fathoms. Six-foot fall. It's about low tide now," said Boone. "There's water breaking at the far end of the shoal. Slow down a little," he told the engineer.

"*Ja*," said the German, whose English was somewhat limited, and shifted to half-speed.

Boone stood in the bows.

"You fetchalong buoy," he commanded the native, who went aft and brought the contrivance to Boone, coiling the chain for a clear delivery. The purple water had changed to brown that turned to amber in the center of the unborn atoll. A bank of seaweed spread its great fronds to port.

"Stop her," cried Boone. "Steady, Haley." The launch rocked on the swell as the young skipper heaved the lead. "Two fathoms," he announced, as the launch moved slowly ahead. "One and a half—less a quarter. Back her. Over with it, Torua! Smartly now! That's good. Half-speed reverse. Now ahead. Swing her out, Haley!"

The vermilion drum bobbed and swung to its anchor, the tin can on its top flashing in the sunshine.

"Due east, Haley. Straight for Vaenga. We've got work to do."

The launch drove for the island still hidden behind the sea-rim and Boone settled himself to search the horizon for signs of a sail.

"They may wait till morning, but we can't afford to lose time," he thought. "When we make the island, Haley," he said aloud, "there's an opening on this side, Torua says. There may be some natives there, but the village is to the east. No use disturbing them. They may be standing in with Sleeth."

"He may be there now," suggested Haley.

"Got to run the chance of that. We've got to mask the launch."

Running at top speed, they soon raised the palms of the low-lying island, and, skirting the barrier reef, found the opening under the pilotage of the native. Boone dropped anchor in the quiet lagoon and leaving the engineer they rowed the little tender to the sandy beach. In half an hour they had felled two young cocopalms and cut some heavy branches of broad-leaved breadfruits, stowed them aboard and were speeding apparently unnoticed toward the shoals once more.

Giving them a wide berth, Boone ordered the engines stopped five miles to the westward of them, and all hands went to work under his directions. The palms were lashed to the port gunwale, one heavy clump of leaves masking the wheelhouse, the other the combined engine-room and cabin. The breadfruit branches were woven here and there in a natural tangle until the screen hid the port-side completely, with little openings here and there for peepholes.

Boone took the tender and rowed off to survey the effect. Even at a short distance the launch was completely masked behind what seemed a mass of driftage, common enough in those wind-swept waters, where every sudden gale uproots the shallow-soiled palms and shrubs and sends them voyaging to plant new islands from their nuts and pods.

"The drift sets right," he said returning. "Keep her broadside on, Haley. We'll turn over the engines often enough to keep her well up. I hardly think they'll come tonight, but we'll keep close watch. Moon-rise at twelve-fifteen. Let's eat before it's dark."

All about them the stage was being set in the never-wearying transformation-scene of a tropic sunset. To the east and windward the trade-clouds, banked in a mighty argosy, began to glow like masses of opal matrix. The western sky changed swiftly in chameleon hues, from blue to orange, then to a vivid green in which swam clouds of crimson and purple, golden-fringed, blending, fading, faster than the eye could pass. Swiftly, as if some invisible hand were letting down curtain after curtain of gauze across the mighty auditorium, the zenith deepened to violet, grading down to olive at the sea-line.

Another instant and all the sky-dome was deep translucent purple, save where the ghostly trade-clouds, warm gray with hints of chrome, sailed in stately squadron. A myriad stars broke through their glittering points simultaneously, switched on by the Master-electrician. The waves took up their flecks of light here and there, a little zephyr wandered from the land in puffs that gradually strengthened to a steady breeze, the ocean—or the sky—seemed to give a long, low sigh of contentment, and the world settled down to sleep.

"The wind's setting us over too hard," said Boone. "They couldn't spot us now anyway. Head her up toward the shoals for about fifteen minutes, Haley, then put on this headgear for a spell. If the call comes from Von der Mehden it will be in five short taps, three long ones, then five short again, repeated twice. After that, I've got the code in my note-book."

The hours slipped by, marked by the march of the stars. Every little while

Boone ordered the engines started, and, despite the drag of the trees, they made half-speed till the shoals sounded a warning. The launch showed no lights save for the buried gleam of the engineer's electric torch, and Boone constantly searched the sea with his powerful night-glasses for some sign of the *Ghost*.

Close to midnight part of the horizon was suffused with a pearly glow, and presently, on skytime, the great moon peered above the water, then seemed to bound free, eager to pass along its arching trail, throwing a path of molten silver on an ebon sea. Creeping veils of phosphorescence glowed in the wake of the launch.

Just as the lower rim of the moon, distorted from its circle, cleared the sea, the shadow of a schooner, topsails bent, all headsails set, glided across the disk. A moment and she passed, blending with the night.

"The *Ghost!*" exclaimed Boone. "Start her, Bockstatt. Haley, keep her up."

He dived into the cabin and brought out two repeating-rifles. One he gave to Haley as he took off the helmet and went forward to the wheel, one he had already left with Bockstatt, the third he retained for himself. He felt the automatic at his belt, hesitating as he glanced at the native, sitting aft by the wires.

"Better not," he muttered and took up the glasses.

Held by her helm the launch sidled toward the shoals, keeping clear of the moon-path. The oncoming schooner, reaching on the breeze, now slackening once more, crossed the silver trail, her side-lights darkened, one light burning aft in her cabin like a malignant eye. Boone kept her covered with his shaded lenses, a dark, swiftly gliding blot upon the water. The light disappeared and the faint rattle of boom-tackles came across the water.

"She's heading up for the buoy," said Boone. "Hold us as we are."

The moonlight played upon the breakers at the southern end of the reef, sounding more softly as the tide raised. The wind had died to puffs again as the schooner, gliding ghostwise as befitted her name, shut off the sight of the argent-sheeted foam. The rattle of a chain came to their ears, followed by the sounds of lowering a boat.

"She's anchored," said Boone. "Breeze is all gone. She's likely to stay there for the dawn wind. Hold us steady. Have your rifles handy. They may get suspicious and try to investigate. If they do, we'll cover them from ambush. If we can hold up a boatload, we can take them off for hostages and soon clear up the trouble."

The lookouts on the schooner had evidently seen the buoy and had no eyes for the launch behind her mask of foliage. The click of oars came to the watchers. A shout sounded, then the sound of oars again, and, presently, the rattle of the in-haul of the anchor-chain.

Then came the pulsing of an engine, the gleam of the cabin-lamp as the schooner came about.

"By thunder, she's got an engine," said Boone.

"*Zwei* cylinder," said Bockstatt. "She don't make more den eight knot, yet."

"How big a radius have we got?" asked Boone. "How far can we follow her?"

"Von der Mehden gif us all der gasoline in der station," said the German. "We come eighty, ninety miles. Yes? Ninety back. We are gut for three, four hunderd, maype. Der engine run fine."

"After them, then! If we can't hold 'em, we'll cut loose the trees, though I'd rather hold them till daylight if we can. Then we'll hide till she's topsails down. Keep on her quarter, Haley. Don't lose that light."

The chase commenced. Despite the drag the big launch held the light of the schooner at even distance to Boone's delight.

"Up to date, is Mister Sleeth," he said. "If his headquarters are anywhere within our radius, which is likely, we've accomplished our end. At the worst, we can get some idea of his general course before he shakes us. I wish we could have cut out that boat, though."

For two hours they trailed the light, fearing every moment it might be extinguished and bring the risk of closer convoy. Suddenly they seemed to gain upon it rapidly and Boone slowed and then stopped the engines. There was no sound of another exhaust in the silent dark. The wind had entirely failed.

"That's funny," muttered Boone. "They couldn't have anchored out here."

The engineer put his head through the cabin window.

"Engine proke down, berhabs," he said.

"Then they could hear ours. I don't like it. Torua, you get along boat with me. We tow *lele* while."

He wrapped the thole-pins of the little tender with cloth to muffle them, and, tugging lustily at their oars, the launch crept onward toward the light, which appeared to remain stationary. In about half an hour Boone stopped rowing and took up his glasses. The light showed clear in the lens, but there was no bulk of a vessel surrounding it. Close by, as it rose on the swell, a star gleamed like a twin.

"Throw off that line, Torua!" he commanded and bent to his oars. In a few minutes they were up with the light, a lantern swung from a triangle of light spars, lashed to a hastily assembled raft.

"Tricked!" exclaimed Boone as he surveyed the piratical will o' the wisp. "We've lost them. They must have seen us after all."

To guess the direction taken by the schooner in that dark sea-wilderness was impossible. The moon soared mockingly, the stars glittered coldly, but nowhere, strain his vision through the glasses as he would, could he catch a glimpse of the *Ghost*.

"Sneaked off under bare poles, I suppose," he said bitterly. "Played me for a shallow-brained kid. I guess I am."

The quick reversal of his hopes filled him with momentary despair and self-denunciation, but, true to type, his spirit rebounded with a call to action. They took up their oars again and picked up the launch. Haley was waiting for them at the gunwale, peering anxiously into the night.

"I got the call," he said before Boone could speak. "Repeated the whole thing three times. I put it down."

Boone took out his note-book and opened it at the page where he had set down the little code, reading aloud by the moonlight, that, serving them this purpose, helped by the very contrast of its brilliance to aid in the escape of the schooner.

> "Call: five short—three long—five short. Twice. Come back.
> Urgent: Six short—six short. Concerning Miss Newell: Four long—
> four short."

"They gave me the whole thing," said Haley, handing over his scrap of paper for comparison. "Got to go back? Where's the schooner?"

"Lost it," said Boone curtly, and described the ruse. Haley responded with a volley of sea-oaths.

"Sandalwood Sleeth!" he ended. "*Slippery* Sleeth, I call him."

"Thanks for the swearing, Haley," responded Boone. "I haven't your gift. Let's get this truck clear and then full speed back."

A little after three o'clock, Boone awoke Torua.

"Pretty close along Reva Reef?" he asked.

The native rose and went forward.

"*Aore*—no!" he said returning. "Reva no come longtime yet."

"You're deaf or crazy," cried Boone angrily, as his trained ear caught the low beat of breakers ahead.

He ran to the bows, leaving the native alone in the cockpit. He could see the gleam of the nigh end of the shoals, nearly covered now, not a quarter of a mile away and dead ahead. He swung angrily, to feel the launch losing way.

"Here!" he cried. "Full speed astern, Bockstatt. Full speed *astern*, I tell you!"

The German, tinkering over his engine, growled in foreign guttural.

"Der engine proke down," he snapped over his shoulder.

A sheet of gray foam hissed to starboard, another to port, as, still forging slowly ahead, the launch entered a lane in the trap of sharp-toothed coral reef, awash in the flood.

"Fix it!" Boone cried. "Torua, tumble into that tender. Over with it! We've got to tow her out."

The native was nowhere to be seen. Boone jumped to where the little dinghy had been stowed inboard. As he strained at it, the keel of the launch grated, bumped, grated again and came to rest.

Boone shouted to Haley and the two tossed the tender into the water, bent a line to the bows of the launch and strove with cracking muscles to budge the heavy craft, without success.

"Tide's falling, too," said Haley pantingly. "—— that Kanaka. Where'd he go?"

"To the sharks, I hope."

"Slippery Sleeth again?"

"I suppose so. He'll have a long swim before he earns his reward."

"Can he make it?"

"Swims like a fish. Went off under water. If it was only daylight I'd put a leak in his skull. Come on, we've got to fix that engine."

"I god id," Bockstatt announced as they clambered aboard the launch. "Look here." He exploded again into a volley of German expletive.

"Torua!" commented Boone as he followed the beam of the electric torch.

The copper feed-pipe from the main gasoline-tank aft in the covered stern was pinched flat, nipped in three places by some blunt-nosed instrument.

"Carried a pair of pliers in his loin-cloth," said Boone. "Waited his chance and did a good job. Can you fix it?"

"Sure I can," said the engineer confidently. "Put id dakes time. Hold der torch."

He entered the cabin, lit the lamps they had kept dark in the vain pursuit and triumphantly emerged with a coil of copper tubing.

"Dubligate barts," he said with a grin. "I wish id was daylight."

"We've got to get off before that," said Boone, "or we'll scrape the bottom off her on the falling tide when the wind gets up."

By the light of the lamps and the torch they toiled under the directions of the competent but deliberate engineer with growing impatience. The sky-curtain began to tremble in the east, as if about to rise. The stars paled, the phantom clouds took on warmer hues and more definite shape, and the dawn wind began to blow softly. At last the sweating German lifted his head.

"She goes now," he said.

He spun the flywheel and the powerful engine snorted, roared, then settled to a steady clutter. Boone and Haley took to the tow again while Bockstatt threw his levers to reverse. Grating and ripping, the launch backed off the coral. Boone searched for a leak, but the well-chosen timbers seemed to only have been scored beneath. From the stern he directed Haley as they worked out of the treacherous maze of the shoals.

"See anything of the Kanaka?" asked Haley as they finally backed into blue water.

"He's three miles away by this," answered Boone. "I hope I get a chance to settle with him some time. That was a close shave for being hung up for all day. The treacherous cur!"

The launch was headed north once more, cleaving the crystal waters. The sun came up in sudden splendor and the grim chase of the preying and preyed-upon fish commenced with the new day.

"Now I gets me some coffee und a pipe," said Bockstatt complacently, regarding his engine now throbbing regularly. "If I find dot nigger—"

"I wonder," said Boone to himself, "now I wonder if Louis knew just the kind of a blackguard that Torua was?"

At eight o'clock, with Viti Levu well in sight, they picked up the topsails of a schooner standing toward them.

"The *Acme*," pronounced Boone. "They must be in a hurry to bring the news."

In an hour they were within hailing-distance. Von der Mehden, flourishing a megaphone, came to the rail of the schooner.

"Miss Newell!" he shouted. "She has disappeared!"

IV

THE GRATITUDE OF LEVUKA LOUIS

IN THE CABIN OF THE *ACME*, Boone, Thurlowe and Von der Mehden held council while the launch made its own course to Levuka under the guidance of Bockstatt.

"All I know, and it seems all there is to know," said Thurlowe, "is that a message of some sort came to the Queen Hotel early last evening, while I was aboard Adams' barkentine trying to persuade him to join us. Miss Newell, accordin' to Mrs. Johnstone, was all in a ferment. She paid her bill an' packed her bag an' off she went to meet you."

"To meet me?"

"The message was supposed to be from you. Ef I'd bin there I'd hev held her back or gone with her, but I hadn't bin able to see Adams an' I calculated on gettin' back to the hotel inside of an hour." The skipper spoke deprecatingly, tugging at his beard as if in self-punishment. "They've played us for a set of suckers clean through," he growled.

"They took me for one," said Boone, and rapidly told the incidents of the floating light and Torua's treachery. "I might have known they wouldn't have played so open a hand without holding the cards. I had the launch masked all right, but either we were spotted on Vaenga or Torua got some signal to them unknown to us."

"Soon as I found the girl was gone," went on Thurlowe, "I tried to get track of her. Three schooners cleared about sundown, an' one, the *Crest of the Wave*, went out earlier in the afternoon. That's the one that turned the trick, I'm thinkin'. I know the rest of the skippers."

"*Crest of the Wave*? I never heard of it," said Boone.

"Nobody else till a few days ago. Came up from the Loyaltys, the skipper said. A sallow-complected chap thet kep' his mouth shut. Said his name was Capwell an' he was after turtle. He was at Louis' night afore last an' he was one of them that left soon after you did. He didn't show himself ashore again—maybe you potted him after all on the beach—an' as I say he went out afore the others in the afternoon. Took a tack offshore, an' squared for the south'ard, they tell me. I reckon he made for some anchorage between Levuka and Moau—there's sev'ral breaks in the reef—an' sent his message from there."

"Who brought it?"

"Native, Mrs. Johnstone claims. Spoke fair English. I feel pretty sure it was Capwell. Anyways the gel's gone."

"Sleeth, or Cree, has had track of her right along," declared Boone. "They were anxious to see who she talked with. Of course she had to get some one to help her set the buoy, but they relied on her anxiety for her father to keep her away from the authorities. Then this Capwell saw me read the letter and they made sure by kidnapping her in my name. I've messed it, thoroughly," he concluded, his clenched fists resting uneasily on the table as if they were already at grips with Cree.

"Don't see what else you could have done," said Thurlowe. "But we'll get her and Newell, too. There's a long score to be wiped out, once we get started."

"Adams coming with us?"

"He's got to go up to Vanua Levu. Got a charter from there to Malayta. He's not altogether his own man. Menzies may go, but I doubt it, unless he sees his way clear to a pot. He's over canny—which is the Scotch for stingy, I take it. Now the point is, where do we go first?"

"*Ja*," said Von der Mehden. "I'm with you to the finish, but where do we go? We thought you'd want to come back when Miss Newell was missing, under any conditions, so I started sending about midnight."

"I'm glad you did," said Boone. "It's no good going on a wild chase after Capwell. Worse than hunting a needle in a haystack with his start. We've got just one card, that's Matemotu."

"Hmph!" ejaculated Thurlowe. "More needle hunting."

"We've got to find it," cried Boone, hitting the table with his fist. "Why, think of it! That girl exposed to the will of those blackguards! It sets me crazy to think of it. There's more to it than you realize."

He told them of the episode of Sam Cree aboard Newell's schooner the *Pleiades*.

"*Gott!*" exclaimed Von der Mehden standing up. "As long as I can travel, Captain Boone, count on me."

He extended his hand across the table, and Boone, rising, gripped it. Thurlowe followed their example, and the three pledged their manhood in the little cabin.

Lives are simple in the South Seas, and impulses primitive, all the stronger for being unhampered by the dictates of conventionality. Love and hate, honor and friendship are affairs of reality, weighed in the scales of action and seldom found light. Men are measured by simple standards and such judgments do not often fail. Boone and Thurlowe knew the other by what each had achieved and both accepted the chubby, impulsive German on the rating-gage of those latitudes, the ability to sense the innate worth of another.

The task before them challenged their manliness and in each other's eyes and hand-grips they knew they were equal to the test.

"Matemotu it is," said Thurlowe. "I've a strong suspicion Louis could give a close guess to the position, but I'm leery of Louis. He's in too many deals that are shady, to say the least of them. I don't say he's in open league with Sleeth, mind you, but—"

"I've a way to get Louis to talk," said Boone. "I'll try it."

"It's our only chance," answered Thurlowe. "If you've got any real call on him, he'll pay the debt, I'll answer for that. I'd hate to be his debtor, though. The man's a smug spider. We must be close in. Let's go on deck."

"If you'll get hold of Menzies," said Boone as they stood at the rail, the schooner heading for the reef entrance, "Von der Mehden and I will tackle Mrs. Johnstone again. If you'll come," he added to the German.

"*Ach,*" replied Von der Mehden. "I told you this was my vacation. This will be better than visiting trading-stations. They can wait. And anything you want from the company you can haf—on one condition."

"What's that," asked Boone.

"You call me Otto."

Mrs. Johnstone received them in melancholy mood, her favorite attitude toward life.

"Hit's 'orrible, gentlemen," she said, dabbing at her eyes with a dingy handkerchief. "Hif Hi'd hany hidea hanyfing was wrong, Hi'd 'ave chased the Kanaka hout hof the 'ouse wif a kettle of b'iling water, I would, afore 'e hever set heyes on the young lydy. The pore, sweet, trusting young thing."

"Was it a letter he brought?" asked Boone.

"A note, hin a henvelope. Sealed, hit was."

"Maybe it's in her room," suggested Von der Mehden.

"Hi've done hup the room," said the landlady. "But hit might be hin the desk. Hi didn't look. She left most hof her fings be'ind 'er. Just took a bit hof a bag, she was in such a 'urry. Hit's from Captun Boone, she ses, hall heager hand hexcited like. Hit's noos from my farver. Hand mebbe both hon hem's dead."

She dabbed at her suspiciously tearless eyes with the dingy rag as she led the way to the girl's room, and opened the door.

Boone lingered on the threshold, glancing into the cool chamber, furnished simply with old-fashioned walnut furniture. Flowers in a bowl stood on a little table by the open window that looked out upon the garden and the sea. Above the odor of the blossoms Boone distinguished the subtle fragrance that he had noticed on the *lanai* when he first met her. The room seemed still to hold something of her identity and he entered it quietly, as if it had been a sanctuary, as indeed it seemed to him. The desk stood by the wall near the table, an empty waste-basket beside it.

"It wasn't in that?" he asked. "Did you empty it?"

"There was nothing hin hit, Captun," said the widow, still sniffling, letting down the front of the desk and exposing a blotting-pad and inkstand with some papers tucked into the pigeonholes that formed the back.

Boone looked over them, then opened a little door that closed the middle partition.

"This looks like it," he said, taking out an envelope that had been hastily opened.

He hesitated a moment, then took out the enclosure.

"The dirty scoundrel!" he said. "Of course he knew she had never seen my writing. He overheard us when we met and knew we were strangers. Read that."

He passed the note to Von der Mehden, who read it aloud.

> "DEAR MISS NEWELL:
> 　　Successful beyond all hopes. But you must come with the bearer at once. Your father is waiting for you. You'll soon be with him again. He is doing well but needs you. RICHARD BOONE.

"He is cunning, that fox," commented the German, folding up the note and handing it back to Boone. "I should like to make him eat it. Do you suppose that means they will take her to her father?'"

"I hardly know. I hope so, but I doubt it. They probably put it in to make sure of her coming."

"Brains they haf. But we haf better."

"We'll need them," answered Boone with quiet finality. "That's all, Mrs. Johnstone. Better not say anything about this to any one. I'll keep the letter."

"Not a word parses my lips," declared the landlady. "They're sealed."

Boone glanced at her and took a crackling five-pound note from his pocketbook.

"For your trouble," he said, handing it to her. Protestingly grateful, she vanished. "That's the best kind of sealing-wax for her type, Otto."

"Ach, Otto is *gut!* As to money, Dick, I haf plenty, if you need any."

"Thanks. I'll call on you if it's necessary. Here comes Thurlowe and Menzies. Let's go on the *lanai*. It's cooler."

"I'll be with you in a minute. I want to be sure the beer is cold." And Von der Mehden vanished in search of the liquid refreshments without which he deemed every prolonged conversation a failure.

The quartet, finally established on the veranda with cigars and liquors convenient to their hands, proceeded to a discussion of ways and means, though it was evident from the first that the Scotchman was not keen on becoming a part of the expedition.

"It's no that I'm not approvin' the idea, ye ken," he said to Boone, stirring the ice in his long glass of amber Scotch and tan-san. "But, man dear, ye're gropin' for a black cat on a dark nicht wi'oot a lantern. The guid Lord may ken wheer Sleeth is, but he'll no be tellin' us, I'm thinkin'. An' the de'il looks after his ain.

"He's in Melanesia—somewheer. Draw a line fra' New Guinea to the Fijis here, an' twa lines fra' those points down to Tasmania; thirty degrees o' latitood to cover an' nigh to forty-five o' longitood. It's a far cry! An' ye've naught to go on. Ye canna catch a fox wi'out a scent to follow."

"We're going to Matemotu," said Boone. "I have means of getting the position of that, I'm almost certain."

"An' if ye find it, which I misdoot, tho' I'm no tryin' to dampen your enthoosiasm, ye ken, how d'ye ken ye'll be findin' aught when ye get there? No, laddie, I'm too auld to gang ghost-chasing, though I wish ye luck. Ye're naught but a pack o' children. Thurlowe there, for a' his gray hairs, is just a wanderin' reckless bairn o' the nicht. It's no the siller, mind ye. Thurlowe was tellin' me ye'd recompense me for the loss o' time. But I'm past the age when the crack o' a pistol made me wishfu' to find oot who fired it.

"But I ha' a lad for ye," he went on. "A red-heided whip o' a lad who's a de'il at the fechting. 'Tis Campbell, my supercargo. The lad's been most

things, amang them a doctor, as he wad be the noo but for his desire to pu'
corks. But he's a rare ane for the fechting, an' I'll lend him to ye."

"Thinkin' of firin' him, Menzies?" queried Thurlowe dryly.

"Nay, he but signed for the trip. I can spare him fra' noo on. He's a restless
lad, he'll hae to dree his ain weird, but he's guid bluid i' his veins, an' if ye
keep the grog-locker tight he should be a gran' help to ye, what wi' the
makin' o' wounds an' the fixin' o' them. He's keen to go, ye ken."

"You've not been talking much about the matter, have you?" asked
Boone. "It's not every one we can trust just now."

"Tut, man," said Menzies reproachfully. "We're Scotch. At least
Campbell's Hielan'. He'll not babble, e'en in his cups. Northern tongues are
na hung i' the middle."

"A good man is welcome," said Boone. "Especially since we have to
reckon on ourselves. There's no one else you can think of, Thurlowe?"

"No one. But there'll be ten of us whites with your mates and supercargo
and mine, counting Von here and Campbell. You can have any of my native
boys you want. I can recommend three or four of them. You'll take the
Roamer, I suppose. She's faster than my *Acme*."

"Yes. I wish I had an engine in her," answered Boone. "I've eight native
boys and Ong Chuck, my cook. He's worth three of them. He's by way of
having been a pirate himself, I believe, but he's true blue to me. That, with
four boys from you, makes twenty-three all told. I hope we can get on more
even terms with them by some stratagem or other, but we ought to give a
good account of ourselves. It's good Campbell's a doctor. We may need
him."

"I can help you with the guns," said Von der Mehden. "We haf a reserve
for the new stations. Rifles you'll need, pistols and a little dynamite. It may
come in handy. Also Bockstatt comes. He has served and is a good man."

Thurlowe looked at the chubby German approvingly. Von der Mehden
radiated enthusiasm.

"Then that makes twenty-four," he said. "Good man." And nodded at
Boone.

"I'll tackle Louis," said the latter. "If you, Otto, and Thurlowe 'll look
out for the weapons and provisioning. Charge anything to the *Roamer*. Will
you have Campbell here by supper, Menzies? Early. We'll leave before
sundown."

"I will, an' sober," promised the Scotchman. "I'm sorry I'm not ganging
wi' ye, but I'm a fearsome body wi' firearms."

Boone and Thurlowe laughed. Menzies' reputation for bravery was far
greater than for his interest in other folks' affairs.

"That's all right, Captain," said Boone. "And thank you. Campbell can be
your proxy, though I doubt if he'll share the loot with you."

"I like to see what I'm playin' for on the table," said Menzies dryly, finishing his glass and absent-mindedly taking a handful of cigars.

Boone found Levuka Louis at the Snuggery.

"Can I speak with you alone?" he asked the Frenchman.

Louis looked at him with close-lidded eyes and shrugged his shoulders.

"Of a certainty, *mon brave*," he answered, and led the way through the garden to an open summerhouse, thatched with dried palm-fronds.

"Here I am, *chez moi*," he said. "If any one comes, we see him first. Vat ees it, *mon ami*?"

He seated himself, twirling the fierce spikes of his mustache, surveying Boone keenly the while.

"Louis," said Boone, "my father told me if I ever needed help badly—very badly—to come to you. He said you were in his debt and he assigned it to me."

The little Frenchman clasped his hands across one knee.

"Did he tell you what the debt was?" he asked.

"No."

"Then weel I tell you, since I am to pay. Once, longtime since, I am married."

A mild light came into the trader's shrewd eyes and he looked silently for a while beyond the palms to where the white surf broke on the distant reef. He fumbled in the breast of his silk shirt with one hand and left the fingers there, as if holding a locket.

"She—Marie," he went on presently, "lies on Nukahiva, in the Marquesas. We had a daughter—*petite* Marie. She was like her mothaire, Deeck, *belle, ah, belle*, a lily of France transplant. I am hard, *mon Capitaine*, but with her I am soft, like honey-wax. Too soft sometime, sometime too hard. So I send her to the good Sisters at Tahiti. Ven she come back she is voman. I make the story short. There comes an Englishman to Levuka—I leave the Marquesas ven my vife die—tall, handsome, blond. Marie, she sees him often, too often, and, ven I am away one time she runs avay weeth him on his sheep. Perhaps he means to marry her. I do not know—he is not all bad, this Englishman.

"*Mais*, ven they get to sea—she is young—and of my blood, the blood that runs fast and strong even ven it is old, like good *vin*—she forget vat the good Sisters teach her. And he—he is man—and at each port he forget to marry an' laugh an' kees her from sadness. An' at Tahiti she is ashame to see the Sisters, ashame to see any one, for, look you, there is to be another, an' yet she is not vife. But your father, Deeck, he meets her, an', because he is my fren' an' good man, she tells heem, an' so he has a little talk with the Englishman. An' so they are wed. *Bon*. An' the little one is not bastard, an' "—his eyes flashed—"I do not hav' the blood of my Englishman on my hands."

He paused, his fingers fell idly to his lap as he gazed reefward.

"She is happy?" asked Boone presently.

"*Mais oui, mon ami*," said Louis gently. "She is happy. She lies, she and her *bêbe*, by the side of her mothaire at Nukahiva. But, because your father save her *honneur*, I, Louis, make heem my promise. And my promises I keep, always. Vat ees it you vant? Do not speak too loudly."

Boone lowered his voice.

"I want you to tell me the position of Matemotu, Louis. If you can, the position of Sleeth's headquarters."

Louis sat silent, his eyes narrowed once more, looking steadily out to sea.

"If it is too much—" ventured Boone after a little.

"Perhaps you ask more than you theenk," answered the Frenchman. "It ees not easy to live as I do an' not make strange connections. *Savez vous?* But I hav' promise. Where Sleeth is I do not know, I do not vish to know. This I vill tell you for the sake of my Marie, for the sake of your father and of yourself, Deeck. I think you vill not go wrong eef you go to Matemotu. Ven do you sail?"

"Sunset."

"*Bon.* You shall haf it before you leave. Let us talk of something else and then part. It ees best not to be togethaire longer. I vish you *bon voyage et bonne fortune*, an' your heart desire."

He looked at the young skipper with keen kindliness and reached up to lay a friendly hand on his shoulder as Boone flushed slightly.

"Nevaire be ashame of love, *mon ami* Deeck," he said. "Go always to meet heem. An' Mees Newell is *belle—comme la lune*."

The sun was sinking with a swift rush as it always does in the tropics, as if eager to plunge beneath the waves after the day's work. The *Roamer*, chain short and ready to break, headsails loosened for the hoist, flapped her fore and main sails in the eye of the wind. Thurlowe, Von der Mehden and Menzies' *protégé*, Campbell, a quick-eyed, undersized but wiry man, were grouped aft with Boone, watching the shore.

"I think your friend Louis has given you the double cross," said Thurlowe.

"I don't," answered Boone. "Anyhow, we can't leave without the information."

An outrigger canoe joined the fleet of native craft that was gathered about the schooner, the paddlers dickering and chaffing the native crew, endeavoring to sell the last of their fruit and chickens to the imperturbable Ong Chuck. A stalwart islander hailed Boone.

"You want coconut, *Capitani?*" he asked. "Veri fine coconut. This-a-kind

Faranki (French) nut. *Maiti no*—very good—"

Boone caught the emphasis on the word *Faranki*.

"All right," he said. "You chuckalong one dozen."

The Fijian tossed the green nuts over the rail, holding the last for a second of delay.

"Thisa nut, he best, *Capitani*," he said.

Boone caught it and felt the husk give slightly between his fingers. He threw a dollar to the native.

"*Mahoro*" (thanks), he said. "*Aroha.*"

He turned toward the mates.

"Break her out, Haley," he commanded. "Up jibs. Lively now."

The canoes scattered as the *Roamer* gathered way, and swinging on the land breeze headed for the reef passage. As they cleared the channel, Boone left the deck to Haley, and, with a nod to Thurlowe and Von der Mehden who followed him, went below.

The husk of the twelfth nut had been deftly split and rejoined by the interlacing fibers. The kernel had been cleaned of milk and flesh and held up a scrap of tough paper, folded and sealed with wax.

Boone broke it open, read the contents and passed the paper to Thurlowe, who held it so that Von der Mehden, peering under his arm, could see it.

The message was a brief one:

Matemotu 24. 18. S. 172. 40. E.

V

THE ISLAND OF THE DEAD

DRAW A STRAIGHT LINE BETWEEN SUVA, southern port of Viti Levu, and Norfolk Island, the same line the cable takes that angles from Brisbane to Vancouver, and, a little to the east, lies Matemotu, midway from nowhere—as the traders have it—remote, desolate, a burned-out crater thrusting itself up among a tangle of reefs to stem the surge of the great Pacific rollers that ever chafe and beat upon its fire-scarred cliffs.

The steamer lanes from Sydney to Suva, and to Apia, leave it far to north and south, the chart shows the vicinity speckless, the Directory of the Pacific ignores its existence, as it does that of scores of lonely islets and atolls far off the beaten track, many of them unknown to any habitant but the bo'sun birds and their feathered fellow travelers of the windways.

Six hundred miles south-southwest from Levuka, the steady northwest trades sent the *Roamer* reaching toward her goal, topsails set, at a pace that saw five hundred miles registered by the patent log at the end of forty-eight hours.

Swiftly as the schooner sailed, seething through the crisp blue seas, with sheets well started, every inch of canvas urging her onward, the hours dragged to Boone, impatiently pacing the deck, watch in and watch out, handling his sails as if he were trying to beat time allowance in an international race. His mood, shared by his comrades, did not hold for them all that it did for him. Though their chivalry was aroused by the thought of the girl's peril, none of them save Thurlowe had ever seen Miss Newell.

The thought of her dainty beauty, of the mind that looked out so serenely from beneath the archway of her brows, becoming seared by contact with the brutalities of Sleeth, Cree and their followers, filled Boone with a frenzy that threatened his self-control from sheer lack of definite action.

He urged his spirit desperately to win self-mastery in the hours he trod the deck, and emerged from the struggle in full control, after a fight in which the last of his boyishness sloughed from him, leaving him with a steadfast light in his dark eyes, a firmer line to his lean jaw, and a set invincibility of purpose that drove the native sailors at top effort before him and gave him the utter fealty of Von der Mehden and Campbell, of all his own and Thurlowe's officers. Bockstatt openly praised him, Thurlowe followed him with an approving glance.

"Boone, he goes far," said the engineer to Thurlowe. "He iss *gut* stuff, dot poy."

"Comes of good stock," answered the skipper, "and will hand down better. Also there's a little more than sheer duty in it for him, I fancy, though perhaps he's not aware of it. Miss Newell's a wonderful type of girl. They'd make an ideal pair."

"So? *Romanz*, eh? Dot vill nod hurt any, *nein*."

To Von der Mehden and to the fiery Highlander, Campbell, lean to scragginess, marked with early dissipation, the trip from a jaunt became a mission, leavened by the high resolution of the young leader.

Campbell swore deep and binding oaths to leave liquor alone until the venture was safely ended, a resolution in which he had the full sympathy of Von der Mehden. At the suggestion of Boone, all were served out rifles, pistols and ammunition and practised assiduously at improvised targets aboard and afloat till all showed a certain proficiency.

Von der Mehden, with a German sporting-rifle of high power, easily proved himself the crack shot, performing miracles with drifting bottles. Then came Boone, with his naturally steady nerves and eyes soon assuring him accuracy, and Bockstatt, quick on sight and trigger out of his old army experience. Thurlowe and Sanders, his first mate, were the pistol experts. Ong Chuck, looking on, once took up a rifle and impassively punctured a floating tin with a series of well-placed bullets. The native sailors, never first-class shots, were nevertheless good men, picked and tested in the events of many voyages.

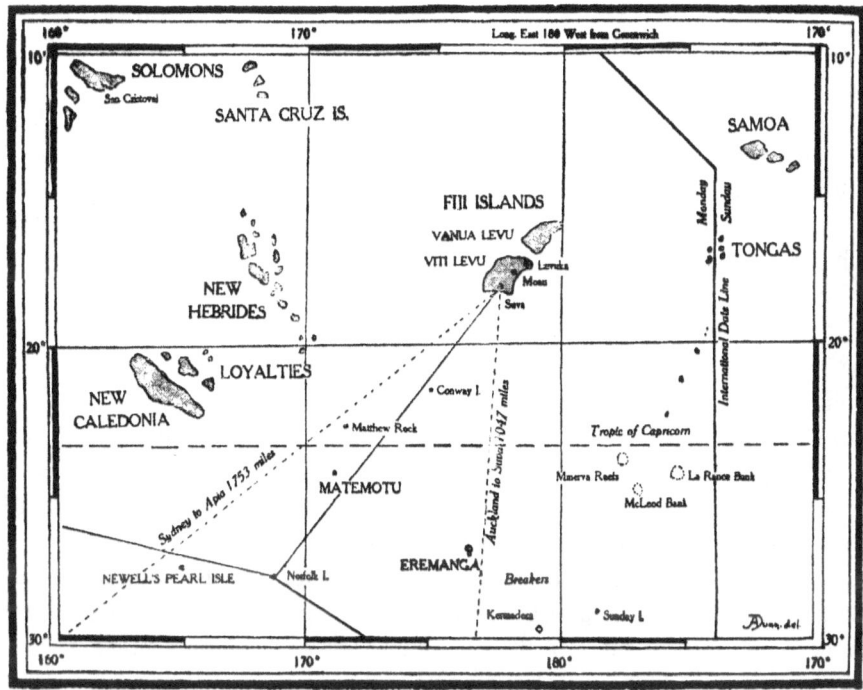

"If we get an opportunity," said Thurlowe, the second night out, "I have an idea we may be able to win over some of Sleeth's crowd. A good many of them must have joined under pressure, to save their skins, and I reckon they're sick of it. If it comes to a showdown scrap—but it's small use figurin' on what we'll do beforehand. We ought to pick up Matemotu at dawn, eh Boone?"

"Pretty close to it, if the wind holds. We'll want daylight for the shoals we may run into. I figure to tack at sun-up for the last leg. The way the current's been setting us up there's less than twenty miles of leeway to make. I am going to circle the island first for signs of the *Ghost*, though I hardly think we'll find her. But from what Louis said, we'll not draw altogether a blank."

"Who goes in the landing party?" asked Von der Mehden.

"We can take six in the whaleboat besides the boys," said Boone. "That will be Thurlowe, you Campbell—we may need your medicine chest—Haley, Sanders and myself. We may all get ashore before we leave," he added for the benefit of the disappointed ones.

"Better you take me," put in Ong Chuck. "Me heap sabby pilate."

There was a general laugh amid which the Chinaman grinned complacently.

"S'pose one man he velly sick," he said. "He want good soup, nice fli' chicken. I take along. I fix."

"All right, Ong Chuck, that's not such a bad idea," said Boone. "We'll crowd you in."

At the first signs of dawn the topsails were lowered and the *Roamer* headed, closehauled, for Matemotu. At four bells a dot declared itself in the clear horizon, and half an hour later the barren cliffs of a volcanic islet, apparently a little less than a mile in diameter, loomed in plain view, its steep walls whitened by the refuse of birds that rose in a screaming cloud at the approach of the schooner.

Strictly speaking, between the monsoon gales and the trades, there was no true weather side to Matemotu, and the lava cliffs were everywhere hollowed by wind and wave into caverns where the surf roared and spouted. Off shore the bare crests of conical rock masses lifted and breakers showed in white patches at frequent intervals.

Haley stationed himself in the fore-spreaders to con in and two men were set in the bows to cast a constant lead.

"Nice looking mousetrap," said Boone to Thurlowe as, with slackened sheets, they made a circuit of the island. "The cat doesn't seem to be home though. No sign of the *Ghost*. Not much sign of a landing either, so far, though of course there must be somewhere."

"There's deep water clear up to the cliffs in some places, they say," replied Thurlowe. "I imagine it's goin' to be no easy job gettin' on top though."

There was a hail from Haley in the foretop.

"Smoke ahoy!"

A faint line of brown fumes stained the blue of the sky in a thin column, coming steadily from the interior of the crater.

"A fire," said Boone. "Some one's alive there, that's certain."

"Deep water, clear in," shouted Haley.

Boone and Thurlowe studied the gray, seamed heights that rose so grimly from the water. Even in the brilliant sunshine the place held a sinister gloom of its own, a sepulchral suggestion that well fitted the title Matemotu—The Island of the Dead.

The northern rim of the outlet fire had built so defiantly in the realm of its opposing element was notched irregularly. The glasses discovered one great slab of smooth, wave-chiseled lava that rose sheer for a hundred and fifty odd feet from what appeared to be a natural wharf of flat rocks. At the top of this slab projected a stout spar, driven into some crevice of the cliff, and from the spar to the rim showed faint traces of a trail.

"There's the landing." The two skippers spoke the sentence simultaneously.

"The schooner'll stand off and on," ordered Boone. "Cover the landing with your rifles from the rail, Brown," he commanded his second mate.

"Ready away with the port boat there."

The landing-party assembled their equipment, the native boys swung the whaleboat into the water, quiet save for a long rolling ground-swell, and made the stout ash blades bend as they raced for the landing, Thurlowe at the steering-oar, Boone in the bows, watching the best means of approach to the wharf which on closer inspection showed signs of having been squared to a better level by man's handiwork.

As the natives handily brought the whaleboat alongside, fending off from the rocks, Boone sprang on the slippery basalt, wet with the spray, the white men following him, Ong Chuck close at their heels. Stout rings had been set in the rock and to these the boat was moored, two boys remaining in it to keep it clear while four joined their officers. A cable's length away the *Roamer* sailed in short tacks with Bockstatt in charge of the covering-battery of rifles.

Boone coiled in his hand a light lead-line he had brought in the boat.

"Stand clear," he said as the end of the line with the lead whirred in a close circle from his hand.

His arm suddenly lengthened, the lead shot upward, arching the cord above the spar, and falling, bearing the slack with it, to his feet. He bent on a stouter line of tough manila and soon had a double rope about the spar. This the native boys held taut as their skipper, a block and line about his neck, clambered up the surface of the cliff, using his feet against the lava wall to aid the muscles of his arms. Once on the spar, he seated himself astride and deftly lashed the block and reeved through one end of the rope. Thurlowe tied a loop in the other and set foot in it.

"Tail away there," cried Boone, and the husky natives hoisted Thurlowe, followed by the rest of the party, up to the side of Boone, on a narrow ledge from which ran a rough path to the summit.

From the rim they looked into the basin of the crater, dipping down in an abrupt slope hummocked with lava and crumbling tufa, whitened with guano, down a hundred feet to a rocky plain sparsely covered with low shrubs. One side lay in deep shadow that sprawled across the floor to the sunnier slope where myriads of birds, their first alarm stilled, gathered in the sunshine, straddling their eggs or squawking in ever-shifting groups.

Here and there appeared the mouths of rifts and caves, and, in front of one of them, level with the bottom of the bowl, rose the thin thread of smoke from a smoldering fire of brush. Aside from the perpetual squabble of the birds, there was no sound of life, and they commenced to scramble down the brittle slope.

The gaunt figure of a man, heavily bearded, clad in torn shirt and canvas trousers, appeared in the mouth of the cave by the fire, gazing upward, with one hand above his eyes. Suddenly he uttered a hoarse cry and came striding toward them, scattering the fire in his unheeding haste.

Thurlowe looked at the approaching figure through his glasses with a puzzled expression. Then he lowered the binoculars.

"By God! it's Huddy," he cried. "Huddy, ahoy!"

The man broke into a staggering run, stumbled to his knees and stayed in that position with outstretched arms, his face working, tears streaming from his eyes, little inarticulate sounds coming from his cracked lips as they grouped about him.

Boone knelt beside him with a flask of brandy. The marooned skipper sucked chokingly at the fiery liquor and gained his feet, looking at them with wonder that broke into laughter that he could not check.

"Steady there, mon," said Campbell, slipping one arm about him. "Ye're gettin' hysteerical. Tak' another sip o' the liquor."

Huddy stared about the little circle.

"At last," he said chokingly. "Thurlowe—and Boone's boy!" He grasped their hands as if in the grips he found tangible proof of safety. "Years it's been," he went on, "though Newell says it's only three."

"Is Newell here?" cried Boone.

"In the cave," replied Huddy, some color coming to his cheeks, his nervous ague ceasing. "He and the Other One. Both alive. Three of us alive—and a thousand dead."

He pointed at the crater walls.

"The caves are full of their bones," he went on, lowering his voice. "Their ghosts come out of nights, hundreds of them. I used to talk to them, till Newell came. It's not good to talk to ghosts. They tell you too much." He shuddered. "The Other One, he hardly talks at all. He's afraid of the ghosts. It's silly to be afraid. I always said so when I was my own man. I was a captain once, you know," he asserted. "You may not believe it, but I was."

"Surely, Huddy, we know," assured Boone. "And will be captain again. As soon as you've rested up a bit and got away from here."

"Who's the Other One?" asked Thurlowe.

"He won't tell. He's"—Huddy's voice sank to the merest whisper—"he's one of Sleeth's men."

"Sleeth's?"

Huddy nodded.

"He's got the mark on his arm. But he hates Sleeth. He hides when Sleeth comes. He wants him to think he is dead. Some day he's going to kill Sleeth. He's living for it. So am I."

His emaciated form wavered and Campbell let him sink to the ground gently.

"Give me some of that soup," he said to Ong Chuck.

The Chinaman produced a thermos bottle, part of Von der Mehden's equipment, and the Scotchman slowly fed him beef tea.

"Haley, you stay with him," said Boone. "We'll find Newell. Campbell, we'll likely need you. He must be too ill to show himself."

They started across the crater floor for the cave, relieved at the news, yet fearful of Newell's condition.

"It's evident Miss Newell hasn't been brought here," said Boone. "I hope we can get the position of Sleeth's headquarters from this Other One, as poor Huddy calls him. I suppose he's quarreled with Sleeth and they've marooned him here. That's what Louis meant, Thurlowe, when he said I'd not be wrong in coming to Matemotu."

Thurlowe nodded. His face was set. The sight of Huddy, half crazed by his imprisonment in that hell-hole, had filled him anew with the grim determination of a private *vendetta* of his own.

They entered the low mouth of the cave, a blow-out in the lava, and explored its tortuous recesses with an electric torch. The air was tainted, the floor foul with the bones and feathers of sea-birds. Dried twigs covered the rough floor.

A tunnel led to a rudely circular chamber in which a man lay moaning feebly, a dirty bandage about his head, his shoulder bound in another soiled cloth. His open eyes were bright with fever, a mat of hair covered neck and chin and cheeks, but failed to hide the deep hollows of starvation and disease.

Campbell lifted a wrist to test the pulse and laid one hand on his forehead.

"Burnin' oot wi' fever," he pronounced. "We'll ha' to get him oot o' here."

A voice, weak and broken, came from the blackened lips. For all its lack of vitality it held a dignity of purpose that told of the will, still master of the fever-beleaguered brain.

"It's no use, Sleeth. No use, man. I won't tell."

It was hard for Boone to realize that this wreck, unkempt, foul, a shell of manhood, was the Captain Newell he had known, firm of flesh and muscle, with clean-shaven, ruddy face, the father of Marion.

"Is he dangerously ill?" he asked Campbell, thanking the impulse that had prompted Menzies to turn an unsatisfactory supercargo into a helpful doctor.

"He's had a bullet thru' the shoulder," said Campbell who had been examining his patient with deft tenderness. "But it's oot. An' another ploughed a furrow i' the side o' his heid. They've no been tended, but the man's bluid must ha' been pure an' he'll pu' thru wi' care. He's been a gran' upstandin' man."

"Thurlowe, will you undertake rigging a sling at the spar?" asked Boone, and the elder skipper left the cave.

Huddy came in with Haley, walking like an aged man, but steadily. Something stirred at the far end of the rock chamber. Boone flashed the torch at the sound and saw a shadow disappear into a rift.

"That's the Other One," said Huddy. "He thinks you're Sleeth's men. He's not afraid of me. I'll get him and we'll give him something good to eat. You get terribly tired of eggs and seagull," he said with the plaintive childishness that marked his deep voice with curious pathos. "And the water's bad," he added, "and not much of it."

"We're going to get Newell aboard," said Boone. "You'll come, Huddy, and the Other One?"

"I'll come," said Huddy eagerly. "But get Newell there first. I've been afraid he'd die and then there'd be another ghost. I couldn't stand that. There are too many now. There's Barkhausen and Renton, Kennedy and Wahlgren and Gregg—"

"You mean they are all buried here?" asked Boone, aghast at the apt roll-call of the missing men he had listened to Thurlowe reciting at Levuka Louis'.

Huddy nodded.

"Dead and buried. I've talked with them," he said earnestly. "Gregg was the last. He buried them in a cave. There's no soil. They have no real graves. That's why they can't rest, I suppose. Gregg wrote all their names on a board, but it isn't a regular tombstone. Then he died. And there are natives, hundreds of them, with an old chief leading them. I'm not afraid of them.

They are all waiting for Sleeth."

"We're not," said Boone. "We're going after him. Do you know where he is? Or Newell?"

Huddy shook his head.

"The Other One does, I think. But he won't talk, you know."

One of the native boys who had been left on the wharf entered the cave.

"*Kapitani* Newell say all ready walkalong," he said.

Outside were three more natives and, in a litter improvised in a spare sail, they bore Newell to the rim of the crater and lowered him gently to the spar where he was transferred to the bosun's chair arranged by Thurlowe.

As they carried him he babbled incessantly his steady thought.

"It's no use Sleeth. No use, I tell you, man. No use. I won't tell."

They soon had him stowed in the whaleboat, Campbell and Thurlowe going off with him to the schooner. The rest stayed with Huddy in the hope of getting some information from the man who had once been one of Sleeth's piratical gang.

"You stay outside the cave," said Huddy. "I'll get the Other One."

He disappeared and they could hear him calling coaxingly to his mysterious companion. Presently he came out with a cautious finger to his lips.

"He's listening," he said warningly. "He says if you will swear by the Holy Virgin that you are not in league with Sleeth, he will come out." Raising his voice, he called: "Listen, Other One. Here are five men. They will take the oath. Answer one at a time"—he turned back to them—"do you swear to the Holy Virgin that you hate Sleeth and all his works?"

Boone glanced at his companions.

"I swear," he said loudly, followed by Von der Mehden, Haley, Sanders, and, at a nod from his skipper, Ong Chuck.

A dark face, like an ancient skull, with its hollow eyes, protruding bones, the tight-stretched skin, pox-pitted, the color of weathered bone, black hair straggling in wisps from a cotton handkerchief about the brows, peeped furtively from the cave-mouth, the eyes looking about with the fearfulness of a trapped animal.

Boone raised his hand once more.

"We swear," they repeated in unison.

"We are going to wipe Sleeth and his gang out of existence," said Boone earnestly. "We are on your side. Don't be afraid."

The figure came out into the sunlight and stood blinking at them. His only garment was the remnant of a pair of canvas trousers, barely covering his loins. His bony, sun-leathered body was marred by scars. On one side crushed ribs had healed in a great puckering scar. His right hand had turned inward at the wrist, the fingers seemingly grown together, like a withered claw.

On the forearm, through the dirt that scaled him, showed the tattooing of a skull with a bone between its teeth. He looked from one to the other, seemingly gathering courage at their reassuring nods and smiles.

Ong Chuck offered him the thermos bottle, still half filled with savory soup. He sniffed at the tempting odor and put out the uncanny claw, taking the bottle in its stiff hollow and tilting it grotesquely toward his mouth. Ong Chuck patted him on the shoulder.

"You all light," he said, as the man gulped noisily at the beef tea. "Me you flend. You sabby? All flend."

"That's strange," said Huddy almost petulantly, "He never let me touch him. And we've been friends for a hundred years, though Newell says it's only three."

"You handle him, Ong Chuck," said Boone. "He seems to have taken a fancy to you. Try and get him aboard."

With the Chinaman's hand about his shoulders, the man suffered them to lead him to the top of the cliff and looked eagerly and long at the schooner. But when they attempted to get him to the sling, he protested, shaking his head and struggling violently.

"He won't leave the island," said Huddy. "He's waiting for Sleeth, I tell you. Some day, when he's not afraid, he's going to kill Sleeth. Isn't that right, Other One?"

The man nodded vehemently.

"Well," said Boone, "you'll come, Huddy? We'll bring him back some clothes and food. Ong Chuck, you stay with him."

He drew Huddy aside.

"You say he knows Sleeth's whereabouts?"

"Yes. Sometimes he talks. I think he was one of Sleeth's best men."

"Well, he's our only hope. They've got Newell's daughter, you know."

Huddy sank his grip into the muscles of Boone's forearm.

"Ned's girl!" he exclaimed. "Then we've got to go soon—now!" He tugged at Boone's arm, urging him to the trail. "I tell you we must sail now. You don't know those devils."

"I know," said Boone grimly. "But we've yet to find out where—from him."

The Other One was hunkered on the rim of the crater, huddled in a bony heap. Ong Chuck was asquat beside him still patting his shoulder soothingly. At Boone's gesture he left the man and came over to the rest.

"He all light with me, Cap'n," he said. "You think he sabby where you want go?"

"Yes."

"I find out sure. Cap'n, you find topside my chest, in galley, one plate. He in sandalwood box in cloth. You bling when you come back. You bling sure. You see."

They left the strange pair together and reached the whaleboat which had returned for them.

"What's he going to do with the plate?" asked Von der Mehden.

"I don't know," confessed Boone. "He's a strange proposition, is Ong Chuck. Best judge of pearls I know. Got plenty of money of his own. He dares not go back to China for some reason and he appears to have adopted me. He seems to be well read in his own lore. I know that everywhere we go the Chinks all seem to think he is a big Joss. I'll fetch the plate."

"The Other One never let me touch him," complained Huddy. "And we've been friends for a century, in there."

He pointed back to the crater with the two figures still asquat on the rim.

They found Newell clean and comfortable in a bunk, asleep. Campbell pronounced him certain of recovery.

"Sleep an' nourishment, an' kindly faces are what he wants," he said. "I've reduced his fever. He'll be fine when he wakes up this evening. Noo, Mister Huddy, we'll fix you up wi' a bath an' some clean linen."

"A bath," exclaimed Huddy. "That's fine." And he went off with the Scotchman happily.

"Three years in that hole," said Thurlowe, joining them. "And see what it's done to him. He's childish."

"He'll be all right again soon," said Boone. "What do you think of the Other One, as Huddy calls him?"

"I imagine he's been in some run-in with Sleeth or Cree and they beat him up till he was useless and then marooned him. Thought it a better joke than killing him. He seems more scared than demented. We've got to get that position out of him. Why didn't you bring him along?"

"Couldn't without driving him insane altogether. Are you going back with me? He's made friends with Ong Chuck and the Chinaman thinks he can make him talk. Otto, you'll come. We'll take Campbell."

They found Ong Chuck and his *protégé* at the mouth of the cave. The former was talking in pigeon English and the skeleton face of his listener bore a smile. On Campbell's advice they refrained from giving him more food, but handed the clothes they had brought to Ong Chuck, who spread them out garment by garment, indicating by gestures that the gift was for the creature who gazed at them with timid rapture and with a sudden rush gathered them up and fled into the cave.

"You bling plate?" asked Ong Chuck.

Boone produced the shallow box of sandalwood, cunningly carven, wrapped in silk brocade. The Chinaman opened the strange brass lock with touches on protruding studs and revealed a plate set snugly in the lining of padded raw silk.

"You tell me what you want find out, Cap'n," he said as they examined the plate.

It was of exquisite translucent porcelain, set with designs in red and black of concentric circles and square ideographic figures, like miniature plans of intricate mazes. As Ong Chuck took it from the box and gently moved it in a circle the patterns whirled and blended with a strange effect of dizziness.

"Hypnotism!" cried Von der Mehden.

Ong Chuck chuckled.

"All same hypnotism," he said. "You speak what you want. I think. He speak."

"I believe he can do it," said Boone. "We've solved the mystery, Thurlowe. You know, Ong Chuck, we want to find out the latitude and longitude of where Sleeth is."

"I sabby plenty. Better you go away *lele* while."

The three walked off and sat behind a rib of lava that protruded from the crater wall.

"Ong Chuck is a good navigator himself," said Boone. "He can handle a sextant as well as I can. Look, here comes the Other One."

The Other One, clad in fresh white ducks, his hair and beard black against the coat, appeared at the entrance of the cave. Ong Chuck spoke to him and they sat down facing each other. The Chinaman showed him the plate and shifted it gently in narrowing circles, the man watching every movement. Presently they saw the thin figure stiffen and Ong Chuck bend forward, making passes before him with his hands. A few sentences were exchanged, the man sitting rigidly, and then the Chinaman laid the relaxed body of his subject in the shade, set back the plate in its box and came triumphantly toward them.

"All ri'," he said quietly. "He sleep now, long time."

"Did you get it?"

"Sure. He look plate. Bimeby he go sleep. I speak, you all same officer fo' Sleeth. You sabby island. No this island. Other place Sleeth stop all time. You want go there. You speak me how sail ship. Latitood, long'tood. He speak ri' away. Twenty-fi' ten sou', one bundled seventy-fo' nineteen. Elemanga Island. Leef open sou' side. Bealing three palm one notch in mountain. Lagoon ha' mile west."

"Eremanga. Twenty-five ten, one hundred and seventy-four nineteen. Fifty-two miles south and just about a hundred east of here. Call it a hundred and ten sou'-sou'east from here on one long run. Thurlowe, we can make it by dawn. It's barely noon. You've got it straight, Ong Chuck?"

"Twenty-fi' ten, one hundled seventy-fo' nineteen," repeated the Chinaman. "I speak him too how many men? He say sixty-thlee."

"Sixty-three! Three to one odds, practically. But we can handle it, eh,

Thurlowe?" asked Boone. "How long will he sleep, Ong Chuck? No use taking him if he's so afraid."

"He sleep all same baby. Bimeby, long time, I think, maybe twenty-fo' hour he sleep. Velly ti'ed now. He all light."

"We'll leave him the grub and pick him up when we come back. Thurlowe! Otto!" He held out both his hands. "We're on the track at last, and, please God, we'll have Miss Newell out of it before we sleep."

"I like shake too," said Ong Chuck, and the four joined hands in the little crater beneath the blazing eye of noon.

VI

THE BUCCANEERS

THE TRADE WIND, THAT OFTEN AT THAT SEASON, when the northwest trades shift to the monsoon gales from the opposite direction, languishes at noon, blew true and strong. The *Roamer*, wing-and-wing, left a long trail of bubbling, sparkling foam behind her as she held straight course for Eremanga.

The heads of the expedition were assembled aft, watching the full-drawn sails, kept constantly wetted by the native sailors to get the full benefit of the breeze, speaking little, intent upon their own thoughts. Unafraid of the hazards of their quest, they reviewed its perils more clearly as they grew closer, with the quietness of men brave in the full consciousness of danger, intent upon playing their parts to the best advantage in the rescue of the girl and the avenging of their comrades.

The risk of a trap seemed imminent. That Sleeth would have an established lookout was only to be expected, and, with an arrival at dawn, discovery appeared certain. Yet in the face of all odds they must effect a landing, if possible, undetected. It was barely possible that the pirates, secure in their loneliness, might be lax in the matter of watchfulness, and this chance they hoped would break on their side.

No definite plans had been discussed before sighting Eremanga, and Boone hoped to secure some definite information concerning its characteristics and the habits of Sleeth and his followers from Newell and Huddy, both of whom, under the ministrations of Campbell, were asleep. Huddy indeed seemed to have had his reason shaken by his sojourn on the ghostly crater of Matemotu. He had taken the opiate given him with the willingness of a good-natured child and would probably be lost to consciousness for many hours. But Newell, Campbell assured them, would probably awaken about sundown, or he could, if necessary, arouse him without risk.

The only present arrangements made were in the disposition of the landing-parties. Boone was to command the port whaleboat, taking with him Von der Mehden, Campbell, Haley and Ong Chuck. Thurlowe, with Sanders and Dixon, his own two mates, and the two supercargoes, the starboard boat. Four native boys were to row in each, leaving four to remain with the second mate of the *Roamer* on board the schooner in company with Newell and Huddy, both of whom were out of the reckoning as fighting-men.

The after-deck was turned into an impromptu armory with a litter of guns and ammunition that was being apportioned and overhauled. Von der Mehden was busy with batteries of dry cells, coils of fuse and insulated wire. A box marked "dynamite" was close to him, under a tarpaulin. The young German had great faith in being able to employ his explosives in some effective manner and blithely superintended the work of his assistant, Bockstatt; a German love-song on his lips, utterly unconscious of the incongruity of the air and words he hummed with the deadly intent of his work.

> *"Ob ich dich liebe? Frage die Sterne,*
> *Denen ich oft meine Klage vertraut;*

"Cap those fuses, *landsmann!*

> *"Ob ich dich liebe? Frage die Rose,*
> *Die ich dir sende, von Thranen bethaut."*

Bockstatt, with grim dexterity, handled the fuses and arranged the wires, attaching them to the batteries.

"There," said Von der Mehden. "Mines we haf for land and water. And a couple of bombs to leave on the schooner. Drop those in their boats and *Guten Nacht!* There won't even be a splinter."

He laughed as he went to the rail. A great school of dolphins played on the quarter, swimming and leaping in a gay escort that was eagerly watched by the sailors as a certain harbinger of good luck.

The *Roamer* was making ten knots easily. The wind was due to lighten through the night and there was need of every mile they could cover while it held. By sunset the two skippers calculated they should have made between sixty and seventy miles, leaving about fifty for the dark hours. The risk of shoals had to be offset by the guard of constant soundings and the vigilance of all eyes and ears.

The essence of success was concentrated in getting under the lee of the island, on its south coast, before the light should uncover them and give the pirates too ample time for preparation of offense and defense. Occasionally, as the hours passed, one of the officers watched the course or hauled the patent log, reporting progress.

Ong Chuck served the sunset meal on deck. From a quietly deft, soft-footed, ever-smiling ship's cook, he had metamorphosed himself. His queue, which he maintained despite the mandate of his countrymen, was coiled tightly to his head, and about it he had wrapped a handkerchief of vivid yellow silk which seemed at once to transform his mild countenance to one of concentrated, if subdued, ferocity. His smile became a grin of menace, in harmony with the broad sash that held a curving, sheathless knife. Across his bare shoulder ran the strap of the holster of an automatic. His muscular body, smooth as ivory save for old cicatrices, showed yellow as old bone. Short, loose trousers ended at the knees. His feet were bare.

"If Sleeth sees you, Ong Chuck," commented Thurlowe, "he'll make you his first lieutenant."

"Suppose Sleeth, he see me, all ri'," answered the Chinaman. "Suppose I see Sam Clee?" He patted the blade of his long knife suggestively.

"What's your grudge against Sam Cree?"

"Long time ago he kill my blotheh," said Ong Chuck. "He catch um junk belong along my blotheh, all full-up sandalwood, in Little Colal Sea. My blotheh he fight. No good. Clee he take um sandalwood, put evellybody no dead in hold, shut um hatch, burn junk, burn evellybody."

"How did you find out about it, Ong Chuck?" asked Boone.

"I fin' out. One cousin of me he hide in wateh-ballel. Junk he plenty smoke, my cousin he jump ov'bo'd. Clee he no see. Bimeby, junk he bu'n to wateh-line, my cousin he climb back. Lain come. He get plenty dlink, not much eat. Bimeby canoe come. He save, my blotheh he burn. You likee tea, or Scotchysoda?"

Soon after sunset Campbell came on deck.

"Captain Newell asking to see you, Captain Boone. An' for the Lord's sake," went on the haggard medico, "some one talk to me an' keep on talkin'. Tak' it in turns. I'm nigh crazy wi' the abstinence."

They gathered around him as Boone went below. He found Newell awake in his bunk, fresh bandaged, his eyes—not so dark a gray as his daughter's, Boone noted—alert once more.

"Your Scotch friend patched me up, you see, Captain Boone," he said. "Though I'm afraid I won't mend soon enough to help you out much in the fighting end of it. Campbell has given me a hint of things," he went on. "What about my daughter?"

Boone told him, giving a swift review of the happenings since Marion Newell awoke in the night at Apia to find the message on the floor.

The wounded skipper sat upright amid his pillows, his thin hands clutching at the covers, his eyes ablaze.

"The scoundrels!" he cried. "And I'm lying here weaker than a child."

He sank back exhausted, unnerved and ashamed, the tears dripping between his bony fingers as he sobbed convulsively. Boone laid a hand on his shoulder. The sight of the brave mariner he had known, crying like a woman, brought home to him more clearly than ever the cruelty of Sleeth and Cree and the danger in which the girl was placed.

"That's why we're here, sir," he said.

Newell's hands dropped from his twitching face.

"You'll do your best, boy?"

"Surely, sir. For her sake as well as your own, Captain Newell."

"You're Boone's own boy, Dick," answered Newell, regaining self-control. "It's that dog Cree. I'd cheerfully give half of what life I have left to get a fair chance at him. And I had been congratulating myself on not letting Marion take the last trip with me.

"Campbell tells me you have got the position of this hidden island of Sleeth's from that poor wretch who was on Matemotu with Huddy and me. And only a scant hundred miles away. But you've got it. I tell you, lad, this is the time of Sleeth's reckoning. I feel it. He must be wiped out, he and Cree and all the piratical crowd of them—shown no mercy, given no quarter, hanged as high as Haman!"

His voice rose to a painful pitch and he fought for mastery of himself.

"Pretty much all in, Dick," he said presently in a more assured tone. "I haven't told you my end of the yarn yet. Sleeth on the *Ghost* cornered me between Phillip Island and Middleton Shoals—that's where my island lies. I must charter the *Roamer* to take me down there for a final clean-up, seeing I have no ship of my own. He had me marked down as a prospect, of course, for a year or more, and this time he caught me in a dead calm. Came up on us out of a rain-squall that had passed by us breezeless and dry as a bone. Chugged up with that infernal engine of his to within half-cable's length, and started talking as if we had come together for an ordinary gam.

" 'Good morning, Captain Newell,' he said. 'It has taken some time to arrange this meeting, but here we are and I hope it proves profitable.'

"His decks were swarming with men, a mixed crew of proper villains, black, brown, yellow and white, pock-marked every mother's son of them. The whole gang had been swept by the scourge, it seems, though, if it was intended as a lesson, they failed to learn it.

" 'I'm coming aboard, Newell,' he said. 'See that all your papers are in order.' And grinned, as if he'd been a boarding-officer, damn him!

" 'I'll see you in blazes first,' I called back. Meanwhile Yates, my supercargo, was serving out arms as fast as he could. I'd always carried a few rifles for protection.

" 'It's possible, Newell,' Sleeth sang out. 'But I'm not going to be there myself for a while.' Some of his rascals stepped aside and there was Cree, grinning that split smile of his from behind the breech of a quick-firer.

"Stevens, my first mate, lost his head. Not that we could have put up much resistance against them, but I might have picked off Sleeth and maybe Cree with lucky shots. But Stevens was wild with rage. He'd been decoyed ashore and drugged and his arm broken at Noumea by Cree, the voyage before—but you know about that. Stevens took a shot at Cree with an automatic. Missed him.

"A volley came back before the flash faded, you might say. Stevens dropped, done for, a bullet clipped me across the side of my head, and, the next thing I knew, I was in a bunk aboard the *Ghost* with a groove in my head and a hole through the shoulder. What happened to Bostwick, my second, and Yates, I don't know. Sleeth burned the schooner. As for the native boys, one or two of them fell at the first shots and I suppose they joined Sleeth to save their hides. Only natural.

"They kept me without attention, without water to drink or for my wounds, while Sleeth tried to make me give up the position of my island. There are pearls enough in the lagoon to make it worth his while, but after my experience with Cree on my last trip, when he shipped as mate, I had kept no log, except from day to day, so I stood it for two or three days—I don't know how long it was—till I petered out. Then they fed me, and one day they bandaged me up and got the bullet out of my shoulder, and Sleeth came to my bunk, as sleek and contented as a cream-fed cat.

" 'You needn't overstrain your memory, Newell,' he said. 'I've arranged to get that position from Miss Newell.'

"I lay there and swore at him while he chuckled. He must have tortured it out of one of my poor fellows that I was going to meet Marion at Apia. Yates, likely enough, he was always a bit of a coward. Then he laid the plans you have told me of, which went through only too well. They were through with me. I don't see why they didn't make away with me, some scruple of Sleeth's about killing a brother skipper, perhaps. He's full of queer quirks. But they took me to Matemotu, hauled me up the cliff and left me there.

"If it hadn't been for Huddy, I'd have handed in my papers all right. I used to wish I could, lying in the cave, thinking of those devils setting a trap for my Marion. She's all I've got, Dick. If anything happens to her, it's the end of me. They let me write to her and I did, warning her not to tell in the hope I'd get clear. But no one ever got away from that crater unaided. I owe Louis something for that.

"It's pretty tough lying here, helpless, Dick, thinking of what those dogs may have done to Marion."

"I've been thinking of that too, sir," answered Boone, "and I figure it out pretty clearly that they haven't harmed her yet. In the first place, it doesn't look to me like a scheme of Sleeth at all. It was too risky. He'll disapprove. As long as she holds the secret of the pearls, the men are not going to have her mistreated, even by Cree. They'll want to be sure of their share and she's not the kind to weaken under fire. We have a day or so's leeway waiting for the answer to that cable she is supposed to have sent, you know."

"You're right there, Dick. That was a saving idea about the cable. It's the best hope. You must let me be on deck when you reach the island?"

"Surely. That'll be tomorrow morning early. You'll be feeling fine after a night's rest. Can you tell me anything about the place?"

"Not much, but a little. I pretended to be worse than I was, lying in my bunk on the *Ghost*, and I overheard a few things that I pieced together. The island seems to have a double lagoon, joined by a creek that is navigable for the schooner only at high tide. There are natives, Papuans, who have been mistreated by Sleeth and his men until they are ready to rise. Sleeth is getting old and cranky. Has strange streaks of religion, if you can term it religion when it's quoted by that kind of a scoundrel. Cree aims to lead. The men are taking sides and discipline is slack. You may get in unseen after all. The camp is in the inner lagoon. There are about seventy of them, all told; about twenty, I think, are Kanakas.

"Is there anything I can do for you?"

"I think not, Dick. Unless that Chinaman of yours can get off these whiskers for me. I don't want Marion to see me like this."

"I'll send him in to you."

"Thanks. Then I'll try to get a little more sleep so as to be on hand tomorrow."

His eyes closed, and Boone left him, going on deck with the news he had gleaned. The wind still held fitfully and the luminous wake showed they were still making progress—though the canvas flapped idly at times—that should show the island close-to by the first light of dawn. Midnight came and the log registered ninety miles. Boone set double watches for signs of breakers and started the leadsmen to heaving at the bows. Every one on board was a volunteer lookout, every pulse on deck beat high beneath the stars as they drifted on through the night to Eremanga.

The vague oscillation of the sky-curtain that invariably presaged the coming of the dawn found the *Roamer* slowly holding steerage-way, true to its course in the spasmodic breeze, over the long heave of the sleeping sea. It was still dark and the leadsmen continually cast and recast their twenty-fathom lines for unexpected shoals, though so far all precaution had proved unnecessary. There had been no sleep on deck. Eyes had strained through the veil of the darkness, watching for the loom of land or lights, ashore or afloat; and ears had strained for the sound of breaking water.

Ong Chuck, who had spent the night squatting on the cathead, suddenly raised his head, sniffed the breeze, sniffed again in the spells of calm, peered long across the starboard bow, then padded aft on naked feet to his skipper.

"I smellee land," he said, his nostrils dilating. "You come look see."

Boone followed him forward and turned his glasses in the direction of the Chinaman's pointing hand and arm. Beyond the jibs, to starboard, a little dead patch showed in the star-set sky, close to the horizon-line. As the *Roamer* rose to the lazy swell he caught it again.

He gave swift orders, the sheets came in, the *Roamer* heeled a little on its new tack and headed up for the vague blot that meant Eremanga.

The dawn rushed swiftly up behind them as they neared the island, closehauled under its lee. Two peaks loomed high, the nearer, evidently of more recent upheaval, showing bare and blasted, rock-ribbed and forbidding, lower and of less extent than the farther, emerald with verdure, purple-valleyed, cleft like a bishop's miter. A few sea-birds wheeled in the sunrise, the surf drummed perpetually on the outer reef, but there was no challenge of shout or gun, the land seemed desolate.

"There's your notch," said Thurlowe to Boone, as the latter ordered the sheets eased, and the schooner, on her port tack, skirted the barrier reef. "Now for the palms."

A little promontory jutted from the land, set with pandanus, a straggling line of coconuts, and, in advance of the rest, three palms standing seaward like sentinels that gradually aligned themselves with the notch in the high peak. A gap showed in the spouting reef.

"How's the tide, Haley?" asked Boone.

"Running slack, sir."

"Head her up for the channel there. Haul in on your sheets. Smartly now. Take the wheel, will you Thurlowe, I'll con you in."

The crew jumped for the boomtackles and headsheets, the booms swung in, headsails flattened and the bowsprit pointed in line with the three palms and the cleft. Boone sprang to the foremast, and grasping the halyards footed swiftly up the rings to the spreader, scanning the entrance and giving an eye to the cliffs for some token of their having been observed.

"Channel's clear. Straight in to deep water," he called down to Thurlowe.

"No sign of trouble. Guess they're all asleep."

The schooner glided into the calm and limpid waters of the reef lagoon and headed slowly westward in the reflection of the volcanic cliffs, searching for the opening to the lagoon told of by the Other One in his hypnotic trance.

Passing a buttress of the sloping walls that towered high above the masts, a fissure opened up in the cliffs, stained red by the scanty soil through which protruded masses of somber lava. It grew wider and revealed the hollow interior of the mountain, lying dark and cool.

Boone announced a favorable channel, and standing up once more, the *Roamer* entered the water-basin of a flaring-lipped crater, the shell of a volcano, purple save where the mounting sun stained the western rim with a widening band of rose. The gentle lap-lap of the water at the stem was the only sound that broke the solitude. Almost opposite the entrance showed another gap where the crater walls had crumbled down. Mangroves grew rife in the bottom of the V, and above them gleamed the trees of the higher mountain.

Everywhere the cliffs rose sheer from the water save for a tiny beach at the gap, where a group of huts straddled on high stilts at the water's edge. The glass showed them abandoned, their thatched roofs destroyed by fire.

Within the bowl the wind failed utterly and the schooner drifted as the lead gave fifteen fathoms. Boone ordered the cable exchanged for a hawser to avoid the rattle of the chain, and the anchor was lowered without a splash into level water, blue as deepest cobalt, unflawed. The sails were handled with the same care and the schooner came to anchor as quietly as a floating swan.

"Well, here we are," said Boone. "Now for the next step. A landing-party, Thurlowe?"

"It's altogether too quiet to suit me," returned Thurlowe. "I don't like it. They probably feel tolerably secure. I don't suppose they've ever been disturbed, but I don't like it a little bit."

"That's the creek, by the mangroves, that ties up with the inner lagoon," said Boone. "I promised Newell I'd call him as soon as we made land. How about it, Campbell?"

"It'll be all richt," replied Campbell. "Huddy's still deid to the worl'. Newell's better on deck. I'll bring him up. He'll fret himsel' into a high fever below."

VII

EREMANGA

EREMANGA HAD THE GENERAL SHAPE OF AN HOUR-GLASS, with one bulb larger than the other. A creek, navigable at high tide for schooners, passable always for canoes and light-draft boats, connected the two craters, the one raw from the making, the other with its scars covered with densely forested sides that sheltered the Papuan natives, who, driven from their beach-dwellings, were in rebellion against their enforced servitude with Sleeth.

Both basins were water-covered, the inner, about a mile in diameter, roughly circular, fed by streams and partly brackish. Its walls shelved less steeply, and, on the western side, dropped to a level crescent beach backed by a lava wall, at the base of which the bush grew rankly in the talus. On this shore were the tents and encampments of Sandalwood Sleeth & Co., buccaneers.

Smoldering fires sent up lazy volumes of smoke. About them a number of the pirates lay huddled. At either end of the beach two sleepy sentries sat, arms about their knees, rifles beside them, on guard against the Papuans.

The *Ghost*, gray-hulled, sails snugly furled, swung at anchor in mid-basin, a solitary figure patrolling her decks. Her boats were hauled up on the sand at one horn of the crescent.

On top of the rock wall that backed the encampment another sentinel leaned upon his rifle and surveyed the sleeping camp. His call was answered by the watchers on the beach and taken up by yet another watchman, high on the rim where he could command the outer basin and the sea. Some of the sleepers stirred lazily, and, reassured by the hails, turned on their sides for another hour of sleep.

The man on the rim laid down his weapon and gazed anxiously into the seaward lagoon at the strange schooner riding there at anchor, as he had watched her make a confident entrance through the reef and find the channel to the outer basin. Now she rode short to her anchor, sails loosely furled, a whaleboat at the davits ready for launching; a brisk, noiseless bustle going on on deck.

Stunted, ill-nourished, a look of fear in his eyes as if in constant apprehension of a blow, the man glanced back irresolutely to the pirate stronghold. A second look at the *Roamer* seemed to strengthen his purpose. He stripped off his dingy shirt and scrambled painfully, barefoot, down the lava wall toward the abandoned huts, pausing frequently to wave his garment and to press his hand against his side, where a dark bruise showed plainly on his scrawny ribs.

"It's Boone's *Roamer*, sure enough," he muttered, flourishing his shirt. "They came in as if they knew the way. I wonder—"

He slipped and barely saved himself by clinging to the rough *tufa*.

On the *Roamer*, glasses were leveled on him as he toiled downward at evident risk of life and limb.

"That's a rum go," said Thurlowe. "He's trying to wigwag us all right, but the fool don't know any code. What d'ye make of it Boone? A trap?"

"It hardly seems so. More likely warning us, I should think. Wave back to him, Haley, it can't do any harm. Seems to me I've seen him before, without whiskers. Haven't you?"

"Let me take a look," asked Newell, lying on a mattress.

He propped himself on one elbow and took the glasses Boone offered him. He shifted the focus as he gazed, then handed them back.

"It's little Yates, my supercargo," he announced. "They must have pressed him. Get him aboard, Boone, he'll have news of my daughter. You can trust him. He's a coward, but he means well enough. Hurry, Boone, for God's sake, hurry man!"

The boat was already in the water. Boone and Thurlowe dropped into the stern.

"Von der Mehden, get Bockstatt and cover us with the second boat," shouted Boone. "Haley! Sanders! You go with them. On board there, stand by with your rifles. It may be some sort of a trap, after all."

Yates, ex-supercargo of the *Pleiades*, had reached the abandoned huts and stood at the edge of the water, beckoning. The first boat grounded and the two skippers sprang ashore. The covering boat hovered close by, ready to attack at the first sign of treachery. But no other figure appeared on shore or cliff.

"Yates, isn't it?" asked Boone. "I'm Captain Boone of the *Roamer* there. Captain Newell's aboard."

"Ah!" answered the trembling Yates. "I thought it was the *Roamer*. I know you sir, and Captain Thurlowe too, by sight. Is Captain Newell all right?"

"Yes. Pull yourself together man. Get in the boat."

"I can't. I've got to get back. I'm the sea-sentry. I have to call down to the cliff-man every hour. If they miss me, they'll be down on us. Have you got a drink? I'm all to pieces."

Boone produced a flask of whisky from the boat-locker and Yates held it to his chattering teeth.

"Brace yourself, man," said Boone sternly. "How's Miss Newell. Is she here?"

The man stared at him.

"She's here, and safe so far," he said. "I don't know how you got here, but thank God you did. They're asleep in there"—he jerked a wavering chin toward the creek—"all except the sentries. Hell's just ready to pop. Sleeth's acting like he was dippy of late an' Cree's workin' up a mutiny. Some of us will join you. Men who've been captured an' held like I was. We've no shares an' they treat us like a lot of niggers. Cruel. Nearly kicked my ribs in two days ago.

"Cree's just waiting to start his ructions when the *Crest of the Wave* gets back from Suva. They've sent her there with a note from Miss Newell to get a cable she's expecting. She sailed yesterday. Capwell, her regular captain, didn't go. He's crazy about Miss Newell. So's Cree. But Capwell swears he'll protect her. He's the first man Cree'll attend to if he wins out. But he hasn't done it yet. Sleeth's a wise one. Miss Newell's in a little cabin above the camp.

"She's safe for a bit. You see Sleeth's got most of the loot hidden somewhere, even Cree don't know where. That's holding the men back. The natives here have all quit. Cree used to flay 'em alive an' they've gone off an' hidden in the woods. They've got no guns and Sleeth burned all their canoes an' fired the huts. They can't get by us back of the camp, but they wait each side of the creek daytimes and the boats can't get out 'count of the rocks they throw down. They broke the foregaff of the *Crest* yesterday. Funny you didn't see her. But she sailed due north, of course, an' you come up to south'ard. I've got to go, they'll be missin' me."

"Wait a moment," said Boone. "How many are there in the gang?"

"Sleeth killed a man yesterday for swearin' at him. He's goin' dippy, I tell you. That leaves fifty-five, counting out my crowd. Besides the women, an' they're a tough lot."

"Who follows you as sentry?"

"Emory. He's one of my crowd. Used to be mate with Barkhausen. They don't trust us, but they make us take the outer watch. They'd kill us if we didn't report. But we'll take our chances with you."

"You'd better," said Thurlowe emphatically.

"We'll stick. I've got to get back though." He shivered apprehensively.

"Take this with you." Boone handed him the flask. "Get back to your post and warn Emory when he relieves you. Any danger of any one else seeing us?"

"No. They gamble all day when they ain't plotting or sleepin'. No one's ever come here before. An' they're too scared of the natives to tackle the creek daytimes, except in the schooner."

"When it's dark," went on Boone, "you and the rest you can trust—make sure of them, you're between two fires—come down to the creek. We'll be there. Can you get away safely?"

"We'll meet you at the bend."

"Can you get a message to Miss Newell?"

"I take her food to her."

"Then get word to her her father's here—with me—and to look out after dark for a rescue. Get back now and brace up, or you'll give us away."

"I've lost my nerve," whimpered Yates. "They've treated us cruel. But we'll be careful."

He started up the cliff as the boat backed off to join the other, both returning to the schooner.

"I'd like to take a look at the entrance, Dick," said Von der Mehden. "It's narrow, and Bockstatt agrees that we could put in some sticks of dynamite with a long fuse or a battery and choke it. Bottle them up, you know, if we haf to, in no time."

"All right, Otto. Go to it," said Boone. "But make as little noise as you can."

Armed with explosives and batteries, Von der Mehden went happily off with Bockstatt in the boat, joyful as a schoolboy about to tackle a wasps' nest. On board there was an eager discussion of the news Yates had brought. Captain Newell seemed to take on new strength and hope as he listened.

"Miss Newell's the first consideration, of course," said Boone. "I propose to reconnoiter after dark, with a view to getting her away without a general fight. It looks to me as if we might be able to."

"I hate to leave without one good try to clean out those pirates," said Thurlowe. "And there are the pearls. If we could surprise them from the cliffs we could come close to wiping them out. That may sound like a massacre, but I don't feel squirmy about it, when I look at Huddy and Newell here an' remember the others left to die on Matemotu."

"There are the natives," said Boone. "We don't want to overlook them. They are liable to be against any white man."

"Once get my girl aboard," said Newell, "and then tackle the crowd. Marion will be as strong on that point as any of you. As for the pearls, I can afford to lose what they took from me, but Huddy's lost everything and there are the widows of the skippers we know have passed out at the hands of Sleeth and his murderers. Flood's somewhere about dawn or a little later, you say, Boone. They can't bring out the *Ghost* till then. We go in with a clear retreat.

"If Von der Mehden can blow up that channel, we've all the best of it, even if we don't get away till after the flood is full. Get me my girl and then clean them up. If I could only stand on my feet for more than five consecutive minutes I'd be with you."

"That suits me," said Boone. "It's agreed we'll try for Miss Newell first, without arousing the camp, if possible. With her aboard, we'll tackle them at dawn, attacking from the cliffs and the cover of the mangroves. It isn't flood till two hours after dawn and, if they try to get their boats down the creek, I've got a plan to block the channel with one of Ong Chuck's Chinese pirate stunts. As for the natives, we'll have to take a chance on them. They haven't got any firearms, anyway. So as soon as it's well dark we'll be off for Miss Newell."

Boone set the native boys to work making a score or so of stakes about fifteen feet in length, using the piles and timbers of the huts. These were hewn at both ends to sharp points.

But for the risk of discovery from smoke, these would have been hardened in the fire, but, for the short use for which they were needed, Ong Chuck, superintending their manufacture, deemed them satisfactory. They were to be driven, later, under cover of darkness, into the soft bed of the creek at a sharp angle to cover their own retreat, if necessary, or serve as a barrier for any exit Sleeth might attempt, a formidable obstacle for oncoming boats propelled swiftly or a schooner gliding on a flood tide.

Toward the end of the afternoon Von der Mehden and Bockstatt returned triumphantly from the reef, where they had worked valiantly, drilling holes below and above watermark, wiring and assembling the capped sticks of dynamite.

"You leaf me on der rock," said Bockstatt. "Ven der schooner gome! So!" He pressed an imaginary button with a vigorous thumb. "Pouff!" And he tossed his fingers upward in a crumpled heap and smoothed the air with his palm in a comprehensive gesture.

Despite the work and the spur of the fear of momentary discovery, the hours dragged. Twice the alarm was given, as glimpses were caught of figures high on the cliffs, but as nothing came of these discoveries they determined that the observers must have been some of the rebellious natives who were powerless to attack them in their present position.

At eight bells, as soon as Von der Mehden returned, Boone took advantage of the ebb and had the *Roamer* towed through the crater channel, with its mines, to the reef lagoon, anchoring by the little promontory of the palms. There had been little or no wind all day and the barometer steadily dropped with a pumping action that was ominous. The trade-clouds were scattered in broken masses and the sea beyond the reef heaved sluggishly, dull of hue, unglazed.

The sun went down in a clear sky of tawny orange, blending into vivid green and so to the deep blue, almost violet, of the zenith. The three captains consulted over the weather signs.

"Looks like a three-days' calm to me," said Newell, and Thurlowe nodded his acquiescence. "This time of year's ripe for it. Then we'll get a gale from the south'ard and the monsoon season will be on."

"It'll blow in the right direction for us going back, anyway," said Von der Mehden cheerfully.

He was armed to the teeth with rifle, bandolier, two automatics and a hunting-knife, almost as spectacularly as Ong Chuck, and constantly humming his German love-ballad.

> *"Ob ich dich liebe? Frage die Wolken,*
> *Denen ich oft meine Botschaft vertraut;*
> *Ob ich dich liebe? Frage die Wellen,*
> *Ich habe in jeder dein Bildnis geschaut."*

"We're not going to get any good out of a calm," said Boone, "with Sleeth able to turn over his engine in the *Ghost* any time he wants to come out. A calm is the last thing we're looking for. But we can't change the weather."

"Much good their engine will do them when I press my little button on the reef," said Von der Mehden. "I only hope they come out after all the hard work Bockstatt and I haf done."

Well after dark the second mate and supercargo of the *Roamer*, much to their disgust, were left aboard with two of the native sailors and Newell and Huddy. The latter had frankly volunteered to stay with his wounded comrade.

"I'm too jumpy for much good," he said. "I'd fight in a corner, but they've got my goat for the time being. If anything is doing 'round here we can't handle, I'll send up a couple of rockets. Maybe you'll see them. But there's not much risk here."

The two boats started as appointed, Boone in charge of one, Thurlowe of the other. Skirting the cliff they entered the outer crater once more, a bowl of ebony cliffs and inky waters, waveless, reflecting the stars that blazed above the mouth of the great funnel, so that the boats seemed afloat in the heavens making their way between the planets.

With muffled thole-pins they rowed silently across the pool and reached the mangrove-guarded creek. The natives shifted their oars, using them as paddles dipping them silently into the velvet water, feeling their way through the narrow channel, guided by the opening where the fringing mangroves showed a strip of glittering sky.

No alarm came from the tangle of boughs and roots deep-set in the water, though the maze seemed an ideal hiding-place for lurking savages, armed with poisoned spears and arrows. Boone held a theory that the Papuans might have sensed that the arrival of the schooner boded no good to Sleeth and were waiting to see how events would aid their own reprisal.

They paddled for a long half mile to where the creek curved. Beyond the bend they saw the slopes of the inner crater opening up. The native boys climbed noiselessly overboard, knee deep in the water, and set the sharp stakes in a slanting palisade across the channel, the points out of water, hidden in the darkness until the rising tide should finally submerge them.

The work was done silently, the stalwart natives driving the stakes deep into the sandy bottom of the creek by sheer weight. As the last spear was being placed, a low hail came from the bank, followed by the whisper:

"This is Yates."

The matted roots of the mangroves formed a crude overwater trail and on it crouched six men, revealed by a swift flash of an electric torch. The two boats were moored to the tree-roots and all listened eagerly to the supercargo's report.

"There's a big palaver going on tonight, later," he said. "Cree and his crowd have been drinking all day and they're ripe for a row. That gave us our chance and we got away without being seen."

"Did you get a message to Miss Newell?"

"Yes. She ain't had much use for me. Seemed to think that I went back on the skipper, though I thought he was dead and only tried to save my own life. But I wrote two names on a slip of paper and hid it between two biscuits—Newell and Boone, I wrote, and when I went back for the dishes she crooks her eyebrows and I nods.

"Capwell was hanging around, an' I couldn't say a word. As soon as supper was over, Cree an' his bunch starts to hittin' the booze again an' I gets our crowd together an' we sneaks. I tell you we was scared pink of some of them Kanakas spittin' us with a spear in the dark, but it ain't far. You can see the fires from just round that bend. Listen!"

The sound of a chorus came clearly through the still night, then the tones of a rollicking baritone voice in the solo. The words sounded plainly.

> "A skull is the cup that tastes the best,
>   Ho for the red, red wine!
> Swallow the draft with an idle jest,
> The next turn may be thine, be thine,
> The next turn may be thine."

Then the chorus again trolled in unison, women's voices shrilling above the deep notes of the buccaneers.

> "Over the seas with a quickening breeze;
>   Ho for the life of a rover!
> At the point of a knife we fashion our life,

Ever the wide world over.
Though we die in our shoes with our neck in a noose,
We've only ourselves to blame.
So a fig for the priest and the black crow's feast.
Die game, my lads, die game, die game,
Die game, my lads, die game!"

"That's Black George singing," said Yates. "He's a Britisher and a bad one. Listen to the women."

A burst of high-keyed voices repeated the final line.

"Die game, my lads, die game."

"They're the worst—the women," said Yates, shivering. "They tortured me, they did, —— them."

"Did you tell Sleeth about Miss Newell waiting at Apia?" asked Boone sternly.

"I couldn't help it, could I?" he whimpered. "So help me, you'd have told. Had me swinging down, head first, over a slow fire. They'd have cooked me. Cree's woman was running it. It was in the galley of the *Pleiades*. They told me Captain Newell was dead an' they wasn't goin' to harm the girl."

"So Sleeth was in on that scheme, after all," said Boone. "Do they carry their women to sea with them?"

"It's against orders, but Cree does. She's a devil. Jude Demoulins. She's crazy jealous of Miss Newell an' she's threatened to knife Cree more'n once. He beat her up this afternoon, but she'll turn a blade in his ribs yet."

There was a grunt in the darkness from Ong Chuck.

"Can you guide us to the cabin where Miss Newell is, without our being seen, Yates?" asked Boone.

"After a bit. We can't pass Cree's gang yet. They're close to the trail. They'll go over to the other fire for a talk with Sleeth, presently. Then we can slip up."

"What about sentries?"

"I'm supposed to be one of them an' Olsen here the other. But they won't be watching out for us tonight. There's too much doing."

"The less go on this trip the better," said Boone. "I'll go ahead with Yates. If you don't hear from me in, say, half-an-hour, Thurlowe, come after me with one of the men to show you the way. We don't want to risk any open fighting till we get Miss Newell safe. Come on Yates."

The two disappeared, creeping noiselessly over the interlacing boughs. There was a little stir in the dark and Thurlowe turned to miss Ong Chuck, who had followed his skipper into the darkness.

Boone and Yates followed the creek to where it widened into the deeper waters of the inner basin, and, with bodies bent, stole into the jungle growing densely at the foot of the cliff that skirted Sleeth's encampment. Close to the foot of an upward trail it thinned out and there they halted in the pandanus where the shadows danced by the light of the fire, about which were gathered Cree and his followers, chanting their ribald songs.

A keg of liquor was tended by several women, dressed in tawdry finery, who, as they replenished the cups and mugs, tossed the heeltaps on the fire where they sent up little bursts of blue flame.

They were a rough lot, these latter-day buccaneers, who, in childish love of display, had evidently modeled their garb in emulation of earlier sea-rovers. But for their more modern weapons, they might have been a band of Morgan's or Bluebeard's desperadoes, come back from Gehenna to sport about an earthly, cooler fire. Bright bandannas bound their heads, earrings showed amid the shaggy locks, vivid sashes beneath leather belts holding up-to-date clips and cartridges. Most of them were bare-legged and footed in the soft sand.

They seemed of all nationalities, to judge from their jumbled accents, though sun and wind had tanned them to a universal swarthiness. Beards and mustaches were plentiful, with here and there an evident dandy. Cheeks glowed deeply red and eyes glistened in the glow of the fire while the two secure in the shadows crouched and listened.

The song ended and Cree, his puckered eye and awry smile plain to see, arose to his feet, swaying a little as he stood, though the liquor he had taken seemed to have rather inflamed than mastered him.

"Mates," he cried, while a shout of approval greeted him. "We'll hav' the confab with Meester Sleeth. He's bin a hog too long. He'll make good bacon. Listen"—his raised hands checked the laughter and cheering—"we mak' heem giv' up da loot you work for. Share an' share alike say I. Me—I giv' you my share. I tak' da girl. Vat you say?"

The circle broke into applause of hands and voice, a mêlée of fierce gesticulation and rapid talk. Boone clinched his fists to resist the impulse that prompted him to shoot Cree where he stood.

Yates laid a hand on his arm.

"Look," he whispered, his mouth close to Boone's ear. "To the right."

The face of a woman, handsome in its Gipsy type, the black hair, blended with the shadows, framing the strained features, showed plain in the ruddy firelight, peering from the pandanus, a scant dozen paces away. There was a bruise on one cheek, the eyes shone crimson like a beast's; one could imagine the figure poised for a spring. All the attention of the woman was riveted on Cree with an intense vindictiveness.

"Jude Demoulins," whispered Yates.

Boone could feel him shake with fear.

As he spoke the face disappeared, dragged back forcibly. There was a swiftly choked cry, the rustle of stiff leaves, lost in the crackle of the leaping fire and the sound of the voices about it.

"*P'st!*" sounded from the bush, followed by a low, crisp whisper in Ong Chuck's voice.

"You come here, Cap'n."

Boone crept across, snakewise, on his stomach.

The woman lay on the ground, pinned down by the Chinaman, one strong hand across her mouth. The other crept back and the blade of Ong Chuck's knife flashed as he pressed its keen steel to her throat.

"You cly, me cut," he said, and removed his hand cautiously from her mouth.

She lay without resistance or outcry, panting.

"Who are you?" she asked in a low whisper.

"I've come after Miss Newell," answered Boone. "What shall we do with her, Ong Chuck?"

"Better me kill, I think."

"You are a pair of fools," said the woman. "Lie close."

There was a movement around the fire, and the pirates, kicking the keg into the flames, trooped off to the other end of the beach where the remainder of the crew was gathered about another blaze.

"You want the girl?" asked the woman, as the two groups mingled. "You shall have her. You are her lover? If you want her, you are welcome to her, the pale, cold thing. I could choke the life out of her with one hand—the weakling! I would have before morning if you hadn't come. Now I shall kill Cree instead. Take away that knife, you fool."

"Better you leave Clee alone," said Ong Chuck. "Me fix Clee."

"He'll drive you into the sea, you fools," she answered. "Take the girl and go."

"You must come with us to the cabin," said Boone. "We know where it is. No treachery, mind."

"She cly, I fix," said Ong Chuck grimly.

"I'll do better than that," said Jude Demoulins. "Capwell's on guard. He's your rival." She laughed softly. "I'll get his attention while you kill him. He's no loss, the soft-hearted fool. Come, while Cree settles with that doddering Sleeth."

Boone called to Yates, and getting no answer crept back to where he had left him. There was no trace of the man.

"Lost his nerve again," commented Boone. "Come on."

They moved through the bush toward the trail. Ong Chuck had bound the woman's wrists with the kerchief from her neck. She led, followed by the Chinaman. Now and then he pricked her neck with his knife-blade.

"Bette' you lemember," he muttered. "No make cly. Sabby?"

They reached the summit of the cliff and looked down upon the beach. Both fires still burned brightly, though the deserted one was dying down. Voices came faintly to them of two men in dispute, the first Cree's, the other a deeper rumble.

"That's Sleeth," said Jude Demoulins. "He loses his last game tonight. Quietly now, there should be a sentry at the turn."

"If it's Yates, you won't find him," said Boone.

"Turned traitor, the sniveling coward? I pity him if Sleeth catches him. I smoked him once. Next time the fire will be hotter."

"Use your tongue when I ask you," said Boone sternly.

The woman laughed.

"There's your sweetheart," she said. "Better take the upper trail."

A light showed ahead from a little window. A passing shadow extinguished it for an instant, then it shone down the trail once more.

"Capwell's there," said the woman.

She led the way, climbing nimbly despite her fettered hands. Presently they were standing on a wide ledge twenty feet above the lower trail where the cabin closed the path, its outline vaguely visible in the starlight. Before it paced Capwell. The glint of a rifle barrel twinkled dully from his shoulder.

Boone heard the thumping of his heart as he knelt on the ledge, watching the sentinel parading in front of the lighted window behind which the girl was watching, waiting for some sign of rescue. He knew in that moment, the supreme one of the quest as far as he was concerned, with Marion almost within reach, within sound of his voice should he choose to raise it, that the pulsing beat within him was not merely the excitement of the issue close at hand, but akin to the mysterious thrill the mere thought of her never failed to bring, an alarm drum-call to love and arms.

Capwell stopped and listened to a shout from below, then strolled a short way down the path to where he could overlook the encampment.

"Will you trust me to go down and hold him in talk?" whispered Jude Demoulins.

"No," answered Boone curtly. "Stay where you are."

She turned her head toward him.

"Eh, but you are young," she said. "You know little of women. Have it your own way. Here he comes back again. I'll call him from here. Are you ready?"

Boone crouched, his thighs tense beneath him, as the unconscious Capwell returned. He had no wish to kill the man, who, however crude his chivalry, had at least aided in the protection of Marion. He came directly beneath them and the woman called to him.

"*Hist!* Capwell!"

"Who's that?" he cried, wheeling swiftly to face the cliff, his face upturned, his rifle ready.

"It's Jude, you fool," she answered. "Lower your gun."

He dropped the muzzle and Boone hurtled down upon him from the ledge, striking him full on his chest, bearing him violently to the ground. The man's head thumped on the hard rock and rolled limp from the neck.

"Want me?" called Ong Chuck softly.

"No," answered Boone, trussing and gagging the unconscious Capwell with his own headgear and sash. "Keep your eye on the woman."

He ran to the window, unglazed, rudely barred with wood. A face was already there, pressing close to his.

"Marion!" he cried.

"Dick!"

The door was fastened with a heavy beam, stapled into the frame. He tossed it aside and stood on the threshold.

"Come," he said.

Pale, her gray eyes larger than ever in their shadows, her hair pale gold in the light of the lantern on the wall, she came swiftly toward him.

"I knew you'd come," she said. "Where is dad?"

They left Capwell, bound and gagged, lying in the hut, the door barred upon him, and stepped swiftly down the trail. Ong Chuck and Jude Demoulins joined them where the paths met.

Cree's mistress laughed sneeringly as she saw Marion.

"Well, pigeon," she said. "Your mate has found you. Thanks to me, do you hear? Thanks to me."

Marion Newell looked at her quietly, without shrinking from her fierceness.

"Do you know what would have happened to that slim throat of yours tonight if he had not come?" went on the woman. "Do you know what would have happened to those lips he cherishes and that I hate? I would have sliced—"

She stifled a shriek as Ong Chuck sunk half an inch of his blade between her shoulders. Boone, his face burning, stood itching with desire to strike the furious mouth. To hear himself styled as Marion's lover, as the rightful possessor of her lips, must, he felt, raise a barrier between him and the sensitive girl.

"Keep silence, you," he said fiercely. "Let us go to your father, Miss Marion. He is waiting for you."

"He is well?"

"He will be when he sees you. Can you walk all right? I don't want to use the torch."

"Oh yes," she answered. "Let us hurry."

Ong Chuck, ahead with Jude Demoulins, laid one menacing hand on the woman's shoulder and held up the other warningly. The noises from the beach had died away, but there were footsteps on the path close by, a bold voice singing:

> "Red are the lips that wait for me,
>   Ho for the blood that flows!
> Eager for lovetime's revelry,
> Ho for her bosom's snows!
> Ho for her bosom's snows!

> "Over the seas with a quickening breeze,
>   Ho for the life of a rover!
> At the point of a knife we fashion our life
>   Ever the wide seas over.
> Though we die in our shoes—"

The song broke off.

"Capwell, you slinking dog," cried the singer. "That's you. Goin' to die in your shoes. Ri' now. Come on, you cur. Come out the shadow.

> "Red are the lips that wait for me—"

Cree lurched around the shoulder of the cliff. Jude Demoulins uttered an involuntary cry. Cree flattened against the wall and a bullet sang by Boone's ear as he thrust Marion behind him.

"That you, Capwell?" cried the pirate. "Eh? Why don't you fight back?"

Boone flashed his powerful torch full in Cree's face, dazzling him, while he felt for his automatic. The face in the glare was a-snarl with drunken passion and ferocity, the crooked lips drawn back, the eyes, maimed and dree, glaring through slitted lids. Jude Demoulins flung herself, bound as she was, upon Boone, biting, kicking, in a frenzy of revulsion as she shouted a warning to her lover.

"You shall not kill him," she panted. "I love him. Do you hear? I love him."

Boone glimpsed Ong Chuck darting through the ray of the torch toward Cree as he struggled with the desperate woman. The Chinaman and the pirate swayed on the narrow path. Ong Chuck's hand closed on the wrist that held the pistol, there was the flash of a knife, a groan, and the two fell.

In a moment Ong Chuck rose, wiping his blade on his sash. Jude

Demoulins flung herself on the prostrate form.

"He kill my blotheth, I kill him," said Ong Chuck. "I gut him all same fish. Betteh we hully."

Leaving the woman with her dead lover, they ran down the trail. The shot seemed to have passed unnoticed and they reached the bush at the foot of the cliff in safety and hurried on toward the creek.

Suddenly shriek after shriek sounded behind them. Looking over their shoulders they saw Jude Demoulins rush past the dying fire at the end of the trail, her dress sopped with Cree's blood, her hair streaming behind her.

Boone took Marion's hand and guided her across the treacherous pathway of tangled mangrove boughs, using his torch freely to blaze the way. Shouts came from behind, dying away, to their astonishment, until Boone sensed the reason.

"They've gone for their boats," he said. "We're nearly there now."

There were more shouts, this time ahead, and the beam showed Von der Mehden, pistol in hand, Thurlowe, and the rest close behind.

"Back to the boats!" shouted Boone. "They're after us!"

As they cleared their moorings the sound of oars in swift stroke came down the creek. They paddled swiftly to the bend and waited.

Splashes of light showed on the twisted trees and in the water, thrown from burning palm torches as two boats crowded with men, the red glare reflecting from their weapons, came surging down the stream. At the curve the creek widened and they drew abreast with wild halloos. The flaring brands gave little light ahead and they were upon the stakes without a hint of their presence before the crash of impact.

Both boats struck at almost the same time. The rowers fell back on their fellows amid curses and utter confusion as the water poured in through the shattered planks. From Boone's and Thurlowe's boats came a constant volley as the men emptied their repeaters into the struggling mass. The pirates sprang over their thwarts into the water and made for the shore as best they could, firing scattered shots that went wild and high.

"Back to the schooner," shouted Boone. "Row, don't paddle."

His boat led the way, Marion in the stern. The shouting buccaneers were soon left behind and they shot out into the outer crater, beneath the quiet stars, pulling lustily for the entrance.

"Man dear, yon was a gra' trick," said Campbell. "Ye staked them like we did the English at Bannockburn. It was gran', but we had to leave just as it was gettin' to be interestin'."

Lights showed on the *Roamer* in response to their shouts. The side-ladder had been rigged and Captain Newell, supported by Huddy, stood at the rail. The bandage on his head had been replaced by plasters and he carried his wounded arm in a sling.

"Is she safe?" he cried. "Did you get her, Boone?"

"I'm here, Daddy," answered Marion, and the next instant she was against his breast.

VIII

THE LAYING OF THE GHOST

THERE WAS A MIDNIGHT COUNCIL ABOARD THE *ROAMER*. Marion Newell was below with her father, the native sailors were clustered forward seeking the sleep their masters still denied themselves in the excitement of the quest, and the five men from Sleeth's marauding company who had come in with the still missing Yates were grouped by themselves amidships, uneasily conscious of the fact that, as renegades, they had yet to prove themselves before they were again admitted to equal rights and rank with honest men.

Though the first part of the expedition was successfully brought to an issue with the rescue of Captain Newell and his daughter, with the finding of Huddy, and the death of Cree for extra measure of satisfaction, the clash with the buccaneers had warmed the blood of the adventurers aboard the *Roamer* beyond any consideration of the affair as closed.

Boone felt his own instincts at war within, the wish to see the girl in absolute safety combating with the intense desire to clear the seas of every remnant of the buccaneers, and, at the same time, to recover all that was left of the treasure they had wrested from Newell and Huddy and the dead captains, lying huddled in the cave on lonely Matemotu.

"What do you think of the situation, Thurlowe?" Boone asked, as they sat with pipes and cigars aglow on the after deck. "Are we right in exposing Miss Newell to any further risks? Now that we know Sleeth's headquarters it would be an easy matter to hold him here, for a while at least, by exploding Von der Mehden's mine, long enough to see Miss Newell safely to Suva and call on Government House for help to capture the gang without further bloodshed. The sight of a gunboat and a well-aimed shell or two would soon bring them to terms."

"Well," answered Thurlowe, tugging at his beard, "that sounds like sensible advice, though I doubt if it comes from your heart, Boone. Of course the main idea of the trip was the rescue of Newell an' his daughter. That's done. But I hate to leave a job unfinished once it's well started. Here's Huddy plumb busted, and there's the fam'lies of Wahlgren, Barkhausen, Gregg, and the rest, sheer up against it for somethin' to eat, for all we know.

"You know what'll happen by the time Government House gets to workin' an' starts a gunboat down this way. Sleeth'll have vamosed, an' the loot, you can lay your bottom dollar, will be tucked away somewhere even tighter and safer than it is now. No, sir, I for one want to see justice handed out full-peppered to that nest of robbers, but I for one want to have a hand in it. An' if ye want to get back what they've stolen there'll have to be harder persuasion put to Sleeth than the methods of a British board of inquiry."

"Man dear," broke in Campbell, as Thurlowe stopped talking. "If ye turn back to Suva wi'oot anither crack at yon pirates, ye'll be takin' me back a corp. I've foresworn liquor till we feenish the job, an' let me tell ye purely fra' a pheesician's stan'point, that a man canna rin his internal economy on alcohol as long as I have an' shift to a change o' fuel wi'oot a breakdown.

"Ye can't rin a gas-engine on coal-oil wi'oot a new style o' carbureeter. Cree's dead, the rest o' the de'ils must be in a gey turmoil. We've gi'en them ane lesson, an' ye'll surely no be closin' the school yet. Ye promised me a bonny fecht, Captain. I've done naught but pu' the trigger a time or so, an' I'm no certain I did much damage at that."

He spoke lightly, but there was a wire edge to his voice that told of the genuine strain upon his vitality. His words brought a murmured echo of agreement from the rest.

"I potted two that I know of," said Von der Mehden. "I'm not over bloodthirsty, Dick, but *Donnerwetter!* this is no time to stop."

"As a matter of fact," said Boone, "I think the matter's settled for us by the weather. The barometer's still pumping for a change, but there'll be little wind if any before morning. Captain Newell spoke of a three-days' calm, Thurlowe. What do you think of the prospects now? Did you notice the phosphorescence as we came back?"

"Yes. Newell was speakin' of average conditions, which generally mean three days of dead calm at the monsoon change, but I'm inclined to agree with you that there'll be something doin' inside of twenty-four hours at the most."

"But at present we're due to stay here a while," said Boone. "So that ends it, and I'll confess it suits my mood. After all, I entered on this trip and asked you to join me at the instigation of Miss Newell. She is the real leader of the expedition."

"Then if that is the case, Captain Boone," said a clear voice, "the leader commands you to go ahead."

Marion Newell had come quietly into the midst of them and stood, one little fist clenched tight at her side, the other resting on the companionway, her head thrown back, her eyes flashing in the starlight—the personification of pluck and determination.

"Bravo!" cried Campbell, and a spontaneous cheer broke from the circle.

"I came on deck to thank you, Captain Boone," she said, "and all the rest of you gentlemen for your bravery and your—gallantry. We, my father and

I, don't know how to thank you, though we shall try to find some way. But on one thing we are assured. Indeed my father had asked me to deliver this message—to go ahead. Don't stop to think there's a girl aboard, please," she pleaded. "Think I'm a boy, as indeed I wish I were just now, and, if you'll give me a gun, I can at least try to use it."

The little speech brought more cheers, under cover of which the girl retreated to the cabin.

"That does settle it," said Boone. "If we can reflect some of the spirit Miss Newell shows when we tackle the job, I'm sorry for Sleeth. Now let's see where we stand. To start with, we've lost any advantage of surprising them. On the other hand, they've lost their boats. We're becalmed at least until morning, there's not the whisper of a breeze, but"—he held up a wetted forefinger—"they've got an engine in the *Ghost*. They can come out when they want to. We can go in, in boats, so long as the channel is open.

"Cree's dead, probably one or two more are accounted for in the scrap we had there in the creek. If Von der Mehden thinks he hit any one he probably did. We're eighteen whites with our new recruits"—he lowered his voice—"and I don't count heavily on them. Their nerve has been pretty well smashed. But call us eighteen, with eight natives and Ong Chuck, making twenty-seven in all. That's only two to one for odds. We can get away with that.

"Here's what I propose. At dawn, unless I miss my guess, when Sleeth sees us becalmed here in the lagoon at sun-up, he'll think us easy picking and bring out the *Ghost*. He can't get through the creek till full flood. That's somewhere about an hour after dawn. When he gets to the channel—"

"Pouf!" cried Bockstatt.

"We don't want to set off the mine unless we are sure he is coming through. We want to leave entrance in case we have to carry the fight to him. And we don't want to blow the *Ghost* up either, Bockstatt, just to put the cork in the bottle. Then we can talk terms to them."

"What terms?" asked Thurlowe. "You don't propose to load fifty odd prisoners, not to mention their women, aboard the *Roamer* and guard them all the way back to Suva! There isn't room in the first place."

"It could be done, I think," answered Boone. "But my idea was to land them all except Sleeth on Matemotu, and leave them there until the authorities took hold and sent for them."

"All of which is hatching your chickens before they are counted, *nein?*" put in Von der Mehden. "So! Put me ashore on the cliff with Bockstatt by our mines and I will close the door of your chicken-coop, so that you can count them at ease."

"In the meanwhile," said Boone, "we had better get what sleep we can. An hour or so will freshen all of us. Dawn is a little before five; high-tide about an hour later. We should start at eight bells, so as to take up positions before it gets light enough for any of Sleeth's lookouts to see us. Otto, are both sides of the entrance mined?"

"*Ja*. The wires lead to a ledge on the port side going in, where you can leave Bockstatt and me safely. We can peep over the edge of the cliff easily. On the other side of the channel there are caves big enough to hold your boats at high water, and there are ridges too, where you can climb and watch, and, if necessary, shoot from and be protected."

"Fine! Ong Chuck! Hot coffee and grub at eight bells sharp! Thurlowe, just a minute before you turn in."

The two skippers went to the after rail together, as the rest of the adventurers made themselves comfortable for three hours of much needed sleep.

"This is likely to be desperate business, Thurlowe," said the younger man. "If I am dropped and it looks as if it might go against us, you will take command, of course, and look out for Miss Newell's safety. I'm going to leave your mate Sanders aboard the *Roamer*. I know you consider him reliable.

"About the five men who joined us. They've proven themselves weak brethren once, and if things seemed to turn in favor of Sleeth they are liable to switch again. I don't fancy leaving them on the schooner with Miss Marion. Suppose you take two along in your boat to row, and I'll take the other three. At least we'll have them under our own eyes."

"Good idea, Boone," said Thurlowe. "And the first sign of treachery I get from mine I'll put a bullet through their heads with a great deal of pleasure. I've small use for their kind of cowardly turncoats."

"At least they came to us of their own accord," said Boone. "We'll give them a fair show."

"Ye'll never win a prize in a dog-show with a coyote," countered Thurlowe. "I'm for forty winks. Good-night, Boone, you're handling this thing in fine style, lad. Good night."

There had been a good deal of light-hearted chaffer among the members of the *Roamer's* crew from the outset, whatever thoughts lay beneath the surface, but something of grim purpose began to show on their faces as they busied themselves in preparing for the second encounter. Captain Newell, visibly improved since the restoration of his daughter, stayed aboard with Huddy and Sanders, the latter in command of the disconsolate schooner-guard. Marion Newell came to the rail in the darkness to wish the boats success.

"I wish you'd let me come with you," she said. "Good luck and thank you again, Captain Boone and all of you!"

She laid her hand on Boone's arm as he stood by the rail, and the thrill within him quickened to a demand that he take her there and then within his arms. He glanced down at the little fingers, pale and fragile in the starlight, and laid his own over them for a second.

"Thanks," he said, his voice sounding oddly gruff and far away in his own ears.

"Fair Maiden," said Von der Mehden with easy gallantry, making light of the occasion as of all others, "you are about to send your knights forth to battle for your fair sake. Wait for the explosion. Give me a token to wear as talisman. I haf no helmet to which to bind it, but I can fasten it to my sleeve. It will assure that the dynamite goes off in the right direction."

Marion laughingly unfastened a ribbon from her neck and gave it to the light-hearted German who tied it about his arm and took his place in the boat. Boone felt a sudden pang of jealousy, vexed at his own lack of wit, envious of the gage that Otto carried proudly.

But the mood passed as the boats left the schooner and passed through the luminous water of the lagoon toward the crater entrance.

Violet fire dripped from the blades of the oars as they rowed under the cliffs, a green veil of phosphorescence trailing in their wake. Now and then the leap of a fish broke like a sudden water-firework. Even for those latitudes, where the sea is never untenanted by the ocean fireflies, the display was unusual, a certain portent of an imminent change in the weather.

The ripples lapped against the cliffs with weird reflections and the waves that topped the reef shattered their crests in ghostly illumination. Boone did not forbid conversation, as there was practically no danger of being overheard with the pirates cooped up in the inner crater, a mile or more away.

"I'm thinkin' the water o' the River Styx must be like this," said Campbell. "Only the fire o' this is cauld. There'll be some o' the de'il's yonder crossin' the tide wi' Charon before another nicht, likely."

"Here's hoping we're not in the same ferry," said Boone. "Where's your lodge, Otto?"

"Right here. Up you go, Bockstatt."

The two Germans were landed and clambered up the cliff to a shelf well above high water, where their wires connected with the batteries. There was the flare of an electric torch as they examined the contact wires.

"All ready for action," reported Otto.

"I'll get up to where we can see each other, Otto," said Boone. "We'll let the *Ghost* get close enough to talk before you set her off. I'll give you the signal and you can pass it on to Bockstatt. If they don't come out, we'll reserve the mine for later developments. How far along are the caves?"

"Close to the other side of the channel. You can't miss them. *Auf wiedersehen!*"

The two boats crossed the entrance on the flood, already swirling through the narrow channel, and readily found the wave-worn hollows in the cliff with the aid of their torches. There was water enough to enter, and, leaving the native boys to look after them, the white men, including the new recruits, waded across the weed-coated rocks and found a way up the face of the wall to a ledge where they waited for daylight to reveal the best place of vantage.

As they settled down, making themselves as comfortable as they could on their rocky perches, Boone climbed higher till he was looking into the star-sown void of the crater. The silence that always deepens just before dawn seemed to brood around and above him, like the shadow of heavy wings, broken only by the low sound of the combers at the reef-barrier, rising in shadowy hills, falling in luminous foam.

From across the channel where Bockstatt and Von der Mehden clung like limpets to the rocks came the low, clear tones of Otto's voice in his perpetual love-song. Boone could see him faintly, humped up on the rim of the cliffs, hardly a hundred feet away. He was singing softly, but the words were distinguishable in the stillness, though Boone failed to understand all their meaning.

> *"Ob ich dich liebe? Frage dich selber.*
> *Hab' ich auch nie dir meine Lieb' vertraut.*
> *Ob ich dich liebe? Frag' meine Augen,*
> *Immer hast du's in ihnen geschaut."*

Ich dich liebe—Ich liebe dich. Boone remembered an engraving he had seen above that title. Two lovers at an open window. *Ich dich liebe.* His tense mood softened to thoughts of Marion.

Love seems, to us purblind mortals, to choose strange times for the pushing of his claims. Boone—on war and death intent—found himself dawn-dreaming of the girl whose touch, whose presence, the lightest thought of whom, set quivering deep within him the mysterious thrill that, first inspiring sympathy and protection, now bid fair to assume the mastery of all his being and guide his thoughts into new ways of tenderness and longing.

Through the swift stress of the pursuit, the finding and the fight, he had thought but little of Marion, save as a woman in distress. Cupid had apparently been inert, while all the time that master-musician had been quietly setting his stops, preparing for a triumphal strain that hinted in its subtle harmonies a wedding-march.

Not that his thoughts were altogether pleasant ones. First-love, not of youth, but early manhood, is generally self-deprecatory, and Boone, with a real man's lack of appreciation of his own worth in a lady's eyes, set aside the value of his superb, clean-living body, making the frequent error of lovers that love is a child of the brain, not the elemental call of fitting mate to mate, an irresistible power behind, beyond the reason.

Otto's facile gallantry haunted him. The German, with his resources of education, travel, means and rank, seemed to Boone a man much more likely to be desired by Marion, whom he invested with all a lover's magic mist of infinite delicacy, than the rough, uncultured sailor he deemed himself. The only sign of preference the girl had shown, to his mind, had been manifested in the ribbon token Otto, singing love-songs on the opposite cliff, now bore upon his sleeve.

A touch on the arm aroused him from his reverie. Thurlowe had climbed to his side.

"Daybreak," said the elder skipper.

The horizon shivered and turned gray, then coppery rose. The sun thrust itself abruptly from its sea-couch, not radiantly, as usual, but with the sullen glow of a bronze shield reflecting fire. The sky as it lightened seemed covered with a film. The sea, emerald within, deep blue beyond the reef, was dulled in its hues like the tones of an ancient rug. Below on their ledge the men yawned and stretched, shivering a little from excitement and lack of sleep, like dogs in a blind, waiting for the fight.

With their feet resting on a narrow shelf some five feet below the rim, the two captains cautiously viewed the basin and the cliffs beyond. The tide curled snakily as it still surged through the channel, lifting the seabeards of the rocks at the foot of the inner cliffs. There was no sign of the *Ghost* yet, no movement by the mangrove-hidden creek or on the distant slopes. A band of pink stained the rim of the crater, slowly widening as the sun rose.

Across the channel Von der Mehden had descended to the side of Bockstatt and the two stood staring upward at the rim of the crater. Von der Mehden turned and catching sight of Boone beckoned earnestly.

Boone made a shell of his palms and called across.

"What is it, Otto?"

"Come over here."

Boone glanced down to the lagoon. There was some risk of sharks in the flooding tide, but he decided to take it.

"Hold my guns, will you Thurlowe?" he asked. "I'll swim across. They might see the boat. Can't tell where a lookout may be hidden now."

He stripped at the water's edge, borrowing a knife from a native boy in case of some intruding sea-wolf, set it between his teeth and swam across, keeping under water as he passed the open channel. He scrambled over the rough rocks to where the two Germans still gazed upward. As he gained their side his eyes followed Otto's directing arm. To the left, from the rim of the crater, in a little notch of the lava, an extended arm projected stiffly, the clenched fist palm downward. On the wrist showed Sleeth's Mark in tattoo, the skull with a bone between its teeth.

"Dead?" asked Boone.

Otto nodded.

The three climbed to the rim. Across the cliff-top lay the emaciated body of a white man clad in canvas trousers. Ribs and backbone protruded through the scant flesh covering. A livid bruise covered one side. In the other an arrow was sunk deeply.

Boone pulled it out with an effort and turned the body face to the sky.

It was Yates, the renegade supercargo.

"Poor devil," said Boone. "That's what he got for funking it last night. The natives got him. Evidently they are out for business, seeing we've started matters. They are likely to give Sleeth trouble as he comes out. On the other hand, they are liable to keep him busy inside. It's to be hoped they leave us alone."

"What shall you do with this?" asked Von der Mehden, covering the dead man's face with a handkerchief.

The rosy sunband, creeping onward, touched the putty-colored flesh and gave it a semblance of returning life.

"We can't leave it here," said Boone. "Probably Newell would want to give him decent burial. He was his supercargo, you know. It wasn't all his fault that he was a coward. He was probably always getting licked, from school up. Let's get it down by the water in the shade. We can get it aboard later."

They set the battered, pitiful shell of Yates in the shadow of a great boulder, Von der Mehden stripping off his own silk shirt to cover the naked chest. Then he and Bockstatt climbed back to their posts while Boone swam the channel.

Dressing swiftly, Boone rejoined Thurlowe and found the latter looking through his binoculars at some moving figures on the top of the cliffs by the creek.

"Natives," he said, handing over the glasses.

"I expected something like that," replied Boone. "They got Yates over there on the other side of the channel. They're on the warpath it seems. All the better, as long as they leave us alone."

The lenses revealed a drawn-out file of Papuans, seldom more than one showing at a time, crawling antlike along the summit of the cañon that dominated the stream joining the inner and outer basins.

"Looks as if Sleeth was getting ready to come out," said Boone. "I guess he's caught a glimpse of the *Roamer*. It's up to him to get clear of the island whether he does us up or not. He'll be afraid of our having told others the position of the island. He don't know where we got it, probably, and hardly thinks it safe to linger."

"Did you find out anything about the chap we left on Matemotu?" asked Thurlowe.

"The Other One? Yes. Doane, down there"—he indicated one of the renegades perched below them—"says he was Sleeth's right-hand man till Cree joined. He split with Sleeth over Cree's advancement. Sleeth set him down, cut off his share to the same as the men's, and, when he kicked, manhandled him. He was afraid to kill him on account of the chap's popularity, so he shipped him to Matemotu, crippled up and off his head. Thinks he's dead, I suppose. You know the poor devil hides whenever Sleeth shows up."

"Reckon the tide's about full," said Thurlowe. "Looks that way to me."

From the rim across which they peered the inner wall sloped sharply to the water where the weedy rocks were now submerged. Hummocks of lava stood out here and there from the tufa and there was a rough trail, like the bed of a dried torrent, forming a rude stairway up and down which desperate men might climb.

"Listen!" warned Boone.

The *chug-chug* of a gasoline-engine, tossed back and forth by the cliffs, came to them across the basin. Boone spoke to the men beneath them.

"Haley, you and Mr. Campbell get the men ready. Don't come up here till I tell you. See that every one's magazine is full."

The crack of a rifle sounded from the creek cañon, followed swiftly by others, the echoes multiplying and magnifying the reports to a fusillade.

"Here they come," said Boone. "Look out, Otto!" he shouted to the German, who, his head close to the crater-rim between his folded arms, waved a hand in signal of readiness.

"The Kanakas are getting in their work," said Thurlowe as the scattering shots turned to a constant volley. "There she blows!"

The bows of the *Ghost* showed gray through the mangroves and the schooner, stripped of sails, glided into the basin. The Papuans, now helpless to attack with their primitive weapons, circled the lips of the crater in vain pursuit.

"We'll have to keep those natives off if they get much closer," said Boone.

He kept his glasses trained on the *Ghost*. No more shots came from her decks in what would have been largely wasted ammunition, and men came up from below till there were half a hundred or more of them crowding the decks. One man distinctively bigger than the rest, his head wrapped in a black scarf, directed a group that labored amidships about some object that stood between the two masts.

"Those Kanakas have put that machine-gun of Sleeth's out of business," announced Boone delightedly. "Smashed it up with a rock, I guess. They're working on it like beavers. Now they've given it up. By Jove, Thurlowe!" he exclaimed as the schooner, the exhaust of its engine sounding steadily, forged across the quiet water of the basin, "there are women on board."

"Afraid to leave them behind, I reckon," commented Thurlowe. "Or as you said Sleeth is figuring to clean us up and make a clear getaway."

Whang!

A bullet struck the rock below and between them with a vicious impact.

"Good shooting that!" said Boone. "Must have caught the flash of the glasses. It's that tall chap with the red sash. Look out."

Another bullet whistled overhead as the two skippers sought and found cover behind an outcrop of flinty rock.

"Nice looking gang," said Thurlowe. "Going to take a pot at 'em before you let loose the mine?"

The gray schooner was rapidly nearing the channel, its crew gazing upward at the cliff. Practically all were naked to the waist and barefooted, many wore only loin-cloths, but all were gay with vivid headcloths and sashes, above which belts carried knives and pistols. Aft, about the dominant, bull-like figure, were grouped a dozen or more gaily clad women, applauding the shots of the tall marksman.

"We might hit the women," answered Boone. "We'll have them all where we want them in a few seconds." He raised his voice. "All right, Otto!" he shouted.

A volley of shots flew above them as they crouched, waiting for the explosion.

The seconds passed and the *Ghost*, headed direct for the center of the fifty-foot channel, was practically immediately beneath them. They could have tossed a cartridge on to her decks.

"Mine's fizzled out," said Thurlowe. "Wish we had a few loose rocks handy. We could sink 'em easy."

"Otto!" cried Boone again, risking his head for a look across the strait.

The men on the schooner were firing straight up the face of the cliff. Von der Mehden's head was still sunk between his shoulders, resting on his folded arms. His figure seemed strained, curiously rigid.

"They've potted Otto!" cried Boone. "Bockstatt, fire the mine. Bockstatt!"

As he shouted, the crater wall heaved beneath them and seemed to lift with the dull roar of the exploding dynamite. Masses of rock hurtled upward and outward, a column of green water spouted—white-maned like a rearing dragon—and fell.

Smaller geysers leaped as the rock fragments dropped into the gut, piling one on the other, until as silence came with the dying echoes the passage showed in a great raw gap of red rock, like a bleeding maw, with jagged boulder-teeth rising here and there from the water.

The *Ghost* lay, her bows high lifted on a submerged reef, raised by the explosion, the foremast snapped, the stays dangling, her crew crowded aft in consternation.

The stout leader rushed forward to the shattered bowsprit and stood defiant, shouting curses at the cliff-tops where the adventurers stood looking down on the confusion, with rifles covering the deck of the schooner at short range. About the crater lips the Papuans were scrambling with the agility of baboons down the slopes and gathering by the ruined huts at the mouth of the creek.

Boone, still in the shelter of the rock, disposed his riflemen along the ledge on which he stood, cautioning them to keep to cover closely, and called down to the stranded vessel.

"Tell your men not to fire, Sleeth," he cried, "and we'll talk. We've got you covered, and if you start trouble we'll riddle the schooner like a sieve."

Sleeth, his legs wide apart, braced on the sloping deck, ceased his futile tirade. His great frame was wadded with fat that hung in folds from age-slackened muscles. His bull-neck had outgrown to fill the natural incurves from the chin and base of the skull. His protuberant paunch was flabby. His big arms, from elbows to finger knuckles, were covered with the same tangle of red hair that masked the barrel of his deep chest.

His face, heavy-jowled to meet the neck, was hairless and heavily pitted. He wore a black sash and leather belt about his coarse canvas trousers for his only covering. Yet, with all the drag of years of ill-living showing in his lax bulk, he loomed eminently the leader. The defiant glare of his eyes, deep-socketed in the fleshy cheeks, could be felt rather than seen. He retreated to the wreck of the machine-gun and bellowed an order to his men.

"Who are you?" he cried.

"Well," said Boone, "here are Thurlowe and Newell, Huddy and Boone, with enough more to amply take care of you." He bent down and whispered to the ledge of men crouching with their rifles ready, eager to take active part. "Give a cheer, boys, a loud one."

Led by Haley and Campbell, they shouted at the full of their lungs. The native boys below with the boats echoed them, and from Bockstatt, who had mounted to the side of Von der Mehden, came a stentorian "*Hoch!*"

The hurrahs had a palpable effect. The buccaneers on the *Ghost* stirred in uneasy clusters. One of them, the tall man with the red sash who had been the sharpshooter, joined Sleeth and talked with him, gesturing earnestly.

"Send a boat over for Bockstatt and Von der Mehden, Haley," ordered

Boone. "You go with it, Campbell, and see what you can do for him."

"Dinna start the fechtin' till I'm back then," replied the Scotchman, as he started for the water's edge.

Sleeth dismissed his adviser with a sweep of his hand.

"What do you want?" he called up.

"You," answered Boone. "And your loot. That's first. We take you to Suva. The rest of you we'll leave on Matemotu till the British government sends for them. Throw your arms overboard and come through the channel six at a time. Swim if you can't wade. We'll get the women later."

The ultimatum was received with loud talking from the crowd of buccaneers and their women. They shouted counsel to Sleeth with violent gesticulations. He silenced them with a bass roar.

Cupping his hands he bellowed furiously back to Boone.

"I'll see you in hell first!" he shouted.

"By the Eternal, you'll be there yourself in a minute," cried Thurlowe. "Look yonder, Boone!"

Out from the little beach by the huts came a floating barricade of poles and timbers and bits of the unburned thatch, pushed steadily across the basin by the lusty arms of swimming Papuans. Behind it bobbed ten-score of frizzy heads. Weapons glinted and arms flashed wet in the sunrise, while shrill cries sounded fiercely across the watery sounding-board.

"Better make up your mind quickly, Sleeth," called Boone. "We'll treat you better than your friends in the water there. If you lay down, we'll hold them off. If not—"

Sleeth's only reply was a voluble string of oaths. The buccaneers commenced firing at the floating shield, apparently without effect. The barrier split and came on, one half to the left and one to the right of the stranded schooner, the Papuans evidently intending to attack their trapped masters from both sides. The war cries grew louder and more triumphant, the eyes of the revengeful savages showed as they rolled exultantly while the rafts steadily closed in on the ill-fated *Ghost*.

"We can't let those brutes get at the women, Thurlowe," said Boone.

"They can for all of me," answered Thurlowe. "They're worse devils than the men. Didn't they smoke that poor devil of a Yates?"

One or two of the shots were taking effect on the swimmers, but there were two hundred Papuans behind the shields, water adepts, diving and swimming beneath the surface, their positions hidden by the rafts; hard targets for the best of shots, relentless in the memories of a thousand wanton cruelties suffered at the hands of their late masters, at last within striking distance.

Confusion broke out on the *Ghost* as the barriers simultaneously neared the sides of the schooner whose lowered stern presented but a low freeboard to the attack. A ring of men surrounded Sleeth in excited argument. Campbell, followed by the native boys, mounted to the cliff-top. "The Dutchman's no deid," he said. "Shot through the right palm an' clipped senseless by a spent bullet. He'll do nicely. Bockstatt's wi' him i' the boat. Am I in time?"

"Well, Sleeth, what's your answer?" shouted Boone, as the pirates prepared to repel the Papuans, now swarming on to their rafts preparatory to climbing the rail of the schooner.

Sleeth broke from the crowding men, shook both fists in imprecation, rushed aft to the companionway and disappeared below.

"He's quit," said Thurlowe. "Gone to get the loot. He's a bit late in making up his mind."

The buccaneers were furiously endeavoring to repel the onslaught of the savages, women as well as men firing pistols and thrusting back at the natives with improvised weapons.

"That ends it, an' naught fired but the mine," said Campbell dejectedly. "Man Boone, do ye ca' this fechtin'?"

The Papuans were gradually gaining foothold on the decks, thrusting with spears and smiting with heavy war clubs as they shouted, when Sleeth reappeared, coming forward to the bows.

"You'll go back empty-handed after all, you bloody man-hunters," he yelled, foam flecking his lips. "Now, lads"—he turned to his crew, engaged in hand to hand conflict with the savages—"the chorus, out with it!"

> "A fig for the priest and the black crow's feast,
> Die game, my lads, die game!"

His deep voice hoarsely trolled the chorus. Some of his men took it up half-heartedly as they repelled the Papuan rush, then catching his meaning, changed to a shriek, half rage, half despair, and those near the companionway shrank from it, regardless of their foes, as they noted the coils of smoke rolling sluggishly upward. Threads of vapor writhed from the after hatch.

"Ha! Ha!" laughed Sleeth insanely. "There's twenty casks of gasoline and oil aboard! Die game, my lads, die game!"

"The man's stark crazy," said Campbell.

The buccaneers ceased resistance to the Papuans who still struck fiercely, as if unconscious of the danger or careless for anything but revenge. Some of the pirates sprang overboard, others rushed below in an attempt to stay the flames.

"Between the de'il an' the deep sea fu' o' his servants," said the Scotchman.

A sheet of flame burst from the companionway. The deck appeared to rise intact, then to crumple like paper. The schooner was instantly enveloped in a searing blast of exploding gases like the roar of a bursting volcano. Masts lifted through the dazzling glare, the air scorched the lungs of the watchers, the cliffs reverberated with sudden thunders and settled to silence.

There was hardly a sign left of the *Ghost*. The fumes of the gas, red in the morning sunlight, floated high above the crater, here and there blackened fragments floated where burned swimmers strove in agony. The rafts of the Papuans had disappeared and the savages who had escaped the explosion, diving deep at the flash, were swimming fast for the shores.

Boone and his men stood aghast at the spectacle.

"God, but that was awfu'!" said Campbell. "Wiped oot like marks fra' a slate. But the de'il takes care o' his ain. He's some man, yon Sleeth. Look at him!"

Striking out for the shore beneath them, with a vigor that seemed incredible, came the leader of the buccaneers. His scarf had been blown from his head, exposing its absolute baldness across which ran a smear of blood. Behind him struggled four others, one a woman.

"It's Jude Demoulins," cried Boone. "She's swimming the wrong way. She must have been blinded. Get down the slope, men, and help them. Pick off those Papuans!"

A dozen savages had turned and were swimming rapidly to overtake the survivors. As the shots pattered and ricocheted about them, one warrior with a yell reached his victim. A knife flashed, the buccaneer disappeared, and the Papuan, fast swimming under water, presented only a momentary mark as he escaped.

"That's ane," said Campbell, as a shot from Boone reached its target and a savage threw up his arms and sank. "An' that's twa!" And his own bullet smashed into a dusky skull.

Another pirate went down with a shriek as his savage opponent clubbed him. A Papuan grasped for the woman, who grappled with him as they swam, striking at him with a knife she held in her free hand. They went down together in a swirl of water that had not yet smoothed when Jude Demoulins reappeared, gasping but triumphant, her knife left in the breast of the savage, twelve fathoms below.

Haley waded out to meet her, guiding her by his shouts. She touched the shoal that had been made by the exploding dynamite and stopped irresolutely.

"It's all right," said the mate. "Come ahead, we're not fighting women."

He reached her hand and led her to the shore and up the slope.

Sleeth was stumbling among the slippery rocks, a savage close behind him, intent on transfixing him with his spear. The other buccaneer had reached the shore and fallen exhausted, face downward, regardless of foes ahead or behind.

"Cover Sleeth," cried Boone to Campbell as they raced to the water, automatics in hand. The pirate leader was in the direct line of his own fire and he emptied his clip into the two Papuans about to strike the prostrate man.

"Drop, you loon," cried Campbell, and Sleeth slumped forward into a pool. The Scotchman fired as the savage lunged. Both fell, the frizzly head of the native plunging beneath the water as he dropped dead across Sleeth, half submerged in the pool.

From higher up, Thurlowe and the rest fired at the retreating Papuans while Boone ran to Campbell's side. The hardwood spear of the savage had sunk deep into him below the ribs, the shark's-teeth edge tearing a ghastly wound.

"I'm done for," said Campbell faintly. "It wasna much of a fecht, but it was better than nane."

He fainted, and at Boone's orders was borne carefully up the slope.

Thurlowe turned his pistol on the buccaneer saved by Boone's pistol. The man had recovered sufficiently to sit up. His face and naked torso were black and crimson from smoke and burns, his hair and long mustache were singed to a crisp, but he essayed a smile.

"Don't shoot, old chap," he said. "No need. I'm all in. Honor bright! Look after the guv'nor, will you?"

"You nearly potted me on the cliff from the schooner," said Thurlowe sourly. "I've a mind to show you I can shoot straighter and save hemp."

"Sighted too low, y' know," answered the tall marksman. "You've got me where you want me. Bear a hand with the guv'nor, there's a good scout."

"He's cheated the gallows," said Thurlowe, glancing to where the men were dragging the heavy, limp body of Sleeth from beneath the Papuan in the pool.

"Not half," protested the singed pirate. "Not the guv'nor. Not born to be drowned, y' know."

It seemed as if his hopeful diagnosis were correct. Sleeth, under the ministrations of two men, commenced to moan as they attempted to get the water from his lungs. Presently he sat up weakly between them, coughing feebly but eminently alive.

The two boats bearing the body of Yates and the three prisoners was rowed back to the schooner in silence. Campbell remained unconscious, moaning a little continually, and Von der Mehden, while there seemed to be no real fracture of the skull from the spent or glancing bullet that had struck his forehead, was also senseless for the time. His head had been bound up by Campbell, who had also bandaged his hand. For Campbell himself there seemed nothing more to be done than the stanching of the flow of blood, which had been already accomplished.

Sleeth sat slumped in the stern of Boone's boat, between the skipper and Bockstatt. The man was evidently at the fagged end of his strength, but his spirit still sat behind his eyes, which were greenish-gray, cold and set as a shark's, and the renegade oarsmen uneasily endeavored to avoid his sinister look of contempt and derision.

Jude Demoulins and the tall buccaneer, identified by one of the rowers as Black George, maker and singer of songs, blackguard and discarded son of British gentry, were in Thurlowe's charge. The woman's wild beauty had vanished utterly, the searing gas that had destroyed her sight had been, in a measure, merciful, hiding from her the face that was doomed to perpetual disfigurement.

Her mane of hair was burned away, her neck and arms badly scorched. She seemed sensible of her lost attractions, though she disdained to complain of her hurts, and wrapped her head in the red sash given her by Black George, who, singed but jaunty, smoked a cigarette he had begged with as debonair a manner as if he had been the successful leader of the raid.

Once aboard the *Roamer*, Sleeth and Black George were stowed in the afterhold, lightly fettered to the mainmast. Campbell and Von der Mehden were borne to their bunks, where Thurlowe, aided by Bockstatt, tended them to the extent of his rude skipper's surgery. The body of Yates was laid in the shadow of a rail, and, at Boone's orders, covered with a flag in recognition of the aid he had given to the best of his spirit's poor ability.

Marion Newell had taken charge of Jude Demoulins with an instant cry of pity for her plight and ready forgiveness of the evil the stricken woman would once have perpetrated upon her. Cree's mistress mutely suffered herself to be led below, without murmur of thanks or show of distress.

"Better be careful, Miss Marion," warned Boone. "I wouldn't trust her too far. She may have a weapon somewhere about her."

Marion Newell flashed him an indignant look.

"She's suffering terribly," she said. "We're not afraid of each other."

Boone turned away as they went below. The dignities of leadership were more than offset by its difficulties and responsibilities, he thought, and there was much in hand to be done. A look at the barometer had revealed a drop of five points since he had left the schooner, the signs of foul weather close at hand had grown plainer.

The mounting sun still glowed like reflecting copper, and sky and sea held their unnatural hues. From sea to zenith the sky arched cloudless in a dome of dull, brassy metal; the water inside the reef was opaque, cloudy green, and the ocean outside the color of dishwater. The life had gone out of it, the foam of the reef was thin, like greasy soapsuds, and the air seemed to leave a sour taste upon the tongue as it came in hot puffs that set the palms and undergrowth on the little promontory tossing uneasily.

"We've got to get out of here," he said to Haley, his first mate. "It's going to blow like Sam Hill presently, and, if it comes from the south'ard as it should, we don't want to be caught on a lee shore if we can help it, much less in the lagoon. We'll have to tow outside. The native boys have had a rest; they can tackle it. We'll set a kedge on the reef from the stern and haul up short on the bow anchor.

"Bend a line on the kedge, we may have to cut and slip cables in a hurry if we get any wind, for I don't believe for a minute we're through with those natives. And tell Ong Chuck to fix up a hot breakfast, will you? If the rest are as hungry as I am, he'd better double his rations."

Haley departed and Boone went over to where the five deserters stood near the body of their late comrade.

"We're going to tow outside, men," he said. "The native boys will take the boats. You men have behaved well. Now I'm not going to set myself up as judge of the circumstances that made you join Sleeth. Yates there has atoned and we'll give him sea burial. But it's up to you from now on.

"Those natives are not going to let us get away if they can help it, and if the calm lasts much longer there's going to be trouble that will take all hands to ward off. I don't know if I am doing the right thing, or the wise one, but if you stand by in good shape I'm not going to hand you over to the authorities at Suva. I'll set you ashore on Vanua Levu, and if you keep quiet a while you can set your own plans for steering straight after this. Meanwhile you can fix up quarters for yourself in the trade-room. Do we understand each other?"

The men answered him gratefully in protestations of past hard luck and resolve to keep clear of trouble in the future. They realized their position. It would be a hard matter for them to prove that they had thrown in their lots with Sleeth under duress, and the consciences of all of them were not entirely clear from having shared in the profits of the pirate's raids.

"Poor devils," thought Boone as he walked away. "They had to save their skins, I suppose; they're not made of the stuff that walks the plank. I expect they've wished themselves dead many a time. And they'll carry that brand of Sleeth's on their wrists until they are."

The boats were swung out and the *Roamer* towed slowly through the sluggish water that seemed to have lost all its buoyancy, beyond the reef into deep water, where they anchored South Sea fashion, swinging between two cables, one holding to the coral of the reef at a sharp slant, the other dropping with its heavy anchor to grip the bottom, thirty fathoms down. Boone overlooked the giving out of fresh ammunition, and, after a hearty share in the meal provided by Ong Chuck, who still retained his piratical make-up, went to see Von der Mehden.

Bockstatt had swathed his head in wet bandages beneath which the German's blue eyes opened with some of their old twinkle as Boone entered.

"*Himmel*, Dick," he whispered. "Such a *katzenjammer*. I've got a lump the size of a cocoanut up here and I'll have a headache for a month. I hope my brains aren't scrambled. They fixed me so I can't use my right hand, too, and I can't shoot worth a *kreutzer* with my left. Bored a hole clean through the palm. How did it all come out?"

Boone told him. The plucky, light-hearted chap's eyes filled with tears as he heard of Campbell.

"That's bad news. I suppose it's all up with him. I liked him, Dick. He was game all through. He—"

Haley entered the little cabin abruptly.

"Natives gettin' busy on the beach, sir," he announced. "Seem to be building some sort of a raft again. Goin' to try the same dodge on us they did on the *Ghost*."

Von der Mehden tried to sit up, but dropped back again groaning.

"Ach, my head," he exclaimed. "Just my luck. I don't believe I can even crawl out to see the fun. Don't forget those extra bombs I made, Dick. Bockstatt, you look after them. I'll be all right."

On the promontory the Papuans were busy amid the palms and brush and on the sandy beach, repeating their tactics of building something that would act partly as a shield and partly as a base from which to board the schooner. They had felled several trees, and the glass showed them working about a rude catamaran built of two trunks rudely platformed with boughs. To this they were attaching outriggers.

Boone tried a shot or two, but the savages dragged their craft behind a pile of rocks and he gave up the attempt and turned to watch Bockstatt at work upon his infernal machines.

The bombs were simple enough. Two clusters of dynamite sticks had been capped and joined by a quick-fire fuse, which the German was shortening to the limit for quick explosion.

"That was a good thought of Mr. Von der Mehden's," said Boone. "We'd have been hard put to it without dynamite, Bockstatt. I have a few sticks aboard which I use for fishing, but I would never have thought of the mine."

"Der poy iss a gut poy," rejoined the engineer. "Also he has prains which he uses. We stop dem, dose natifs. They haf no guns. If they gome on der raft, it iss simble. We drop dese—und the sharks haf preakfast. If dey swim in der water I haf somedings else to gif them for a surbrise barty. Yes?"

He displayed a number of half sticks, each with a short fuse—a battery of hand-grenades frightfully destructive at short range.

"Good work, Bockstatt," said Boone. "A dose or two of that medicine will soon cure them. We'll try picking them off as they come through the reef channel. I wish the wind would start, gale or no gale. I'd rather take a chance with the weather for a change. I'm sick of this butcher business."

The revulsion of the past twelve hours—it was barely that since they had entered the creek to rescue the girl—was still to manifest itself fully to all of them. As yet the horror of it all, with the burning of the *Ghost* and the awful death of the buccaneers, was still too close to seem real. And there was action enough forward to fully occupy their minds. The catamaran was setting out from shore, propelled by clumsy paddles and the thrusts of swimming Papuans.

Boone turned to place his riflemen along the rail and found Marion by his side.

"You had better go below," he said bruskly. Then, more gently, "How is your patient?"

"She is in great distress," answered the girl. "Mental as well as physical. Just think what she has been through, Captain Boone."

He shrugged his shoulders. He had little sympathy with the woman in the light of her attitude to Marion on the crater trail, and he was still smarting from the position the latter had placed him in upon his warning her against Jude when she was first brought aboard. Neither did he relish the "Captain Boone."

Once having progressed to the intimacy of first names it is hard for masculine admirers to understand the tactical withdrawals of privilege by the lady. And he was really anxious to get her below, not merely from danger, but to spare her the sight of a conflict which promised to be as desperate as the one just ended, mercifully hidden from her eyes within the crater.

"Go below now, please," he said. "This is no place for you."

As she went, a trifle indignantly, he felt that he had made another blunder of clumsy speech and knew the masculine impatience of feminine insistence upon all the courtesies, at a moment when there was urgent work ahead.

"Get ready, there," he called to the men kneeling by the rail, their rifles ready. "Try and stop them at the reef. Watch your splashes."

Despite their best efforts the rifle-fire was comparatively ineffective. The range was at an angle and the view obscured by the mounting waves breaking on the reef. Most of the Papuans were in the water, and the clumsy catamaran came on slowly.

"Better hold your fire," said Boone. "They can't hurt us yet. Look out for arrows till they get closer up. Bockstatt, wait till I give you the word. I'll let them get where you can reach them, but I'll have to swing the schooner or we'll be blown out of the water. Here comes the wind, thank heaven."

"*Ja*, I wait," said the German laconically, blowing on a spare length of fuse to keep it ready for lighting his bombs.

The puffs of wind were commencing to join forces in a breeze that sent the waves curling nastily about the raft, on which the savages were beginning to clamber, yelling fiercely and brandishing their weapons, evidently encouraged by the lack of firing, which Boone still reserved, into the belief that the white men were short of ammunition. Balked of personal revenge on their late tyrants, the buccaneers, the *Roamer* with its fittings was a rich prize, to say nothing of their blood-lust and the feast that would come afterward.

Thurlowe came over and stood by Boone. Arrows began to fly, quivering as they stuck in the deck and masts.

"Look out," warned Boone. "Keep in cover of the rail. They may be poisoned."

The wind was beginning to hum through the rigging. The light failed, the sun losing its power to cast shadows, glowing in the hazy sky like an overheated metal bowl. Between the yells of the oncoming savages a low moan sounded from seaward. The schooner chafed at her bow cable and the seas began to pound at her timbers.

"Set a trysail on the main, and a storm jib, Haley!" cried Boone. "Jump to it! Stand by to cut the stern-line and slip the cable. Look out, Bockstatt! Are you ready? Wait till I give the word."

Bockstatt, his burning fuse in one hand ready to light the perilously shortened fuse of the first bomb, crouched by the rail. The catamaran, boiling with savages, was close alongside, the Papuans shouting in anticipated triumph.

"All ready, sir," reported Haley.

Boone glanced around. The native boys were belaying the sheets of the storm canvas. The catamaran bumped against the side of the schooner. Dusky fingers clutched at the rail.

"Take the wheel, Thurlowe!" he shouted. "Let go your bow cable, Haley. Smartly there!"

Sanders, ready with a hammer, smote at the shackle and the bolt dropped clear. The *Roamer* swung before the incoming seas, tearing away from the raft, paying off rapidly till it was almost parallel with the reef.

"Now, Bockstatt, let 'em have it!"

Boone ran to the stern and seized the ax from the man who held it. The German rose from his crouch, the fuse sputtering fiercely, and hurled the bomb into the midst of the savages as Boone severed the line that still held them to the reef.

There was a shattering roar, followed almost instantaneously by another, as the engineer tossed over his second bomb. Sheets of brown water spouted.

The *Roamer* heeled to the shock of the dynamite, righted a little, and, leaning to the gale, plunged off at a tangent, gradually brought closer into the wind by Thurlowe, straining at the wheel.

Springing to the side Boone looked vainly for a sign of the Papuans, the schooner leaping, close-hauled under her scanty canvas, into the heart of the mounting storm. The waves, foamset now, rose high in tawny hills out of the roar of the monsoon. The lower headlands of the island were hidden as the *Roamer* dropped into the deep valleys, gallantly bucking the angry seas.

The force of the wind was terrific, the loose ends of ropes stood out stiffly like iron bars; the spume, cut from the crests by the fury of the gale, swept horizontally across the deck. The rigging shrilled like an orchestra of mighty harps. Thurlowe's long beard streamed over his shoulder. Boone, with a swift glance over the side, joined him at the wheel, adding his strength to the stubborn spokes.

He set his lips to Thurlowe's ear.

"No damage," he shouted. "We swung clear in time. How's she making it?"

"Can't keep—her—up," gasped Thurlowe as the wind strangled him. "Got to—run for it."

"Got to clear that headland!" Boone yelled back, looking over his shoulder at the cape of the higher mountain, showing black and menacing against a sky that had turned the color of slate. "We can—just—about—make it."

The gale shredded his voice to a whisper, but Thurlowe caught his meaning and they set themselves to hold the struggling schooner off the land.

They succeeded. Buffeted by the wind, blowing eighty miles an hour in its sudden wrath, the *Roamer*, clawing at the gale that buffeted it in anger that seemed to wax with every minute of the fight, as if furious at the presumption of the man-made thing, battled desperately, driven slantingly to leeward until the thunder of the reef, close in to the threatening headland, was scarce a cable's length away. As the skippers watched their chance to come about, growing more risky every second, the trysail on the main burst from its hold and was lost, a speck flying against the land, with a clap like a cannon shot.

The wheel whirled, the ready vessel spun on its keel. For an instant great masses of water seemed about to engulf her as she raced, beating the clutch of the sea, pounded by the fury of the monsoon gale, far, far to the southwest, Eremanga, if not its memories, blotted out in the wrack.

IX

Black George Tells What He Knows

Boone, with thurlowe and newell, stood in the little cabin by Campbell's bunk. Marion Newell was seated beside the dying man, trying to soothe his last few moments. The doughty Scotchman was conscious, though hardly capable of the speech he tried to utter.

"Drink this," said the girl, holding a glass to his lips with difficulty as the schooner reeled in the storm. Some of the liquor spilled on the covers.

"*Na, na*," said Campbell, mustering his final strength. "I dinna like the smell o' it. I'll die a blue-ribboner. Ye'll be writin' hame for me, one of ye, hame ta Lairg. 'Tis i' Sutherland, ye'll fin' the address i' my coat. Tell them I died sober. 'Twill be a shock for them a', na doot, but they're used to them fra' me."

He turned his eyes to the weeping girl.

"Dinna greet, lassie, I've been a sair wastrel," he said faintly. "But i' ye hav' a Bible aboard there's a bit aboot green pastures an' the valley o' the Shadow my mither used to read, lang syne. I used to think it puir readin', but I remember it weel.

"Aye, an' still waters it spoke of," he added. "Listen ta the storm."

Marion hastened from the cabin. Campbell closed his eyes again, his fancy wandering back to Sutherland and the misty hills of Loch Shin.

"The loch's in a gey turmoil the nicht," he muttered, "an' the burn's in spate. There'll be no fishin' the morn. 'Tis awfu' dark, lads, but ye'll see the licht i' the tower i' a minnit."

The girl came back and started to read softly.

"Ah, that's guid," said Campbell. "I wonder now will there be heather yonder. Eh, yon's the licht, comin' over Ben More. 'Tis sunrise, surely—"

He closed his eyes, the haggard features relaxed and Captain Newell led his daughter from the cabin as Boone and Thurlowe composed the features of the gallant Highlander.

Three days the *Roamer* ran before the monsoon, until at last they cleared its path and headed up for the long beat northward to Matemotu under blue skies mottled with the torn fleeces of high-sailing cloud. The double funeral of Yates and Campbell had taken place with all the ceremony the gale would allow, and all hands drank in the sweet breeze and invigorating sunshine with delight. The past seemed to have been wiped out in the storm, vanished like a nightmare at morning, and, as they relaxed, laughter came back to lips that had been long foreign to it.

But the stress of fight and storm had left its effects on all of them. The men seemed to have grown older. Boone wondered at his own gravity, while he tried to throw it off in the hope of soon seeing an end to the quest that had borne so many wild adventures.

Marion Newell was quieter, too, he noted. The dimples rarely showed nowadays, and she busied herself with tending Jude Demoulins and Von der Mehden, now able to sit up, and even walk dizzily, his arm in a sling, a great bump on his brow where the thwarted lead had left a souvenir.

Sleeth and Black George remained in the afterhold, close-guarded but unbound, the better to cope with the hardships of the storm. The latter had remained defiantly reckless of the gale, roaring snatches of song, taunting his leader, who seemed slow in recovering. Sleeth had begged for a Bible and striven to read it by the light of the lantern that dimly lit their prison, regardless of his comrade's jeers, moving a flabby finger continually across the page, quoting passages aloud. The men who took turns in guarding him believed him insane.

Jude Demoulins, blind and marred, her power for evil gone, was a close ward of Marion Newell's, who, in the necessarily close quarters, shared her cabin with the stricken woman. The young girl openly avowed her belief in Jude's repentance. She told Boone that her charge had repeatedly asked for him, but the skipper had put off his visit, facing repeated responsibilities he deemed superior to her claims.

Now as he started to visit her, Haley stopped him.

"There's some wreckage off the port bow, sir," he said. "Sternpost and a few timbers. There's a name on it, but I can't make it out for the wash."

"Lower a boat," ordered Boone. "I'll go in her. Want to come, Thurlowe?"

The low-lying driftage was soon reached, evidently a relic of the gale through which they had won. The gilt had been washed from the lettering, but a sailor caught the planks with a boat-hook and they readily made out the deeply carved letters:

CREST OF THE WAVE
SYDNEY

' "That clears up the bunch of them," said Thurlowe. "More hemp saved the stretching."

"Saves a heap of trouble," agreed Boone. "I was wondering what we could do. Fate seems to have decided this was the time-limit for Sleeth and his gang!"

He forebore mentioning the incident to Marion. Conversation had languished between them in some manner inexplicable to him, and he did not feel like starting it with news of this kind.

"No use saying anything about it," he gave orders. "Not even to Sleeth."

He found Jude Demoulins listless in her bunk, her head covered with bandages. Marion was on deck reading to Von der Mehden who lay in a deck-chair in the sun. The constant unrest of the gale had kept him weak and feverish, and he was content to lie in drowsy lassitude, listening to the tales in the old magazines Marion had discovered.

"Is that you, Captain Boone?" asked Jude in a rich contralto voice that had lost the selvage of her wilder days.

"Yes," replied Boone, seating himself. "What is it you want? Miss Newell told me you wanted to see me."

"Miss Newell is an angel," declared the woman. "If there were more like her in the world, there would be less devils like me."

"It is on her account I have come to see you, though I doubt if I shall be able to do anything for you. I hardly feel qualified to deal with your case. I prefer to leave that to the proper authorities."

"Miss Newell has forgiven me. I do not ask you to follow her example," she went on with a touch of her old defiance as she sensed Boone's hostility. "But Miss Newell tells me you have given the five men who joined you from Sleeth another chance."

"They were pirates by force, not choice. They aided us all they could. They have in a measure redeemed themselves."

"Did I not help you?" she asked. "Could you have mastered Capwell so easily without me? Have I not suffered enough? I have lost the only man I love. He died in my arms, loving me again. My name was the last word he uttered. I have lost the power of making men look upon me without loathing. I know what these bandages hide, a face that will make men and women both shrink from me. I have lost the hope of ever caring again myself. Is not that punishment enough?"

"It hardly sounds like repentance."

"Repentance! What is repentance but an excuse to avoid punishment? Surely I have found my hell. Darkness and desolation. What more could your prison give? You say those men were forced to join," she went on hurriedly—vehemently. "What do you know about me? I had wild blood in my veins, born in me. Was it my fault that when men sought me, as they did, every pulse in me raced to keep pace with theirs?

"I'll not keep you long," she said as Boone moved in his chair. "I was kept close, too close, first in a convent, then by my brother who gave full swing to his impulses while he sought to chain mine. I met a man at last, who married me and took me away as I begged him. He was wild like me, and loved as he punished—fiercely. He was a devil, too. He taught me everything of evil, nothing of good. At the end he joined Sleeth, after he had made every port unwelcome. He was in Sleeth's confidence till Cree came.

"Then he and Sleeth quarreled and they said he was dead, and so I became Cree's dog. I loved him as I had never loved my husband, with such love as you could never understand. I loved him well enough to hate him, and the woman you love as well, in the jealousy that is only dammed up, rejected love. Now"—she choked down the hard sobs that shook her, grasping the side boards of the bunk with white, fierce fingers—"everything is gone. And you, who have won, have everything. If repentance means atonement, I shall repent all the hours of my life. Help me to do it—if you believe in it."

"How?"

"Let me go back to the convent where I was brought up. They will take me. I will take the veil. Behind it I may find peace for my soul and hide the face that is now a hideous mask. The girl you love asks it with me."

She lay exhausted by her violent emotion, panting, shaken again by the hard sobs. Boone could fancy tears that could not fall welling in the fire-scorched sockets beneath the wrappings. Marion wished it, would judge him by it. It was not much to ask. Justice could not demand much more than she was suffering and to suffer. Death, to such a nature, would be relief.

"Do you want me to take you to the convent?" he asked gently.

"No," she said, hope revitalizing her. "Take me to Levuka. Let me stay aboard and tell Louis Bodin that Jude Demoulins is there. He will do the rest when he knows all."

"Louis Bodin. You mean Levuka Louis?"

"Yes. He is my brother."

Boone sat silent and amazed. This, then, was the secret of the intrigue he had suspected existed between the Frenchman and Sleeth. This was what Louis had meant in granting the redemption of the debt of his father, when he told him that he asked for more than he knew.

The blind woman's hand groped appealingly from the bunk.

"Well?" she asked.

Boone took her hand and gripped it firmly.

"All right," he said, and left her sobbing, her tears freed at last.

Marion Newell glanced up as he came on deck and walked aft. He nodded and was about to speak when she put a swift finger to her lips and motioned with a side tilt of her sunny head to Von der Mehden, who had fallen placidly asleep in the deck-chair.

Boone stopped, piqued. It seemed to him that she might readily have left the man who had the ill grace to sleep while she read to him for a word with the man who had served her as he had in his promise to Jude Demoulins.

Marion was beginning to seem hourly more desirable to Boone, even as something impalpable seemed to have entered into their friendship, coming between them. He failed utterly to realize that this veil of hesitation, instead of separating them, might be the tentative beginning of folds that should finally bind them the more closely. The more desirable she appeared, the less he calculated his chances to be.

He was finding out many things about her lately. He noted that her hair in the sun seemed to hold splintered rainbows in its mesh; he had discovered a tiny mole close to the one dimple in her left cheek and likened it, privately, to the star that the crescent moon sometimes holds in its embrace. He had loved the simile, not finding himself ridiculous. Had there been a volume of poetry aboard, he would probably have read it at night, secretly, in his bunk. As it was, he invested Marion with all the romance that his nature held, in a measure that would have surprised him had he suspected it.

He was genuinely angry at Von der Mehden for the slight he felt he had put upon Marion. He envied the German his facility of badinage and continually imagined that he discerned signs of a growing intimacy between the pair. He turned on his heel to meet Thurlowe's first mate, Sanders, coming up from below.

"Sleeth's bothering the head off the men on guard, sir," he said. "Demanding to see you, when he's not talking Bible. I think he's plumb crazy."

"Or playing it," answered Boone. "I'll see him."

He passed through the forecastle to the forehold and through that to the main. Both were practically empty and reeked with the odors of rancid copra and dried turtle. Inside, by the heavy door-hatch sat Thurlowe's supercargo, smoking, automatic in hand. Sleeth and Black George sat on the floor by the mainmast, beneath the lamp.

Sleeth was reading in rambling fashion from the book on his knees, the same Bible from which Marion had read to Campbell. His head was sunk into the folds of his thick neck, tortoise-wise, his bald cranium reflecting the light.

Black George had a pack of cards spread in front of him, gained, like the pipe he was smoking, from his guards, in virtue of his cheerful bravado. He shifted his cards in the game of solitaire, singing the while, to the obvious annoyance of Sleeth, who paused now and then in his reading to give his comrade a look, the malevolence of which ill suited the nature of the book he held.

Boone waited for a moment by the door, the sliding of which had passed notice in the song that Black George sang while he deftly placed one card on the other.

"Where are the gallant ships? Lost in the tide-rips.
Where are their gallant crews? Lost in the coral ooze.
Where are the arms that bound love-wreaths about them?
Where are the tender hearts, lonely without them?

"Oh the life of a man is a short, short span,
And the bloom of a maid fades early.
Go, gather your plunder while you can;
	Oh ho, for the teeth so pearly!
Rubies and diamonds, lips and eyes,
Arms of ivory. Gather your prize.
The anchor's up and the Roger flies:
	Gather, ye seadogs surly!

"By Jove," he said as he ended the rollicking refrain. "Here's the gallant Captain himself, come to pay us a visit. Glad to see you, y' know. Don't mind Sleeth. No manners. Never had any. He's the original 'seadog surly.' At his devotions. Trying to learn a new system of bookkeeping so he can square his accounts. What, guv'nor?"

Sleeth looked up, his eyes sparking maliciously in the shadow of his hairless brows.

"I ask you, sir," he said, addressing Boone, "if this is a place to keep a man thrice your age, old, weak, unarmed, forced to listen to the gibes of this fool. I am ill. My days are few—"

"And the hairs of your head jolly well numbered," broke in his comrade with a guffaw. "Well, Captain, so far as I'm concerned the jig's up, and I know it. The music was rippin', but it's all over but the Dead March. There he swings! What? Take us out of here. The cockroaches are good company compared to Sleeth here, but the bilge is bad and the copra takes away my appetite. Take us out. We'll be good little boys, won't we, guv'nor? And for pity's sake, Captain, give us something to wear."

Boone looked at them. They were still clad in the scorched remnants of their canvas trousers. Black George's beard had sprouted and he looked a proper villain. The pox-pits that had hardly left their mark with him had seemingly killed the roots of all Sleeth's hair as far as his head was concerned, but the pirate leader's face glistened with sweat and dirt, and the blood from the blow on his head that he had got during his escape from his burning schooner was caked in a black smear.

"I'll send you some clothes," he said. "Are you ready to talk, Sleeth?"

The buccaneer's face looked like a dinted mask through which peered living eyes.

"Talk is vain and availeth nothing," he said.

"I've just had a long talk with Jude Demoulins," said Boone, fencing for an opening through the hypocrisy of Sleeth's talk, assumed, he felt sure, as a guard.

The mask seemed to slip for an instant, and the jade eyes gleamed in sudden cunning.

"Jude?" said Black George. "How is the old girl?"

"Blind," answered Boone. "And sorry."

"It is good to repent," said Sleeth. "I am glad she knows that the ways of evil are false."

Boone moved in disgust of the canting singsong of the man's glib speech, and Sleeth changed his tone.

"Might I ask our position, Captain?" he said almost whiningly.

"We are heading up for Matemotu."

Again the mask shifted. Black George stared blankly, then laughed.

"I can't stay any longer wasting time," said Boone. "Once again, Sleeth, are you ready to talk?"

The pirate countered.

"Are you taking me to Matemotu?" he asked.

Boone regarded him watchfully. The men had both been searched without avail. He had hoped to discover a hidden belt of pearls on Sleeth, or some chart or indication of the hiding-place of the treasure, which he felt sure had not been left behind on the schooner when Sleeth set it afire. One main object in making Matemotu was to bring off the Other One, and Marion had expressed a desire to visit her father's crater prison. Now it flashed across him with instant conviction that the treasure was hidden somewhere on the Island of the Dead.

"Yes," he answered. "First, then to Suva."

"Where the kindly British government will send us—further," said Black George.

Sleeth sat silently with eyes cast down upon his book.

"If I show you where the pearls are," he said at last, "will you leave me on the island?"

"I'll promise nothing," answered Boone. "You will both be brought before Newell and Huddy, with Thurlowe and myself, tonight. They will judge what to do with you."

Sleeth seemed to fall into a reverie, muttering as if to himself.

"Lay up not treasure unto yourself," he muttered.

"Oh, chuck that rot, guv'nor," said Black George impatiently. "The game's over and you've lost. Pay the stakes."

"The pearls will go back to their owners and the families of the men you have made away with, whose bones lie on Matemotu," said Boone.

Sleeth threw aside his mask and struck the Bible in sudden rage with his clenched fist.

"Some fool has babbled," he cried. "But it was not Jude. You don't know where they are. I thought Jude had blabbed. I thought Cree had told her before he died. No one knows where they are but me. They are well worth my life," he went on, lowering his voice, a cunning look creeping into his eyes. "Half of them well worth the year or so I have left. I'll strike a trade with you, Captain. My neck, it will not serve me long, against half the pearls?"

"I promise nothing," answered Boone.

"All of them, then, Captain. All of them. And the rest of the trinkets. There's"—he lowered his voice to a hoarse whisper, looking fearfully at Black George, who had returned to his game of Canfield—"there's nearly half-a-million dollars there, Captain. Half-a-million! I'll show you where they are. You can say you gave me all of them and keep half. Just to leave me alone on the island?"

Boone shook his head and turned away.

"Then the families you prate of can starve and rot!" shrieked Sleeth. "Don't be a fool, Captain. My life against the pearls. Come."

"What about mine?" asked Black George. "Eh? What about mine, guv'nor?"

"Yours, you singing fool!" snarled Sleeth in a fury. "Beg for it yourself, you cur. The pearls were mine—mine, you whining minstrel!"

Black George looked at his leader with a sinister change on his careless face, handsome despite its disfigurement of burned hair and mustache.

"Maybe I will," he said quietly and built his ten on the jack of spades.

"I'll send you some clothes as I promised," said Boone. "We'll settle the matter tonight."

"And a razor and scissors, old chap," begged Black George, as the skipper left the hold.

At noon the reckoning showed that the *Roamer* had sped before the monsoon far below the thirtieth degree of latitude and was now close to the direct steamer lane from Auckland to Suva, with Matemotu some six hundred miles to the north and east. The brisk wind was directly aft with the certainty of a steady breeze from the monsoon quarter, and Boone, the schooner wing-and-wing once more, making better than eight knots hour in and hour out, hoped to fetch the crater by the third night or early the morning after.

With level decks, the Roamer was overhauled and the minor damages done by the storm restored. Many hands made light work and short watches, aside from the guarding of the two pirates in the after-hold, and Boone at last found himself with comparatively little to do.

He was still chary of forcing his company upon Marion, and the girl, after one or two puzzled glances in his direction that he failed to notice or interpret, resumed her reading to Von der Mehden, who lay back in his comfortable chair watching her through half-closed eyes that missed nothing. Once or twice she lost her place after she looked up to see Boone standing at the lee rail smoking, and the German's eyes held a hidden smile. Finally she closed the magazine.

"It's a stupid story, don't you think, Mr. Von der Mehden?" she said. "I thought it was going to be interesting."

"*Ja*," assented the German, yawning behind his hand. "It is not very awakening. You could write a better one about what we've been doing. If you do not mind, I think I'll drop off again. Nothing like sleep for all sorts of headaches, Miss Newell."

He closed his eyes. The girl arose, hesitated, then with a mounting flush walked to the rail.

"Captain Boone," she said, conscious of her blush but meeting his eyes squarely, "aren't you going to let me thank you for what you promised that wretched woman? It was generous of you."

"I am glad it pleased you," he answered.

"Do you know that you are a very difficult person to talk to of late?" she asked him. "Especially these days, after you have buried me under all these obligations. Do you want to avoid a settlement?"

"A settlement?"

"Yes. Father tells me you expect to find out about the pearls tonight from Sleeth. You said once I was the leader of the expedition. You haven't rendered any accounting of expenses even. I don't know how deeply I may be involved. I'm beginning to feel terribly in your debt."

She spoke lightly and Boone tried to meet her tone.

"Are you anxious to pay me off then?" he asked.

Their eyes met again. Hers were dancing with a merriment he failed to grasp.

"No," she said. "But I have talked with father and perhaps you would rather discuss this with him?"

Boone shook his head.

"You are still the leader," he said.

"Well, then, we have decided that our share of the pearls should be divided into two parts, one for us and one for you. Father suggests that part of the remainder may be set aside to recompense Captain Thurlowe and the rest, but in case you don't all agree to that, we'll split our share in three and repay them for their trouble that way. That is fair, isn't it?"

"Your father can repay my expenses," said Boone, "but I did not, do not, wish for any reward."

"None?" she asked, her roses blooming again in her cheeks as Boone's gaze grew more intent.

The signal was thrilling deep within him, her blushes, a something that dimmed yet deepened the luster of her eyes, the quality of the mood that seemed mutual, urged him to claim the reward his heart desired. Then his glance fell on Von der Mehden and caught the flutter of his eyelids. The thrill ceased abruptly, the mood dissolved and he felt himself suddenly a fool for having misinterpreted a girl's eyes in mistaking gratitude for love, for having thought a schooner's deck at midday the fit place for an uncertain wooing.

"There is none that I can name," he said.

Her face changed suddenly. Its softened outline seemed to grow harder. Then the dimple suddenly danced again in her cheek and the merriment that had puzzled him returned to her eyes.

"In that case," she said, "as soon as you have made up your mind exactly what you want—perhaps you had better—see father."

She left him bewildered as she hastened below, with a flirt of the white skirts she had achieved from the trade stock to replenish her wardrobe.

Boone walked toward Von der Mehden in a daze, pondering the meaning of her last words. He halted beside the deck-chair to find its occupant regarding him quizzically.

"Awake again?" queried Boone.

"*Ja*. Wide awake. You, my friend, look as if you were day-dreaming. So?"

"Your head is still buzzing, Von der Mehden."

"So. You think so. Von der Mehden? Poor Otto! He is dismissed. Dick, you are a fine skipper and a brave man, and a strong. But you haf your weak spots, my friend."

"Yes?" Boone was conscious of a growing irritation as he spoke.

"*Ja*. With all your virtues you haf one big fault. Dick, you are what they call in English a chomp."

"How's that?"

"A choomp, Dick. Perhaps I do not pronounce it exactly, but that's the word. Chomp!"

Boone felt a foolish desire to pick a quarrel with the sick man, but turned away biting his lip as he heard the German complacently humming—

"Ob ich dich liebe?"

Boone stayed away from Marion for the rest of the day, avoiding her later when she resumed her place with Von der Mehden. There was no more reading and their casual laughter jarred upon him, fancying himself the subject of their conversation, imagining that they were discussing his qualifications as a "chomp," which he rightly interpreted as "chump."

After the evening meal, the *Roamer* seething serenely beneath the stars and the thin sickle of a new moon, the four skippers, Boone, Newell, Thurlowe and Huddy, sat in impromptu court about the cabin table, waiting for Sleeth and Black George to be brought in. Huddy was fairly his old self once more and the quartet prepared to sit in equable judgment.

On two things they were already decided—to make every endeavor to secure the pearls, and, in case of success or failure, to make no compromise, but to deliver both the men over to the British authorities. Newell and Huddy were both British subjects and the piracy committed on their ships alone rendered Sleeth and his companion liable to direct punishment.

Boone, after disclosing the relationship between Jude Demoulins and Levuka Louis, readily obtained the consent of the rest to his promise.

"That's a different matter," summed up Thurlowe. "But pearls or no pearls, by the way, we've got to be careful the British bigwigs don't get their hooks on the treasure after we find 'em under pretext of 'Crown rights' or whatever they call 'em, like they did with a chunk of ambergris I found on Vanua Levu and was fool enough to brag about. Those ghosts that the poor loon we left on Matemotu thinks he talked to are not going to be laid until Sleeth's own life has paid forfeit. If we do get the pearls, what are you goin' to do with 'em, after Newell and Huddy here get theirs back?"

"Why," said Boone, "it's my idea we ought to form a trust-fund of the rest, advertise for the families of the men that have been made away with—you know most of 'em, Thurlowe, and Louis can help us with the rest—then divide it up among them according to their needs, since we'll never find out the exact amounts, in all probability—I don't suppose Sleeth has kept books—keeping out something for prize-money for all hands. How does that strike you?"

"Fine, after we get them," said Thurlowe.

Haley came in ahead of the two prisoners, who followed under guard.

"All right, Haley," said Boone. "You can leave them with us."

He ostentatiously shifted an automatic in front of him and motioned to a locker where the buccaneers seated themselves, facing the four captains, grouped about three sides of the table to form their court.

The stern gaze of their judges seemed to have little effect upon Sleeth and his comrade. Both were dressed in white ducks from the trade-room and Black George had managed to barber himself to some degree of nattiness.

Boone had offered the position of inquisitor to Newell, but the three skippers had insisted upon his assuming the office, declaring that he was the least biased and the actual head, as master of the schooner and leader of the enterprise.

Sleeth sat stolidly with set face and implacable eyes. Black George fingered his trimmed mustache with an air of unconcern.

"There is no time to be wasted in this matter, Sleeth," commenced Boone. "You offered me your life against the pearls. Both are already forfeited. The pearls were never your property. If you care to restore them, it may have some effect upon your ultimate sentence from the authorities, to whom we are resolved to deliver you. It's pretty evident that the treasure is somewhere concealed on Matemotu. Ultimately it will be discovered, with or without your help."

"You can search till the sea gives up its dead," said Sleeth, "and you will never find it. I do not ask you for my life. Give me a chance for it by leaving me on Matemotu and you can sail with the pearls.

"Judge not that ye be not judged," he went on in monotonous bass, his eyes cast upward. "There were robbers mentioned in the book that I have been reading. Had I not neglected its teachings I would not be in this position. Barabbas, there was, and two others who were shown mercy."

"This is sheer blasphemy, Sleeth," said Newell severely. "You are going to Suva to suffer for your crimes. You can make up your mind to that. It would be barely justice, and a sentence that would be well approved, if we strung you up to the main spreader. If your canting talk means anything, restore the pearls."

"So I go to Suva, do I?" asked Sleeth.

Boone affirmed his question.

"Then you may all burn in hell before I give up the pearls," he snarled with sudden fury. "Yet it is a pity"—he softened his tone—"there are many of them, and other trinkets. Almost half a million dollars. Much more than the pitiful remnant of my life is worth, far more than the chance I ask for on Matemotu."

"We've given you our final decision, Sleeth," said Boone. "Haley!"

The mate appeared.

"You can take them away," said Boone.

"I'd like to say a word or two, y' know," said Black George. "I have no bargain to make, but I rather fancy you'd like to hear what I've got to say."

"Go on," said Boone.

"Thanks. My esteemed pal, the guv'nor, seems to be inclined to leave me entirely out of the deal. If I remember right, he called me a 'whining minstrel' today and told me to beg for mercy on my knees. Now I'm not going to do any crawlin', but I rather fancy I can make him do some singing, even if the tune won't be to his liking. Cree didn't tell Jude where the treasure was hidden, guv'nor, but he *did* tell another woman when he was drunk, and she told the 'whining minstrel,' and he's going to tell where it jolly well is, without fear of you, old chap, or favor from these gentlemen. It's—"

Sleeth sprang to his feet with astounding nimbleness and sank his apparently nerveless fingers deep in Black George's throat, till the latter's face turned purple and his eyes started from their sockets. It took all the strength of Boone and Thurlowe to break the pirate leader's desperate grip. All the old vigor of his mammoth frame seemed to return for the moment and as suddenly ebb again, leaving him limp and flabby between the two skippers.

He spat in Black George's face as the skippers forced him apart, and sank weakly to the locker.

"You spawn!" he ejaculated. "You cowardly slime of the pit!"

Black George, solicitously feeling his neck where the marks of Sleeth's fingers showed clearly, cleared his throat, attempted to speak, and made an appealing gesture for a drink.

Boone mixed him some whisky and water, which he swallowed with eager difficulty.

"Thanks," he said, leaning against the wall of the cabin. "I think I jolly well earned it. Let me tell you a few things about this bloodthirsty gentleman who is so apt with his names. He had the strength of two men once—he gave us a little exhibition just now."

Black George ruefully felt his throat again and mutely looked at the whisky bottle.

"He was just as brave as his strength, a grown-up bully among a lot of cowards who had landed where they were in his crowd because they were more afraid of hard work than anything else. Oh, I was one of them. I'm a proper blackguard myself, I acknowledge it. But Sleeth there was what you Americans call a bluff. Give him the whip-hand and he was a good driver. He handled us all nicely until Cree came along. Herded us like cattle and branded us with his private mark."

He turned back his sleeve and showed the tattoo of the skull with the bone between its teeth.

"You won't find it on him," he went on. "He was always figuring on leaving us in the lurch some time and scooting with the lion's share of the loot. Precious little we got. But he didn't want us to get away. With this brand advertised all over the South Seas, there wasn't a chance for any poor devil to quit and earn an honest living. Not that many of us wanted to. It was a merry life enough. But Sleeth would have dug out long ago, only Cree joined. He was a proper man, Cree was. He was your master, and you knew it." He turned on Sleeth, limp on the locker. "He called your bluff. You were not as strong as you used to be and you were a little bit afraid of cracking your whip too much. And we knew it. Cree was our man.

"Sleeth's main hold was knowing where the treasure was hidden. He was always promising to divide it up, but he never meant to, and the night your schooner came in Cree and the most of us who had joined him called Sleeth for a showdown. He came through and told Cree the secret. Told it straight too, for he knew what would happen to him if he lied to Cree. Cree was to have been leader, and one to follow. We were goin' to put the guv'nor there on Matemotu where he'd left the men he robbed—we robbed, if you like—to starve, because he didn't have the nerve to kill them.

"Then you showed up and Cree got killed, on account of a woman. That was Cree's weak point, he had three of them for that matter: wine, woman and song—the old story. He would never have called me a 'whining minstrel.' He was drunk that night. All of us were, more or less, or we wouldn't have blundered on to those infernal stakes you set in the creek, which was a smart trick, at that.

"I wasn't so drunk as some of them, a hard head is the only inheritance I haven't been cut off from, and I got a girl who was fond of me to play Delilah to Cree's Samson. I'm no leader, but I wanted a good share of that loot myself. I'm too lazy to crack the whip or I wouldn't be where I am, but

I sometimes use my head, and here's the key to Sleeth's treasure-house."

He broke off suddenly.

"You'd better look after the guv'nor," he said. "He's goin' to have a stroke. Always thought he'd go off that way with that neck of his. Had one once before. They're goin' to have a hard time hanging him. Better let him go this way."

Sleeth's head, congested with blood, rolled on the fat column of his vein-swollen neck. His eyes still held their venomous stare, but his fingers worked convulsively as he labored for breath.

They laid him on the floor, still glaring with set eyes, in which consciousness appeared to linger, loosened the collar of his shirt and dashed water into his face. Haley came in at Boone's call and Sleeth was carried into the trade-room, which opened out of the main cabin.

"Harris is a bit of a doctor," suggested Black George. "One of the men that came over to you. Little red-headed Whitechapel Jew. He handled him the last time he had one of those fits. That is, if you are anxious to save him for gallows meat," he added callously.

Boone gave instructions for the renegade to be sent for to aid in Sleeth's recovery and resumed his seat at the table.

"Not much bluff about his sickness," he said to Black George, "and there wasn't much bluff about his blowing up the *Ghost*."

"He jumped, didn't he?" answered the pirate. "Gave himself a good start over the rest of us. Got right up in the bows. I don't say he's not dangerous. Dogs bark often enough, but they bite too. Now, about the treasure."

"We can not guarantee you any immunity, you know," said Boone.

"Don't you worry about that end of it. I've come to the last of my string. No one to lament me. Not goin' to do any lamentin' myself. Got to stand by my own words, what?

"Though we die in our shoes, with our neck in a noose,
We've only ourselves to blame.

"I've made a proper mess of it all 'round," he went on, "but I've had a fairly good time. Got to pay the bill."

If it was bravado, it was excellently well done, and the four men could not repress an involuntary feeling of admiration for the man, hardened though they were in their determination to deliver him over to justice.

Thurlowe poured out another drink and pushed it across the table. Black George accepted it gratefully.

"That's sporting of you," he said. "Now for business. You have to stand directly above the spar that's set in the cliff by the landing at Matemotu. Know it? Then face the crater, walk thirty paces along the rim to the right.

Look across the crater for the skull. That's some sort of a lava formation, I fancy, I've never noticed it. You can only see it from this position in early morning sunlight when the shadows are right. Just below it are a lot of fissures in the rock, straight up and down.

"The junk is buried somewhere in the floor of one of these caves. They all join each other in a kind of labyrinth. You can tell the right one by the water dripping in it and a pool of sour water a little way inside. If the guv'nor comes 'round, better take him along. It may save you a lot of poking about. So there you are."

He drained his glass.

"I hate to be a hog," he said. "But have you got a spare cigar?"

Boone took half a dozen from the box they had been using and went to the trade-room door.

"Have this man taken back, will you, Haley," he said, and passed in to where Sleeth lay stretched on the display table.

One of the five renegades, the English Jew named Harris, a shifty-eyed individual with a spoon chin, was bending over him, trying to force some whisky between the tightly closed teeth. Sleeth still breathed stertorously, but his face had regained some of its natural color.

"Better leave 'im 'ere tonight, sir," said Harris. "Hit's a stroke. 'E's 'ad 'em before. 'E'll come hout hof hit hall right hafter a bit, mebbe a hour hor two, but 'e'll not be hup to much before morning."

Boone felt Sleeth's pulse and turned back his eyelids. The balls were uprolled, the whites suffused with blood, and the pulse pumped with feeble jerks.

"I hold you five responsible for him," he said, addressing Harris and his four comrades, who were sitting by their makeshift bunks on the long counters.

"Aye, aye, sir," they answered, echoed by Harris. "Hall right, sir, we'll look hafter 'im."

"Call me or Mr. Haley as soon as he comes to himself," ordered Boone as he returned to the main cabin. The captains had left and Black George had been taken back to the hold.

When Boone went on deck he found Marion alone at the stern, watching the shining wake. Von der Mehden left her as Boone came up, and went forward, humming. Boone's first impulse was retreat, but the girl nodded and made a place for him at her side.

"You let your patient keep late hours," he said.

"Von der Mehden? He's doing capitally. Looking forward to the end of our adventuring is doing him good."

"Are you looking forward to the end of it, too?"

"Why not?"

There seemed no appropriate answer he could think of, and he remained silent.

"Were you successful?" asked Marion presently. "About the pearls, I mean. I haven't seen father since he went below."

"Yes. Black George has told us where they are hidden in a cave on Matemotu. We'll be digging for them at sunrise on Thursday, I hope."

"Thursday! It seems strange to talk again about the days of the week. We seem to have been out of the world of clocks and calendars, though of course your chronometers have had to do their duty. What's today?"

"Monday. Do you realize it's only ten days since we walked on the beach at Levuka?"

She turned her head toward him in the darkness.

"It hardly seems possible," she said softly.

All sorts of impulses jumbled together in Boone's brain. To tell her the time had passed all too quickly, to say he felt that he had known her for years—both of which apparently paradoxical statements were true—to tell her he wished the trip would never end but they might go on sailing together forever; to take her in his arms and make her own she loved him, through the sheer fervor of his own desire to have her and to hold her as sweetheart and wife through all the years to come. All these surged within him till he felt himself leaning toward her, words thronging to his lips as he looked into her upturned face in the starlight, ivory pale, deep gray eyes whose color he could not distinguish but knew so well, little glints of pale gold in the hair of her dainty head.

Then, as the scent of a cigar was blown faintly to them, came the sudden reversal, the remembrance of Von der Mehden standing where he now stood, of his own comparative poverty, of the German's wealth and the girl's own heritage, about to be added to through Black George's disclosure.

He steadied himself, and the girl, swaying a little, turned her gaze seaward again with a little sigh.

"Will you go direct to Suva," she asked in a little while, "after Matemotu?"

"Yes. Are we to say good-by there?"

"I don't know. We could go home by the steamer to Auckland, of course. I thought father wanted you to run down to his island for the rest of the pearls, unless it's getting too late in the season."

"Pretty late for rotting out. The rains will be coming soon. He did mention it. I understand there's only a comparatively small patch left, though he expects it to be rich. Would you go?"

"Perhaps," she hurried on before Boone could speak, "Mr. Von der Mehden is anxious to get to Suva. He's expecting important mail from home, you know."

"Yes?"

"Hadn't he told you?" I thought you knew. He's going to be married as soon as he gets back to Germany—to the loveliest girl! He showed me her photograph. I'm going to write to her, for him. Of course he can't, with his wounded hand."

All the constellations seemed to Boone to rush together in a blaze of glory. He was his own man once more.

"Marion," he said. "If—"

"There's father," she said quickly, and Boone fancied there was more than a tinge of disappointment, even annoyance, in her voice. "Have you spoken to him yet, about the reward?"

"No," said Boone. "I've decided not to mention the matter until after we leave Matemotu. Then I'm going to take it up with you."

The three captains bore down upon them and Marion took an early opportunity to escape. Boone looked into Von der Mehden's cabin, which he shared with Bockstatt, before he turned in himself. The engineer was snoring rhythmically and Von der Mehden was reading in his bunk. They chatted for a few minutes. Then Boone said casually—

"By the way, Otto, you never told me you were engaged."

"Is that so, Dick? I meant to. Like to see her picture?"

Boone looked and admired.

"You've been taking pretty stiff chances," he said. "If I'd known you were going to be married, you wouldn't have been shipped. Good night, old chap."

"How about yourself, Dick?" asked Otto with a twinkle. "Good night, old chomp."

All the next day Sleeth remained in a stupor. It was evening when Harris finally sent word that the buccaneer was conscious once more. Boone found Sleeth in a comfortable chair, usually reserved for trading chiefs, apparently himself again. Three of the five renegades were above on duty, but Harris and the other man seemed to wait upon their ex-leader with a fawning deference that Boone did not altogether relish.

"Feeling better?" he asked Sleeth not too sympathetically.

"Patched up, sir, patched up," answered the pirate in a weak voice. "I'm pretty well broken down, Captain Boone," he whined in a tone strange to his ordinarily booming bass.

He lifted an arm from his knee with an effort and let it drop heavily. His jaw sagged, his mouth was drawn at the corners and moved in a noiseless mumble when he ceased to talk. His eyes were almost lost between the fat creases of his brows and the puffy pouches beneath. One hand picked at the cloth on his knee.

Attitude and action denoted a feeble, senile old man, yet Boone sensed again the presence of a mask, a warning of danger, as from a maimed and trapped tiger, waiting patiently hour after hour for its captor to come within striking distance. He was not inclined to entirely accept Black George's estimate of the man. Whatever of weakness lay in Sleeth he set to the account of age, not any lack of courage. Black George's speech had been, not unnaturally, tinctured with venom. In this his fellow captains agreed with him.

"Sleeth is a scotched snake," Thurlowe had said. "Dangerous until he's dead, and I'd let him lie a long time before I made certain of that. Ever see a pizen snake's fangs strike after his head was whipped off?"

Boone resolved to handle the pirate leader with care until he was off his hands.

"I was nearly taken, Captain," went on Sleeth. "Truly it is written, 'Vengeance is mine, I will repay.' A sorry hulk you'll deliver to justice, sir. I feel that I shall not live for the trial. But you have been kind. If I could only have my Bible. There is joy over a repentant sinner. Do not scoff," he added as he caught the look on Boone's face. "I have been on the border and seen death face to face as I lay here. The scales have fallen from my eyes. I would clear my deck as best I may before going into port."

Boone listened disgustedly, his subconscious senses still warning him, as he noted the narrowed jade eyes steady between their puckering slits, at strange variance to the flaccid face and trembling frame.

"I'm no priest, Sleeth," he said. "You'll find your Bible back in the afterhold."

"He ain't fit to be moved, sir," put in Harris.

"That will do my man," said Boone. "Remember you're not altogether at top rating yourself yet. Tell Mr. Haley I'm ready for Sleeth to go back to the hold."

The man slunk off with a sidelong glance at Sleeth, and Boone continued:

"Black George has told us all about the cave with the pool, Sleeth. We know the treasure is somewhere buried in the floor. I'm going to take you with us. As long as we are bound to find it, you can show your repentance by saving us some digging. It will make a difference in your treatment while you are aboard, too."

"Willingly, Captain Boone, willingly. I tell you I am a changed man. I believe the rush of blood to my brain has cleared something away. I have read of such things. I will prove my good faith and show you the spot. The pearls are in a teak box, with other things and money. I will prove my good-will once more. I will open it for you. There is death in the lid. It is well guarded. Death, above the pearls!" He disclosed a momentary glimpse of opening eyes that seemed to glow with lambent flame. "But I will open it for you in safety."

"Don't try any tricks, Sleeth. Not anything like the blowing up of the *Ghost*, for instance."

Sleeth covered his face with his hands.

"I was mad when I did that. I must have surely been mad, Captain. No, no, Captain! There is only death for one—one who is careless. But I shall be careful. You shall see. There will be no danger for you. Black George and I will dig it up together. He will do the lifting, for it is heavy and I am weak. Then I will open it. You can stay outside if you like, and I will bring it to you. Half a million dollars in luster pearls, in trinkets and gold coins. A king's ransom. A great restitution."

"A bit tardy," said Boone grimly. "Make sure it's genuine, as far as it goes. Ah, Haley! Better keep them separate, I think. Put Black George in the forehold. Keep some one watching both of them. And Sleeth won't need Harris any more."

"I thank you," said Sleeth humbly. "I shall feel safer. Black George may bear me a grudge. I deserve it. But now I shall be alone in peace to read and learn much that I should have learned long ago."

He rose to his feet totteringly as Haley called in the man detailed to guard him.

"Pah!" said Boone as he and his mate entered the main cabin. "The man sickens me. He's a mass of hypocrisy. Keep those five chaps away from him. I don't trust them overmuch."

"Nor me," said Haley. "That Harris is a bad one, clean through."

During the next day the landing party was arranged for Matemotu, then a scant two hundred miles distant. Huddy, healthy minded and active once again in the company of his fellows, still felt a strong aversion to the place and had no desire to revisit it, but Marion begged hard to accompany her father and see the place where he had been imprisoned.

Somewhat against his will, Boone consented, and places in the boat were set apart for her, Captain Newell, himself, and Ong Chuck, to cajole the Other One aboard the schooner. Boone held no particular desire to hand the Other One over to justice, neither did he fancy leaving him alone with his ghosts upon the lonely crater to gradually become a maniac.

Von der Mehden elected to remain aboard, feeling his dizziness a bar to the trip up the rope and subsequent climbing. Boone decided to use his own boys at the oars in his mistrust of Harris and his comrades, whom he suspected of still being too much under the influence of Sleeth to be chanced on the trip. He had no desire to risk the slightest possibility of a slip in this winding up of the voyage, neither did he purpose making a picnic of the final visit to Matemotu, and decided, against all requests, that the one boat would be sufficient, with the three captains and Ong Chuck well armed with automatics to handle the two prisoners.

In the new understanding he felt now existed between Marion and himself his hopes ran high as he checked off reckonings with Thurlowe at noon, and pricked off the position of the *Roamer* on the chart, a hundred and thirty miles south and east of Matemotu, the weather logged as fair and a following wind full and steady in the stretching sails.

X

THE END OF THE QUEST

THE MOUNTING SUN WAS CHASING THE STARS FROM THE SKY, as a pickerel scatters a shoal of minnows. The aroma of Ong Chuck's coffee arose like grateful incense. Boone, by the wheel in the morning dusk, was joined by a lithe little figure, gray in the half-light one moment, rose-radiant the next in the first glance of the sun god, who seemed to have timed his arrival to greet it.

The level beam searched the face of Marion Newell, smiled audaciously into her eyes until the white lids sank in defense against his shafts, turned a searching light on her hair and pronounced it pure gold, kissed the fresh red lips, caressed the firm young throat, and, finding all flawless, passed on to severer duties.

When Marion reopened her dazzled eyes, she found Boone gazing at her with an ardor, more human, but as intense as that of Phoebus himself. Her blush matched the hue of a little, rosy, out-all-night cloud, high in the zenith, caught by Watchman Day.

"I'm on time, you see," she said. "You promised we'd be in sight of Matemotu at sunrise."

· "There it is," answered Boone, pointing to starboard. "Come forward, we can see it better."

They walked to the cathead, hidden from the deck in a little world of their own by the screen of the hauling headsails. Flying-fish in lustrous blue and silver livery leaped in the sunrise. Dolphins scattered flakes of molten gold as they pursued in a deadly chase, that, in the primrose and hyacinth dawn, seemed only a playful game of tag. The tragedies occurred out of sight, below the surface. Two miles ahead, and to starboard, a blue mound, flecked with purple shadows, lay upon the sea.

"That's Matemotu," said Boone.

Marion gazed at it earnestly.

"It looks like a great turtle, doesn't it?" she said. "Or an enchanted isle fresh risen from the sea. Yet you say the crater holds the bones of hundreds left there to slow starvation. Matemotu! The Island of the Dead! Horrible!"

"It's not a pleasant place to visit," suggested Boone. "I wish you'd give up your idea of going."

"I want to see the place where father was sick and imprisoned," she protested. "Besides, you promised. Why do you always persist in treating me as if I were an everyday, make-a-fuss-over-me girl?"

Boone's look was an eloquent answer, and she went on hastily.

"I want to visit the graves of those poor captains, too," she said. "What are you going to do about them?"

"We've talked that over. We'll send back and bring them to Suva or Levuka for proper burial. I don't want their bones aboard with us. I want it to be a pleasure trip back to Viti Levu," he said meaningly.

Marion flushed again and didn't seem to mind it.

"Have you found it terribly hard," she asked, "to realize all the terrible things that have happened? I can't. Of course you spared me the sight of most of it, but it all seems as if I had read about it or dreamed it."

"I'm thankful for that. I don't think about it more than I can help, but, now that the actual excitement is over, it all seems fairly real. You see I saw it."

"Of course," she shuddered a little. "It must have been frightful. Sleeth burning his ship, and then the killing of all those savages. Thank you for sending me below. It was bad enough there. I thought the schooner was blown up. I can't forget, though, the sending of all those men and women into eternity without warning. What sort of a monster is Sleeth? Father thinks he is insane."

"More cunning than insane, I'm inclined to think. Yet, after all, his act was more merciful than the law would have been, though he was thinking of his own motives just then, I fancy. He's mad to some extent, but the line between his cunning and his madness is a slight one. As to the savages, we had to protect ourselves, and you. But we're through with all of that now. We'll have the pearls within an hour or so and then we're homeward bound for Happy Harbor."

A clamor on a gong disturbed them.

"Ong Chuck getting impatient," he said. "We'll get the boat off as soon as we've had breakfast. Fresh flying-fish, hot biscuits, coffee and marmalade. How's your appetite? Curiously enough I don't seem to have lost mine."

"Why should you?" she asked mischievously.

Boone looked at her with a twinkle matching her own in his brown eyes, his eyebrows raised a trifle, and he made a little movement toward her.

"Oh!" she said, rose-red once more, and fled.

Boone followed her smilingly.

"I'll make Otto take back that 'chomp' before the day's over," he said to himself, wondering somewhat at the assurance of happiness that possessed him.

It was six o'clock when the whaleboat left the schooner, swiftly rowed over the dancing sea by the native boys. Sleeth and Black George, who seemed to show no enmity against his leader, were set in the bows, Ong Chuck, armed with knife and pistol, between them, a grim, effective warder. Both the buccaneers had been searched for arms—Boone in his suspicions of

Harris, or rather of Sleeth's ascendancy over the renegades, deciding to take no chances. Black George smoked one of the cigars Boone had given him overnight with as much serenity as if the occasion were a pleasure excursion organized in his benefit.

Marion, trim in white duck, sat between her father and Thurlowe in the stern. Boone handled the steering-oar. Besides the automatics of the four men, Marion herself carried one of smaller caliber, slung in a holster suspended across one shoulder.

"I'll be as much of a man as I can," she told Boone laughingly, as he filled her clips with cartridges before they left the schooner.

He had looked at her, wondering at the transformation the coarse stock of the trade-room had received at her hands. Out of the cheap duck she had achieved a middy blouse that caressed her rounded figure and disclosed an adorable little V at her throat. Boone made up his mind there and then to kiss it at the earliest opportunity, if his interview after the recovery of the pearls turned out as he hoped it would.

A blue handkerchief was tied in a sailor's knot—which is also a true lovers' knot, smoothly joined, evenly balanced. The short skirt hung jauntily midway to narrow arching insteps and ankles not to be matched, south of Capricorn at any rate. A sailor's canvas hat had received jauntiness and style from some feminine twist of the fingers. The native sailors gazed in open admiration. Von der Mehden, at the rail, waving his left hand in greeting, whispered to Boone, who was giving final instructions to Haley.

"If I wasn't going to be married, Dick, I'd try and cut you out."

Ong Chuck was first ashore, herding Sleeth and Black George against the cliff while the rest landed. The boat was secured again to the iron rings, one native fending clear while the others prepared to haul on the tackle that still swung from the spar. Boone and Ong Chuck ascended first and received the buccaneers. Then came Marion in the bo'sun's chair, followed by her father and Thurlowe, the sailors staying below.

In the same order they climbed the track to the summit and stood on the edge of the crater, the wind blowing fresh about them, making tiny pennants of the tendrils of the girl's hair where it escaped from the jaunty hat, the desolate crater-bowl below them.

The trade-clouds swam in a sky that was but a shade less deep than the sea beyond the reef, sea-birds wheeled, joined every moment by others from the bowl of the crater till the air was full of them, planing bright-eyed and unafraid, almost within handgrasp. The gullet of the crater, crusted with the ashes and clinkers of its dead fires, lay in heavy shadow, somber, desolate.

Boone looked toward the cave where they had found Captain Newell and the Other One. The fire smoked no longer, but the box in which they had brought the food had vanished.

"There's my cell, Marion," said Newell. "We can get a better view of it over this way. Later you can go into it, if you want to. It's not much of a show-place."

"The whole place is dreadful," she answered as they walked a little apart, Boone with them. "It's a mortuary." She shivered in the bright sunlight, thinking of the skeletons within the caves whose mouths showed black in the purple shadow. "And to think, daddy-chum," she went on, "you might have been here till you were—like the rest—if it hadn't been for Dick."

She held out one hand to her father, another to Boone, and the three stood for a moment united in happy presage, thought Boone, thrilling with the "Dick" of many long years to come.

"We mustn't forget Louis," he said. "It must have cost him something to tell me the position of the island, knowing we would be likely at any moment to discover what he has always concealed, the fact of his sister being identified with Sleeth."

"I hope he'll do what she asks," said Marion. "I really believe she's sorry. Do you think he will?"

"I do," said Boone confidently. "There's more heart to Louis than most people give him credit for. But we'd better be getting busy. There's no sign of the Other One. His fire's out, but I suppose he's been finding cold canned grub an agreeable change from sea-gull. He's probably been watching us, recognized Sleeth and gone into hiding. He doesn't realize Sleeth is a prisoner. We'll get Ong Chuck to look him up later."

They went back to the others. Sleeth, who had been silent all morning, turned to Boone.

"You'll go straight across, Captain?" he asked, an eager note in his voice, apparently anxious to get through with the affair. "There's the place."

He pointed to some clefts in the opposite wall.

"Where's your skull?" asked Thurlowe.

"You'll have to walk the thirty paces," said Black George. "Got to get the sun just right. Want to see it? Rather interestin' formation. Quite natural. Sort of trade-mark of the shop, y' know. I've never seen it, but I've heard them talk about it on Eremanga."

Boone looked at Marion, who nodded. They walked westward along the uneven rim, Black George, counting off the strides, leading. Behind him walked Ong Chuck, knife in one hand, patting the curving blade with the other as if more than willing to use it. Two crowbars were tucked beneath one arm. Sleeth came next with Thurlowe behind him, his pistol ready for any desperate move. Sleeth walked with dragging steps, his whole body expressing utter weariness.

"Thirty!" proclaimed Black George, halting and facing the bowl. "There you are. Right opposite. Curious. What?"

Marion gave a little cry of wonder, echoed by the others. A great mass of lava stood out from the cindery slope, some fifty feet from the irregularly notched rim of the caldera. The eastern sun, now mounted above the crater, struck sharply on its bosses and cavities, showing the striking semblance of a gigantic skull, fire sculptured in high relief. All the grim details were plain, the smooth cranium, the projecting under jaw, gloomy eye-sockets, sunken hollows for the cheek-gaps, a triangular pit for the nose, a ghastly rent for the mouth, in which showed horribly suggestions of crumbling teeth. It was the symbol of Matemotu, as Black George had put it, "the trade-mark of the shop," the sign of the Island of the Dead.

Below showed the vertical rifts, in one of which the pirate leader had hidden his ill-gained hoard.

Marion swayed a trifle, covering her eyes. Boone passed his arm about her shoulders.

"I'll be all right in just a second," she said, trying to smile. "Let's look the other way for a moment. You see, I'm only a girl after all."

They went slowly down the slope, deep with fine ash that turned up sulphur-hued to the foot. As they descended, the gristly mockery of the skull changed shape, fading back into the cliff to a misshapen block of lava.

They passed through the colonies of protesting gulls and crossed the bottom of the bowl, set sparsely with crackling clumps of bushes, dried and dead, as became the place, ascending the slope before them till they stood on a little level in front of the tall fissures, narrow, jagged-edged from the gases that had torn them open.

"Which one, Sleeth?" asked Boone.

The buccaneer, who had staggered up the cliff in apparent exhaustion, pointed at the central fissure, flanked on either side by two others.

"Remember, there's death in the lid," he said. "Who's coming in? Or shall we bring it to you?"

"We'll go with you," answered Boone, and thought he saw fleeting disappointment in Sleeth's eyes. "Ong Chuck, go ahead with a torch. Sleeth, you and Black George follow. I've got you covered, remember, with eight shots in my automatic, and another torch. No tricks. Captain Thurlowe follows me. Captain Newell, you'll stay with your daughter?"

"Can't I go too?" asked Marion.

Boone shook his head.

"No," he said firmly. "You heard what he said. You'll stay outside. We'll bring out the pearls."

The girl made a little *moue* of protest.

"I thought I was the leader," she said.

"Not now," answered Boone. "You've resigned."

"Not yet," she said, but her eyelids dropped under his gaze.

"That's right, Boone," applauded Newell. "You'll have to learn to take orders, honey."

The five entered the narrow cavern, cold with moist air. The torches illumined the ragged walls and shone on water that slowly trickled from the roof and dripped from points of lava. Dark openings gaped here and there. The place seemed honeycombed. A hundred feet in, the passage curved and sloped downward to a little pool, stinking of sulphur. Thurlowe dropped the crowbars Ong Chuck had carried and they fell with a clang on the flinty floor.

"Go to work, Sleeth," ordered Boone. "No tricks."

With Ong Chuck holding both torches, Boone and Thurlowe standing ready to fire at the first hint of treachery, the two pirates took up the iron bars, and, wading in the shallow water, began to probe under Sleeth's direction.

"Where first, my gallant leader?" asked Black George. "Here? Right-o!"

He began to sing, his voice resonant in the little chamber.

> "Every gem is a brave man's life,
> Each coin a drop of his gore;
> Every pearl is the tear of a wife,
> Yo ho, for the glittering store!"

Sleeth stopped probing the bottom of the pool.

"Dig, you chanting fool," he said.

"What? Silence under the skull? As you like. Hullo! Here it is."

He bent down, groping in the ooze.

"Here's a handle," he cried. "Got yours, guv'nor?"

Between them they lifted a heavy box, slimy, encrusted with salts, and set it down beside the pool. Sleeth straightened up with a groan and a sigh.

"Half a million or more," he said. "Better leave it. There's a curse on it."

Boone and Thurlowe bent to look more closely. The chest was of hardwood, black with age and exposure, bound with heavy iron. On the lid, deeply carved, was the design of the skull with the bone between its teeth, and the words—

SLEETH, HIS MARK

"That's the curse," said Boone. "We'll chance that. Open it—carefully!"

They stepped behind a buttress of the rock, their guns trained on the two buccaneers, half expecting the explosion of some infernal machine that would bring the walls about them.

"Suppose he blow up?" said Ong Chuck. "Goodbi'."

"Only death for one," repeated Sleeth. "Bear on that stud," he snarled at Black George. "Hard!" He pressed on the head of another bolt.

There was a whirr and a creak. The heavy lid snapped back. Sleeth, with lightning agility, thrust his hand into the chest. Something flashed in the blent circle of the rays from Ong Chuck's torches, and Black George sank to his knees, clutching at his breast.

Boone and Thurlowe fired simultaneously, emptying their magazine-clips at Sleeth. Ong Chuck dropped one torch and sprang forward with his knife. The bullets thwacked into the heavy wood, the reports rattled in a hundred echoes and the place was filled with the acrid smell of smokeless powder.

Sleeth had disappeared—gone like a fleeting shadow into one of the dozen openings that grinned at them on either side.

Black George lay gasping at their feet. In a widening crimson stain on the bosom of his shirt the handle of a knife still quivered. His mouth opened, quivered as if about to speak and the jaw dropped. The eyes glazed, staring horribly. One arm lay about the chest, where the light diffused a milky radiance from a tray where a cluster of shimmering pearls showed, surrounded by a medley of tarnished jewelry, a sparkle of jewels gleaming here and there from the tangle.

The three looked at each other confusedly for a moment. Ong Chuck moved toward the chest and Thurlowe knelt to place a hand above Black George's quiet heart.

"Back to the entrance. Hurry!" cried Boone, stricken with a sudden dread.

They stumbled through the passage to meet Marion and her father hastening in.

The girl ran to Boone with a little cry, and he caught her in his arms.

"Thank God!" he exclaimed.

"Thank God!" she whispered back.

"We've got to get back to the schooner," he said. "That devil knew what he was doing. He may have weapons *cached* in there somewhere."

They hurried from the cave, Ong Chuck lingering, grumbling at leaving the chest.

"Hang the pearls!" cried Boone. "Come on. We'll get them later."

As the Chinaman reluctantly joined them on the little plateau, a hail came from above them. They looked up apprehensively.

Sleeth, a rifle at his shoulder, stood outlined against the sky, above the lava mass that formed the skull, some two hundred and fifty feet higher than the level on which they stood.

"Ah!" he shouted. "Throw up your hands. Don't try to shoot. I've got the range of ye. Up! Up with them, or I'll start in with the girl."

"We can't reach him," groaned Boone, raging.

"Now, you brave man-hunters," shouted Sleeth. "The deal's in my hands. I'm a bluff, am I? Ask Black George if I'm a bluff now. You girl, throw your gun away. Throw it! Throw it! Now, take the others and throw them after it. Lively, or I'll make a mash of your slick lover's head.

"Stay where you are, you yellow cur!" he yelled at Ong Chuck, who was cautiously shifting his feet, bending his hips for a sudden spring to cover. "Take his knife, too, my lady."

He shifted his rifle to the hollow of his arm, the discomfited men standing helpless, Marion, pale but facing steadily upward, between Boone and her father.

The pirate seemed transformed. His assumed weakness had been shaken off and he raged above them, on the rim of the crater.

"Thought Sleeth was played out, didn't you?" he cried. "Thought he was old and toothless, ready to be led to the gallows like a dog on a leash. You came to the old wolf's lair and you found him ready for you." His voice mounted in a gale of ferocity. "Do you know what I'm going to do to you? In one of those caves there's what's left of a dozen better men than you are, a heap of bones under the skull. Sleeth's Mark!"

He snarled down, spitting at them.

"Maybe I'll put you there after a while. I'm going to let you bleach first, when the gulls have got through with you. Come, I'll give you a chance to beg for your lives. On your knees. Then I'm going to pick you off, one at a time. Don't try to rush, or the girl goes first." He threw his rifle to his shoulder. "I don't intend to kill her yet, unless I have to. I may find use for her as a hostage.

"Do you know what happens when this rifle goes off? There's going to be something stirring on your schooner, Captain Boone. Harris is my man yet. You young fool! It may be my schooner after all. And there's another card you've overlooked. The *Crest of the Wave* is due. They'll bring her here when they find my message at Eremanga.

"Kneel, you fools, kneel! Say your prayers, Captain Newell. You're first. You don't escape this trip. Pray, you skulking—"

He saw something in the upturned faces. Boone had started to tell him of the wreck of the *Crest of the Wave*, but refrained, preferring to die, if he must, in silence. His hand reached out to meet Marion's when he saw a figure rise up behind Sleeth.

The pirate glanced over his shoulder, wavered in his aim and suddenly shrieked, as a lean arm was thrown about his middle and another, ending in a twisted hand and wrist, stole about his neck. The rifle fell to the ground at the shock of the unexpected attack and the two figures strove for mastery on the brink of the cliff.

"It's the Other One," cried Boone. "Come on!"

• • •

Marion, faint in the revulsion of safety, was caught in her father's arms as Boone and Thurlowe clambered upward, skirting the side of the great skull, clinging precariously for hand and foot hold.

As they reached the top of the lava outcrop and stood for a second on the smooth dome of the skull before the last rush, Sleeth toppled to his knees, the hook-like wrist still sunk deep into his fleshy neck, helpless, his face contorted and discolored, while the Other One dragged him slowly backward.

"Do you know who this is?" the Other One cried, tugging desperately, heedless of his own safety. "You thought I was afraid of you—and I was. You kicked the soul out of Jean Demoulins once and left his body here to rot.

"But my soul came back!" He jerked the choking pirate closer to the rim. "The ghosts told me not to be afraid.

"Let me alone," he screamed as Boone neared the struggling pair. "He's mine. Ah, you would!"

He had relaxed the grip of his claw ever so slightly and Sleeth's arm shot upward in a final effort. Demoulins lost his balance on the crumbling *tufa* and they fell, writhing for a second on the lip of the crater wall.

Boone and Thurlowe reached the cliff-top to see them whirling, sliding with frightful momentum down the steep slope. Still locked, they rebounded from the face of a precipice that fell sheer to the sea and dropped like a plummet into the surf.

"Demoulins," said Boone. "Jude's husband! No use telling her about this. She thinks he's dead."

"He is," said Thurlowe laconically. "So's Sleeth. Black George was wrong. He was born to be drowned, after all, unless that chap choked him first with that hook of his."

He wiped the sweat from his forehead.

"I hope that's the end of it, Boone. I'm sick of it. Next time I'll follow the advice Menzies gave us, and stay home. I've had all the excitement I need to last me."

"The same here," said Boone. "Poor Campbell's the only one we have to regret, though. The rest got what they deserved. Let's go down. Where's Ong Chuck?"

They found the Chinaman sitting outside the cave on the chest. He had picked up the guns and his knife and grinned at them.

Marion had recovered and they started back.

"Come on, Ong Chuck," said Boone. "We'll send back for that."

"Betteh I stop along tleasure," said the Chinaman. "Maybe, Sleeth, he come back. Bimeby you send Kanaka."

"You're not going to turn pirate again yourself, are you?" asked Thurlowe. Ong Chuck grinned again.

"Pilate bus'ness he no good," he said. "Lele while plenty fun, bimeby."

He stretched his neck to an imaginary rope and drew a phantom knife across it.

"Me want live long time yet," he said.

At the trail head they saw the *Roamer* serenely coming about. A figure waved from the stern in response to Boone's shout. Below, the native boys sat on the rock landing, fending off the whaleboat with their feet, chatting carelessly.

"It's Haley," announced Boone. "Harris evidently didn't materialize. I'll attend to those chaps later. All right below."

"Any trouble on board, Haley?" he asked as they gained the deck.

Haley stared.

"How did you guess that?" he asked. "Nothing to amount to anything. Harris and the rest of his precious bunch were getting excited over something forward and Sanders figured they were going to start something. He found a gun on Harris and the rest had knives. So I stowed them away in the hold, with something to remember me by. They're a rotten crowd. Hanging's too good for them."

"I agree with you," said Boone. "The boat's going ashore for Ong Chuck and the loot. Send them with it. Haul them up and leave them on the island. They'll be there any time they're wanted."

"Aye, aye, sir," replied Haley. "I'll see the beauties ashore myself."

The treasure glittered on the cabin table. The pearls had been admiringly passed from hand to hand and roughly appraised. There were over four hundred of them, round and oval, all shades from blue-white to pink and black, all sizes, including a dozen kingly gems, all perfect.

Sleeth had been a connoisseur. Some of the pieces of jewelry were engraved, and these were set aside as the owners were identified or guessed at. The chest beneath the tray had been filled with rouleaux of gold coins, British, French and American, to the value of sixty thousand dollars.

After Newell and Huddy had set aside the value of their losses, recognizing some of the pearls, a rough estimate put the value of the remainder at close to four hundred thousand dollars. This was to be placed in trust of Newell, with Boone and Huddy, for restitution to the families of the missing men, under the plan proposed by Boone.

"We'll deduct triple pay for every man from this," suggested Newell, "with proportionate shares from a tenth of the entire amount as prize-money. If that's agreeable to all?"

"Surely," said Thurlowe, "and the quieter all hands keep, the better. Now we've no prisoners to deliver there's no need shouting about it. We don't want the Britishers chucking the whole thing into Chancery, or whatever they call it. We got it, and we'll do the distributing."

"That goes," said Huddy. And the council broke up.

"Dick," said Newell, as they went on deck together, "I want to have a private talk with you about a proper recompense for all you've done."

"Thank you," said Boone, looking to the after rail where a figure was standing, the sight of which set him a thrill with longing. "If you don't mind, I'll talk that matter over with Marion."

Later—much later—some one knocked at the door of Boone's cabin. It was Von der Mehden, in resplendent pajamas.

"Dick," he said, extending his sound arm, "I take that back."

"What, Otto?" asked Boone abstractedly.

"That 'chomp.' "

Adventure Vol·11 No·1 Nov. 1915

The GOLD LUST A COMPLETE NOVEL by J·ALLAN DUNN

I

BURIED TREASURE

Lust of Woman and Lust of Life,
Lust of Travel and Lust of Strife;
Never a one has the grip to hold
And the power to curse—like Lust of Gold.

"THREE QUARTERS OF A MILLION DOLLARS IN GOLD. Ye gods! Did I understand you to ask me what I'd do with it?"

The speaker, Jim Winton, once successful man of leisure, now, by a spin of Fortune's wheel, a tardily equipped and struggling architect, came from the long tables where he had been working under the north-light windows of his studio and faced his friend.

"I'll tell you what I'd do with it," he went on with mock earnestness, a twinkle in his brown eyes. "I'd pile every blueprint, tracing, plan and specification in the middle of the floor, warn Peggy and Selim, put the cat in safety, mail my insurance policy to the owner and set fire to the studio.

"If you ask me what I'd do *for* three quarters of a million I can tell you that also without hesitation: Commit with cheerfulness every crime on the calendar. But I don't believe there is that amount of loose coin in the world."

"I didn't say coin," said Archer Addams. "This is gold-dust and nuggets, at sixteen dollars to the ounce, twelve ounces to the pound, Troy weight, say close to two tons of the precious metal."

He stood by the fireplace in the light of the hickory logs, glowing brilliantly in the big studio, dusky with the shadows of the late wintry afternoon, a brave figure of a man, well over six feet, lithe and alert, weather-bronzed despite the bleach of winter, a trifle over thirty at a guess, scaling close to a hundred and ninety at another.

He possessed a quality of vibration, a plus of vigor beyond the average that was communicative, seeming to charge the atmosphere with magnetic energy and a sense of conviction. His quiet mention of a sum to which his listeners had been strangers—even in hope—for many a day, seemed matter-of-fact. Somehow one would not have been surprised to hear a second announcement that the gold was outside, waiting to be signed for. Even Jim Winton, the flippant, was impressed. Yet, to the general world, Addams was a failure. To himself, he was a man with a bad start who would yet challenge the leaders in the stretch.

He turned to the third occupant of the studio, Jim Winton's sister, who had risen at Addams' entrance a few minutes previously and cuddled down again among the cushions of a long-used, much-abused, but hospitable Morris chair.

"Well, Peggy?" he asked. "You purry, comfy thing, what would you do with it?"

She raised her head, the firelight on her rounded throat deepening the natural carmine of her cheeks, heightening the red-gold of her hair to match the curling flames.

"The answer's easy, fairy godfather," she mocked. "Get your wand ready. I've been fire-dreaming for an hour while Jim has been finishing up those plans he's working on. I was a thousand miles away when you arrived. What would I do? I'd clamber out of this rut we are all in and I'd start in whichever direction my nose pointed."

"Then you'd arrive in Heaven before your time, sister mine," broke in her brother.

Peggy made a face at him that was more of a reward than a punishment, and, the suggestion that her perfectly well-chiseled little nose was tip-tilted being largely a fraternal fallacy, went on placidly.

"I'd start and I'd keep going till I'd seen everything there was to be seen, and I'd get hold of dad and mother and—but don't get me going. It's your turn to answer foolish questions. Archer Addams, what would *you* do with three-quarters of a million dollars?"

"It's really only a quarter of a million, Peggy," he replied. "It has to be split three ways."

"Only a quarter?" exclaimed Winton in a voice of exaggerated interest. "Then I refuse to play any more. I'm going to finish this job, which represents one hundred and twenty-five dollars in real money."

He went back to his tables, and Addams, looking down at the girl, answered her question.

"I know what I'm going to do with mine," he said. "I worked that out coming down here. My law library of thirty-odd volumes, more or less in repair, my desk and two chairs, my typewriter, my one near-Persian rug, well worn by bill-collectors and book-agents, I am going to turn over to a young chap I know who is trying to 'get by' with a pine table and one chair, first endeavoring to persuade him to give up the law and learn barbering or something definitely lucrative. Then I am going to get the gold, buy one of Jim's very best plans, build me a house and marry the girl I'm in love with."

"And settle down as a country gentleman. That sounds nice and sensible," she said.

"No, not settle down. The girl wants to travel."

It might have been a sudden leaping of the flames, but Addams fancied the flush on the girl's face deepened as he spoke. He hoped so. She sprang to her feet.

"Stop work, Jim," she ordered. "Sit down, Archer. I'm going to make tea. Then you, sir, can explain what you mean by coming into our humble studio and talking about quarters of millions as if you had brought in a bag of oranges for general distribution."

She busied herself with the tea-things while her brother gathered his papers together and Addams lit a shaded lamp.

They were good friends, these three, chums of all the years from childhood. The two men, college mates, were about the same age, thirty; the girl seven years younger than her brother. A few years before, their fortunes had been lost in the failure of a common speculation, a catastrophe that had set the boys to a hasty attempt at developing their capabilities for business. Peggy kept house for her brother who struggled with the task of designing ten-thousand-dollar bungalows for five-thousand-dollar clients. Archer Addams studied law for the benefit of clients as yet conspicuous by their absence.

The news of failure had found Addams cruising in the Caribbean on his sixty-foot sloop, Winton in England looking over prospective polo ponies for his string, and Peggy as a popular débutante of one season. The elder

Addams, his wife already dead, soon followed her, crushed not so much by his own misfortunes as the knowledge that reliance on his judgment had led others, his friend Winton among them, into practical insolvency. Winton Senior and Mrs. Winton had retired upon a tiny competency to a small holding in the Berkshire Hills, while Jim, with Peggy as his housekeeper, set out upon a belated attempt to woo Fortune by designing tasteful dwellings for those who desired only show, and Addams set up his law office.

All three had faced the issue with laughs which had persisted in the face of persistent lack of success. Addams was a frequent visitor at the studio. To former liking had been added mutual respect. Friendship had stood the test. With Addams, towards Peggy it had ripened into something deeper that he rigorously imprisoned in a very secret chamber of his heart.

They had all gaily avoided the pertinacity of "old days' " friendship with their offers of help or pretense that nothing had happened; but Addams, recognizing Peggy's vital charm of beauty and vivacity, almost deluded himself into hoping that some man, more in favor with Fortune than he, would restore her to the status she had promised so well to adorn. But these things in the false pride of poverty he barely discussed with himself, even in his most intimate moments of privacy.

But, at last, when it seemed that, square his broad shoulders and smile as he might, he was doomed to drudgery and denial, Fortune had at least shown a disposition to flirt.

"Now Archer," said Peggy, when they were all cozily disposed about the little fire and she had played her part as dispenser of things to eat and drink, "on with the tale. There's been an air of secrecy and general puff-uppiness about you, ever since you arrived."

She cocked a merry thumb and forefinger at him.

"Stand and deliver, sir!" she ordered. "Or you may sit, if you prefer it, but deliver you must."

"Well," said Addams. "It's a long story, but I'm going to tell you the preface, and if you have no objection I'll let the man who made the story finish it. You remember the old chap I found in Union Square one night, half frozen, half starved, half conscious, with a policeman playing the nightstick rally on his poor old feet?"

"The one you say looks like Walt Whitman, and Jim calls your pirate?" asked the girl.

"He is a pirate," asserted her brother. "I met Archer mooning with him in Battery Park one day, and the old boy looked like Captain Kidd trying to masquerade as Santa Claus."

Addams set down his teacup.

"Well, you're not so far wrong after all, Jim," he said. "He was a pirate, once."

The girl clapped her hands.

"A real pirate!" she exclaimed. "Oh, go on, Archer! I can see John Silver and Blackbeard and Sir Harry Morgan standing in the dark corners."

She looked around the studio with a delicious little shiver, half real, half assumed.

"He won't measure up with those worthies," said Addams. "He never murdered any one, though he was in the middle of a lot of it. He was grateful to me for what little I did for him."

Jim grunted, knowing a soft side to his friend's character.

"And after a while I got interested in him. That started by my looking him up in his cubby-hole of a room in a dismal little court off Macdougal Street, a dingy place enough—but clean and shipshape as he could keep it. When he got better I used to meet him afternoons at the aquarium, when I'd got tired of playing at being a lawyer to nobody except cranks with imaginary grievances.

"We'd sit up in the gallery and watch the fish, and he'd tell me long yarns about schools of them, little bits of living rainbows, swimming over beds of live coral set with jeweled anemones and gaudy seaweeds, as he had seen them in the South Seas.

"He seemed perpetually and fearfully on the lookout for some one, but for a long time he did not tell his secret. This morning he tramped down-town to my office and unburdened himself."

"The treasure?" asked the girl, her eyes alight.

"Yes. Seven hundred and fifty thousand dollars' worth of dust and nuggets, at sixteen dollars to the ounce and twelve ounces to the pound, Troy weight, close to two tons of virgin gold—taken from the riverbeds of California sixty-five years ago, buried, and waiting for some one to dig it up and put it into circulation!"

"Has he handed you the usual bunk, Archer?" asked Jim with lazy sarcasm. "A sunken galleon full of tarnished gold, a map, skulls and crossbones, and a dying curse?"

Archer flushed.

"I'll admit the average buried treasure stunt is more or less of a joke," he said, "and usually ends in a fizzle. But I think you'll admit I'm not over gullible, and he tells a story this afternoon of a treasure, tarnished by a curse, that seems to me to hold the elements at least of truth.

"I suppose," he went on, "it's different, this matter of treasure-trove, when one is personally interested. But you shall hear the story as it was told to me by this old man of eighty-five, sane and clear-headed, from his own lips, and judge for yourselves."

"But I don't see where Peggy and I come in on it, Archer?" said Jim Winton. "He's *your* pirate!"

Then he shrugged his shoulders, admitting his interest in the tale, looking a little like a boy discovered stealing jam.

"Haven't we all been pals before and since our respective fathers went up in the same smash? And wasn't the entire unfortunate speculation made on the advice of my poor old *pater*?" asked Archer. "This is another speculation to be entered into on the advice of his son, with at least nothing to lose and a chance of recouping heavily. Of course we share alike. Jim, you're ridiculous."

"I understand, Archer," said the girl softly.

"Thanks, Peggy," he said. "I'm sure you do. So does Jim, really. Then it's all right if I bring the old boy 'round about eight o'clock?"

"Sure! We've nothing doing," answered Jim. "But honestly, Archer, didn't your pirate dream it? Do you really mean there's a chance of our putting hands on a chunk of coin? It sounds too good to be true. If you knew how sick I am of this grind of turning out cheap bungalows and punk garages—"

"Me too, Jim," answered Addams. "The practise of the law, what little I get of it, is neither attractive or lucrative. But I honestly believe this is true and that the money's there for the finding. We may have to fight for it, though."

Winton took his hands from his pockets and stood up.

"Fight! Why didn't you say so, long ago. That sounds more reasonable and interesting at the same time. You must admit that to quietly walk in on us and start talking about three-quarters of a million dollars as if it were thirty cents was somewhat staggering?"

"Well, we'll see," said Addams. "I've got to go now. No, I can't stay to dinner, Peggy, thank you. I've got to get some charts and things together that I left at the office. I'll have dinner downtown somewhere, but I'll be here at eight o'clock with the pirate."

II

THE GOLD PIRATES

THE KNOCKING AT THE BACK DOOR continued vigorously as Jim Winton tugged at the tardy bolts.

"Bring a light, will you, Peggy?" he called. "It's black as ink in the passage."

Peggy Winton appeared at the door of the studio. The apartment ran the full length of the building from Washington Square to an alley used partly as mews, partly for converted studios by the painters, sculptors and artists who had made that quarter of New York their own. The door at which Winton was struggling was a private one practically unused in favor of the entrance from the square.

"Here's the electric torch, Jim," said the girl, directing its beam on the stubborn door which opened suddenly as the last screeching bolt reluctantly left its socket.

A rush of wintry night air brought with it a few flakes of snow, and Archer Addams appeared, steadying the arm of an old man, muffled in an ulster that fell from beneath his long white beard to his feet.

The ray of the torch fell full upon the aged face, vigorous yet in spite of the telltale traces of years. The cheeks, tanned long since to leather, held a glow where the blood still ran rather than crawled through the veins. The gray eyes beneath the hoary penthouse brows were clear though in the strong circle of light they seemed to hold something of alarm as their owner glanced across his shoulder into the bleak, snow-set mews, before he tramped, sturdily enough, across the threshold.

"Easy as we go," he said in a deep, rumbling voice. "A bit of that light for the feet, miss. Thank'ee."

Addams shut and bolted the door and Peggy led the old man into the studio to a big chair in front of the fire. On a little table beside it were pipes, a tobacco-jar, a box of cigars, a brass kettle above a spirit lamp and the materials for the brewing of hot toddy.

The stranger surveyed the table with eloquent eyes while the girl applied a match to the lamp beneath the kettle, as Addams entered the studio.

"Why the back door, Archer?" queried Jim Winton.

"We had a fancy we were followed. We took a taxicab from Macdougal Street where Fellowes has his room in a little court, and as we came out some one tagged us. Fellowes rather expected something of the kind and we planned to dodge. The chap was handicapped with a lame foot, but we couldn't go over fast on account of the heavy snow tonight and he kept pretty close to us till we got to the Arch. Fellowes was strong for him not knowing where we were coming and we whipped around Washington Place into Ninth Street, down Fifth Avenue and up the Mews before he'd turned into the Avenue. It's still snowing a little and the tracks are pretty well mixed up, so I figure we've lost him."

"Will you have some toddy, Mr. Fellowes?" asked Peggy.

"It's a cabin welcome you're givin' me," answered the old fellow, basking before the grateful warmth of the fire. "I don't go much on grog as a rule. I stopped usin' it forty year ago; but I'm old now, and on a night like this it's welcome. Seein' as Mister Addams has told me I'm to spin my own yarn, why, I'll wet my whistle once in a while an' be obliged to ye."

Within a few minutes the group was established, the girl leaning forward interestedly from her chair, elbows on knees and her chin between her hands, Addams and Winton on the lounge with their cigars, centering their attention on Fellowes who sat, stroking his beard, looking meditatively into the fire.

• • •

"We'll have to go a long ways back," he commenced at last. "Back before any of your daddies was born, I reckon, likely enough; back to Californy an' the gold rush—the days of forty-nine. I'm eighty-five, I am, an' good for a few years yet. I'm hearty an' sound, an' my brain can box its own compass. Thet's because I've left this stuff alone."

He pushed his tumbler away from him, took a cigar and lighted it, watching the smoke spirals in silence.

"I'm tryin' to get the yarn all shipshape without makin' too many tacks," he said. "There's sixty-five years to cover, an' there's no sense in wasting time."

Addams brought a book and a roll of papers over to the little table.

"Here's an atlas and some charts that will help us to follow the story better," he said. "And some papers that would naturally be termed supporting evidence."

"Mostly for my benefit, I suppose," laughed Jim. "Wait till I put some more wood on the fire, Mr. Fellowes, before you start in."

He replenished the andirons and the flames leaped lustily, besieging the dusk of the great studio, unlighted save for the fire and one shaded lamp raised on a standard.

"Selim will bring some more wood in presently," said Peggy. "Now, Mr. Fellowes, we're all comfy and curious."

The old man looked at her eager face with kindly eyes.

"If my gal had lived," he said, "she'd be twice your age by now. She had the same kind of hair you've got, miss, beggin' your pardon—color of gold with flames reflected in it. But she's dead, long since, dead from the lust o' gold, dead from the gold an' the curse that lies upon it.

"I wasn't born so far from here," he went on. "Up in Maine on a farm that run down to the sea at Penobscot Bay. I used to sail about in a catboat an' the water always suited me better than the land, when it come to ploughing of it, though I didn't dream I was goin' to sail the seas I did before I'd get through my adventurin' an' back to Maine again.

"I was twenty when the gold fever broke out. They was a ship goin' 'roun' the Horn to the diggin's, an' with a lot of my pals, wild ones they was, the fever caught me an' we shipped to make our fortunes. It was a tough trip 'round, nine weeks tryin' to make westing. When we wasn't soaked through an' tired out we'd talk off-watch of just one thing—gold! We'd brag how we was goin' to get it, an' what we was goin' to do with it. At Frisco we did what all the crews did, deserted an' started off for the diggin's on the American River—that was the richest place goin' when we arrived.

"There was a fellow named Henley aboard. A bad one—"

He lowered his voice and looked furtively about him.

"A bad one! But he was older than most of us an' we thought he was a fine sort, as youngsters will, lookin' for short-cuts to be smart. He got to be the leader of a gang of about a dozen of us, all off the ship 'cept a chap named Chappell—'Chappie' we used to call him. He'd come from Australy—some said he was a Botany Bay man, a convict who'd cut loose. He was another bad one. I reckon they wasn't a heap to choose between any of us, on'y some knew more'n the rest. But we was all eager to learn.

"The upshot of it was that we got into trouble at Fort Sutter; Henley, Chappie, me an' a couple of others. They suspected Henley an' Chappie of crooked work with the cards an' we was identified with 'em. If they'd bin sure they'd likely have lynched the crowd of us, but they give us the benefit of the doubt and ran us out of the fort. That queered us in Sacramento an' most everywhere for that matter, so we split up.

"I got a job washing dishes, when I was hungry enough to eat the scraps off 'em, an' makin' beds for better men. I called 'em luckier men then. What they *was*, was honester. But the gang had all taken up Henley's an' Chappie's p'int of view, which was to let the other fellow do the diggin' an' get the gold out of him some easier way.

"I was pretty sick of playin' chambermaid, an' when Henley showed up one night I was ripe to listen to him. His talk sounded good to me. I suppose there never was a kid yet who didn't think it great to be a highwayman or a pirate, an' I was only a half-baked kid, at that.

"There were four men staying in the place where I was working who had made a big clean-up on the North Fork of the American. They had been the first to work on the big placer bars an' they had struck it rich, mighty rich, so that folks pointed them out on the street.

"They'd cleaned up half a million apiece, talk said, though we found out later that it was about two hundred thousand, an' they had declared themselves as ag'in goin' down to San Francisco on the river steamers. The steamers was jest plain floatin' hells, what with the gambling goin' on and the crowd that hung 'roun' the men who'd made their stakes. So these four—they'd come 'roun' the Horn, same as we had, an' had some workin' knowledge of seamanship—figgered on gettin' hold of a schooner an' a skipper an' sailin' direct to the Isthmus, doin' their own work, sailors bein' scarce, an' so keepin' out of the way of the rough crowd on the steamers an' in San Francisco, an' playin' guard to their own gold.

"Henley put it up to me to find out their plans, an' I, like a young fool, was proud of the job. I used to be in their room on an' off servin' drinks, an' I learned easy enough that they had made a dicker with the captain of a schooner to hire the ship at a top price to take them to the Isthmus. The skipper would pick up a crowd there bound for the diggin's an' make good money both ways. The skipper's name was Ellersby. He was a hard drinker in spells an' generally a rotten lot, but he could navigate and they didn't have much choice.

"First off, Henley had the idea of a crowd of us shippin' as sailors, but he decided it 'ud look too suspicious when nobody, unless they'd made their pile, was leavin'. Also we was still liable to be recognized in a bunch as the crowd that was run out of Fort Sutter. So he got to makin' friends with Ellersby, the skipper, drinkin' with him an' stickin' close while the schooner was gettin' provisioned up, an' one night he got the bunch of us together—they was four, outside of Henley, Chappell and me—an' told us the skipper had promised to come into the scheme for an equal share, meanin' an eighth.

"There was a sloop, not seaworthy but good enough for a calm river trip, that he figgered on stealin'. The seven of us was to run down to where the San Joaquin River runs into the Sacramento at Carquinez Straits, up at the north end of San Francisco Bay. There's a lot of islands there—a delta, they calls it—an' we was to 'stablish ourselves on one of these an' wait for Ellersby to come along at nightfall an' run the schooner on to a mud flat.

"It worked out to a charm. We got the sloop an' ran down with the tide, hidin' up in a slough that divided one of the islands. 'Cordin' to schedule the schooner come along after dark, buckin' the start of the flood. There was a mist, what they call a tule-fog, all over the river, an' Ellersby slid the schooner on the mud so soft that the four miners, asleep in the cabin, didn't know a thing till we'd boarded the schooner in a small boat, an' when Ellersby called down to 'em to come on deck they found us waitin' for them with belayin' pins.

"Henley showed a bit of himself there, if we'd had sense enough to see it. He was all for gettin' rid of the miners, claimin' dead men told no tales. Chappell backed him up, but the rest of us wouldn't stand for it. So we set 'em, bound an' gagged, on a little reedy island, all bog, an' floated the schooner off easy enough on the full tide, runnin' on the ebb down San Francisco Bay, out through the Gate, a Golden Gate to us that trip all right, with the dust an' nuggets stowed away in the hold—ours!

"Once free an' fair of the Farallones we held a palaver. There was a chance of the miners gettin' picked off the island sooner than we expected. That might mean we'd reach the Isthmus to find the news ahead of us an' a law-an'-order committee waitin' for us. The same thing might happen in Honolulu, which port we figgered on for a long while, or in any of the South American ports. A trip clean 'round the Horn was out of the question in the schooner, let alone that we didn't have grub enough for that long a trip.

"Finally, Ellersby, who had been mixed up in opium smuggling in the Hawaiian Islands—Sandwich Islands they called 'em those days—proposed to sneak quietly into Pearl Harbor, eight miles from Honolulu, hide up in one of the arms of the big lochs there, find out if the coast was clear as far as news of the affair was concerned, an' if everything was all right buy or charter some other craft an' sail to New Zealand or Australy in her or, better still, ship the gold as parts of machinery an' take passage in a steamer.

"We settled on that plan finally, though if we'd carried it out, we'd have run right into trouble, for the news of the robbery was in Honolulu long before we'd have made it."

Fellowes paused and took a sip of his toddy which Peggy had made hot again.

His auditors were silent, transported from the New York studio by the straightforward vividness of the old man's delivery to the pirated schooner on the Pacific Ocean outside San Francisco, with the eight buccaneers in council in the tiny cabin.

Addams broke the pause by picking up the papers he had deposited on the table and separating them.

"I'll read you a couple of extracts while Fellowes rests for a minute," he said, unfolding a newspaper yellowed with age.

"This is the Sacramento *Bee* of July sixth, 1850," he announced. "I'll read you the article:

"PIRACY ON THE SACRAMENTO

GANG OF VILLAINS ROB MINERS OF THEIR HARD-EARNED TREASURE

The River Steamer *Chrysopolis* brought back to Sacramento today four miners whose luck on the North Fork of the American has been the comment, and possibly aroused the jealousy of many. These men, Rivers, Thorn, Edwards and Burns, who chartered the schooner *Lady Mine* from Captain Ellersby to convey themselves and their dust, amounting to about eight hundred thousand dollars, to the Isthmus, were waylaid by a ruffianly gang of pirates, acting in consort with Captain Ellersby, who is, it appears, himself somewhat notorious, and robbed of their gold. They were captured without the chance to make resistance for the treasure they had wrung from the river-bars, and set, bound and gagged, on a little island, while the schooner, with Ellersby and the ruffians aboard, sailed through Carquinez Straits, presumably for the Isthmus or some other port.

The villains were something short of a dozen in number, consisting of two men appearing to be the leaders, by name Henley and Chappell, the last suspected of being a convict from Australia, and their followers. Henley and Chappell were recently run out of Fort Sutter for suspected trickery at cards. Another who was recognized by the unfortunate miners was a young man named Jared Fellowes who had been employed out of charity at the Davis House as dishwasher and bedmaker, where, it is thought, he learned of the plans of Rivers and his three companions.

Rivers managed to work the gag from his mouth and succeeded in getting the attention of the up-bound *Chrysopolis* from which Captain

Rollins promptly despatched a boat in answer to the call for help. The unfortunate men are now penniless, but, with the spirit of true Argonauts, leave within a few days for the North Fork where they hope to recoup themselves for their stolen fortunes.

The news will be sent to San Francisco on the hope of apprehending the men. All outgoing steamers will carry the story of the outrage and it is trusted the rascals will soon be apprehended. Should they be returned to Sacramento, we recommend them to the attention of the Vigilance Committee. It is high time that some semblance of law and order be maintained.

"That's the *Bee*. This other is a copy of the San Francisco *Chronicle* of a little later date, where the story is practically reproduced. There is also a copy of the *Commercial Advertiser* of Honolulu, dated August the third, with a reprint."

"Thankee, Mister Addams," said Fellowes. "Of course, we didn't figger for a minnit the miners would be picked up that soon, but, as you'll see, if we'd made Honolulu they'd have been all cocked an' primed an' waitin' for us.

"But we didn't get there. Three days out, nothin' would do but we break out the gold an' figger out just what the shares was. We counted twenty boxes, made up of hooped iron over heavy timber, weighin' close to two hundred apiece. One of 'em we took into the cabin an' opened up. Two men was on deck, an' when the rest of us ran our hands through the dust—heavy colors an' rough grains all of it—an' began shoutin', they left the schooner to itself an' come down to join us. Ellersby swore at 'em but at last he went on deck by himself, leavin' the rest of us handlin' the glitterin' heavy stuff like a lot of kids in their first sand-pile. That's where the trouble started.

"Some sort of devil crept out of that case and took charge of all of us. We got the gold-fever. You don't know what that means, but I've seen it work a hundred times—a hundred places. It means greed an' hatred an' murder. I've seen a man's eyes change to hold the gleam of the gold in it, an' his nature change at the same time. That's the way it was with us.

"We spent that gold a thousan' ways, an' cursed because we couldn't get to where we could toss it on counters an' across bars. They was eight of us, with a tenth of a million apiece, an' not able to use it. Of course we started gambling an' drinkin' with it.

"We'd arranged watches, but nobody would leave the table. We ate stuff out of cans without cookin' it, an' when anybody took the wheel it was usually some one tryin' to sober up. The skipper started to drinkin' in his cabin. He turned nasty an' went 'round with his revolver threatenin' to shoot any one who wouldn't take his trick. We had sense enough left not to break with him, 'count of his bein' the only navigator on board. But Henley used to nod an' wink when he was absent, an' tell how we'd get rid of him soon as we were in sight of land. 'We'll cut up his share alike,' he said.

"That meant fourteen thousand more for each of us. An' they wasn't one of us but what figgered how much more would come to him if the rest should die. It sounds pretty terrible to think of murder breedin' that way; but it was the curse of the gold, an' the lust of it. If we'd come by it honest it might have been different, but we was outlaws anyway.

"Henley, first, an' Chappell next, began to win all the time at cards. We all suspected them of cheating, but we didn't catch them at it. Then, after fourteen days, we run into the doldrums between the northwest an' southeast trades, an' slatted sails day after day in a dead calm.

"I got sick of the cards, not bein' able to win an' not willin' to go on losin', an' spent most of the time on deck. It was bad enough there, but it was a little hell in the cabin. The schooner had carried pearl-shell an' copra an' trepang. She was dirty in the hold an' sour of bilge. You can figger what it was like under the steady sun with the pitch squeezin' out of the seams. The skipper was in his cabin most of the while, drinkin' steady. There was nothin' to do in workin' the ship, an' the wheel spun any way it wanted.

"Next thing, the water went bad. Then every one began to get sick eatin' the canned grub, uncooked. Not a drop of medicine aboard, an' the only doctor in sight was Doctor Shark. They was five of *them* trailin' astern, one for each man that was goin' to be served to 'em. The curse had started."

Fellowes stopped and passed his hand in front of his eyes. The two men sat silent with frowning brows. Peggy shuddered and stirred the fire.

Suddenly she sprang up with an exclamation.

"The window!" she cried. "There, at the window!"

III

THE FACE AT THE WINDOW

THE BIG NORTH WINDOW OF THE STUDIO was a-steam from the cold without and the warmth within. Winton, working late, had neglected to cover the lower panes with the blind, and, as the younger men sprang up, turning swiftly, while Fellowes elbowed himself from his chair and Peggy stood pointing, a swift, evasive shadow showed for a second against the misty glass and then vanished.

"It's Henley!" hoarsely exclaimed the old man, his face working. "He's trailed us."

"It may not be he," said Addams. "Come on, Jim! Where's that torch of yours?"

The two men passed through the little passage and out into the crisp air of the Mews. An electric arc at the alley's entrance to Fifth Avenue dimly illumined the lately fallen snow, stained faintly here and there by the orange light from a window. The snow had ceased. Along the narrow sidewalk, halting in front of the studio window as if some one had been peering within, a trail showed clearly defined, one sharp imprint and the blur of a dragging foot, coming and going back to Fifth Avenue. There was no one in sight. The mews seemed utterly deserted.

"That's the lame chap who followed from Fellowes' lodgings," said Addams.

"Fellowes said it was Henley," said Jim. "Did he mean the chap that was the leader? He must be about a hundred, by all accounts. He's pretty spry in his old age."

"No, his son. You'll hear about him later. He's got the old boy pretty nervous. Trying to force him to tell where the gold is. Come on in, Jim. It's freezing. And pull down that blind."

"It was Henley?" asked Fellowes anxiously. "He's getting desperate, I tell you—"

"He can't get in to do you any harm here," soothed Peggy. "Won't you sit down again?"

He suffered himself to be made comfortable again, but his corded hands were shaky and the look of alarm had come into his gray eyes once more.

"See here," said Winton, "you don't have to go home tonight. Archer, you'll stay here. Your usual room's ready for you and we can fix up Fellowes here with a shakedown in the studio. Eh, Peggy?"

"Easily," she answered. "I'll tell Selim."

She pressed a button and the tinkle of a bell sounded distantly.

"This is what he's after," said Fellowes, reassured somewhat. "This—and this, meanin' the whereabouts of the gold—only he don't know just what shape I carry them in."

He took from his inner pocket a piece of stout paper, creased in its well worn folds, and laid it on the table near Addams, while he fumbled at his waistcoat and finally brought out a thick, old-fashioned silver watch.

"You keep it," he said to Addams. "I've always meant you to have 'em. I'll feel safer."

Addams carefully spread out the paper which proved to be a roughly drawn map of an island, marked here and there with faded lettering.

"I'll come to that presently," said Fellowes, as Addams laid it on the table. "Who's that?"

He covered the map with his great hand, staring fearfully at a figure that glided silently out of the shadows. A lithe, swarthy man, with black almond-shaped eyes and thin, straight nose, black-browed, his crisp black hair barely topping the shoulder of Peggy Winton who gave him some quiet orders to which he bowed and departed as quietly as he had come.

"That's Selim," explained Winton. "Our butler, cook and man-of-all-work. We couldn't get along without Selim. You needn't be afraid of him."

"He looks like a South Sea Kanaka," said Fellowes, still keeping his big hand over the map.

"He's an Arab," said Winton. "Peggy picked him up at an employment agency, and he's *some* cook. She nursed him through an attack of pneumonia and he worships the ground she walks on. Don't worry about Selim. He's eaten our salt and he's true as steel."

"He's brown!" said Fellowes suspiciously. "And if you've seen as much of brown skins as I have, you wouldn't trust 'em out of your sight and not too much in it, though some of them was mighty good to me once."

He watched the Arab when he returned with fresh logs for the fire, and waited until he left the room before speaking. Then he attempted an apology.

"I ain't aimin' to say anything against your servant, miss," he said. "Only, three-quarters of a million is enough to turn any man's head, white or brown. Where was I?"

"Fourteen days out, in a dead calm, with five sharks following on behind," said Winton in a voice the affected calm of which betrayed his eagerness, while Addams smiled quietly across at him.

"Five sharks waitin' for five men," repeated Fellowes. "Well, they got 'em, three of 'em, in the next ten days. Ptomaines, it was, only we didn't know the name of it those days. Then another went. He was in his bunk for a day before any one got away from the cards long enough to get rid of him. This is a pretty rough yarn for a woman to listen to, miss?"

He turned to Peggy.

"No, no. Go on," she said. "It's really happened and I'm not afraid to hear of such things, or see them if I have to."

Fellowes looked at her admiringly.

"It happened, all right," he said grimly. "Henley went on winning till he owned pretty nigh half the gold, outside the skipper's share. A chap we knew as Zeb, a Southerner, thought he caught him slipping an ace—an' he told him so. I was on deck an' didn't see what happened, but I heard the shot, an' that night Zeb went to Doctor Shark.

"That left three of us, not countin' the skipper—Henley, Chappell. The convict, an' me. I had held on to most of my share an' I wouldn't play cards any more. Chappell an' Henley kept at it for a bit an' then they quit. Henley tried to make up to me an' pretty soon proposed we get rid of Chappell who, he claimed, wanted to do *me* up so's there 'd be more to share.

"I was in a funk by this time—as we used to call it—a blue funk. I was only a kid, sick of the whole trip an' scared of Henley. He was just plain devil. I used to see him lookin' at me an' at Chappell, stealthy, an' I knew if we ever got our fingers on any of the gold it wouldn't be his fault. He quarreled with the skipper, too, but he couldn't bluff Ellersby. Then Chappell an' Henley sulked. Ellersby was a wonder. He was drinkin' steady, but it didn't seem to have any effect on him, 'cept that his eyes looked sometimes like a mad dog's, with a red light in them. He watched Henley all the time with a snarl on his lips, just like a dog that's suspicious of ye.

"We got to the last of the good water—you use up a lot of it in that kind of weather—an' things looked pretty bad when we run into a rain-squall, at last, an' filled up everything we could. Then a roarin' monsoon come up out of the south an' whirled us away on the fringe of it, 'way off the course. All four of us did what we could to work the schooner, but you can't do much with a monsoon. When it threw us off its track an' left us, the schooner was leakin' badly an' the two main boats, whalers, was smashed to bits. That left only a little square-sterned dinghy, hardly big enough to carry four men, let alone the gold.

"An' it looked as if we'd have to take to the boat. The foremast had sprung a steady leak. The skipper thought a butt had started somewhere else, an' the best we could do at the pumps couldn't keep the water from rising. At last you could hear it sloshing about in the hold where the gold was stowed.

"Ellersby talked it over with us. There was an island reported by whalers once in a while, an' known to the natives, that was somewhere near where we was. But he wasn't sure that it was really there or that we could find it. He didn't have its position an' the South Pacific is full of islands that are reported an' can't be found when they're looked for.

"If we could reach it, he proposed to careen the schooner an' fix the leak. We could do that or take a chance in the boat without the gold, or we could bury the gold on the island if we found it an' couldn't fix the leak, an' make for Hawaii in the dinghy from there, a trip of about eight hundred miles, he told us.

"We took votes on it. I voted for the island. That gave me another chance that I knew I'd lose if it came to a question of leaving the gold out of the boat rather than me. My weight in gold was worth a whole lot more than I was, right then. The skipper voted with me, wantin' to save his ship, an' then Chappell sided in. He argued that a small boat arrivin' at Honolulu, with or without gold, was goin' to be an object of more curiosity than we was lookin' for. So we agreed to try for the island an' do what we could with the ship.

"It was touch an' go. The water came up till the schooner slogged 'roun' like a water-soaked log. Any kind of a sea would have finished us. It was the tenth of August, thirty-nine days since Sacramento, when I saw a little speck on the horizon, early in the afternoon.

"We slapped each other on the back, all except the skipper who was surly with the responsibility. We got the sodden schooner close-hauled to the course at last, under jib an' mainsail; Ellersby took the wheel, Chappell, who had been feelin' sick, went into the cabin an' Henley an' me stood by to handle sheets. Henley was sore at Chappell. He wasn't feelin' over an' above good himself, but Chappell deliberately turned into his bunk an' stayed there.

"I can see the land as it opened up, now," said Fellowes, looking into the fire. "There was a low peak with a long low cliff runnin' out from it to a cape, an' beyond the cape a little island the shape of a thimble. When we got close, the gulls lifted like the top of the island was comin' off. The slopes was white with guano. The surf was thunderin' on the reef an' we couldn't make out an opening. The only chance was to go between the cape an' the little island. The water was boilin' an' swirlin' in the channel, but the schooner was sluggish an' hard to steer an' we had to take short-cuts. Accordin' to reports there was an entrance somewheres in the reef—an' we had to find it.

"Ellersby orders Henley to get Chappie up to help on the tack, an' he went below while we edged in closer to the reef, the schooner gettin' slower an' more logy every minnit. I went down to hurry the two of them up an' found the pair of 'em rollin' on the floor. Both had knives out an' they were shoutin' an' cursin' too much to listen to me, though I told 'em we'd be on the rocks in a minnit if they didn't lend a hand. All of a sudden Henley gets Chappie's hand between his teeth an' he drops his knife.

"Like a fool he grabbed for it, an' Henley stuck him. He grunted an' huddled up an' Henley an' me races on deck. Just as we reached it the schooner smashes into the reef, scrapes across, staggerin', an' wallows through the lagoon, rail awash. They was no one at the wheel, the main-boom had broke away from sheet an' tackle an' must have thrashed the skipper overboard. A blind breaker took us like it would a surf-boat an' flung us on the sand, buryin' the bows deep an' firm.

"We picked ourselves up an' stood lookin' at each other on the slantin' deck in the sunset—red like blood it was, I remember—two of us out of the eight, a lonely beach an' lava cliffs frownin' down at us, the schooner with its back broken, a dead man in the cabin an' three-quarters of a million in gold in the waterlogged hold."

He stopped and sat with his hands on his knees, breathing hard, staring into the heart of the fire as if it were the sunset on the lonely, bird-haunted isle, trembling with the excitement of his tale.

IV

THE FIGURES IN THE WATCH-CASE

PEGGY WINTON GOT UP AND WENT OVER TO FELLOWES' CHAIR.

"You're tired," she said gently. "You must go to bed and tell us the rest in the morning. It's a shame to sit listening here, never thinking of how you were feeling."

"That's all right, miss," assured Fellowes. "I'm tougher than you think. I'll rest a bit an' take another drop o' somethin' hot, if you don't mind. But I'll finish the yarn tonight, if you'll listen. There's some things Mr. Addams ain't heard yet that I want him to know. It's gettin' close to the end of the voyage for me an' I want to tell it while I can."

He looked fearfully at the window, where the blind had now been drawn, and about the dark corners of the room, then leaned back, closing his eyes.

Addams picked up the map again and the three of them examined it. On it was shown the island of the wreck, the cone drawn as a hollow crater. Near the cape were two crosses, one lettered "wreck" the other "caves here." The reef was indicated with an opening on the opposite side of the promontory from the two crosses. At the bottom was the word "*Kapukalipelipe*."

"That's the native name for the place," explained Addams. "Means 'the wide-mouthed hole,' Fellowes says, referring, of course, to the crater."

"There's no position marked on the map," said Winton in a low voice.

Fellowes sat forward in his chair.

"I'm coming to that, sir," he said, "in just a minnit. So far that's a secret. I haven't even told Mister Addams, an' if it wasn't for him I'd have been underground in a pauper's grave a month or more ago. I'm ready now for the rest of the yarn.

"That night Henley an' me slept on the beach by a fire. He was pretty sick, but I made shift to get some stuff from the lazarette an' cook a warm meal. That heartened us both up a bit. Next morning we found the body of the skipper washed ashore an' buried it. Then we got Chappie's body up from the cabin an' did the same with that. After, we explored the island, what they was of it—one big crater, choked with lava, another one on the cape, smaller, an' I reckon still another on the little island. Not a thing grew on the place 'cept a spiky-leaved plant all covered with silver hairs. There was nothin' livin' but the sea-birds, an' no fresh water.

"Down not far from where the schooner was ashore we found some caves with funny carvings of men an' animals all over the walls an' roof. I've seen just the same sort of picters out west in Indian caves. You could only get in the caves at low tide, an' then some of the carvings was under water. I figgered that the island had been higher out of water once an' had sunk down in some volcanic breakout, like lots of the South Sea islands have.

"We took stock. Henley was gettin' weaker an' we was pretty well up against it. We didn't have more than thirty gallons of good water. It wasn't the rainy season, as the skipper had told us, an' we had the chance of making Hawaii, eight hundred miles away, in a little open boat, or dyin' of thirst either there on the island or in the boat if we was too long on the trip.

"The boat, which had been stored amidships, was in fairly good shape. Henley started to tinker it up an' rig up a mast an' sail while I went below for grub. I reckon we was both scared after sizin' up the water. I worked in a sweat pilin' up cans an' tryin' to make up my mind what to take, listenin' to Henley draggin' an' scrapin' on deck with the boat. I was afraid of him, too. I still figgered he might get rid of me an' put my weight into gold in the boat. It 'ud help with the water, too, if I was out of the way. So I went into the skipper's cabin, hopin' to find a pistol of some sort, an' come across the log.

"I turned over the pages an' found what I hoped for. Drunk as he was, the skipper's habit was strong enough for him to set down the position regular an' keep up the log. His reckonin' that noon was on the last page. That was as good as a pistol to me. We'd have to leave some of the gold anyway. Even if Henley made away with me he couldn't pack it all. So I figgered I'd hold the position of the island as a weapon. Then we could come back for the gold, an' I figgered we'd have to leave enough behind to make it worth while for Henley not to shoot me in the back.

"First I thought I'd keep the figgers in my head. Seemed as if I must remember them, but I wasn't sure of myself. I started to tear out the sheet an' then I thought of my watch. I took my knife an' scratched the figgers on the back lid which screwed off."

Addams had set the watch as a weight on top of the map. Fellowes unscrewed the case from the back of the old-fashioned key-winder and passed the lid to Archer who read the figures by the lamp.

"See if you can make them out, Peggy," he said.

The girl took the silver case.

"One-six-five-four-naught-W?"

"One-hundred and sixty-five degrees and forty minutes west longitude from Greenwich," he explained.

"One-two-two-naught-N—that's north I suppose?"

"North of the Equator, south of the Tropic of Capricorn. Twelve degrees and twenty minutes north latitude. Look it up on that chart, Jim. You'll find it easily enough."

Winton obediently unrolled a U.S. hydrographic survey chart of the southern Pacific and looked up the position.

"It's marked here!" he said excitedly. "Not under any name, though. There's just a dot and the lettering 'E.D. reported 1901.' "

"Meaning that some ship reported that they had seen, or thought they had seen, an island about that position. That was in 1901. E.D. stands for 'Existence Doubtful.' That's the chart for this year. The first official recognition of possible land was in 1901, and the last. But it corroborates Fellowes' yarn. There's nothing to tie it up with a treasure island without Fellowes' story and nothing then to show where the treasure is without the map indicating the caves."

"An' nothin' *then* to tell which cave it is or how it's hidden," chuckled the old man. "Without I told it—an' I've told it to no one, mind you—you could dig an' prod about the caves for twenty years an' never find it. That part of it, miss, I'm goin' to tell to you, because you've been kind to me, an' because you look as my daughter might have looked if she'd lived. That gives you a share in it, though I've got an idea"—the gray eyes twinkled as he glanced at Addams and the girl, standing together by the lamp—"that you would have a share in it anyway. Will you come over here where I can whisper it to ye?"

Peggy, with bright eyes, came lightly over and perched on the arm of the big chair.

"Remember now," said Fellowes, "it's still a secret. Just between you an' me. You're not to tell it unless I say so or unless something should happen to me. An' then tell it when you want to. Only don' be in too much of a hurry. It's worth three-quarters of a million!"

Addams and Winton stepped aside while the old man cupped his horny palm and whispered into the shell-like ear of the girl, who nodded her comprehension as he whispered the information.

"I understand," she said. "And under no conditions am I to tell it to any one but you, Archer," she said, blushing a little.

"That lets *me* out," said Jim. "I see where I have to be a private in this expedition."

"Then you are beginning to think seriously of it?" queried Archer not without emphasis.

"Oh, I've caught it," acknowledged Jim, "the gold fever, or the gold lust, or whatever you call it. I'm infected. Go on with the yarn, Mr. Fellowes. Have a fresh cigar."

"Thankee kindly, I will," said the old man, and lit one.

"Let me see. Oh, I'd scratched the figgers in my watch. Well, I tore out the sheet from the log, anyway. I rolled it into a spill, filled my pipe an' lit it with the page. I burned it to the end an' smeared out the ashes with my foot. Then I shoved the rest of the logbook 'way back in the lazarette. I felt better then. I bumped into the skipper's coat hangin' by the door as I was comin' out, an' struck somethin' hard. It was a pistol, loaded up. I stuck it in my pocket and felt equal to Henley any time. Then I took the grub up on deck.

"Between us, though Henley was so weak he had to sit down every little while, we got the dinghy into the water an' stowed the provisions. We got into it to test it an' the gunnels were pretty low. I caught Henley lookin' at me an' shifted so he could see the pistol in my pocket. He didn't say a word till we got the boat afloat an' tied an' was both in the cabin takin' a last look 'round. Then he stopped by the box of gold that had been broken on the trip.

" 'We better bury the rest of this in the caves,' he said. 'We can take this along, I reckon, if we dump one of those kegs of beef. How far's Hawaii, did Ellersby say? Where's the logbook?'

"He started to look for it, me watchin' him. Presently he turned and looked at me. 'Where is it?' he asked.

"I had my hand on the grip of the pistol an' I looked back at him an' says, 'It's no use lookin' for it. I chucked it away.'

"He watched me steady for a minnit. 'You artful devil,' he says. 'You must have got the figgers somewheres. You're a fox, you are,' he says. 'I always knew you for a smart 'un, that's why I made a pal of you. Let's have a look at the figgers, Jared, an' we'll map things out.'

"I kept my hand on the pistol an' my eyes close on his. I could see he was wonderin' whether he should make a jump for me, but he was pretty weak an' I reckon I must have looked as if I was ready for him. 'The figgers is in my head,' I says, 'an' goin' to stay there.'

"He shook his head at me as if he was admirin' me for bein' smart. 'Foxy, Jared, foxy,' he says, 'but foolish. You might forget 'em. Better put 'em down while they're fresh.'

" 'Not me,' I told him. 'Hawaii's about eight hundred miles, due northeast. That's all you'll get out of me. I'll play square with you,' I told him, 'an' now you'll have to play square with me.'

"He kept lookin' at me close, wonderin' whether I was lyin'. Then he give it up. 'All right, Jared,' he said, with a smile that looked like the start of a bite, 'I see I'll have to take good care of you.'

"That afternoon we worked like stevedores handlin' the gold. It was hot, an' we stripped. Once Henley said he was played out an' lay down for a bit of a nap while I finished hidin' the chests where we'd put 'em away inside the cave. I left him in the shade of a rock an' when I came out he was still there with his eyes shut, but, when I picked up my clothes, I could tell he'd been through 'em, looking for a paper with the position set down on it. He didn't think of the watch though.

"I'd packed my pistol with me so he couldn't take that. I hadn't thought of it when I took my duds off, but it was a good move to let him go through them—or he might have murdered me in the boat when I was asleep, for I c'd see he hadn't been satisfied about what I said of the figgers bein' in my head.

"Finally we got everything stowed in one of the caves—you know where, miss."

Peggy nodded.

"We got the opened chest into the little boat an' was so done up we slep' on the beach all night, too tired to make a fire or cook a meal.

"Next mornin' Henley was in a high fever an' I had a hard time to get him into the boat. He was off his head at times an' wished we should stay by the gold, but I got him quieted down. I rowed around the point, inside the reef, to the opening on the other side of the island, got up my rag of a sail, fixed Henley so he'd be in the shadow of it on the bottom boards, an' steered northeast by the compass with a steady breeze drivin' us due from behind.

"I've often laid nights when I couldn't sleep an' thought about that trip. There was a long time when it was all out of my head, as I'll tell you, though now I remember everything that happened as if it was yesterday. There was me in the stern with the opened box of gold between my feet. Then Henley, moanin' for water an' me givin' him all we c'd spare, an' more. Stowed all about was a keg of beef, the water-cask an' canned crackers an' stuff. The bows of the cranky little boat was cocked 'way up. I had a canvas over the water-cask an' kept it wet with seawater to let the wind hold the stuff as cool as possible.

"It was sun—sun—sun, fourteen hours of the day, dryin' you to a mummy, crackin' your lips, swellin' up your tongue an' spoilin' the canned stuff so I had to throw it all overboard. The beef went pretty bad an' there was nothin' but that, the crackers, some cans of tomatoes an' the water—hot water, at that.

"The third day a big shark slipped up astern an' kep' trailin'. He was the one of the five, I figgered out, that hadn't had his share, an' I wondered which one of us it was goin' to be, an' didn't care much. There was his fin, night an' mornin' like a V upside down. After a while I got to talkin' to him. Henley was unconscious most of the time. My hands cracked an' I didn't want to eat—couldn't keep the food down when I did.

"I never was a navigator. Anyway, all I had was one watch an' no chronometer, so I cu'dn't have even figgered out latitude if I'd known how. I had no idea of dead reckonin', no log, an' I didn't know what current might be swingin' me. I figgered that the gold-island was the point of a big triangle with the Hawaiians makin' the base line of about four hundred miles. I wanted to hit that base somewhere. In a straight line, it was an eight-hundred-mile course I had to run. It didn't seem I could miss them altogether if I wasn't blown off my course or drifted too far when I was asleep. To offset that I lowered the sail nights when I napped. If I did happen to miss the Islands it was the end, of course, with nothin' closer than two thousand miles on the course an' small chance of pickin' them up again if I once passed 'em.

"I figgered to make eighty miles a day, sleepin' an' wakin', if the wind held. It was guesswork, of course, without any log. At the rate the water was goin' I had enough to last out.

"Five days along I began to get faint an' confused. I couldn't see anything for minnits at a time. Henley was dead, I thought. I crawled over twice an' wet his lips, which was all black, an' he never stirred. I was burned to toast an' more cracks come in my hands. The boat was too low in the water, an', when the breeze was fresh, the spray 'ud hit the bows an' wet me so that I got sea-sores all over.

"Late that fifth night I come to with a start. It was starlight though it was close to dawn. I could see Henley. He'd moved an' was all huddled over the chest. The sky began to shake an' the sun jumped up, an' there was his eyes starin' at me, his lips grinnin', one hand mixed in with the gold.

"The boat tipped high on a wave an' water came runnin' to my feet. Somethin' told me what it was, but I tasted it. I was right. It was *fresh*. I got by Henley an' found the plug out an' the keg bone dry, 'cept the inch or so beneath the bung. Somehow or other Henley must have had a rally an' got out the plug.

"I sat there a while. Then I mopped up what I could with a rag an' squeezed it back into the keg. It wasn't much. The shark come glidin' up alongside an' swirled over showin' his teeth. That set me crazy. 'You ain't goin' to get *me*,' I yelled at him an' I tumbled Henley's body overside. That was the last I saw of the shark.

"Then I began to see yellow. The sun was shinin' into the open chest of gold. I remember grabbin' a pannikin an' scoopin' up the dust, a thousand dollars at a throw, I reckon, an' scatterin' it on the sea like it was yellow seed. I must have emptied it an' then fainted.

"I come back, maybe that day, mebbe the day after, with a squall tippin' the boat over an' my body soakin' in torrents of rain. I must have taken the rain up like a sponge. An', if I hadn't spilled that gold, the boat would have capsized for certain. My sail was down, an' that helped. The squall passed, the sun came out an' I was glad to see it for the first time for many a day. I got some food into me, ran the rainwater off the folds of the sail into the keg, hoisted the sail an' got on the course once more, with a bit of courage still left in me.

"I was afraid of passing land in the night now, an' used to sleep daytimes, under the sail for shade. The stars an' a new moon was enough to make me sure of pickin' up anything the size of the Hawaiis as long as I kept awake. I knew I was makin' longitude by the way the Southern Cross was dippin' close to the horizon. My time was all mixed up, but I figure it was the fourteenth or fifteenth morning when I raised land on either side of me. You'll find them there on the map, Mister Addams, Laau Point on Molokai Island to port of me, an' Kaena Point, on Lanai, to starboard.

"I wasn't out of it yet, till I could get through the reef. I've seen double-ender whaleboats since then rolled end-over makin' an opening, many a time, in the rollers that snake across where the reef is low enough for you to tackle it. I guess the sight of land heartened me up an' put some strength in me, for I caught a comber an' shot across the lagoon an' up the sand on to a bay like a crescent, walled in by lava cliffs with their horns running out far into the sea on each side.

V

THE LEPERS OF MOLOKAI

"THERE WASN'T A SOUL IN SIGHT and I knew the natives were friendly, so I lay down in the sand under the shadow of the boat an' slept, with the tide goin' out, till noon, or after, when the sun sneaked over an' got into my eyes. I got something to eat an' started exploring. I was on the lee coast of Molokai, though I didn't know which island I was on then, an' for a bit it looked as if I had jumped out of the soup-kettle on to the stove.

"The little beach was like a prison with the cliffs an' the sea. All the water I had left was about half a gallon, not extry sweet at that, an' there was none in sight. On top of the cliffs I could see palms fringin' the summit an' I knew there was water there if I could make shift to climb up. They was a few big cracks in the cliff wall that looked as if it might be tackled, an' it had to be. But I rested an' slept good all that day an' that night. The sand made a good bed—I could stretch out full length, anyway, an' I slept like a kid.

"Next morning I felt better, an' after breakfast I started to climb. It was hard goin', an' the lava cut like flint. My hands went first, then my clothes, what they was of them, then my shoes. But I had to keep goin', the water was all gone.

"They was a ledge or so I managed to rest on a bit, an' finally I reached a little valley like a pocket, about two-thirds of the way up. It was covered with long grasses, but there wasn't any water. The cliffs up to the palms at the top was worse than the ones I had tackled, but I was afraid of gettin' stiff an' I was about all in so I went to them.

"Half way up I got stuck. I couldn't get up an' I couldn't get down. I stuck there clingin' somehow, the way a sick cat might, gettin' dizzy an' dizzier. A lot of faces like apes was grinnin' at me from the top. I lost my grip about then, fainted, I reckon, an' flopped to the bottom.

"When I come to it was like a nightmare. They was a ring of natives round me, gibberin' Kanaka an' lookin' down at me. They was just scraps of humanity, pretty bad to talk about, let alone look at—the lepers of Molokai. They was kind enough, an' after you got used to 'em you couldn't help but like 'em. They had seen me creepin' up the cliff an', when I fell, climbed down somehow an' hauled me up. They could climb like goats, all of 'em. I had a pretty bad smash in the side of my skull, how bad I never knew, but they fixed it up with plasters of red mud an' herbs an' pulled me through.

"I had headaches for weeks steady an' never got rid of them till years after, an'—I couldn't remember a thing of what happened before I fell from the cliff. I used to sit in the sun like a skeleton, gettin' well little by little an' puzzlin' over who I was, where I come from an' what I'd done. All no good. They brought me my hat, a knife, a watch-key, the watch an' a few coins.

"There was a name in the hat—Jared Fellowes—which I supposed was mine, though I wasn't sure of it. I knew I must have come there in a boat, for the natives swam 'round an' got mine, but there was no name on it. I had a hazy idea, or instinct, that I was a sailor. My arm had been badly twisted an' I didn't try to wind up the watch for a long time. Then I saw the figgers in the lid, but they didn't mean nothing.

"The Board of Health come over about three months after I landed. They quarantined me for a while, but I was all right. I didn't have any open wound, an' leprosy ain't contagious, only infectious. Then they released me, sendin' me to Honolulu as Jared Fellowes—on account of the hat—supposed to be an American citizen. A doctor said he might bring back my memory by an operation, but I had no money to pay for it an' I was shy of bein' experimented on as a pauper patient. So I drifted 'round, callin' myself by my real name an' never knowin' it for sure. You see a sailor buys so much stuff from junk dealers or the slop-chest I might easy be wearing some other chap's cap.

"I shipped on South Sea traders and blackbirders raidin' islands for plantation labor, able seaman an' once second mate, without papers. I was on a whaler for four years. I showed the figgers in the watch to a mate one time, but they was nothin' marked on the charts of them days, an' I give that up as a clue.

"When the war came I was in Boston, after the whalin' v'yage, an' I volunteered. I come out a sergeant. They tell me they's a pension comin' to me, but I don't aim to take it. I volunteered, an' that would be like sayin' I had a string on my offer all the time, 'pears like to me. Anyhow, if I'd had that pension I wouldn't have been freezin' an' starvin' that night in Madison Square an' then"—he looked around with a smile—"I wouldn't be here.

"Well, after the war, I drifted back to Californy. There was the keeper of a boardin'-house had a daughter who took a fancy to me, saved me from gettin' shanghaied on a hell-ship once, an' we married. She was a good woman, too good for me, a long sight. Her father's ways driv' her opposite, an' she was strong for religion.

"By an' by I got to seein' things the way she did. We had a little farm on the coast near Monterey an' did fairly well. We had two youngsters, a boy an' a gal. The boy sickened an' passed away when he was five, an' the gal lived till she was ten. Mary, she believed there must be some sin that set a curse on us, an' it made a bit of a shadow between us, me not bein' able to remember the first part of my life, an' she thinkin' in the back of her head all the time that I must have done somethin' to bring the curse on us.

"Fifteen years after we was married she got a cancer that took her finally. Seemed like they was somethin' against us all right. I was a sort of a head man in the church, an' Mary an' me we prayed for light many a time, but it didn't come.

"At the end of the summer of '76 I went to San Francisco about the shipment of some cattle. On the way back the side-rod of the engine snapped an' the train went off the track. They took some of us who was hurt back to San José where the company's surgeons worked over us. I'd got another clip on the head and they raised the bone an' put in a 'pan,' I think they called it."

"Trephined you," suggested Addams.

"That's the word. The doc' told me they was a blood clot an' asked me about my memory. When he told me it would probably all come back I was happy at first an' then a bit afraid, on account of the wife's an' my own beliefs, in case I'd done some crime that had brought the curse on us an' our kiddies. But the doc' said I'd probably have to have some strong clue or link with the past to start things.

"My name didn't mean any more to me than it did before. Doc' said it was all there in the cells ready to light up, waitin' for something to start the current an' turn the switch.

"I saw the figgers in my watch next time I wound it—it was still goin' well—an' somethin' seemed to be tryin' to talk, 'way back in my brain. It give me a headache, but went no farther. I used to moon about, tryin' to think, with my wife boostin' me on, so's if anything was wrong we could fix it. She had got set in the idea that I had a curse on me somewhere; what with broodin' over the kiddies an' gettin' sicker herself each day, it was no wonder. But I couldn't find the switch to those brain-lights of mine.

VI

THE MAN WITH THE DRAGGING FOOT

"ONE DAY A MAN DROVE UP TO THE RANCH in a buggy an' asked for me. I was plowin' an' my wife come out an' told me a man about thirty wanted to see me, a man with a dark fringe of beard an' one foot that dragged, givin' the name of Dave Henley.

"It was just as if a bolt of lightnin' had hit me when I heard the name. Everything seemed to come over me in a rush an' I fell to the ground in a sort of a fit. My wife was beside herself. The stranger come over an' helped carry me in, but he didn't leave. He said he was sure now I was the man he wanted.

"When I come to an' he came in the room I nigh fainted again, for he was the spit of his father as I had seen him on the schooner an' dead in the boat. I closed my eyes an' pretended I was still unconscious, thinkin' all the time. The thoughts came clickin' up like one of these movin' picters, an' soon I remembered everything up to the climbin' of the cliff.

"My first thought was that I was glad it wasn't murder I'd done. Then I realized I'd have to get a grip on myself. I wasn't goin' to let Henley's boy drive fear into me, a man grown, like his father did when I was a kid. So I set up at last and got up an' shut the door on the two of us.

"It was Henley's boy all right. Dave, when he sailed 'round the Horn with us in '50, left a wife, a girl two years old, an' a comin' boy-baby behind him. He didn't say anything to us about it, any more than he did to her about leavin'. But she told the child when it grew up, an' when he was about twenty-five he went out to Californy an' tried to find out something of his father. It didn't take him long to find those papers Mister Addams read you from, but beyond that he could trace nothing. The four miners were gone, clear. Nothing showed beyond the fact that we had got away an' had never been heard of.

"He quit tryin' after a while an' got to minin' himself. That's how he got his lame foot—crushed by timbers. But he never made a strike, an' there was that three-quarters of a million dancin' in his dreams every once in a while. Then he heard my name accidental on the street in San Francisco. It was the only one the papers mentioned you'll recollect, outside Henley an' Chappell and he remembered it. It wasn't a usual one. In the combination my age 'peared to tally up an' off he come to see me an' get his share of the gold.

"I had my nerve back by the time he got through talkin', an' I just laughed at him an' denied everything. He stuck it out, arguin' I hadn't had a fit for nothin', but I got him away till the next mornin'.

"I lay awake that night, pretendin' to be asleep an' sick, but thinkin' hard an' prayin' between whiles. Next mornin' I stood by my guns. Young Henley showed pretty plain he thought me a liar an' said he'd dig up proofs that would force my hand to show him what became of his father an' the gold. It was precious little he cared about the first—he was too much like the old man. His father had deserted his mother an' him still unborn, an' he wasn't wastin' tears or trouble over him, dead or alive. But he went away at last an' left me to face my wife.

"I told her everything. She was just, I reckon, but mighty hard, considerin' I didn't know anything when I married her. But she blamed the kiddies' deaths an' her own-to-come on me an' what I'd done, an' I couldn't disprove it. We tried every way to get some trace of the four miners, but couldn't. Mary got worse all the time an' died inside of a year. Towards the last we hardly spoke. That's what I mean when I say there's a curse on the gold.

"An' it was still working. Everything I touched went wrong, land, crops, speculations, till I was down to bed-rock; an' the older I got the poorer I was. Five years ago I tried to get up an expedition to go to the island. I was sick an' nigh broke an' desperate. I figgered the curse had pretty near worked out, my share of it anyway, after sixty years.

"But I didn't look the part. I couldn't well tell the real story of the thing an' I guess they knowed I was lying. Of course I wasn't goin' to give up the real location till the last minnit or they'd have done me out of it. Mebbe I was wrong, I don' know. But I couldn't get the thing to goin'.

"The papers took it up an' made a Sunday story out of it, all wrong except my name an' a drawin' some feller made of me, which was good. That brought Dave Henley to Chicago, five years ago, sixty years old and broke. All the talk in the world wouldn't persuade him I wasn't the man an' didn't know where the treasure was. He offered to share it with me, as he said it was his right. But I had a little money left then an' I wasn't goin' after that treasure with a Henley as my partner. I figgered that would sure resurrect the curse. So I gave him a little of my money an' got away from Chicago on the quiet.

"I figgered it all out finally. That money had to go to some one clean. There was nothing the matter with the gold. It was intended to be used. But I had no right to it, no more than Henley. So I forgot about it. I had this map made when I tried to start the expedition an' I still had the figgers in the watch. I knew Henley reckoned I had the position somewheres an' I knew he'd stop short of nothing to get it. I wasn't the fighting man I used to be. I was old an' wanted to die in a bed, quiet.

"I figgered on leavin' a letter to some institution tellin' them of the gold, but when Mister Addams here picked me up an' saw to it I didn't need to be cold or hungry, I changed my mind."

Addams felt the girl's gaze upon his face. He raised his eyes and met her admiring glance.

"Then," continued Fellowes, "I made up my mind he was the kind of a man who was clean enough to get the gold. He told me he had partners, so I come around to see you an' spin the yarn. You're the clean sort, too. They ain't no curse goin' to worry you.

"Now you've got the map an' the watch with the figgers, an' Miss there has got the location of the gold in the cave. I'm through with it. I'm nigh the end of my voyage an' I'm lookin' for a quiet anchorage.

"The gold is cursed to me. You get it. Give me a bit of an income from it while I live, if you want to—it won't be long—an' that's ample. But you've got Henley to buck. He's like his father—a bad one! I thought I saw him in my court yesterday mornin' an' again after Mister Addams come in the afternoon. He was there this evenin'. He followed us an' looked through the window. Look out for him! He ain't alone in this, an' three-quarters of a million is a big stake. Keep clear an' start right away."

He stopped talking, his head, hoary-set with hair and beard, drooped as Peggy Winton stirred the fire.

Addams gathered together the papers on the table, folding up the map and setting the watch on top of it.

"Then you want me to take care of these, Fellowes?" he said.

"If you will," answered the old man, rousing himself from his drowsiness.

"I'll sleep all the better for not having them."

Selim, entering to the ring of his mistress, set a screen about the fire and started to prepare a couch for Fellowes. Addams made a low-voiced suggestion to the girl.

"Selim," she said, "bring a cot for yourself in here." She turned to Fellowes. "Then you'll not be worrying about the man who looked in at the window," she suggested.

"I'll worry no more, now that Mr. Addams has the map and watch and you the secret of the caves," he declared stoutly. "I'll not trouble your man."

Remembering his prejudice against brown skins, the girl forebore to press the matter. Addams picked up the watch and map.

"I'll sleep with these between my mattresses," he said. "Jim, have you got a pistol?"

"An automatic," Jim answered. "It's in my room. I'll give it to you."

"That goes under my pillow," said Addams. "Well, what about turning in? We'll talk over ways and means at breakfast, eh, Peggy? We've got enough to dream on."

"Dream!" exclaimed the girl. "I'm going to sit awake all night thinking. It's all too wonderful and exciting to waste on dreams."

VII

THE MYSTERY IN MONROE COURT

WHEN SELIM ESSAYED TO WAKE JARED FELLOWES for breakfast the next morning, he found the old man up and dressed, pacing the big studio as if it had been the deck of a ship. He had started the fire, which was snapping briskly, and seemed himself to be full of hardy life and vigor.

"It's done me a world of good," he announced at the breakfast table, "gettin' shut of that map and the whereabouts of the gold. I feel as if the curse was lifted; not shifted on to *your* shoulders, but done away with, unless Henley tries to keep in touch with the treasure. There's a share of the curse comin' to him, I reckon, if he doesn't stand clear an' by. His father got off easy, in a way, compared to me."

The talk about the table soon centered on ways and means, as Addams had suggested overnight.

"The best thing to do, it seems to me," said Addams, "will be to take the train overland direct to San Francisco, then steamer to Honolulu by the Pacific Mail. Then we can charter a trading-schooner or maybe a yacht without much difficulty, I should think. A small schooner would be all right. I remember enough from the old days to navigate her and, Jim, you're a good man, if you'll come."

"If I'll come!" exclaimed Winton indignantly. "Do you think I'm going to stay here drawing plans for people who don't know the difference between Modern Renaissance and Early Egyptian and couldn't pay for either if they did, while you're looting the caves and standing off Mr. Henley, junior? Not much!"

"Well, then, we'll only need a couple of native sailors to haul and belay. I wonder if Selim knows anything about the water?"

"I'll ask him," said Jim.

Selim, with a flash of his white teeth, declared that he was a top-notch sailor; that he had worked aboard his brother's *dhow* and could steer and row.

"That completes the crew, then," declared Addams. "Selim as cook and bo'sun, and you as first mate, Jim."

"What about me?" inquired Peggy Winton. "I can steer and reef too, at a pinch. You once said yourself, Archer, that I was an 'able seawoman.' Am I to be left behind to watch and wait for the expedition?"

"You can't possibly go, Peggy," put in her brother.

"Why not? It shouldn't be more than a week's trip either way from Honolulu, at the outside. Not so long a voyage as the one we took five years ago to the West Indies with Archer."

"It isn't that you'd be in the way or that we wouldn't be delighted to have you," Addams said slowly. "I think you know that, Peggy. But there's likely to be trouble with Henley and whatever crowd he has got together. They are not going to lose sight of us, neither are they lightly going to give up the chance of getting the money. The risk is too big."

"Archer's right," said Jim. "Sorry, Peggy, but you can't go."

"You forget," she said, "that without me you can't find where the gold is buried. It's my secret. You're with me, aren't you, Mr. Fellowes?"

The old man, keenly enjoying the contest and the girl's spirit, tugged at his beard.

"We might come to terms," he suggested. "I'm not too old to tail on to a rope. Suppose I come with you, if the expense ain't to be too heavy, an' act as bodyguard to Miss Winton. I can still growl—an' bite, too, if it's needed."

"There," declared the girl, her eyes still sparkling. "Mr. Fellowes is with me. If you don't take up, we won't tell you where to dig."

Her brother capitulated with a shrug. She turned to Addams.

"Don't you want me, Archer?" she asked, looking directly at him. "I'll not be left here alone or shipped up to the farm to Dad and Mother."

"Can you ask?" he answered a trifle unsteadily.

"Well, then, that's settled. When do we start? Will you let the Emersons have the studio, Jim?"

"I'll 'phone them right away. They'll be tickled to take it for a few weeks. Emerson's present light is rotten for painting. As for me, I'll be ready to start tomorrow. I'll write the two clients I have on hand just what I think of them, dig out my flannels and yachting togs and be ready to weigh anchor at dawn. How's that?"

"As for you, Peggy, if you insist on going, let's compromise," suggested Addams. "I can see little danger in your coming as far as Honolulu. What do you think, Jim? Then, if there's no sign of Henley, we can discuss it further."

"That's fair, Peggy," said her brother.

Peggy pouted.

"That's because I'm a woman," she said.

"It's because you are our woman, Peggy," corrected Addams. "Jim's sister and my—chum."

"All right," consented the girl reluctantly. "But I'm not agreeing to anything?"

"No. How long will it take you to outfit?" Addams asked as he arose.

"A week?" said Winton sarcastically.

"I'll be ready as soon as you are," she retorted. "When, Archer? You're the leader of the exposition."

"I'll look up the steamer connections and let you know," Addams answered. "No use in marking time in San Francisco, but you can both start in packing. I'm off! I'll draw the remnants of my bank account and report here this afternoon. How about you, Fellowes? I'm glad you're coming. I didn't like the idea of leaving you behind."

"I'll be ready to start an hour after any time you say so, sir," replied Fellowes.

"Good! Clean up what you want from your room. You'll stay here again tonight, and till we leave. That all right, Peggy? Good! Jim, go easy on the wardrobe—we'll travel light and fast."

"Chap's got to look decent on the steamer," protested Winton.

"One steamer-trunk," said Addams. "This isn't a pleasure trip. Peggy, you can have two. Look up your summer things and get whatever you want for that climate. What's missing we'll get in Honolulu. Will you look out for Selim? I'll see you all later. I'll secure reservations clear through, as soon as I get schedules."

"Hold on a minute, Archer," said Jim. "One word about finance, old chap. It's understood that Peggy and I stand our whack of the expense. Otherwise it's off. That right, Peggy?"

"Surely," she said. "Together we sink or swim, gallant captain."

She touched her bright hair in a gay salute.

"All right," said Addams, "that's agreed upon."

"Got the watch, Archer?" asked Jim.

"That's something I want to talk about," said Addams. "Fellowes could carry a watch like that without suspicion. But it's a bulky thing to pack and a dangerous thing to lose. Also, it's palpably an out-of-date thing to be packing around. It suggests in itself it may have been preserved for some special reason. It has served its purpose.

"I propose to have the figures tooled out and put them down somewhere else more practical and less likely to be discovered. So, if you don't object, Fellowes, we'll do that. This chap Henley may be sharper than his father. It's foolish taking unnecessary risks. I'll plan out a way we can all carry a copy of the figures without fear of them being found out. And we might as well destroy the map. It's of no practical value."

"I'm agreeable," said Fellowes. "I kind of hate to lose the watch altogether, though it ain't much on time any more. It was the figgers in it that made me nervous. So I'll pack it again after you've fixed it. The map's better burned anyway."

"Better do it now," said Addams. "I've got them both in a money-belt next to my skin. Wait for me in the studio."

He went into the room always reserved for him at the studio, and came quickly out again with the watch and map. The latter he handed to Peggy.

"Burn it up while I fix the watch, will you?" he asked.

The girl lighted a match and set fire to one corner of the little chart, dropping it when well ablaze on to a brass plate used as an ash tray, where the stout paper sluggishly resolved itself into ashes, the lines showing out from the chart the word "*Kapukalipelipe*" plain until the girl crumpled the wrinkled heap, and one clue to the treasure vanished as she brushed the remnants into the fireplace.

Meantime, Addams had dampened the stamp on a used and opened envelope he took from his pocket. This he allowed to soak until he was able to peel it off and carefully dry it.

"Give me your India ink, Jim," he said. "The waterproof kind. Thanks."

He sat down at a small table, putting the screen between him and the window.

He copied the figures from the watch-lid on to the back of the stamp, comparing them carefully.

165' 40" W

12' 20" N

"Now the mucilage, Jim."

He lightly regummed the stamp and replaced it exactly in its former position on the envelope, padding it with a blotter till it was firm.

"Now for the watch," he said, and, with the blade of his knife, erased the telltale figures from the lid. He handed the watch to Fellowes and put the letter back into his breast pocket.

"They'd puzzle a long time before they struck that," he said, "but I'll think up a better scheme yet."

Peggy Winton's eyes widened at the precaution.

"Don't expect to be held up, old chap, do you?" drawled her brother.

"After Henley's stunt at the window last night," answered Addams, "it's best to expect anything and be prepared for it. Now, I'm off. Good-by!"

It was snowing hard and persistently. From the front of the house the big archway of the Square not fifty yards away was invisible.

Peggy shivered as she opened the front door for Fellowes, clad in one of Addams' ulsters, ready to go to his room and pack and dispose of his few belongings.

"Won't you let me get you a taxi?" she asked.

"Bless you, miss, no!" he declared cheerily. "This is nothin' to the Arctic. In a fortnight we'll be wishing we could see some of this snow again."

She watched him plowing sturdily through the drifts, the falling snow closing him out from sight like a curtain, before she closed the door and went to find Selim. In the studio she could hear her brother singing in his light tenor:

> "Fifteen men on a dead man's chest.
> Yo-ho-ho and a bottle of rum!
> Drink and the devil have done for the rest.
> Yo-ho and a bottle of r-r-rum!"

It was late afternoon before Addams returned. Peggy, in the excitement of packing, had not noticed the time until it grew dark at a little after four. She went into the studio where her brother was delightedly burning up blue-prints and elevations.

"There goes that Court House competition drawing, Peggy," he said. "Watch it flare! That's where I've often wanted to send the whole stack of them—to blazes. I'm burning my bridges, like Archer. Good luck!"

"Shouldn't he be back by now?" she queried. "And surely Mr. Fellowes ought to be here. Maybe something's happened to him?"

"Shucks, no, Peggy! But the old boy is late, isn't he. If you like I'll run over. It's only a few blocks. Monroe Court on Macdougal Street, isn't it?"

He struggled into his ulster.

"Tell Selim to watch out for Henley," he said jestingly.

At the front door he met Addams.

"Anything up, old chap?" he asked, sensing the gravity of Addams' demeanor. "Trip all off? Pirate woke up and found it all a dream?"

"I wish he had," answered Addams grimly, "rather than this had happened.

Come into the front room, Jim. Peggy in the studio? Good. No need to tell her all the details."

Winton's care-free features sobered.

"Henley?" he asked.

Addams nodded.

"Looks like it," he said. "Fellowes is dead."

Winton gave a low whistle.

"Have they got Henley?" he asked.

"No—nor likely to. It may not even have been murder. They caught me at my office at three o'clock from the tenth precinct police station. They had found a card of mine in Fellowes' room. He got there about eleven o'clock this morning, directly after leaving here, I suppose. He told his landlady, who is an Italian, that he was going to pack up to go away on a sea voyage and for her to come up later, as he'd have some things to give her as keepsakes.

"She heard him, off and on, singing to himself and moving about, till her youngsters came in from school and she got their meal ready for them. I imagine the children talking drowned any outside noise except that once she says she heard the sound of a man coming down-stairs—a man with a foot that dragged."

"Henley!" exclaimed Winton.

"Of course. She didn't think much of it—all kinds come and go in that kind of a lodging-house—and she didn't open the door to look because the halls were cold. After the children had gone again she went up to the room and found Fellowes on the floor, half propped against the bed, gasping.

He managed to say, "Too late!" which she supposed to mean she was too late to find him. She called in the neighbors and they got him on the bed. When the ambulance came he was dead. Not a scratch on him, no sign of violence—heart failure. The doctor said it was a wonder he hadn't gone years before. The valves were rotten.

"The drawers were all emptied, so was his sea-chest, with the contents piled up in a heap on the floor. But, as she told the police he'd been packing to go away, they didn't think anything of that. They found a little money in his pocket, and his watch was on the bureau—*with the lid unscrewed*—but that didn't mean anything to them.

"The landlady, between the excitement and her lack of English, forgot about the lame man till after they'd gone and taken what was left of the poor old chap. She didn't really attach much importance to it and only remembered to tell it to me because I talked to her in Italian and she didn't have to worry over her words.

"I didn't suggest anything to her and I didn't volunteer any information to the police. I told the desk sergeant I was interested in the old man since I'd found him that time in Union Square—and that ended it as far as they're concerned. 'Heart failure,' they'll bring it in.

"There's no proof against Henley. It's likely he didn't lay a finger on the old man. Fellowes had left his door unlocked for the landlady, and the sheer sight of Henley may have brought on the shock.

"He wouldn't want us to raise a hue and cry after Henley without a chance to convict of either robbery or murder. What he'd want us to do, is to get after the treasure at once. I imagine Henley will go into hiding though. The less said about it the better. As it is, no one is likely to identify him with the story that came out in Chicago five years ago about his expedition.

"I suppose not," assented Jim. "Good thing, too. If the reporters scented a three-quarters-of-a-million mystery, we'd have the town on us. Who's going to tell Peggy? She's quite fond of the old chap, already."

"So was I," said Addams. "I think you'd better tell her, old man, being her brother. Better just tell her it was heart failure."

So it was dry-eyed Peggy who met Archer at the dinner table and talked sorrowfully over the old man's death.

"I suppose he would think the curse was buried with him," she said. "Poor old man, he paid for his wrong. Sixty-five years of luck against him, his wife and children both gone. It hardly seems right to go without him."

"He would have wished it, Peggy," said Addams. "If he knows, I think he'll be glad that we are going ahead. And the sooner, the better. This chap Henley, when he realizes Fellowes is dead, as he will sooner or later, may give up the idea of finding the treasure, but—he may not."

"I hope so," said Peggy.

Selim entered with a tray on which was a dirty envelope.

"A verree small boy bring this just now," he said. "There was no name, but he say the number correct."

Addams, with a glance at the others for confirmation, opened the note. It was short, made up of printed characters, and occasional words evidently clipped from a newspaper and pasted on the cheap sheet of paper, as a precaution against the identity of the sender. He read it aloud:

> "I know you have what I want. You put in advertisement tomorrow *Herald* position of lat. and long., or look out for trouble. You know who sends this. H."

"Our friend Henley," commented Winton. "What are you going to do, Archer? Bluff him out?"

"I don't imagine that will be so easy," answered Addams, "though he's trying to run one on us. But we'll try. I'll put the advertisement in, all right, but if he follows the figures I give he'll never find the island."

"Good work."

"The hitch is that he'll probably be watching us, or have us watched. If we stay here he may think he's frightened us out. On the other hand, if he realizes we're off on a trip he'll trail us to check up, if he's got the cunning and persistence I'm giving him credit for."

"That's so," assented Winton. "What are you going to do about that?"

"We'll all meet separately at the Pennsylvania Station tomorrow morning. Train leaves at ten. I'll give you your tickets separately. I'll not stay here tonight. Leave the house at different times—and no baggage. We'll have to get along the best we can and get some stuff in San Francisco if we have time. It's close connections, and the overland trains are liable to be late in this snow."

"Oh, I say," objected Winton, who had carefully selected the contents for his one trunk with a view to making his usual dapper appearance aboard the steamer. "We can't go that way."

"Not a grip," said Addams decidedly. "Can you manage, Peggy?"

"Of course I can," she answered blithely. "As long as we have to."

"That's the answer," declared Addams. "Jim, you confounded dude, you ought to be ashamed of yourself. Wait till we come back. You can flirt with all the pretty girls to your heart's content, and marry one of them if you want to, on the strength of your quarter of a million."

"That's so," retorted Winton, determined to score, as he thought regretfully of his well-fitting flannels. "You said you were going to do something of the sort yourself, didn't you?"

He watched his sister's flush and Addams' slight embarrassment with ill-concealed amusement.

"There's one thing I want to do, right away," said Addams, avoiding the issue. "Have you got any marking ink, Peggy?"

"Why I think so," she said wonderingly. "For linen, you mean? I'll go and look for it."

VIII

The Man in the Wheel-Chair

The first day or two of the voyage proved uneventful. They had reached San Francisco in time to get some clothes, much to Winton's satisfaction, whose slight but well-molded figure responded kindly to the ready-made outfit he secured.

The first afternoon found him basking in the smiles of a pretty girl, "making hay while the sun shone" as he lightly dubbed the flirtation entered into in shipboard *camaraderie* by both himself and his charmer of the moment.

Addams found the idle hours passed swiftly in the company of Peggy. All talk of the treasure was *tabooed* for safety's sake, but the excitement of the quest was alive in both of them and they drew closer in the mutual glamour of the venture.

There were no signs of Henley. They had made their individual ways to the train apparently unobserved and had noted nothing on the overland journey to arouse suspicion that they were being followed. The delay of getting their outfits for the sea trip had brought them almost last to the gangplank, but a quiet though close survey and mutual comparisons of the passengers revealed none but the ordinary run of travelers.

Only one person failed to appear, a man named Stevens, kept to his cabin by paralysis, they learned, and represented by his nurse, an austere woman of about fifty, in regulation uniform, non-communicative, attentive to nothing but her duties.

Selim, from his part of the ship, reported nothing that aroused suspicion, and their hopes of gaining the gold without interference mounted high.

On the evening of the third day, Addams, returning for a fresh supply of cigars to the cabin shared by Jim and himself, thought that he noticed some slight disarrangement of the things in the tray of the trunk he had bought at San Francisco.

Closer inspection failed to justify his suspicion. If the cabin had been searched, an expert must have accomplished it. There was nothing definite upon which to base determination. The bedding of the two bunks was immaculately neat, the clothes in the trunk unwrinkled. Yet an evanescent suggestion persisted in Addams' mind that the carelessly recorded mental image of his last look at the state-room differed from the picture before him in some tiny detail, that, while it troubled, refused to be definitely recalled.

He went on deck, rejoining Peggy, luxuriant in a becushioned steamer-chair. He took the one next to hers, smoking his fragrant cigar thoughtfully.

"Seen Jim?" he asked.

"He's hidden in the friendly shadow with Miss Belmont," said Peggy. "He really thinks he's in earnest this time. But then, he always does. She's a charming girl, too. They're going to stay in Honolulu for some time. They've got a cottage on the beach at Waikiki and want me to join in all sorts of plans. Of course I didn't accept or refuse. I couldn't, without hinting at something mysterious in our own trip."

"You're a trump card, always, Peggy," said Addams.

"You'd better talk with Jim," she said. "He's liable to get overconfidential. He does, you know," she went on, "when he's in love, or thinks he is."

"Jim's all right," assured Addams, though making a mental note to once more warn that gentleman against carelessness.

Both approximately the same age, there was a vast difference between the friends.

In the old days, when Archer Addams played center at football, Winton was the volatile yell leader. At polo, with Addams playing back, a tower of strength for his team, certain of stroke, calm of judgment, playing the game every moment for all he was worth, Winton was Number One, a brilliant but erratic forward. With Addams at the wheel and skippering the yacht in race or cruise, Winton handled the jib sheet, and, between tacks, devoted himself to the general entertainment, especially if there was a sailor of the gentler sex aboard.

And yet, through his birthgift of the ability to draw and design, Jim Winton had made better weather of it so far in the commercial field than Addams. But there was no question as to who was the leader in times of stress.

"Peggy," said Addams, lowering his voice. "Have you noticed any disarrangement of your cabin, as if some one had made a careful search of it?"

"Why, I did, yesterday afternoon," she said, "after lunch. But I wasn't sure, so I said nothing about it."

"Ah! I've had the same fancy. Suppose you arrange something—some ribbons, say—in such a way they can't be disturbed without your knowing. Can you do that?"

"Easily. You think—"

She stopped as a figure passed them.

"I don't know anything except they'll find nothing for their pains. If Henley has traced us in spite of all, he must be on this ship to do him any good. Have you any idea what this mysterious passenger looks like?"

"He's a very old man, I believe."

"Well," said Addams, "I may be mistaken. In any case he'll not find out the position, the way we've disposed of it."

The pacing figure came back, a long coat covering it from collar to foot.

"It's the nurse," whispered Peggy as she passed. "What does Henley look like?"

"Tall and thin, with black hair and beard. Heavy eyebrows. The best he can do is to keep on following us if he *is* aboard and, if I can charter the right kind of a boat, we'll lead him a merry chase to the island. Here comes Jim."

The spark of a cigarette glowed as Winton and his companion, a vivacious brunette, came laughing aft.

"Come on down, moonies," said Winton. "This is concert night. Miss Belmont's going to sing."

"So are you," said the girl at his side.

"I am willing to go through my whole repertoire of parlor tricks like a good doggie at your command," said Winton, "providing the usual lump of sugar, or its equivalent, is forthcoming."

They passed on, chaffing. Addams and Peggy Winton followed after a few minutes. At the head of the staircase they heard the piano in the music salon break out into accompaniment, and Jim Winton's tenor caroling—

> "Fifteen men on a dead man's chest,
> Yo-ho-ho, and a bottle of rum!"

Adams shrugged his shoulder.

"He's irrepressible," he said.

"He ought to be more careful," said Peggy.

"Perhaps this is all getting on our nerves too much," said Addams. "We may be imagining everything without real cause. We're as bad as Shakespeare's guilty thief who 'fears each bush an officer.' I confess I thought the chief engineer was Henley the first time I saw him, and I was only relieved when I noticed he didn't limp. Let's join the crowd."

IX

SELIM FOLLOWS A TRAIL

IT WAS NOON OF THE FIFTH DAY OUT from San Francisco. Diamond Head was already in sight and the passengers of the *Korea* were on deck, waiting to watch the unfolding of the panorama of Waikiki Beach with its villas and the harbor of Honolulu with the emerald, purple-shadowed mountains of Tantalus and the Pali-Gap beyond, backed by the ever-present masses of trade clouds.

"It's wonderfully beautiful," said Peggy Winton to Addams, as the *Korea* glided along the reef, where the peacock waters changed swiftly into the transparent chrysoprase of the lagoon. "I suppose our little island will look very different from all this."

"Yes," assented Addams, "I imagine it will. But I don't think you are going to see it, Peggy. Not unless I am satisfied we have shaken off Henley. The risk is too great. You won't miss so much. You see, we'll be sailing for several days through a sea-desert; and life on a small boat, such as we may have to put up with, is not too agreeable."

"Any one would think I had never been on a yacht before," pouted Peggy, looking particularly adorable, Addams thought, in white linen and spotless Panama set upon her well-shaped head, crowned with its curling masses of red gold. "I am almost inclined to think you are sorry I came."

"Honestly, Peggy," said Addams, "I'll be glad to have the trip over, that is, from here on. The fact that we've seen nothing of Henley so far, doesn't convince me that we've got rid of him. The man is a persistent type and he's got a big stake to play for. Frankly, I'm nervous."

"On my account?"

Addams looked over the rail. They were around the bell-buoy now, heading for the harbor. The white houses on shore and clustering up to the slopes of Punchbowl Crater, in their setting of green palms and tropical foliage, gave him an excuse. He was nervous, and on Peggy's account. He had been in love with Peggy Winton for seven years, since she was eighteen and he twenty-three.

The mutual loss of fortune, which he considered due to bad judgment, at least, on the part of his own well-loved father, had set a barrier between them. Or rather he had set it up as a barrier, believing that he should not attempt to link his own poor fortunes to those, no better, of the girl. He did not attempt to deny that he had entirely concealed his love. He had even hoped, in confident moments, that it was returned. The sudden opportunity of a bid for fortune, raised by his meeting with Fellowes, opened up to him, if success crowned their efforts, at least an opportunity for avowal on the standing that he felt a man should occupy, the ability to maintain a woman in the state that she was accustomed to, or had a right to demand.

Jim Winton was frankly out for the money, to relieve him from the commercial grind. His interest in his pretty fellow passenger could not be taken too seriously. For Addams, the gold was a secondary consideration, merely the key of a gateway that had long barred the path to the heart of his sweetheart. Peggy's interest, he trusted, was coincident with his own. It was no wonder, he thought, that he was nervous.

The death of Fellowes had brought a grim reality into the affair that Addams could not shake off. The story of the continuous ill fortune that had hovered over the old man's life for sixty-five years to the moment, when, with a happy if temporary haven in sight, he was suddenly cut down, seemed to presage the still present existence of the curse on the looted gold.

There was nothing superstitious about Addams, healthy and vigorous as he was. The thought of disaster seemed absurd on this morning of tropic sunshine, yet it was persistent, imminent. They had left New York on schedule without hearing from the man with the dragging foot; having nothing of him on the train trip across the continent, it appeared impossible that he could be on even terms with them, and yet—

Addams shook his broad shoulders and accused himself of being morbid.

Peggy Winton had moved forward and was tossing nickels to the swimming boys who surrounded the sides of the vessel. She smiled at him as he came up.

"I'm all out of small change, Archer. Lend me some dimes. There's one duck of a boy—"

She broke off as a wheel-chair came up silently on its rubber tires, propelled by the taciturn, grim-visaged nurse. Addams surveyed its occupant keenly.

The man lay heavily on his cushions, gloved hands limp and seemingly lifeless on his knees. Despite the heat a steamer-rug was wrapped about his knees and above a corpulent stomach. His face was very pale and clean-shaven; deep shadows under the eyes were accentuated by amber-tinted glasses, through which he gazed vacantly ahead. Beneath a Panama hat, the only concession to the climate, its broad brims shading the ghastly face, a straggling fringe of gray hair showed. His eyebrows were slight, straggly tufts of white above the wide-rimmed glasses.

"Not much like Henley," Addams thought with sudden relief.

He lifted his eyes to the face of the nurse. The imperturbable mask of her face seemed to him to shift for an instant, in her dark eyes something that watched appeared to leap to the surface for a second and then hide again, swift as the movement of a camera-shutter.

The wheel-chair moved on conveniently close to the gangway. Addams beckoned Selim to one side with a look.

"I want you to follow that man in the chair, Selim," he said quietly. "Find out where he stops, make sure he's staying there, then come up to us at the Royal Hotel. I'll look after the baggage."

The Arab's eyes lit with intelligence and he unobtrusively moved off.

"There's a good man, Peggy," he said. "That boy Selim of yours."

"He's a jewel," she answered. "I suppose you'll want to take him on the trip."

Winton came up with Miss Belmont.

"All ready for shore?" he asked. "Where do we stop, Archer?"

"The Royal. I cabled. It's in town and they have separate cottages. We've got one to ourselves."

"Miss Belmont's going to the Moana, out at the beach," said Jim. "If you don't need me particularly this afternoon, Archer, Miss Belmont has promised to initiate me into the noble art of surf riding."

Addams gave him a swift glance. The sooner the fascinating Miss Belmont was left in the background, he thought, and the sooner they got to sea again, the more he would be able to realize on whatever use Winton was going to be to the expedition. But it was no part of his plans to antagonize the Belmonts, with whom he hoped to leave Peggy during the trip to the island.

"Go ahead," he said. "I wish I could join you, but I'm going to be busy all afternoon. We'll see you at dinner."

Miss Belmont turned to Peggy Winton.

"You'll come, won't you?" she asked.

"I'd love to," answered Peggy with an indignant look at her brother, which slid off him like mercury from a slanting board. "But I've got shopping that simply has to be done."

On the wharf, among the crowd of friends and onlookers, Addams noticed a man who met the man in the wheel-chair and seemed taken aback at his reception. Addams was too far away to catch the words, but the sound of the invalid's voice was like a rasp as he answered the greeting. The man was a hulking figure in ill-fitting serge, his face repulsive in its low type, with the broken nose and shattered ears that mark the prizefighter.

He seemed to protest, but, at another sharp sentence from the paralytic, turned and walked beside the chair in silence.

"So he was expected," thought Addams. "I don't think much of the reception committee. He seemed to be unwelcome, to say the least of it."

As the chair moved off he caught sight of Selim, gliding like a shadow in its wake, indistinguishable among the many Hawaiians who had thronged to see the steamer come in, according to their idle custom.

X

THE SECRET OF THE CAVES

AFTER DINNER, AT WHICH WINTON DISPLAYED a quaint, emotional mixture of being at the same time ashamed of himself for leaving Addams in the lurch and pleased at how he had spent the afternoon, the three adjourned to one of the big semicircular *lanais* (verandas) of the hotel for a moment.

"Let's go over to the cottage," said Addams.

They walked from the main building by paths bordered with hibiscus and stately royal palms to their bungalow, facing a quiet street, and sat on their vine-clad *lanai*, gorgeous with the orange trumpets of the huapla vine. The perfume of *ihlang-ihlang* and *plumaria* was heavy on the air; the brilliant moonlight spread the lawns with an arabesque of light and shade, unshifting in the calm, breezeless night.

" 'Where every prospect pleases and only man is vile,' " quoted Winton, lighting his cigarette. " 'Man,' standing for Henley. I've got a hunch he's not out of the running somehow."

"That's the way I feel about it," declared Peggy. "I know men laugh at a woman's instinct, but, like Jim, I've got what he calls a 'hunch.' So has Selim. He told me this morning that the omens were bad and we should not start on our trip tomorrow at all events. I wonder where he is."

"I sent him on an errand," said Addams. "You two needn't be ashamed of your hunches. I had one too. That nurse's eyes were alive for the first time since we started, when she passed us wheeling that chair this morning. I sent Selim to trail them and find out definitely where they were stopping. He should be back by now."

"You don't think that helpless old doodlebug was Henley, do you?" asked Jim.

"I don't know, Jim," Addams answered. "It didn't look much like him, but they met a rough-looking customer who didn't fit in with the outfit, and who, if I'm not mistaken, was called down by the man in the chair for showing up at all. There was something in that woman's eyes—but we'll know more when Selim shows up.

"Now then," he went on, "I'm going down to Pearl Harbor tomorrow by train to see if I can charter one of the inter-island schooners. They are slow tubs, but all the yachts seem to be in commission. These chaps sail all the year 'round. There's a regatta on next week and they're all entered."

"Why not?" said Jim. "You'd hardly think this was the middle of January, would you? Want me to come with you? I want to do my share, you know," he said apologetically for his afternoon's dereliction.

"No," said Addams, "I think not. I've dug up a ship's chandler who'll fix us up in twelve hours from order, any time of day or night, and he's working on the list I gave him. But it's up to you tomorrow, Jim, to scare up two sailors, or three if you can get them. Natives preferably. I want men who know a jib from a topsail. Tell them it's a pleasure trip. That's your job."

"I'll get them if I have to shanghai them," answered Winton.

"Want to come with me to Pearl Harbor, Peggy?" asked Addams. "Have you got your shopping done?"

"Everything," she answered. "I'm ready to sail at a moment's notice. You're not going to leave me behind, are you?"

"I may be making mountains out of molehills," said Addams. "The thing for us to do is to drive ahead. You'll go with me tomorrow, Peggy?"

"Gladly. Since you won't promise to let me go with you, I suppose I had better tell you the secret of the caves," said Peggy. "Jim, you're not supposed to hear this. It was only to be told to Archer, according to poor Mr. Fellowes' instructions."

"I'm dismissed, am I?" said Jim. "Oh, very well."

He rose and strolled away toward the hotel, glad at his chance of release, intent upon telephoning to the Moana Hotel to see if the vivacious lady who had captured his fancy was disengaged.

"Now, Sir Masterful," said Peggy, "I think you are nothing less than mean to despoil me of my share in the real adventure, but, as the promoter and leader of the expedition, I suppose I must temporarily bow to your authority. Though, mind you, I have not promised to stay willingly."

"Agreed," said Addams. "We'll argue it out when we get a boat and arrive at some conclusion about Henley."

"Well, then," she said, "there are six caves, all close together. The gold is in the third, counting from the cape."

She spoke softly and Addams bent his head close to listen. The moonlight shone on her face, he could feel her breath on his cheek, and at its soft suggestion his heart beat faster as she went on in familiar confidence.

"We are to look for a group of hieroglyphics. There's a carving of a big fish, then a canoe and a group of five men. Under this is a ring. Poor Fellowes said it probably meant the killing of a whale or a shark by five men who afterwards went 'round the island before they left in their boat. It's the only carving of a fish in any of the caves and it's somewhere on the right-hand wall. Is that plain?"

"Perfectly."

"Archer," she went on after a moment, "I feel I ought to apologize for Jim, and myself, too, for that matter."

"Why?"

"Both of us, in your generosity, are sharing equally with you. There was no necessity for it. I'm a girl and you don't have to take me with you. And Jim's not doing his share."

"That's nonsense, Peggy!" said Addams. "It isn't because I don't want you that I suggest your staying behind in Honolulu. As for Jim, he's almost as much my brother as he is yours. That is—"

He stopped, checking the thoughts that clamored to be put into words.

"Yes, I suppose he is." Peggy's tone had changed. There was mischief in it now. "So, Brother Archer, take Sister Peggy back to listen to the orchestra. They are going to dance later. See that you perform your fraternal duties, sir, and provide me with plenty of partners."

XI

THE SCHOONER *WAVECREST*

"NO, SIR!" SAID THE STOLID GERMAN who did odd jobs for the Pearl Harbor clubhouse of the Honolulu Yacht Club. "You can't get no schooner. Dere iss de *Ahimanu* what iss loading firewood, put she won't pe in for a week, und dere iss de *Lei Lehua*, put she changed charters yesterday."

"Somebody buy her yesterday?" asked Addams sharply.

"Sure did they puy her," said Schwartz. "A man who iss goin' to use her for carrying sheeps ofer to his ranch on Lanai. You vas too late, already."

"Who was the buyer?" asked Addams. "Maybe I can charter her from him for a week or two."

"I should know his name?" answered the German. "Iss it my pusiness? I don't own de poat."

"Then you don't know where I could get a sloop or a small schooner?" asked Addams almost despairingly. He seemed to have come to the end of a blind alley. "I'll pay well for it."

The man's little eyes gleamed, but he spread out his hands slowly.

"I could use de money," he said. "Put—der ain't no poat."

If Addams had known the ancient and unsavory reputation of Schwartz, gained in the days when illicit dealers slipped through the tortuous reef into Pearl Harbor under cover of darkness at the signal of the old boatman, he might have distrusted the slow smile that broke through the dirty features as the German turned away, muttering to himself:

"Sheep to Lanai. Dot vas a gut one! *Dumkopf!* He schwallowed it like a mullet. I charge dot feller Henley extry for dot."

"Well, Peggy," said Addams, "we'll have to buy a *sampan* or hire a steamer, I guess. I suppose I could persuade one of those yacht-owners, but I'd have to take him into the secret of the trip, and I hate to do that. It might leak out, and, aside from the risk of Henley, we've got no mortgage on the island or the treasure either. Some one might beat us out."

"There's a little cove over here," said Peggy, "with some private villas. I walked over while you were talking to that man. And there's a schooner at anchor. It's up for the season, I'm sure; the sails have all been stripped and the deck is covered with canvas."

"Let's go over and take a look at it," said Addams. "It's a case of any ship in a storm. We can go down trying."

The schooner, a trim, modern, overhung craft of about fifty feet waterline, was at anchor off a small wharf running out from the lawn that sloped from a somewhat pretentious bungalow to the water. The blinds were down, but smoke came from a chimney.

"Let's go in," suggested Addams. "If we could get her we'd be fixed. She's a beauty."

A ring at the front door brought no response, and they walked around to the back. A contented-looking Chinaman was scaling fish on the porch.

"Mornin'!" he said. "You wan' speak Misty Steven? He no home. He go San Francisco—no come back one, two, mebbe flee week."

A reflective light came into Addams' eyes.

"You savvy Mr. Stevens' first name," he asked. "You know his initials?"

"Sure. He name Josiah P."

Addams' face was wreathed in smiles. "It's 'Tub' Stevens, Peggy," he said. "Old Tub who went to Harvard with me. I knew he lived in Honolulu, but I had forgotten it."

He turned to the Chinaman.

"Your master a fat man?" He indicated a generous stomach with his hands.

The smiling Chinaman nodded.

"Plenty fat," he said. "He got one mark here." He touched his forehead. "He your flen'?"

"I should say he was!" exclaimed Addams. "He got that scar the night of the freshman rush. He was knocked flat and some one kicked him in the 'scrim.' I stood over him till he got up. We were good friends. Luck's with us, Peggy. He'll lend me anything he owns."

"But he's in San Francisco!"

"The cable's working. You know his San Francisco address?" he asked the Oriental.

"Palace Hotel, I think—mebbe." The Chinaman's friendly interest had been accentuated by the pressure in his palm of a five-dollar bill. "He got office in Honolulu. King Stleet. There they sabby."

"Fine. Let's go down on the wharf, Peggy." He turned to the Chinaman. "Any way of getting off to the yacht?" he asked. "I'd like to have a look at her."

The Chinaman went with them and pointed out a small boat moored at the end of the little pier.

Addams helped Peggy into the dinghy and they rowed off and about the schooner.

"She'll sail rings 'round any wood-schooner!" exclaimed Addams as they reached the pier again. "Thank you, John."

"That all right, thank you. My name, he Ah Sing," replied the man, returning to his fish.

As the train, running back to Honolulu, skirted the shore of the eastern arm of the Pearl locks, they saw a dingy schooner unloading wood, moored to a wharf. The mainsail hung down at the peak. On it was a big patch. The broad stern showed the name, *Lei Lehua*, in tarnished gilt lettering.

"That's the tub we might have got," said Addams. "That schooner of Stevens' will go by her like a steamer."

"What was the name of Mr. Stevens' yacht?" asked Peggy. "I didn't notice."

"The *Wavecrest*. I'll put you in a taxi for—the hotel, Peggy, if you don't mind, while I scout up the office. I hope Jim got the sailors. We'll rig the *Wavecrest* and sail up to Honolulu and load there. We should get away tomorrow night, if I can get him by cable."

Addams reached the hotel at the end of the afternoon.

"I got the cable rushed," he said triumphantly. "Here's the answer."

Winton and his sister bent over the pink slip.

"*Wavecrest* yours," it read. "Take Ah Sing."

"That's something like a pal," said Jim with enthusiasm. "I think I've got the men, Archer. Got one sure. We're to meet him tonight on the water-front at a sailor's hang-out called the 'Fore-and-Aft.' He'll have his mate with him."

"Native?"

"No. Portuguese, named Silva. Claims to be an able seaman. Says he's worked on yachts, and seems to know what he's talking about."

XII

AT THE SIGN OF THE "FORE-AND-AFT"

THE FORE-AND-AFT SALOON WAS ON THE HONOLULU WATER-FRONT, a resort conducted by a pair of partners named Burke and Jewett, reviled in many a port for their success in shanghaiing sailors and, occasionally, when the supply of the genuine article was scarce, landsmen. They were tough customers, able to handle themselves in a scrimmage, and their tactics had led to many a broad hint from the Territorial police that things could no longer be run as they used to be under the monarchy.

So Burke and Jewett opened the Fore-and-Aft and, ostensibly, mended their ways. The saloon was unique and popular. The big room held two bars ranged in circular fashion about stout spars that ran from floor to ceiling in imitation of masts. One of these bars was known as the "Fore," the other as the "Aft," or, sometimes, the "Main."

Set about the room were little tables for those who preferred them. The place was always filled from dusk to closing time with the flotsam and jetsam of the water-front, sailors and stevedores spending their newly earned wages, men down to the price of their last drink, and hangers-on—beachcombers—sneaking up to the lunch counters with a furtive eye on Burke or Jewett, who usually lounged by the circular bars.

There were no women allowed; and the saloon, save for the loud talk, might fairly be considered orderly. Rough-houses occurred now and then at the Fore-and-Aft in the regular routine of business, but to the casual eye the place held no hint of being anything but what it professed to be.

As Addams and Winton entered, an orchestrion was blaring out a popular dance tune, some men were clumsily dancing with each other like trained bears, and the place was blue with smoke. Some fifty men were at the tables and about the bars. The counter of the "Aft," at the back of the saloon, was comparatively deserted and to this they made their way, Winton keeping a lookout for his man, Silva. No one seemed to pay particular attention to them, and they ordered a glass apiece of the resinous beer for "the good of the house."

Addams touched Winton's elbow.

"There's that rough-neck acquaintance of our invalid friend," he said. "The one who met him at the wharf. Over at the other bar. He's with his own crowd, all right. They're a nice-looking lot of uncaged jail-birds."

Winton agreed with him. The half-dozen hulking, ill-kempt men returned his glance, one of them saying something that raised a general laugh. A broad-shouldered man, better dressed than the rest, a big diamond horseshoe in his tie, wearing an air of authority, left the group and strolled over to Addams and Winton.

"Lookin' for any one in special, gents?" he asked. "Or jest sight-seein'? My name's Burke. I'm one of the owners."

"Pleased to meet you, Mr. Burke," replied Winton untruthfully. "You'll join us? I was looking for a man by the name of Silva. He said he'd meet me here with a friend of his. We want to hire them. Perhaps they'll ask for me—I gave them my card. My name's Winton."

"Silva's a common name along the waterfront," said Burke affably. "I reckon your man'll be along soon. Make yourselves at home."

The crowd of men from the other bar, with the broken-nosed man among them, came across and started talking familiarly to Burke, crowding Addams and Winton carelessly as they pushed up to the circle. One of them jostled Winton, who flushed angrily. Addams trod lightly on his foot and edged around the bar.

"Don't start anything, Jim," he said quietly. "I don't like the look of this place. Let's go over to one of the tables."

As they did so the other men left the counter and deliberately brushed them, treading on their feet.

"Git outa my way, you —— dude," said one of them, thrusting Winton aside.

The rude shock and the impudence of the man who set his inflamed face close enough for Winton to catch the whisky-laden breath, infuriated the latter, who was no coward, beyond control. He swung viciously, snapping his right to the jaw and sending his man staggering backwards.

Instantly, as at a signal, the place was in an uproar. Men at the tables jumped to their feet cursing, and the broken-nosed man with his immediate companions advanced threateningly upon the two friends who set their backs to the bar. Addams coolly tossed his untasted beer in the face of one of them and followed it up with a blow that sent him to the floor.

"Make for the door, Jim," said Addams quietly. "Punch the fellow in front of you; keep punching and keep moving."

It was sound advice. The fight had become a free-for-all and men were striking indiscriminately at the nearest to them. But the six who had started the trouble had become a dozen, then a score, all apparently determined to wreak vengeance upon the strangers.

It began to look like disaster. Addams and Winton were forced slowly to retreat. Presently they felt the back wall against their shoulders. Addams picked up a chair and swung it about him. Winton, beside him, was fighting stubbornly.

Then the broad-shouldered figure of Burke appeared, raging through the crowd. The two masts had been fitted up to approximate the real thing as closely as possible, and Addams had noticed a ring of belaying-pins set in a rail about each of them. That these were realities was proved by the way

Burke, backed by two husky bartenders, was handling his.

He fought his way to the wall.

"This is a bad mess," he said to Addams. "They think you're dudes an' they're sore at your buttin' in. There's the back door just to the right of you. Better slip out quick. I'll keep 'em back till you make your getaway."

He was swinging viciously at the crowd which dodged the blows of the hardwood belaying-pin.

"Come on, Jim," panted Addams. "This way."

He found the door and opened it. The fresh, salty air flowed into the stale, smoke-burdened atmosphere. The next moment they had slipped through and slammed the door behind them.

They found themselves in an alley, heavy in shadow. As they turned, uncertain of their direction, a dozen dark forms seemed to spring out of walls and fences and they were borne down, struggling under the weight of their opponents.

XIII

HENLEY AND CO.

ADDAMS REGAINED CONSCIOUSNESS ON A DAMP FLOOR OF DIRT. He felt his head, which was sticky.

"I thought some one hit me a crack," he said to himself. "Jim!"

There was no answer, though he called again and again. The place was absolutely dark. There was a strange smell of spices and the acrid tang of something like incense. He thought he could hear voices murmuring close by and got to his feet, groping towards the sound. He hit his wounded head against a beam and stopped, confused with the sharp pain.

A square of orange light suddenly appeared in the blackness, barred across with a grille. A head showed, silhouetted against the brightness.

Addams went cautiously toward the light, trying to make out the features of the person beyond the grille of stout iron bars that, with the shutter outside that had just been opened, formed the upper part of a heavy door.

"Come to your senses, have you?" asked a voice that he seemed to have heard before. "That's good. You'll need 'em!"

"Where am I?" demanded Addams. "And who are you?"

The man chuckled.

"You're in the cellar of a Chinese hangout," he said. "And your partner's fixed the same way. Twenty foot under ground, you are. You an' me's goin' to have a little talk. As to who I am, take a look. You've seen me before, more'n once, though you may not recognize me."

He held up the lantern, which had illumined the grille, close to the bars, disclosing the face of a clean-shaven man, with black hair cropped close to his face. Despite the absence of the gray wig and the amber glasses, Addams saw the resemblance to the man in the wheel-chair.

"Ah, Henley," he said, drawing at a venture.

The man's face showed disappointment. Then he laughed, showing uneven, discolored teeth.

"You're smart, you are," he said with a grudging admiration. "But it was only a guess, if it was a good un. You didn't tumble to me aboard the steamer, for all your foxiness."

"I suppose you know," bluffed Addams, "that you're wanted in New York for murder?"

The man snarled.

"I didn't murder Fellowes, if that's what you mean," he said. "He was scared to death before I laid a finger on him, because he knew what I'd come after. Something that belonged to me. Something I'm going to get, Mr. Addams, for all your smartness. And you don't want to forget that New York's a long way off from here. It's you that's in a tight place now, not me.

"I thought something was up the night you took Fellowes 'round to your place," he went on, "playing charity to the old thief, so as to get the information that belongs to me, by rights."

"Go on," said Addams, who had found a bale of goods near the door and established himself there. "You mean the gold your father stole and committed murder for."

"I'll show you what I mean," said Henley. "I've got you where I want you now, and here you stay till you come through. Oh, you're a fox, with your fake position in the *Herald* and stowin' away the right figgers where they can't be found! I'll hand it to you. We searched your cabin thorough, and your girl's, too. We've been all through your clothes and your pal's while you was both out of your senses just now, but you're goin' to tell 'em to me before you get out of here.

"I'm a fox, too," he went on, his voice thickening in anger at Addams' immobility and silence. "I thought maybe you wouldn't give me the straight dope in the *Herald*, and I had you tagged all the time. I ain't alone in this. When Fellowes croaked, I ducked, but I knew every move you made. I know when you left for San Francisco and then I was sure of three things: first, that you'd tried to bamboozle me; second, you had got the real dope from Fellowes; third, you was goin' after the gold yourselves.

"I followed on the next train west from Philadelphia. I wired to San Francisco, and when I got there I knew all 'bout you—where you registered and what steamer you was goin' on. When you was shopping I had a pal outside, watchin'. You might be lookin' out for a lame man with a beard, so I got my sister who's been an actress and a good one, to fix me a make-up—a wig, some grease paint, a close shave and some padding—an' play nurse to a poor paralytic who couldn't leave his cabin except in a wheel-chair.

"I know every move you've made," continued Henley. "I knew the gold was on an island somewhere in the Pacific. That fool Fellowes give that much out when he tried to get up an expedition and leave me out of it. It's somewhere not far from here, that's a cinch, or you wouldn't be dickerin' 'round the yacht club an' the water-front for a small craft.

"You see, I lived here once, Mr. Addams, and you can't turn a trick here that I ain't on to. And you couldn't get a yacht, could you? I could have told you that and saved you the trouble. You was just a day late at Pearl Harbor to get the *Lei Lekua*, too. Why? Because me and Schwartz are old pals. We've worked together. His brother-in-law owns the *Lei Lehua* and you had no more chance of gettin' her than you had of flyin'. And she's the only craft that's handy. And I've got her. Not for carryin' sheep to Lanai, neither."

"You might as well use her that way," said Addams. "I don't see what other good she'll be to you."

"Oh, you don't, don't you? Well, I'll tell you. I'm going to load her with gold, Mr. Addams, and you're goin' to tell me where to get it."

"Am I?"

"Yes, you are. You'll stay here, where nobody's going to look for you, till you come through with that latitude and longitude. And you needn't try to stall with the wrong figures. I'm going to get them from you and I'm going to get them from your pal, and if they don't tally you'll both stay here till they do. And you won't be getting fat doing it, either."

"You don't suppose my friends here—and I've got them, Henley—" said Addams evenly, "are going to let me drop out of sight, do you? You're playing a dangerous game."

"Yah!" Henley sneered through the bars. "That's just what you have done—dropped out of sight. You're two floors under the ground. There ain't more than a dozen white men, and they don't include the police, who know anything about it. You think it over, Mr. Addams! I want them figures and I'm going to get 'em!"

At the sound of a low whistle, he turned his head.

"All right, I'm coming," he called. "That's your pal, come to his senses. I'm off for a little talk with him. Maybe I'll get some figures to bring back. Then you can tell me yours. But they've got to tally, see? If they do I'm going to give myself a few days' start, according to the distance, and then you'll get back to your girl again. If I don't get them you can stay here till you rot!"

The whistle sounded again and Henley vanished. Addams could hear his lame foot halting along a passageway and up an uncovered flight of stairs.

He pressed his face against the grille. He could see across the passage into another room, the door of which was partly open. It was dimly lighted and on the one wall shadows wavered. Through the door came an acrid tang, the smell of cooking opium.

He went back to his bale to think it out, feeling for matches and cigars.

Everything had been taken from his clothes to the tiniest scrap of paper. Fortunately he had left most of his money in the hotel safe and persuaded Winton to do the same. Despite his predicament, he chuckled at the thought of Henley's chagrin after searching, probably in the person of his sister, first the cabins, and now the persons of himself and Jim, for the figures showing the position of the treasure island. Their hunting fingers must have passed over them a dozen times without being conscious of their existence.

Henley seemed to have set his plans very nicely: Silva, the fake Portuguese sailor, the row in the Fore-and-Aft, and Burke's apparent kindness in slipping them out of the back door into the very arms of their enemies, done so as not to incriminate Burke, who could profess ignorance of anything happening off his premises. The man was not only determined but clever, and evidently had a crowd of his own kind with him. The situation was serious. He felt sure of Jim, who, for all his surface frivolity, was stanch in times of stress, and resolved, in any event, not to give up the position of the island.

Peggy—whom Henley had called his "girl"—his heart warmed to the word—was his chief worry. She would be alarmed, of course. She had money, and Selim to look out for her, besides the Belmonts to advise and protect her, but in her anxiety she was almost certain to call in the authorities. And, whether he and Jim were found immediately or not, the story of the gold would become public and they would find it almost impossible to carry out their plans.

They would be marked for the rest of their existence until the affair was cleared up, which might not be in a fashion entirely to their profit. Governments might intervene under the treasure-trove law. Private ownership to the island might be assumed and even proven.

He was not particularly afraid of Henley doing anything desperate with himself or Jim. He decided to play the game of delay for a while. Peggy was not expecting necessarily to see them that night. She need not be alarmed until nine or ten the next morning.

He wondered what the time was. Then he groped his way about to discover some way out of the cellar, bumping into beams and over bales. The floor seemed to offer the only chance. It was of dirt, but any idea of digging a tunnel to the street was palpably absurd. He did not even know its direction. As for the walls, they were of hard brick. Consignments of strong-smelling Oriental goods were piled up on all sides.

He resumed his seat on the bale. The thought came to him that he might hide himself among the goods in the hope of some one coming in at last, and take a desperate chance at mastering them and fighting his way out. This idea he perforce set aside as impractical, though he constantly cast about for some way out of the dilemma.

There was the *Wavecrest* at Pearl Harbor waiting for them. Perhaps he could compromise with Henley for a share of the loot, offering to wait behind, and then outstrip him with the *Wavecrest*. It was evident that Henley knew nothing of his having secured the schooner.

A babble of voices aroused him and he went to the grating. Some Chinese were entering the room with the partly open door, across the passage. It was of little use appealing to the opium smokers. More than likely they would fail to understand him, if they were not in league with Henley.

Presently he heard the dragging footsteps coming back. Others, light but firm, followed it.

The face of Henley came to the grating.

"Well," said Henley, "you may as well come through. Your pal says he will, if you will."

Addams laughed.

"Better leave those tactics to the police. I'm not going to tell you."

"We might try the third degree yet—" said Henley.

"Pardon," said a suave, cultured voice. "Your tactics are somewhat crude, Henley, my friend. Open the door."

Henley demurred. The voice repeated the sentence coldly, in a tone as impersonal as the tap of a hammer on steel, a ring of authority in it, a far-off suggestion of an accent, or rather a too perfect precision of vowels and syllables.

"Open the door, you blundering fool. Are you afraid of an unarmed man? Do not try to attempt a sally, Mr. Addams. It will be useless, I assure you."

There was the sound of the removal of a heavy bar and the door swung open. On the instant, the flash of an electric torch was focused on Addams, resting on his face, dazzling him even as he saw by the light of Henley's lantern the dark blue gleam of two automatics in nervous hands.

"Sit down, Mr. Addams," said the suave voice. "There's a bale conveniently behind you. Shut the door, Henley."

Addams obeyed. The glare of the torch was shut off. As his pupils dilated once again in the half-light of the lantern, he saw his visitors before him

Beside Henley stood the figure of a Chinaman, sleek, inclined to stoutness, with the air and attire of a prosperous merchant of high rank. His clothes were of thick brocade in quiet design of dull and glossy black silks. The skull-cap that crowned his bland smooth face, that was more like ivory than flesh and blood, was topped with a coral button. Once, from a finger on the hand that held the automatic, shot a brief dazzle of prismatic sparks as a magnificent diamond flashed out its fire in answer to a movement of the lantern Henley held.

The face challenged Addams' attention. Plump, creaseless, smug, emotionless, it revealed nothing, suggested all things. It was a mask that neither jest nor murder could change. But, between the smooth, sleepy lids, eyes as hard-lustered as polished marble, but ineffably alive, showed the vitality that lay beneath the placid physiognomy. They looked at Addams with the impersonal interest of a vivisectionist surveying a helpless victim, purposeful, implacable.

He spoke, and his voice had lost its metallic ring for a low, smooth-purring quality.

"Our friend here, Mr. Henley," he said, "being lacking in many things that are needful to successfully carry out his enterprise, has appealed to me. He has been very clumsy; he is still inclined to be. You will find, Mr. Addams, if you persist in being obstinate, that we are well equipped in both imagination and practise to persuade you to give up any idea of securing this gold. I can not even suggest a compromise with you. The amount is too small for division greater than already arranged."

He paused to mark the effect of his words.

"I assure you in all sincerity," he went on, the purring voice covering a sinister, insistent menace, "that you will find it very much to your advantage and to that of your friend, who is in the same helpless, unfortunate predicament as yourself, to forego any hallucinations as to your interest in the treasure.

"There will be nothing clumsy, I assure you. The Orient, as you may have read, perhaps seen, Mr. Addams, has reduced the profession of punishment and coercion to a fine art. I trust we shall not have to exercise it unduly. I have come frankly to deal with you as one head of an expedition to another."

Henley let out a growl that subsided promptly as the Chinaman turned the threat of his cold eyes upon him.

"Your friend, Mr. Winton," went on the quiet voice, "asserts that he does not know the needed figures of latitude and longitude. You do! It will be necessary to secure them from you and compare them with figures given by some other responsible party of your organization."

He paused. Addams faced him steadily.

"I am not going to tell you," he said.

"I shall give you a minute," rejoined the Oriental imperturbably. "Use it to balance the value of liberty and your present excellent physical condition against the sum of seven hundred and fifty thousand dollars. My own valuation is largely on the side of the money, in quite a heavy preponderance."

He went to the grille and called across the passage in Oriental sing-song. There was the scuffling of soft shoes and four Chinese entered the cellar.

Addams, his muscles tense, kept silence. The newcomers shifted into the shadows.

Suddenly the torch flared out into his face again and he was fighting furiously in a mêlée of entwining legs and arms that pulled him down at last, writhing, struggling on the floor, conscious all the time of the High Chinaman's impassive face and idly curious eyes, watching the certain outcome of the struggle.

Conquered at last, his wrists bound behind him, his ankles cross-tied, Addams found himself seated on his bale held by the four Chinamen, all of them breathing heavily. He knew by the resistance to a few hard blows he had sent home from fists and knees and elbows, that some of them were not entirely uninjured, and he derived a grim satisfaction from the thought.

At the command of the leader he was jerked roughly to his feet. A rope was run through a hook in the ceiling and attached to the thongs that bit into his wrists. With this hauled taut till his shoulder blades ground in their sockets, two of the men lifted him by the hips, placing him on a little platform of superimposed boards an inch in thickness, a foot in total height. The slack of the rope was taken up once more and its end fastened securely to a second hook projecting from the wall. Then, at a word from their chief, the four coolies withdrew.

"Now," said the Chinaman. "As I promised—nothing clumsy. The pain is exquisite, but there are no marks, no disfigurements, no blood. The dislocation can always be reduced if a satisfactory decision is arrived at in time. The figures, Mr. Addams."

Addams, the pain of the straining muscles already bringing beads of sweat to his forehead, disdained to answer.

The Chinaman flicked an inquiring torch-ray at his face.

"No?" he said. "Henley, take away one of those boards. Quickly, at a level."

The drop of an inch sent a wave of agony through Addams. He sunk his teeth in his lower lip to stop an involuntary groan.

"Once more, Henley," said the suave voice presently.

The sickening jar came again. The blood rushed to the tortured man's forehead and his brain seemed congested. Then the biting pain cleared it.

"Well?" asked the voice of velvet.

The cracking lips parted in an inarticulate "No." Henley dragged out another plank. Addams felt his muscles and sinews tearing away. His brow was wet, dripping with moisture. The torchlight, full on his face, faded suddenly as he fainted.

When he returned to consciousness he was in the same position, racked with pain, though the boards had been replaced. Henley had gone.

"We are going to leave you," said the Chinaman. "It will not be comfortable, but that is your fault. I am sorry you have been so stubborn. Once more, will you tell?"

Addams shook his head. The movement wrenched him till his features twitched.

"I shall slacken the rope a trifle," said his torturer. "If you keep very still you can think better. There are other ways of finding what we want. I may need you presently for comparison. *Au revoir*."

He went out, barring the door after him and closing the shutter of the grille.

Addams, alone in the darkness, half suspended, half standing, gave vent to his bitterness of spirit and the agony he had fought back in a groan.

The grille showed once more in the orange square of light. A chuckle sounded.

"I was waitin' for that," said Henley, as his face showed darkly at the grille. "If I had my way I'd get it out of you if I had to cut it out!" he exploded savagely. "Comin'," he answered in response to some signal, and Addams heard the halt of his foot upon the stairs.

"Other ways." The threat held possession of Addams' brain. What did that mean—Jim, or Peggy?

XIV

The Strategy of the Quong Shing Tong

Peggy Winton looked at her wrist-watch and smothered a tiny yawn. It was close to eleven o'clock, but she had determined not to go to bed until her brother and Archer Addams returned from their attempt to secure sailors for the trip.

She sat on the long veranda of their cottage, vine-curtained from the street. From the hotel, across the dark lawns, set about with high hedges of hibiscus, spattered with the moonlight that fought its way through the tree canopies, came the lilt of the native orchestra, flute and guitar and violin, the voices of the musicians blending now and then in little snatches of song.

All about the girl, as she sat reading casually by the shaded electrics, it was very quiet. The whole life of the place seemed centered at the main building, a block away across the gardens in which the cottage colony was set. At the other end of the veranda, squatting on his haunches was Selim, silent, motionless, save for the occasional shifting of his hands as he smoked incessant cigarettes, little sparks that died and were born again in the gloom.

The glamour of the semi-tropics, the fragrance of the flowers, the velvet feel of the air, invested Peggy Winton with a feeling of elation, an exultant sense of living in a romance of which she was a delightful part. She laid down her magazine and let her thoughts run down the back trail to a week ago, then back again over the swift, vivid incidents of the transition from the firelit studio in Washington Square, the snowy cityscape outside and the old adventurer spinning his yarn, to this land of sunshine and flowers, perfume and moonlight.

The outcome seemed rosy as she projected her thoughts ahead, strengthened by hopes and wishes that she but vaguely allowed her heart and mind to dwell upon. Essentially vital, the girl reveled in the action in which she found herself suddenly projected from the rut where she had seemed doomed to travel. Her spirit rose in mutiny at the thought of being left behind with the Belmonts while the two men rounded out the quest, and she resolved to put up a stirring argument to be taken along. Her brother, to whom she had always acted as a balance-wheel, she knew she could persuade, but she realized, with a little thrill of half resentment, half acknowledgment, the quieter mastery of Archer Addams.

She drifted into a reverie from which she roused herself as some one mounted the steps of the veranda and tapped at the screen-door. Selim rose lithely and opened it. A native, neatly clad in blue serge, came within the brighter radius of the lights.

He bowed respectfully, with a flash of white teeth, and presented a card to the girl. It was her brother's.

"The gentleman give me this," he said. "He say he like this man," he indicated Selim, "to come *wikiwiki*—quick," he translated, with another smile.

"Where to?" asked Peggy casually.

"I show him," said the man. "Mr. Winton say he want him to carry some package."

Selim looked inquiringly at his mistress.

"All right," she said. "Wait a moment."

She entered her room and brought out a coin for the messenger. He looked at her curiously as he took it. Then the two went away together.

Before she had settled herself again the telephone bell sounded.

"This is the office, Miss Winton," came the message. "Can you come over here for a moment?"

Peggy hesitated.

"Who is it?" she asked.

"One moment," said the person at the other end of the 'phone.

Peggy waited and heard another voice, suave, cultivated, with just the hidden hint of an accent, indefinite, elusive.

"This is Mr. Champion," it said. "They tell me Mr. Addams and Mr. Winton are out. I wanted to see them—about a matter of special importance. I would much rather talk it over than leave a message. If you prefer, I can come to your cottage, if it is not too late?"

Peggy considered rapidly. Conventions seemed petty in the light of their enterprise, but it was late and she was alone.

"I'll come over," she said.

She caught up a strip of black lace and threw it over her head above the light gown she wore and ran swiftly down the steps, passing up the little path that split the lawn and led to the main drive.

Two men rose from the shadow of the hedge, one on either side of the path. A soft pad of something was pressed upon her face; pungent, intoxicating fumes filled mouth and nostrils, penetrating, simultaneously it seemed, to lungs and brain, as she swooned and fell, one hand grasping at the shrubbery of the hedge. The powerful engine of a motor-car panted softly on the street.

One of the men looked hurriedly up and down the driveway. Then the two bore the limp form of the girl to the machine and laid it on the floor of the tonneau, taking places themselves on the wide seat. As the door clicked, the driver threw in his clutch and the car, with a whirr, glided rapidly away.

Selim walked with the messenger who had brought the card, down towards the water-front. The native led the way to a saloon, which they entered.

"One minute," he said. "You sit down. I tell them. I think they in back room."

Selim sat at one of the little tables while the Hawaiian crossed the floor and went through a door at the back. The Arab waited patiently, ordering a drink, which he left untouched, watching the random crowd. Several men, he noticed, went through the door by which the native had left the room.

Presently he rose and opened the exit. An alley lay before him, blind-walled, deserted.

At top speed he ran through the quiet streets back to the Royal Hotel and the cottage. It was deserted, the lights still burning. He sped to the ungated opening in the hedge where the path led to the driveway. On the lawn to one side showed the scattered scarlet petals of an hibiscus bloom. Beyond them something darker than the grass showed in the shadow. The Arab picked it up, recognizing it as his mistress' lace wrap.

Like a hound on the trail, he cast swiftly on both sides of the path, noting the faint clutter of footprints on the drive. The hard, shell street revealed nothing, but on the curb where the motor-car had waited, showed a shred of vermilion where a petal had fallen from the girl's unconscious hand.

Not stopping to pick it up, Selim sped westward to Fort Street and on to where Nuuanu Avenue unrolled its white ribbon, leading up to the valley to where the dividing mountain-walls formed the gap of the Pali precipice. In this direction lay the house where the invalid of the wheel-chair was stopping.

The road was barred by shadows, the sidewalks dark beneath the trees. Here and there great poinciana trees, brilliant in daytime as a mammoth scarlet geranium, made great archways beneath which the Arab ran swiftly, bound for the house to which he had traced the man in the wheel-chair.

Practically in the confidence of his employers, Selim's quick wits had pieced together suspicion and situation and coupled up the abduction of his mistress with the man he had been told to trace from the wharf. To Peggy Winton he had attached himself in absolute devotion from the time that he, an alien—unable to attend to his duties, expecting therefore to be cast out as useless—had found himself nursed back to life with tenderness and consideration. The spirit that renders the Arabic emotion absolute, whether for fanaticism, love, hatred or fidelity, was strong within the breast of Selim, as he bent all his energies and primitive, unspoiled capacity for the chase upon the trail.

Presently he reached the quiet cemetery, with its monuments of converted Hawaiians; of the chiefs of the island race, lying in mausoleums of coral and lava stone while their ancestors slept the last sleep in hidden mountain-caves; of Saxon and Latin, missionary or merchant, soldier of the cross or sailor-trader of the yard-stick—adventurers all—at rest beneath the tropical verdure that sought so speedily to cover up the lifeless clay before it reclaimed it to transmuted uses.

A high-powered car, with three men in the tonneau, came plunging by. Selim crouched in the shadow of one of the pillars of the main entrance, watching the machine as it raced townward, trying in vain to discern features as the car fled past him.

High rails of iron shut off the cemetery from the street. By these Selim ran at top speed. The mountain end of the graveyard was uncared for and overgrown, its mounds and tumble-down vaults adrift in the sea of untrimmed growth. At this, its northern border, a ragged hedge separated the cemetery from the garden of the house to which Selim was bound.

Set back from the road a hundred yards, the house was invisible from the gateway, lost in a riot of vines that clambered up the palms, hung in festoons between them and smothered the coral-block walls of the house. Along the outer wall of gray lava sprawled the cactus leaves of the night-blooming cereus, ten thousand of its silver blossoms wide-eyed to the moon. The garden held the heavy, depressing fragrance of a mortuary, the house itself was silent and dark as a tomb.

The hard, convict-made road that led up Nuuanu Valley had shown no sign, but Selim saw in the softer dust of the drive the fresh impression of the tires of a car, entering and leaving.

He crept with swift stealth to the house and circled it. All the lower windows were tight-shuttered, those of the upper story looked blankly to the night. As he made a second patrol a dim light showed through a barred window at the back, and vanished. A coco-palm, standing at a sharp angle, grew close by.

Selim threw off his shoes and socks and nimbly climbed the slanting stem, with clinging fingers and toes, like a man-ape. There was a heavy sill in the deep casement, and iron bars guarded the now dark window. The palm trunk came within two feet of the building. Crouching on the tree Selim looked and listened. There seemed no actual window behind the bars, or else the frames that held the glass had been swung inward.

As he watched, his quick ears caught the shuffle of feet. The light again dimly illumined the room. A woman carrying a candle came towards the window. Selim flattened on the palm trunk. The woman closed the window behind the bars without looking out and the light vanished, the footsteps deadened now by the intervening glass.

Selim slid swiftly to the ground and put on his shoes. He had seen enough. The woman was, as he had expected, the nurse of the man in the wheel-chair, still in her linen uniform, but at her throat his swift eyes had seen and recognized in the lamplight a miniature, set about with pearls and enamel, that Peggy Winton often wore and that Selim had noticed on her gown that same evening.

For a moment he considered the situation. The window he had just been surveying was barred, the others unapproachable save for a ladder, or closed with heavy iron shutters. He felt certain that his mistress was inside, imprisoned, helpless. But, being an Arab, he possessed the rare faculty of summoning patience to his aid when impatience spelled impotence.

He was an alien. The laws of the country he knew nothing of, save that the police were men of darker color than himself, who spoke for the most part a barbarous tongue. An attempt on his part, alone, at the house-breaking that seemed necessary for a rescue, might result in disaster for him and the removal of the only man, outside of her enemies, who knew of the whereabouts of the girl.

That he had been lured by a false message to give opportunity for kidnapping his mistress was plain to him. Her brother, and Addams, recognized by Selim as the true leader of the expedition, might, missing the girl, find their way to the lonely house from his description of it to them after he had traced the man in the wheel-chair to its doorway; but they did not know positively, as he did, that she had been brought there. And they might not miss her until the next morning, believing her asleep in her own room and not wanting to disturb her.

He paused irresolute, then confident that the first and right step was to get in touch with his masters, sped back to the hotel cottage even more swiftly than he had come.

XV

ADDAMS CAPITULATES

THE GRILLE RESOLVED ITSELF ONCE MORE INTO AN ORANGE SQUARE, set with vertical bars. As it brightened, the halting step of Henley, followed by the lighter, firmer ones of the Chinaman, brought back Addams from the borderland of unconsciousness. His shoulders seemed swollen to an enormous size, his cracked lips and parched tongue ached for water as he wondered how long he had been left on the little platform, half standing, half suspended.

The door opened and the two men entered. Once more the electric flash blinded him and Henley laughed while the victim tried to bring his pain-racked features to some semblance of composure with which to face his tormentors.

At the command of the Chinaman, Henley roughly slackened the rope sufficiently for Addams to sit upon a bale, and the blue-white ray of the torch was shut off. The swift and painful release from the strain summoned all his reserves of will to keep from fainting. The Chinaman's voice seemed very far off.

"I have been looking at the matter from all sides, Mr. Addams," the suave tones purred on. "You see, naturally, intending to secure the treasure yourself, you gave a false position in the newspaper in an endeavor to throw Henley off the scent. It has occurred to me that you and your friend, Mr. Winton, might have agreed on a set of figures to use in a crisis like this. I may be overcrediting you, but you seem to have been a very careful man with your secret. So I decided to raise an issue that should settle the matter to treat the affair psychologically.

"You may not rate your own safety, nor that of your friend as worth this three-quarters of a million, but I fancy you may place a higher estimate upon your friend's sister?"

A flick of the electric beam showed Addams' jaw rigid and thrust forward, his lips in a tight line, his eyes steely and determined.

"This is not a trick of the third degree," went on the Oriental blandly. "The lady is in my possession. I should be loath to use any means of persuasion with her. She is very charming. You, I am sure, would be unwilling to have me do so. Don't try to rise, Mr. Addams, or we shall be forced to string you up again."

Addams relaxed, with a mental groan at his uselessness.

"I shall ask you to tell me the position," went on the Chinaman, "and I shall then verify it as far as possible through your friend and the young lady. All three of you will then be kept where I have placed you until such time as we secure the treasure. We shall not return to Hawaii. It will be unnecessary, but I shall arrange for your release within, say—two weeks.

"Now then"—the smooth voice altered its tone to the sound of metal upon metal—"the position of the island?"

Addams opened his lips but only a harsh clicking sound issued from his throat.

The Chinaman produced a silver flask from an inside pocket.

"I thought you might need this," he said, pouring some of the contents into the container that cupped the bottom of the flask and holding it to his prisoner's lips. "It will not hurt you."

Addams sipped, then gulped eagerly. The drink was slightly acidulous, yet fruity and deliciously soothing to the fevered membranes of his mouth and throat.

"Made from tamarinds and limes," said the Chinaman. "You can speak now. There is no need to delay matters. You must be very uncomfortable."

"You say," said Addams, "that you have Miss Winton in your possession. I do not believe it."

"Look," said the Oriental.

He threw on the contact switch of his torch. The beam shone on a tress of red-gold hair that shone alive, iridescent, as it moved in the Chinaman's smooth fingers.

Addams started forward, bound as he was, to fall back at Henley's rough thrust. A groan that all the torture could not wring from him, broke from his lips.

The electric ray was clicked off, the lock of hair, shimmering, even in the dim light of Henley's lantern, was restored to the pocket from which it had been taken.

A vision of Peggy bound, helpless at the hands of this imperturbable fiend, set every pulse in Addams' body throbbing with hot blood. He struggled to burst the cords that bound him and, realizing his absolute impotence, as Henley's rough hands on his shoulders held him helpless, subsided.

"Even with the ropes off you will find yourself incapable of doing much damage for at least the first few minutes," said the Chinaman in tones that mocked in their evenness. "You will give me the position?"

"Otherwise," he went on after a pause of a few seconds, "the lady may have to suffer annoyance."

Addams' fury spent itself at the realization of the position of the girl he loved. There was no question now as to the gold, though, had it been merely the matter of his own safety, he would have fought to the last. Now he was out-tricked by a master of stratagem.

"How do I know you will keep your share of the bargain—that Miss Winton will be cared for?"

"Tut—tut—my dear man," answered the Oriental. "You must take my word for it. All I want is the gold. For your life, your friend's, the girl's, I care nothing. They are absolutely valueless to me. So, in exchange for your information, I shall present them to you. There will be a little inconvenience for a little while, that is all."

The utter lack of sentiment in the cold tones gave them conviction. Capitulation was the only way of escape. Raging inwardly, Addams gave the figures. The Chinaman set them down in a notebook.

"Varying considerably from those in the *Herald*," he said. "Now to verify them."

"You can do that easily enough," said Addams coldly, resolved to end the matter. "If you will rip away the name label in the breast-pocket of my coat you will find the longitude marked on the under side. In the same place Mr. Winton has the latitude."

The Oriental deftly opened Addams' coat and with the sharp blade of a small pocket-knife severed the threads of the label.

"I must compliment you on your ingenuity," he said. "I must confess to having overlooked that, which was very careless of me. Henley will return your valuables and those of your friend. You may rest assured that Miss Winton shall be taken good care of until you see her. As for us, we shall not meet again."

He swiftly cut the cords at Addams' ankles and wrists and motioned Henley, who had set down the contents of Addams' pockets on a bale, to the door.

"I shall leave you this," he said smiling, and tossed something soft and clinging on to Addams' knees. It was the lock of Peggy's hair.

Addams' numb limbs refused to answer to his will. His arms were powerless, as if they had been torn from their sockets. Henley's face darkened the grille.

"Good-by, Mr. Fox," he sneered. "If I'd had my way I'd have taken the gal along, too, to see if her hair matched the gold. I may do it yet!"

With a supreme effort Addams stood up, forcing his paralyzed arms to action and stumbled to the door. Henley with a laugh, spat through the grating at him and limped away.

XVI

AH SING

FOR HALF AN HOUR ADDAMS FORCED the reluctant circulation back into his arms by kneading them. His shoulders were humps of living pain as he worked them as well as he could against the protesting tendons and muscles.

On the bale he found his match-case with the other things that Henley had restored, and he used them one by one in a futile search of some possible way out. He wondered what had happened to Selim, clenching his fists at the way the tables had been turned upon him.

Suddenly he remembered his watch and struck one of his last matches to read the time. It was midnight. He held it to his ear to reassure himself by the ticking, thinking it had been far later.

It was a sad ravel to disentangle and no easy matter for the strongest of men, physically and mentally distressed, as was Addams, to center his best efforts upon the patient untwisting of the snarl. One end of the thread was plain: the prime necessity of getting free from his surroundings. But the following of it was beset with knots and twists.

The whereabouts and welfare of Peggy was aggressively his foremost thought. The problem was many-sided at its best. With Peggy found, Jim Winton loosed, there was a bare chance of getting to the island first. The *Wavecrest* he knew could outsail the lumber schooner, though the course was before the wind and with the latter's larger spread of canvas, the handicap would be larger. Beyond all this, the combination, of which Henley was now palpably little more than a figurehead beside the calm, calculating Oriental, did not know the secret of the caves. If they arrived first, however, they would undoubtedly defend the island easily enough by guarding the solitary reef passage until they had ransacked every square foot of it. In an eight-hundred-mile trip to leeward, he figured feverishly, he could afford to give the *Lei Lehua* eighteen hours' start, and within one hour more they would, in all probability, be on their way.

Then the peril of Peggy, the fear that the Chinaman would not keep his word, the final threat of Henley, sped through his brain in a mental phantasmagoria which his will strove to keep in focus and safe proportion.

He put the lock of Peggy's hair within his breast pocket, telling himself it was a talisman involuntarily bestowed by the Chinaman. His arms, thanks to his chafing, were regaining some of their use, though his shoulders seemed stiffening as he clutched the bars of the grille that Henley had left unshuttered and peered into the gloom of the passage. Far to one side a lamp dimly showed the door of the room where the smokers were sleeping out their poppy dreams. There was little hope of help from that direction. Undoubtedly they were friends or servants of the shrewd head Chinaman who had so suddenly assumed mastery of the situation.

Addams tingled in every nerve with the desire to batter the smooth, shrewd face of his late Chinese captor and to come to handgrips with Henley. He shook the bars in raging inability.

The door across the passage opened, and the acrid tang of opium stole out with the figure of a stout Chinaman who emerged, stretching himself before he closed the door. The light from within and that of the lamp in the passage revealed his features. It was Ah Sing, the Chinaman of Pearl Harbor, the servant of Stevens, the man who was to go with them at his master's suggestion.

Addams hissed between his teeth in a low but piercing note. Ah Sing turned at the sound as Addams lit a match at the grille.

"Ah Sing," he whispered, "come here."

The Chinaman closed the door and came wonderingly toward him, looking curiously at the face behind the bars.

"Ah Sing," repeated Addams. "You know me. You remember, yesterday, at Pearl Harbor? Mr. Stevens' friend? Speak quiet."

"Eyah!" exclaimed the Chinaman. "Sure I sabby you. You write catch Misteh Stevens with cable. You catch?"

"Sure, Ah Sing, I catch," said Addams. "I've not got the cable message here. It's at the hotel, but Mr. Stevens says all right. He says you are to come, too."

"Sabby that all light," answered Ah Sing. "I catch um cable, too. I go 'long of you. Wha' mally you here. You come all same me—smoke pipe?"

"I got locked in, Ah Sing," said Addams, cautiously foregoing lengthier explanations. "Can you let me out? Also my friend is somewhere, locked in, too."

Ah Sing fumbled with some bolts and swung open the door. As Addams stepped free, an old Chinaman came from the room across the passage and spoke to Ah Sing, who chattered volubly with him. The latter led the older man back into the cellar.

"You come along; us make talk one minute," he said to Addams.

"This man he speak Tuan Yuck; he say you stop here one-two week," he went on in a low whisper. "Tuan Yuck he velly big man, all same he head Quong Sing Tong. This man he 'flaid let you go. I don' know, mebbe, suppose you give him plenty money, all li'! He no like Tuan Tuck, plenty hate but plenty 'flaid. You give him, I think mebbe, thlee, fo' hundred dolla, he go 'way, go China mebbe. Tuan Yuck no find!"

"I'll give him five hundred if he'll come with me to the hotel," said Addams.

The two chattered in what seemed to Addams an interminable chant of useless syllables.

"All li'," said Ah Sing at length. "He come hotel. Now he show you your flend, we go."

The older Chinaman, apparently the keeper of the place, with a gesture for stealth, went down the passage and unbarred a heavy door. Beyond, a ladder led down another flight underground. Close to its foot was a door, fastened without by a heavy cross-piece of iron. Ah Sing had brought the lamp from the corridor, and as the door opened Winton appeared, pale and disheveled, a bruise on his forehead, blinking wonderingly in the light.

"Hello, Archer," he said. "Good work! I thought I was in for life. Say, they got—"

He stopped at Addams' imperative signal of silence, and the four climbed three flights of wooden stairs, creaking despite their care, and entered the rear door of a Chinese general store through another carefully protected entrance.

"You stay here," said Ah Sing. "I go look see everything all li'!"

Winton felt for Addams' hand in the darkness and gripped it. "They got the figures out of my pocket-tag," he whispered.

"I know," returned Addams in the same tone. "I'll explain later."

Ah Sing, re-entering the store, called softly to them. In a moment they were in the narrow street where a hack was drawn up to the curb.

"Betteh we lide," said Ah Sing. "This dliver, he my cousin. He all li'."

Addams hesitated for a second and reassured himself. So far the two Chinese had at least set them free.

The four climbed into the stuffy hack, filled with faint Oriental odors. Ah Sing gave the direction to drive to the Royal Hotel. The horse moved off with unexpected briskness as the Chinese hackman cracked his whip, and they were soon rolling swiftly over the practically deserted streets.

Addams held the news of disaster from Winton until they should arrive at the cottage. In his present mood he was disinclined to discuss anything aloud, friendly as Ah Sing appeared.

"Tuan Yuck," said the latter, leaning from his seat beside the keeper of the opium den and speaking softly, "he one time too much beat this man, too much floggee, take his wife, one, two wife. He plenty think Tuan Yuck no good, but all time aflaid. He belong same tong. Me I no belong Quong Sing Tong. I go to this man fo' smoke pipe—number one hop he catch all time. Tuan Yuck, he no good. Plenty lich, plenty stlong. He speak along you? You sabby him? He fat all same me—one velly big diamond he catch?"

"Yes," said Addams grimly, "I saw him."

"Al li'. Hotel we stop now. Bimeby I tell you more."

At Addams' orders Ah Sing directed the driver to the cottage, and the oddly assorted quartet hastily mounted the veranda and entered Winton's room.

"Go over to the hotel, Jim, and get five hundred dollars on the jump," said Addams, curbing his impatience till the Oriental was dismissed. He had hoped against hope to find Selim waiting for them. Now the tangle seemed as hopeless as ever.

The old Chinaman crouched in a chair, looking fearfully about him. Ah Sing pulled down the blinds while Addams paced the floor. The hackman had been told to wait.

"This man he too much aflaid," said Ah Sing. "Fihst steamboat it come, he go China. Now he get money, he hide."

"Tuang Yuck has gone away," said Addams.

The close-fitting lids of Ah Sing's eyes lifted almost imperceptibly then closed to their normal slits.

Winton came in with a clinking double-handful of coin.

"I caught the manager up," he said. "There's a dance on. Here's the money."

He piled the twenty-five twenty-dollar pieces in a glittering rouleau whose yellow glitter seemed reflected in the old Chinaman's covetous eyes.

Ah Sing spoke to his fellow countryman and the latter nodded.

"He say you can tlust him. I say so, too," he said, turning to Addams. "He all li'. He no speak."

Regarding the five hundred dollars as fair pay for their release, regardless of other obligations, Addams clinked the money into the yellow cups of the Chinaman's palms. In the split of a second, by some act of legerdemain, it had vanished, and the man stood looking for his leave to go.

Addams nodded at the door and he disappeared, the padded soles of his slippers noiseless on the veranda.

Addams turned to Winton, but Ah Sing stepped in front of him, pointing at a charm that swung from the chain restored by Henley. It was a Masonic emblem of the higher degree.

"You sabby that?" asked Ah Sing, lightly touching the ornament.

Addams nodded bruskly, eager to tell Winton the news and start search for Peggy.

"I sabby too, plenty much," said Ah Sing.

He wheeled and looked at Winton, on whose waistcoat shone a similar emblem.

"You, your flen', Misteh Stevens, me—all same sabby," went on Ah Sing with glittering eyes. " 'Melican man he call Mason, Chinaman he speak otheh name. All same."

To the astonishment of the two men he swiftly produced a jade charm from beneath his blouse, suspended by a slight chain of gold, carved in practically the identical emblems worn by the two Americans; then rapidly, by signs and pigeon-English he demonstrated the close identity of the fraternal ritual, Occidental and Oriental.

"Now you sabby, I flend, I speak tlue," said Ah Sing. "I sabby you Misteh Steven flend, you both my blotheh, all 'long this." He showed the jade charm before he tucked it underneath his blouse. "Suppose you in tlouble, I think I can help, mebbe. I no flend Tuan Yuck. Plenty Chinaman I know not his flend."

He thrust out his hand and exchanged a secret grip with both the men, then stood back, complacent, smiling.

Addams looked at him with wondering assurance. Here was an unexpected ally. The coil might yet be undone.

"Sit down," he said to Ah Sing. "Here's the trouble. We are after buried treasure, Ah Sing. A man named Henley, a lame man who lived here once—"

The Chinaman nodded comprehension.

"I sabby him," he said. "He smuggle opium, one time."

"Well, he is trying to get there first. Tuan Yuck is helping him with money, I think."

Ah Sing grinned. His opinion of Henley's judgment in selecting Tuan Yuck as business partner was evidently a depreciatory one.

"They got us where you found us," went on Addams hurriedly, "and tried to make us tell. They tied me up—"

The Chinaman made a comprehensive gesture.

"My God, Archer!" exclaimed Winton. "Do you mean the brutes tortured you?"

"Never mind that," said Addams. "I wouldn't tell them. So then they got hold of Miss Winton, your sister."

Winton sprang to his feet.

"Peggy!" he cried. "I thought she was asleep in her room. Where's Selim. What have they done with her?"

"That's what we've got to find out," answered Addams grimly. "They tricked them somehow as they tricked us. Look!"

He took out the lock of red-gold hair. Winton, his eyes blazing, took it in his hands.

"Go on," he said hoarsely.

"They threatened things against her," said Addams, "until I gave them the position. That's how they knew about the figures in your coat, Jim. They promised to release us and her, wherever they've hidden her, after they got clear with the treasure. We've got to find her."

Winton turned, his face twisted.

"How?" he asked. "Archer, it's my fault. Like the trifling idiot I am, I wasted time yesterday with Miss Belmont. It was late when I got down to looking up these sailors, and when this chap Silva offered himself I fell right into the trap, like a blundering ass."

He wilted under the look in his friend's eyes and sat heavily into a chair, his face in his hands.

"Brace up!" snapped Addams. "This is no time for slumping. If your infernal philandering lost her, it won't bring her back again. They may have taken her to the place Selim traced Henley to. But he's missing, too. As it is—"

He strode over to the wall-telephone.

"What are you going to do?" asked Winton dejectedly.

"Do! Everything that can be done. Call up the police for one thing. This is a civilized community. A Chinese tong leader is not running American territory. We know where they've gone, for one thing. We'll charter a tug, if the government won't, and bring them back."

"Then, at the best, we lose the gold, once it all gets out," said Winton.

Addams' eyes blazed as he clicked the hook of the 'phone impatiently.

"To Hades with the money!" he cried. "What kind of a man are you, Jim?"

Winton got up, a new determination imprinted on his features.

"I didn't mean anything like that, Archer," he said. "Don't judge me too harshly. I was only blaming myself for everything."

"Time enough for that later," said Addams. "Hello! Is this the office? Connect me with—"

The door from the veranda opened and Selim stood on the threshold, his dark eyes on his masters, his chest heaving from his long run through the darkness.

Addams turned at the click of the latch.

"Selim!" he cried. "Miss Peggy?"

"I show you," said the Arab. "Come."

XVII

IN THE HOUSE OF THE DEAD

THE HACK, SELIM ON THE BOX BESIDE THE CHINESE DRIVER, quickly covered the distance to the cemetery and stopped a little beyond the entrance to the house to which the Arab had trailed the girl. Addams and Winton stepped out with Ah Sing as Selim jumped from his seat.

"I sabby this house," whispered the Chinaman. "One time befo', Misteh Henley live this place, long time he smuggle opium."

They advanced cautiously through the garden wilderness and rounded the darkened house to where Selim pointed out the palm and the window at which he had seen the woman wearing the girl's miniature.

"I can to the window jump," he said, stripping off his shoes. "Bars a long way apart. I theenk maybe I can get in."

"Try it," said Addams. "We'll tackle the front of the house. If we can't break in we'll create a diversion. Up you go!"

The Arab climbed nimbly up the palm as the rest slipped through the shadows to the front door and mounted the porch cat-pawed, on the balls of their feet.

Addams tried the handle. It yielded and the door opened. Fearful of surprise, he took out the automatic he had brought from the hotel cottage and entered the silent, dusty hall, Winton following his example, Ah Sing close behind.

They stood listening. The house was void of sound. Addams felt for the loose sleeve of the Chinaman's blouse.

"Get one of the hack-lamps," he whispered. "Cover the light as you come back."

The two white men waited until Ah Sing was silently beside them again, the lamp shrouded with his loose jacket.

Addams took the light and they explored the lower floor. All the tight-shuttered rooms, save one, evidently the kitchen, were empty of furniture, the floors soft with dust on which their feet left trails.

The kitchen had been swept and apparently lately occupied. There were four or five chairs and a cheap table, on which stood a half-filled lamp. In the sink were piled some dirty dishes with grimy fingermarked glasses on the drain-board, and beneath it three or four emptied bottles. On a shelf showed a row of unopened canned goods.

Ah Sing approached the stove, looked into the pots that stood there and took off a lid from the fire-grate.

"Stove plenty hot," he said. "Some one he cook, I think mebbe three, fo' hour ago."

A closet disclosed a bundle of dirty rags on the floor beneath empty shelves. Winton lit the lamp and they proceeded noiselessly to the upper story. In one room a pine wardrobe and a cot with the bedclothes neatly arranged set them to greater caution. The room adjoining was similarly furnished. A bath-room held towels, used and clean. The other rooms were as those below, dusty and long deserted. In the last they entered. At the back they found Selim beyond the casement bars, tugging to bend them sufficiently for entrance. Addams opened the window.

"Can you make the tree again," he asked.

Selim, crouching on the wide sill, nodded.

"Then come 'round to meet us at the front."

The Arab turned on his haunches and, measuring his distance sprang for the palm, sliding down its trunk in safety as the three men descended the stairs.

The house was vacant. There seemed to be no cellar. Its coral-stone foundations rested on the solid ground. Selim joined them, and the group assembled in the kitchen in perplexity.

"Tell us your story again, Selim," said Addams. "You are sure you saw the woman at the window."

The Arab recapitulated the details he had already told them in the hack. There seemed no clue, no suggestion of a lead.

"Moon's down," said Addams. "We might find footprints in the garden, but they may have heard or seen Selim and gone away by motor."

The Arab shook his head.

"They not see—not hear me," he declared.

Ah Sing, whose eyes had been puckered to blindness, matching the furrows in his forehead, suddenly threw up his head like a hound that had caught the scent. He caught up one of the empty bottles and commenced sounding the floor of the kitchen. His Oriental instincts had suggested a hidden exit.

"Good man!" said Addams. "We'll try all the rooms."

But Ah Sing's ear had detected a hollowness beneath the boards. He followed it to the door of the closet where he tossed out the rags and knocked with his knuckles triumphantly on the floor below the shelving.

"I find," he announced. "All same Chinaman they fix."

A close examination discovered a plank that tilted, disclosing rope handles in a hollowed space between the false flooring and the lid of a trap-door that rose easily. The rough steps of a ladder were revealed while from the aperture came a dank, musty smell.

Ten steps led to a low and narrow tunnel lined with stones, adrip with moisture and patched heavily with fungous growths that dabbed at them with damp suggestions of ghostly fingers.

Addams, in the lead, was forced to bow his head as he followed the passage, running at right angles to the lay of the house—leading towards the cemetery. His enforced position brought back an almost intolerable pain to his shoulders, forgotten in the excitement of the past hour. The tunnel with its foul, stale air, seemed interminable as he crept stealthily on, pistol in hand, the grotesque shadows of his companions jerking ahead at every step as they closely followed him.

He stopped. In front a light dimly outlined three sides of a door. Addams set down the carriage-lamp he carried and crawled forward on his hands and knees; Winton, Selim and Ah Sing imitating his example.

The door had sagged on its hinges from neglect. A break of the light that marked its opening edge indicated a bar or heavy lock on the inner side. As they paused, the sound of heavy breathing came from the other side.

Addams had noticed, as he placed his lamp on the floor, a stout wooden bar standing against the frame of the door, evidently used for barricading on the tunnel side. This he cautiously handled, passing it back until Winton and Selim grasped it with himself lengthwise, quickly grasping his intention. Ah Sing, behind them, held up the lamp, his eyes agleam with anticipatory excitement.

Three times they swung the impromptu battering ram to get full poise, then, Selim plunging at its end, catapulted it at the center of the door. It gave way, splintering rottenly, and a gust of musty air came through the falling panels as they leaped into a vaulted chamber, Addams seizing the figure of a woman, clad in a nurse's uniform, who sprang from some rugs on the floor at the abrupt intrusion.

As Winton and Selim came to help him, he left her to their not too tender mercies and strode across the flagged floor to where Peggy Winton, her golden hair atumble, raised herself upon one elbow from a rough pallet of matting, her eyes upon his.

"Thank God!" he said, a sob strangling his utterance. "Peggy!"

XVIII
THE *WAVECREST* GETS A CREW

THE PLACE WAS A MAUSOLEUM, the private tomb of some Hawaiian chief's family, as evidenced by the stands of moldering *kahilis*, tall poles plumed with feathers, like mammoth dusters, that drooped above a stone casket set upon a central platform of stone. Coffins were set in niches in the walls. A flight of steps led up to heavy metal doors.

The light of the carriage-lamp and a lantern on the floor sent pale rays searching out the fearsome vault in discouraged fashion. The place reeked with decay.

Addams hastened to get Peggy away. She stood clasped in her brother's arms, pale and still weak from the narcotic she had inhaled. Ah Sing and Selim grasped the woman, who looked defiantly at Addams who confronted her.

"Take off that brooch," he commanded.

The woman sullenly obeyed as Selim gave one hand temporary freedom, unknowing that her covetous vanity had furnished a step toward her own undoing.

"Get Peggy up-stairs, Jim, and into the air as soon as possible," said Addams. "I'll be with you in a minute. Now then"—he faced Henley's sister—"I might have you jailed for robbery," he said.

"Try it," she answered, a defiant gleam in her eye.

Addams reflected. Privacy was still an important factor. The woman might tell, not all she knew, but enough to encumber them in a net of official and public annoyance. There was no chance of any of her friends returning. It had probably been arranged that at the end of the two weeks suggested by Tuan Yuck she should disappear, leaving Peggy to escape and join them as best she could.

The vital thing to do now was to see Peggy domiciled at the hotel with the Belmonts, get the *Wavecrest* in commission and start to overhaul the *Lei Lehua*. But he was determined not to leave the woman in Honolulu, still able to work injury upon Peggy. He looked at his watch. It was three o'clock.

"What time does the first train leave for Pearl Harbor, Ah Sing?" he asked.

"Seven o'clock."

"Then you come with me. Selim, stay here and watch this woman until some one relieves you. I'll get some food to you. Can you manage her?"

The Arab showed his teeth and produced a dagger from the girdle he wore instead of a belt.

"She stay," he said briefly.

"Betteh you tie," said Ah Sing. "Betteh mebbe you cut um throat, put um all same in coffin."

He pointed suggestively to the stone casket. The woman shrank back.

"You can tie her if you want to," said Addams.

He was largely callous about the treatment of one who had played jailer to Peggy in such a place and, in all probability, had subjected her to at least the indignity of cutting off the lock of hair which had brought about his capitulation. He wished that she had been a man upon whom he could have executed summary vengeance.

He left the tomb and hurried up the passage through the trap. As he reached the carriage in which Winton had placed his sister, Ah Sing caught up with him and mounted the box.

On the way back to the hotel, Peggy attempted to make light of her adventures.

She had been unconscious, she said, or practically so, until she had found herself in the tomb with Henley's sister barring the way out. She held a dim recollection of having been carried along a passage, but had no remembrance of being questioned or of her hair having been cut, until her brother told her of the occurrence.

, Winton would have proceeded with a description of their own imprisonment had not Addams placed a compelling hand on his knee, being in no mind to allow the already overwrought girl to listen to anything of the sort.

"It's all right now, Peggy," he assured her. "How do you feel? That's the main thing. Jim and I are all right."

"I'll be fine after I've rested," said the girl pluckily.

"We'll all turn in and get what rest we can," said Addams. "Tomorrow, or rather, later today, we'll get under way and beat them at their own game."

"But I want to hear all about it," the girl persisted. "What has happened?"

"Strict orders of the leader of the expedition," said Addams, lightly but firmly. "No explanations, no discussions, till we've all had some sleep. I confess I'm about played out."

Peggy, weak and a little nauseated from the drug, leaned back in drowsy relaxation until the carriage halted outside the cottage. Addams and her brother helped her up the steps into her own room where she thanked them with tired eyes.

"Sleep as long as you can, Peggy," said Addams. "One of us will be on hand in the morning. Good night."

"Good night," answered the girl as they left her.

In their own room, with Ah Sing in attendance, Addams sank wearily into a chair.

"I'll have to get some liniment rubbed into my shoulders," he said. "I feel as if they'd been sewed together."

"I fix that," said Ah Sing. "You sabby *lomi-lomi*?"

Under his direction Addams lay face down on the bed stripped from the waist up, while the Chinaman kneaded and pulled at the swollen muscles in the Hawaiian massage. The pain at first was intense, and Addams bit at the counterpane to muzzle his involuntary protests.

For fifteen minutes the Oriental pinched and snapped and rubbed, dislocating and relocating the blades and soothing the bruised muscles until the fibers were supple once more. At last, the sweat rolling from his face, he stopped.

"Tomollow, next day, mebbe one time more, I fix," he said. "Then you all li'."

"It's a whole lot better now," declared Addams. "Now for the plan of campaign, Jim. I'm going to Pearl Harbor with Ah Sing—in three hours—to get the *Wavecrest* in commission. We'll sail her down to Honolulu tonight and we'll clear as soon as we get the stores aboard. You've got a full day. You've got to get food to Selim without being seen. You've got to get Peggy out to the Moana Hotel with the Belmonts. And you must see that the ship's chandler is ready to load us up by, say, five o'clock this afternoon. I'm relying on you, old chap."

"I'll not fail this time," said Winton reddening.

"Tell Selim we'll relieve him late this afternoon."

"What are you going to do with Henley's sister?" asked Winton.

"I'm going to take her along," said Addams, coming to a sudden decision. "She's too dangerous to be left loose in Honolulu, and we haven't time to fuss with her. I may leave her on the island and tell the Tuang Yuck-Henley combination to call for her if we get close enough to hail them."

"You think we can get there first?" asked Jim eagerly.

"Think? I know it," declared Addams with conviction. "We'll have to give them twenty-four hours' start, but the *Wavecrest* is a racer and the *Lei Lehua* is, comparatively speaking, a tub. We should clear tonight at ten, by moonrise. We don't need clearance papers, we're on a yachting cruise to the other islands. You might drop that information to the Belmonts, Jim, and 'round both hotels, casually. I'll give you a duplicate of the list I gave the chandler. You'll have to get some rules and ammunition. Get Winchesters. Hire them if you can. Tell them we're going after wild goats on Hawaii."

He was up and walked lithely about the room, a pajama-top about his torso, vigorous and animated, as if the events of the last eight hours had merely aroused his best activity, despite his declaration of tiredness to Peggy. Ah Sing surveyed him with open admiration and Winton felt his spirit rise in response to his friend's."

"Archer, you're a wonder!" he declared. "You can count on me, old man, for all I'm worth. I'll get Peggy stowed away. She'll kick, though, like a steer. But of course she can't go."

"Hardly," said Addams. "This is not going to be a pleasure trip from now on. I imagine there's a pretty large and tough crowd on the *Lei Lehua*, probably half Tuan Yuck's tong men and half Henley's pick-up following. I wish we had a crew."

"That's my fault," said Jim.

"Well, we must make the best of it," said Addams heartily. "There are four of us any way. Maybe we can find some one else."

"I can get good sailorman, one, two men my flen'," said Ah Sing. "Sabby sea plenty. One man, he Loo Chow, in China he sail all same junk. Sabby can plenty fight, too. One man, he Foo Chin, he come suppose you pay. He sabby ship, sabby fight. All same big fighting men for China Tong. Not Quong Sing Tong—Tsue Chong Wo Yick Tong. All same they got no use for Tuan Yuck. They my flen'. Belong all same this."

He touched the hidden jade charm below his blouse.

"I'll give them a share in the treasure." said Addams. "You, too, Ah Sing. There's seven hundred and fifty thousand dollars—"

Ah Sing's slanting eyes opened wide.

"We'll split it into a hundred shares," said Addams, "at seventy-five hundred apiece. Selim gets two shares, so do you, Ah Sing, if we win out. That's fifteen thousand apiece for you. I'll give each of your men one share. If we lose, which we won't, I'll pay them two hundred and fifty apiece for their trouble, and you twice that. Is that all right?"

The Chinaman's eyes were glowing with enthusiasm.

"All same they go to hell for that," he said.

"That's settled then," said Addams, "if you can get them. Jim, you'll have to get six rifles and four more automatics. Split the buy at different stores and have them delivered here. We'll keep the cottage until tonight. Where are your friends, Ah Sing?"

"I go get them now," said Ah Sing. "I take hack. I meet you seven o'clock at lailway station."

He started for the door.

"You'll need some money for the driver and fares," said Addams. "Wait a minute."

"I got plenty money," replied Ah Sing. "Bimeby you pay me. Suppose you no get gold," he went on earnestly, "you pay my flen', no pay me. Misteh Steven, he pay me. He your flen'. I work for you all same for him. So he speak in cableglam. All flen', all blotheh!"

He stepped quietly through the door and in a moment they heard the hack drive off.

"Well," said Addams. "We can thank our stars for fraternalism. We'll be a fine outfit, Jim. Three highbinders, an Arab who was once mate on a piratical dhow, and the pair of us, all armed to the teeth! No place for Peggy."

"No place for me either, Archer, if you weren't the biggest kind of a brick," declared Winton, "after all my falling down."

Addams said nothing, but clapped his friend on the shoulder.

"Let's go over that list for the schooner again, Jim," he said, "if you're not too sleepy. We can catch up when we get to sea."

"I couldn't sleep," declared Winton.

"Then we'll go out on the *lanai* and smoke. It's close to sunup now. We'll get some hot coffee in a little while. I hope Peggy's asleep. Wait, I'll put on my coat."

They tiptoed on to the veranda past the girl's darkened room and discussed the situation in whispers at the farther end of the *lanai* till the sky got gray and Addams persuaded the hotel clerk over the 'phone, all unconscious of the night's happenings, to send them over a hot breakfast.

At half-past six Addams rose.

"I'm off for Pearl Harbor," he declared. "Stick around till Peggy wakes up. Get her out to the *Moana* and see her settled. Then get in touch with Selim and hustle the rest of the things through. Look out for the schooner about the end of the afternoon. We'll have to hustle to get her sails bent and have her in shape. Good-by."

XIX

UNEXPECTED PASSENGERS

AT FIVE O'CLOCK the *Wavecrest*, Addams at the helm, Ah Sing and his countrymen at the sheets, tacked up the channel entrance to Honolulu harbor and glided up to the wharf designated by the ship chandler.

Winton was waiting by the string-piece as the sails came down and were smartly stowed, taking the line Ah Sing tossed to him and snubbing it to a bulkhead.

"Everything ready, Archer," he said as Addams stepped ashore. "Men waiting to load. That's some crew you've got."

Addams glanced with satisfaction at the Chinese, working with a will to complete moorings. Both were of unusual height and evidently muscular. Loo Chow was far from prepossessing, with a villainous squint and a triangular face marked with scar-seams. Foo Chin was a veritable giant, with a bland moon-face that seemed incapable of cruelty, a good-natured smile playing upon it as he chatted with Ah Sing in a conversation that sounded like exploding fireworks.

"They're up to their work," he said. "How's Peggy?"

"I left her with the Belmonts," answered Winton. "She didn't make half the fuss I thought she would about not going. She's feeling fit again. Didn't propose coming down to see us off."

"Sensible girl," said Addams, inwardly disappointed. "We'll be on the jump. We'll have to stow things after we get away."

"She wants us to go out there to dinner, though," said Winton.

"I don't see how we can make it," said Addams regretfully. "We've got to get Selim and that sister of Henley's aboard as soon as it's dark. I'll requisition Ah Sing's cousin's hack again. You go out, Jim, and make good-bys for both of us. I'll telephone to Peggy."

"That isn't fair," demurred Winton.

"It's got to be. Peggy will understand. I've got to watch the loading, Jim. I know where I want things to go. You can explain to Peggy—and say good-by to Miss Belmont," he added.

"I've forgotten all that till we come back," protested Winton. "But it'll make it nicer for Peggy their being here. They want her to go over to the volcano with them."

"Fine," said Addams. "How's Selim and his prisoner?"

"He's got her bundled up in a blanket like a mummy," Winton replied. "She gave me a frank opinion of all of us till I told her I'd gag her. She's like a furious wildcat. Here's our man and his stevedores."

"Goin' out tonight?" asked the ship chandler, looking first at the sky, then to where the schooner flattened the rope puddings that protected her from the wharf timbers.

"Yes. Why?" asked Addams.

"Looks like we're goin' to get a *kona* before mornin'. Been workin' up for it all day. How was the wind comin' down?"

"A bit shifty. What's a *kona*?"

"Southerly gale. 'Sick wind,' the natives call it. Makes a weather shore out of this side of the island, dirty weather at that. Liable to blow forty to fifty an' keep it up for three days."

"Well, we'll chance it," said Addams. "That's the best news yet, Jim," he went on, as the dealer started to superintend getting the stores aboard.

"With the regular trades making a clear run of it to the island it would be a close call to outsail the *Lei Lehua* with her start against her spread of kites. But the *Wavecrest* is a witch at reaching and close-hauled. We can outpoint them and outsail them working into it. I'll set all hands scratching the varnish off the boom if it'll hurry up this *kona* he talks about. Get the rifles? We'll probably have a fight on our hands as it is, but we'll put up a better scrap if we've got the gold, than if our men were fighting against odds to get it away from them."

"The guns are up at the cottage."

"Take Ah Sing and get his hack. Settle the bill at the Royal and then pick up Selim and the woman. It'll be dark by the time you get there. Better gag her and get her into the hack as quietly as possible. You can drive in up to the door. I'll be waiting for you. We'll stow her in one of the staterooms. There are four of them; Stevens spent money on this yacht. Then you run out to the Moana and get back as soon as you can. I'll watch the loading."

"I'll have the guns and Selim and the tigress down here in an hour," said Winton. "And I'll be back from the Moana by eight. Is that time enough?"

"Plenty. Come down to Lycurgus' restaurant on King Street. I'll leave Selim in charge on board, and get a bite to eat before we start. The men will want something, too. I'll phone to Peggy from there. We'll start at moonrise. Ten o'clock. The tide's right for then."

At eight o'clock Winton joined Addams in a private box at the restaurant and the latter, finishing his coffee, called up the Moana on the 'phone. He came back to Winton a trifle disconcerted.

"Did you tell Peggy I was going to 'phone," he asked.

"Yes. Why?"

"She's gone to her room. Left a message for me. I suppose she's upset because I didn't go out. I thought she'd understand."

"I think she did, old man," said Winton. "I explained everything and she seemed to. But she said she was tired at dinner. She's going to be worried about us all the time we're gone. She needs all the rest she can get."

"Of course she does," acquiesced Addams not over cheerfully.

It was not like Peggy to take offense, he thought, and tried to dismiss the unpleasantness, as he remembered the tax that had been set upon her frail strength. He himself was conscious of the strain. So was Jim, he realized, as he looked at his friend's drawn face and weary eyes. As he had said, the rest of the trip in no way resembled a picnic, and the best place for Peggy was a comfortable hotel and the society of the friendly pleasure-loving Belmonts.

At nine o'clock the complement of the *Wavecrest* was aboard, stowing away the goods that cluttered up the main cabin into some temporary order while they waited for the turn of the tide. Their prisoner stayed quietly sullen in her stateroom where Selim had served her food brought from a water-front restaurant. The Arab had freed her bonds and locked the stateroom door on the outside. Addams and Winton were too busy to interview her. The excitement of getting to sea mustered up their reserves of strength into an energy that rushed the work before them. The Chinese worked cheerfully, stowing away the supplies into the lazarette and the plentiful lockers with which the schooner was provided.

At half-past nine a faint glow behind the coffin-shaped mud-crater of Diamond Head announced the coming moon. The wind was blowing more strongly on-shore every minute. The harbor craft had set out extra lines and the *Wavecrest* chafed at her moorings. The trade-clouds had gone from their steady vigil of the inland mountain-tops; the stars were obscured by a filmy scud flying high overhead before the southerly gale.

At ten o'clock the full moon topped the crater, orange through the atmospheric veil. The wharf was deserted as Addams and Winton, clad in oilskins, followed by Selim and the Orientals came on deck. Two reefs were set in mainsail and foresail, and the first swung up and swayed taut. The jib was set, and five minutes later forestaysail and foresail, as the schooner clawed her way out channel in the face of the wind, past the lighthouse, past the clanging bell-buoy, out to sea.

The hollows in the insheeted canvas clutched like fingers at the gale as the waves slammed at the bow of the *Wavecrest*, forcing her passage outwards. Addams was at the wheel.

"Turn in, Jim," he said, his face wet with spray, gleaming in the moonlight and the glow of the binnacle lamp. A surge of foam rose at the bows and smothered the decks and his spirit, spurning the call of the tired body, leapt exultant to the fight. "Get a few hours' sleep."

"I've got to watch the staysail sheets," said Winton, his hands cupped to his mouth. "We can't risk missing stays in a blow like this."

"Good man, Jim!" Addams shouted as Winton went forward, clinging to the rail.

The best of his friend was coming out at the call of need and he warmed to him. It was a ticklish job getting sea-room off that lee shore with the least loss of time and travel. Every knot might count in the stern chase after the *Lei Lehua*. The gusts shrilled through the rigging, and wind and wave pounded at the stanch hull of the schooner with the sound of a furious artillery fire.

The lee they were making was hard to determine. Diamond Head had to be cleared and, after that, the islands of Molokai, Lauai, and Kahoolawe, lying in a southeasterly line, had to be given a wide berth. The *kona* gale swept in furiously from the southwest. The seas, what he glimpsed of them from the spume that swept over the starboard side, were a tumble of gray-green mountains and valleys. Winton was right. There must be no question of missing stays.

Addams put his strength to the wheel, setting his course south-southeast, handling the ready schooner on three spokes, save when he felt by seaman's instinct that a tack was necessary and spun the circle with a stentorian shout of, "Hard a-lee!" He would have liked to grip hands—had he one to spare—with the designer of the sturdy oak-ribbed, sweet-lined boat as she answered to her helm, then stayed for a moment, not hesitating, but eager to take the seas on each new course, laying over till the foam seethed through her scuppers, fighting, buoyant, dominant.

It was a long time since Addams had faced the elements, a deck beneath him, wet sails shining to the moon, spray crashing on his oilskins, the gale singing through the rigging; and in the sheer joy of it all, fatigue, the treasure, Tuan Yuck and Henley, even Peggy, were for the time forgotten.

At two in the morning, the moon totally obscured by the storm, Jim fought his way aft.

"I'm not much good as a steersman in this weather, Archer," he shouted into Addams' ear. "But you can't keep this up much longer. Ah Sing says Foo Chin is a top-notch man. Let him spell you."

Addams, his eyelids feeling as if they were fixed beyond the power of closing, his fingers turned to rigid hooks, called back:

"Send him aft! I'll try him!"

The Oriental came back, his bulk swaying easily to the pitching of the schooner.

"Make it sou'east-by-south and keep her steady!" Addams shouted, and the giant, nodding his comprehension, took over the wheel, peering into the compass-box.

Addams watched him for a few minutes, then joined Winton by the weather-rail.

"He'll do," he said. "We'll both turn in till dawn. Where's Selim?"

The Arab stood by the foremast shrouds, holding to them. Addams reached him.

"Call us at daybreak," he said, and with Winton, the gale sweeping them like a broom, went swiftly aft, reached the shelter of the companionway and staggered on leaden legs to the cabin.

There they threw themselves on the transom cushions.

"We've a clear course till morning, Jim," said Addams. "The men are all right—they slept on the way up."

A snore was his only answer. An instant later he lost himself in the deep sleep of exhaustion.

Selim awakened them. Gray light filtered through the skylight. The seas were pounding at the bows. The Arab stood poised to the slant of the cabin floor, two half-filled mugs of steaming coffee clutched in one hand. The schooner lunged in long pitches as she rose to the seas.

"Fo' bells," said Selim, smiling, his brown face rimed with spray. "I got hot hash for you. The devil woman, she, oh, verree sick."

As their senses cleared they could hear between the slamming seas a high-pitched continuous moan from the cabin where Henley's sister was locked in.

Addams sat up, rubbing the stubborn sleep from his eyes, and began to put on the sticky oilskins he had discarded four hours before.

"Let her rave," said Jim, sleepily following his example. "Gee, but this coffee's good, Selim!"

They went into the galley, forking the hash from the pot lashed to the stove, and then gained the deck.

The sunfire glowed, close to the horizon, far away across a waste of streaking seas beyond the port bow, showing through the cloud-rack as if behind the bars of a clogged grate. On either side of the dim sun was the misty loom of land, far off, the blotches showing now and then as the schooner lifted to the crests.

"Keelai Kahiki Channel, however they pronounce it," said Addams, "lies between Lauai and Kahoolawe. Main's beyond. You can just see the mountain."

The crest of Haleakala, ten thousand feet above sea level, wrapped in a muddy fleece of clouds, revealed itself, a smudge against the working sky.

"We've come seventy miles and over," said Addams. "This is going to be some race, Jim."

Foo Chin greeted them cheerily as Addams took the wheel. Ah Sing and Loo Chow were forward in the lee of the foresail. Addams motioned them to go below.

"We'll take her over," he said, as the tired men gratefully sought the forward companion. "Get something to eat and turn in."

The wind blew steadily at a clip that presaged hours of force behind it. The waves, their crests flattened to the blast like the ears of an angry cat, surged against them as the seaworthy schooner battled with them, rank by rank, shook them off and kept her steady course. Boom tackles had been rigged, but there was no need for tacking; and minute after minute, hour by hour, they sped onward.

"Eight bells passed, the sharp strokes of the cabin clock repeated by Selim, who had come on deck and tapped them off on the yacht's bronze bell. On Addams' order he hauled in the log. It registered eighty-seven knots.

"Take off seven for leeway," said Addams. "That's eight knots an hour, Jim. I'll wager the lumber schooner isn't doing a whole lot better than six with her bows and beam. At this rate we'll fetch the island in four days and a half, and we're gaining fifty a day on her. We'll overhaul her easily."

"Great!" cried Winton. The short sleep, now that the gale had blown its lingering traces away, left them revivified, reinspired with the spirit of the quest. The seas raced by them, bowing their crests as if in acknowledgment of mastery. A frigate-bird swooped above them with hard incurious eye and braced wings, wheeling away to leeward after a brief scrutiny, reappearing again and again at intervals.

"Good luck!" cried Selim, pointing at the bird which squawked an answer as it plunged downward into the turmoil of the wake.

At four bells Ah Sing and his mates reappeared, and the two white men went below to consult their charts. Selim followed them.

The flaps of the cabin table had been raised and the surface set with a cloth, and dishes held in fiddles. In the passageway between the forward staterooms stood a slight figure, lithe to the motion of the vessel, clad in blue serge, the eager face crowned with red-gold hair, smiling at them.

"Peggy!" they cried simultaneously.

"Come aboard, sir," she said, still standing in the little corridor.

"What are you doing here?" asked Winton angrily. "This is no place for you, Peggy!"

"I had to come," she said. "I'm a third partner. You said so, Archer. Treat me as a stowaway if you want to. I'll scrape paint or be a cabin-boy, but I had to come."

"You had no right! You'll only be in the way!" exclaimed her brother.

Peggy's blue eyes filled.

"I'll not be in the way," she faltered.

Addams' heart went out to the plucky girl, swaying with the pitch of the schooner.

"Jim's right," he said. "You have no right aboard, Peggy. This is a man's trip with too many risks for a woman. But—we can't afford to turn back now."

"Would you rather I hadn't come?" she pleaded.

"Much," said Addams, while Winton scowled. Then he relented. "We're a band of desperadoes, Peggy," he said, "out-pirating pirates. You're to consider yourself entirely as a passenger. How did you come aboard? I suppose Selim had a hand in it."

"Don't blame him," said Peggy. "He's my servant. Don't punish him for obeying me."

She left the passage and sat down by the table.

"Come and have breakfast," she coaxed. "I helped to fix it."

"What will the Belmonts think of it?" asked her brother. "They'll be searching the island for you."

"I explained it all to Madeline," she answered, regaining confidence at the assurance the schooner was not to be turned back nor she to be set ashore. "She understands. She told me to tell you, Jim, she wished she could come along. I took a taxicab and came aboard while you were telephoning me, Archer, I guess," she added. "You didn't suppose I was going to let you leave without saying good-by, did you? Or that I could wait ashore and worry myself gray-headed, wondering what had happened to you?"

Addams sat down, and Winton, half appeased, took place beside him. A moan sounded from forward.

"She's terribly ill," said Peggy. "Selim told me you had brought her aboard. What are you going to do with her, Archer?"

"That isn't the problem that's worrying me," he said. "It's what we're going to do with you."

XX
THE RACE TO KAPUKALIPELIPE

AT SUNSET THE TWO SNOW-CROWNED DOMES of Mauna Loa and Mauna Kea on the big island of Hawaii were well abeam to leeward, lifting above the cliffs of the Kona coast. Addams altered the course to south-by-east somewhat reluctantly, but the wind was still forward of the beam, the *Wavecrest* reaching into the breeze, and in his judgment steadily outfooting the *Lei Lehua.*

"We should clear Kauna Point on this tack, that's the southwestern cape of Hawaii," he explained to Winton and Peggy, "by midnight, and clear the big island before morning. If the wind keeps steady from this quarter, as it promises to, it will be abeam when we change to a southeast course on a long leg for the island. At that we can hold up better than the other schooner. They got away with the wind behind them, but they must have run into a baffle-patch of shifts, and I'm sure we're catching them."

The *kona* gale showed no symptoms of blowing itself out; the sea remained a welter of waves that matched the gray sky. All suggestion of the tropics had vanished save the temperature, but all aboard the *Wavecrest* were content in the speed they were making, with one exception.

This was Henley's sister. Towards evening Peggy asked Addams to visit her and see if he could devise some means of relief.

"Her face is absolutely green," she said. "She can't speak, she can't even moan any more. I am afraid she's going to die."

"Good riddance," muttered Jim more than half in earnest. "She's a feminine Jonah. Don't see why you brought her aboard, Archer."

"Easiest way to keep tab on her," Addams answered, following Peggy to the stateroom where the woman lay helpless.

She still wore the nurse's costume, now crumpled and soiled, in which she had guarded Peggy in the vault. She had refused Peggy's ministrations and offers of clothing and glared at her and Addams as they entered, with the venom of a trapped wildcat. Addams prescribed and mixed a dose of bromide, but resistlessly weak as she was, her locked lips and teeth refused passage to the draft, while her eyes shot sparks of concentrated hate. Finally they left her, the medicine beside her.

"She won't eat, or can't," said Peggy. "Is there nothing we can do for her?"

Addams shrugged his shoulders. He had little sympathy for the woman or, though he admired the trait, Peggy's spirit of forgiveness.

"She'll pull through," he said. "A good siege of seasickness may help her general disposition. Though I doubt it," he added, under his breath.

Ah Sing's hatchetmen, as Winton persisted in styling them, hourly proved themselves to be treasures. With Ah Sing, who had resigned the duties of the galley to Selim in favor of seamanship and the closer company of his fellows, they worked willingly and well, establishing themselves in the favor, not only of Addams and Winton, but of Peggy.

"I like them," she declared. "I don't care whether they're pirates or highbinders. They're absolutely good-natured and there's nothing sly about them. I'd trust myself with them willingly. That may be a woman's instinct and you may think it nonsense, but it's the way I feel. Selim believes in them too, and he's usually suspicious."

"I agree with you in the main, Peggy," said Addams. "Aside from Ah Sing's Masonic affiliations they have other things to bind them to our interests. They have small use for Tuan Yuck or the tong he represents, to begin with. Then they have a stake in the success of the enterprise that means a fortune to them. I understand it's a character of the highbinder, or hatchetman caste, to be faithful to employers. I'd rather trust them than some of the crowd Henley has with him."

The *Wavecrest* was being sailed on strict routine. The gale, while it could hardly be said to have moderated, had taken on an even pressure and the schooner, reaching gallantly, was easily managed. Peggy, who possessed a natural trick as helmswoman, an intuitive ability to favor the boat on mounting seas and save rudder play, took her daylight tricks at the wheel. Addams and Foo Chin divided the rest of the time, and Winton at regular intervals assumed charge of the deck.

"Sailing hard all through the twenty-four hours is half the battle," declared Addams. "I doubt very much whether they are sticking as close to it on the *Lei Lehua* as we are. They think you are still in the charge of our seasick friend, Peggy, and Jim and myself locked safely up in that basement. So they are liable to take things fairly easy, especially nights. That's where most long-distance races are won—night-sailing."

Sixty hours out, with more than half the distance to the island covered, the storm began to abate. Addams looked anxiously at the sky, already showing blue through the ragged splits. The wind came in puffy and the waves ran in a cross tumble of hesitancy. The barometer rose in slight but steady gradations, and the afternoon of the third day the breeze began to box the compass, blowing for brief periods from different directions.

The sky, a blue dome once more, showed signs of reforming trade-clouds on the after horizon towards the northwest, a surety of steady wind from that quarter before many hours had passed, though giving an immediate prospect of doldrums and delay.

Addams summed it up cheerfully.

"They've run into the same thing," he said. "It's even up. We'll make the most of what wind there is while it lasts. Set both jibs, Jim, and your fore and main gaff-topsails. Well try the maintopmast staysails if the breeze holds. Even a knot or two may make all the difference. It's the first boat through that reef-entrance that counts."

He took the wheel and humored the schooner along, taking advantage of every flaw of wind. Presently he ordered in the useless topsails and staysails.

At last the fluttering flying-jib came down; main and fore sheets were run out in expectation of a following wind that hinted at fellowship. A school of dolphins, encouraged by the change of weather, gamboled about the ship, then, deciding it was a fine day for hunting, concentrated their activities in pursuing and devouring a flock of frantic flying-fish.

But the hoped-for breeze failed. The heave of the deep blue ocean died to pulsations on which the schooner wallowed with slatting blocks and ropes, the jerking booms dipping as she rolled, until the slack sheets were taken up and they resigned themselves to the inevitable.

With Foo Chin at the idle wheel, they got out the rifles and automatics and all hands practised at floating targets. Addams proved the master-marksman, with Foo Chin, when his opportunity came, a close second, once he got the balance of the weapons. Peggy, to her delight, proved not far behind either.

"Though there is no spare weapon for you, young lady," warned Addams, "and the moment trouble shows up, below you go as a non-combatant."

"I agree," said the girl, smashing the shoulder of a bottle as it danced past the counter, "but, if it does come to bullets, remember one of your very crackest sharpshooters is out of it, strictly on your account, not hers."

Later that day she found a guitar in the cabin and played accompaniments to Jim's tenor with the Chinese clustering by the foresail, listening eagerly as he sang:

> "Fifteen men on a dead man's chest,
> Yo-ho-ho! and a bottle of rum!
> Drink and the devil have done for the rest,
> Yo-ho! and a bottle of rum!"

At midnight they heard the Orientals chanting high-pitched ululations of their own, barbaric versions of the *Treasure Island* chantey.

All night the schooner tossed easily, often without steerage-way, and before sunrise on the fourth morning out, Addams anxiously sought for signs of wind. The horizon was clear and the piled up clouds gave promise that they refused to redeem. The noon reckoning showed their position at five hundred and fifty-four miles from Honolulu on their direct course, with a little less than two hundred and fifty still to cover.

"If we don't get a breeze soon," said Addams, "we'll not make the island until after dark tomorrow night. That will spoil whatever lead we may establish."

"This drifting 'round like a cork ravels the edge of my nerves," said Jim, chewing at an unlighted cigarette.

"They are probably in the same fix," replied Addams. "It can't last long by the look of things. It's starting to blow at last, I believe."

The sluggish roll of the water began to take on new life, forming into companies of crisp, bottle-blue waves, that advanced from trot to gallop, from gallop to charge as with the trades leading them on, they sent the schooner lunging along at top running speed. The main and fore booms were braced with tackles to help the steering in the following waves and offset the risk of jibing. Within an hour the *Wavecrest* was racing with the creaming seas, the wind strong and steady, swinging on as if imbued with the spirit of her crew.

The log, once more revolving briskly beneath the surface, showed a speed of nine knots when it was hauled at two o'clock in the afternoon, a result that cheered the heads of the expedition mightily.

At Peggy's earnest solicitation, Henley's sister had been permitted to come on deck where, under the watchful eye of Selim, she sat by the rail awhile, then walked forward to the bows with a firmness of step that betokened a swift return to strength, since the head-seas had vanished and the *Wavecrest* ran on comparatively level keel. Selim had reported her appetite as fully restored.

Refusing to speak, or even look at her captors, she yet seemed in sullen fashion to have become reconciled to her condition. Keeping most of the time of her own accord to the privacy of the stateroom accorded her, she had been given the practical freedom of below-decks, with the Arab keeping an eye upon her general movements.

She strayed forward, gazing ahead steadily, until mid-afternoon, when she advanced toward the main companion. Every one else was on deck. Selim glanced in her direction and prepared to follow, suspicious of leaving her alone below, when a shout rang out from Loo Chow.

"Shippee!" he cried excitedly, pointing to leeward. "Shippee!"

Addams sprang to the shrouds, taking the deck-glasses with him as he mounted to the main-top. He focused them eagerly in the direction indicated by the Chinaman.

"It's the *Lei Lehua*," he announced as he gained the deck. "We'll overhaul her before dark. "Get a spar into the leech of the forestaysail, Jim, and hold her out. Bend on your flying-jib, it may help. Then wet down the sails."

Every effort was bent to get the last foot of speed out of the *Wavecrest*. The canvas was soaked with buckets of water from gaff to boom, the better to hold the breeze, and all gathered aft as an aid to the center of effort, watching the sails of the chase rise until the hull was seen at last.

The course they were folding promised to bring them closely alongside the *Lei Lehua*, and Addams, anxious to estimate the force against them, held it at the risk of a long-range bullet. As they neared the wood-schooner he sent Peggy mutinously below, a precaution fairly justified within a few minutes by the rip of a bullet through the mainsail, though they neither saw flash nor the almost imperceptible vapor of the smokeless powder, nor heard, with the strong after-wind, any report.

Foo Chin looked longingly toward Addams at the wheel, who shook his head.

"No good starting anything unless we have to," he said. "I fancy that was a lucky shot. We'll clear them by half a mile. Keep under cover of the rail, all of you. If we fire back they'll lay across our course and try to force the issue by bullets. They've got us outnumbered. We can win better by outsailing them right now. I've got the weather gage of them, besides the speed, and we can afford to keep off and away.

"You can get the rifles up, though, Selim, in case we are put to it, and Jim, see if you can make out how many there are of them. They must have been able to recognize some of us or the vessel or they wouldn't have dared to fire. Naturally they're suspicious of anything in these waters, but if they'd made a mistake it might be costly. It's plain piracy as it is."

Winton mounted half-way up the rings of the mainmast and, concealed by the sail, scanned the craft they were rapidly overhauling.

"There's Tuan Yuck. He's got his glasses on us," he reported. "And Henley is walking deck like a lame duck. He's the one who tired, I guess; he's got a rifle. Look out!"

A bullet came singing over the water, but the range was too great for the accuracy of any one unaccustomed to long-distance sighting, and it passed over them harmlessly. The powerful marine-glasses enabled Winton to see clearly what was going on as the two schooners drew abeam, though over half a mile of water separated them.

"There's a row aboard," said Jim. "Tuan Yuck's kicking at Henley for firing. Looks like a general scrap. There are a dozen Chinamen to about six with Henley. Henley's going below now. I guess Tuan is boss of that expedition."

The *Wavecrest* slowly forged ahead of her broader-bowed adversary, and the crew of the *Lei Lehua* set a clumsy square sail on the foremast in an endeavor to keep on even terms. Blanketed by the main and foresails it was largely ineffective, and the *Lei Lehua*, despite her bigger spread of canvas, fell steadily behind."

"Bad steering," said Addams. "She ought to do better than that."

"What's Tuan Yuck's idea in not trying to pick us off, Archer?" asked Winton. "He must know he's lost out."

"He's not the kind to take chances," answered Addams. "And he doesn't figure he's lost, yet. Murder is a more serious charge than robbery and, after all, we've only a treasure-trove right to the treasure. It's the property of the first finder, if he can keep it. Tuan Yuck probably figures on letting us dig it up and meeting us coming away. That's where the trouble will start if we can't outsail him hard enough in the next twenty-four hours to get the gold aboard and get clear of the island. He's still got chances to win. What's that?"

A shrill cry for help came from below.

"Take the wheel!" shouted Addams to Winton, and leaped for the cabin companionway.

Even as he did so a flying figure came from the forward ladder, followed by a gush of smoke. Henley's sister ran to the rail before she could be reached, and with a yell, topped it and sprang into the sea, going rapidly astern as she swam strongly toward the *Lei Lehua*. Her skirt, stripped off, showed free for a moment behind the woman who was striking out vigorously for her brother's craft.

Winton, deserting the wheel, dived down the main hatchway after Addams, in terror for what might have happened to his sister. Selim and Ah Sing, with Loo Chow, rushed to where clouds of black smoke rolled from the forward companion, as Foo Chin grasped the deserted wheel.

Below, Winton found Addams bending over Peggy, seated protestingly on the transom.

"I'm not hurt!" she said. "Not one bit. I screamed to warn you! The galley's on fire."

Smoke was filling the main cabin as they broke through the passageway between the staterooms to the kitchen, where they met Selim already throwing water on the blaze from buckets handed down by Ah Sing from Loo Chow.

"Get back in the main cabin, Peggy," ordered Addams. "Pass me those cushions, Jim; we can beat this out. Tell Foo Chin to keep her steady!"

In ten minutes the confusion was over and the fire out in the galley at the expense of charred walls, broken dishes, and some minor burns to the fire-fighters.

"We got it in time, thanks to you, Peggy," said Addams. "What happened?"

"I was sitting here looking at the chart after you sent me below," said the girl. "I thought she was in her room. Then I heard a noise in the galley and, thinking it was Selim, I went out to talk dinner with him. She was there. She had unscrewed the oil container from the stove and was sprinkling it over the floor and walls. I jumped for her as she struck a match, threw it down and ran forward. Before I could follow her the blaze stopped me. A breeze was coming down the companionway and I slammed the galley door and shrieked. What happened to her?"

"She's aboard with her precious brother by this time," said Addams. "We sighted the schooner just as she went below. She got to work while we were all on deck. You must have hurried her up and prevented her from thoroughly soaking the woodwork. As it is, we're not badly damaged and they've been delayed, picking her up. It was a desperate trick. We're well rid of her. Thank God, you're safe."

"Then I have been some use to earn my passage," asserted Peggy, pale but animated. "If I hadn't been a girl you wouldn't have sent me below and the fire might have gotten away from you."

Addams smiled at her. In his heart he wished her, brave and plucky as she was, safe ashore in Honolulu. Not merely Henley's shots, but Tuan Yuck's masterful repression of present hostilities seemed to him ominous signs of a probable and desperate struggle before they won free with the treasure that had lain waiting under the sand for sixty-five years for ownership.

XXI

THE TREASURE ISLE

THE BREEZE FALTERED AS THE SUN WENT DOWN and at midnight the *Wavecrest* ran into a windhole, slatting aimlessly about on the breathless sea till morning. Far behind them, barely seen from the masthead, Addams picked up the *Lei Lehua*, doggedly on their tracks.

All forenoon the fickle breezes played with them, filling them with alternate hope and disgust, and all day long the *Lei Lehua* haunted the horizon, sometimes rising under the impulse of a partial breeze until her sails were plain from the deck, then, as Æolus favored the *Wavecrest*, falling behind again.

There was nothing to do but make the best of it. They were in the region where the northern and southern trades are in constant dispute, and great patches of neutral, wind-forsaken sea halt the mariner. It was a gamble between the two boats in the lottery of the winds.

At times, while they rolled with slack tackle and slapping sails, failing progress enough for even steerage-way, they could see, half a mile away, a sharp squall ruffling the sea, and, struggling to reach it, behold it suddenly vanish as they touched the margin of the breeze.

They learned more of Tuan Yuck while they waited for weather favor. The head of the Quong Sing Tong had made a fortune in the days of the island monarchy by purchasing from the powers behind the throne a monopoly of the opium traffic. Under the bargain he smuggled and they closed too eager eyes, including their own. Henley had been one of his aides, and the house by the cemetery, with its secret tunnel, one of the main rendezvous of the smugglers. American acquisition had destroyed Henley's usefulness with strictly-carried-out regulations, and he had wandered afield.

Tuan Yuck, a large part of his revenue cut off, remained in Honolulu, still rich and, among his countrymen, powerful. Naturally, Henley, with none too much money to hire schooners or men, had applied to his former leader who had, Addams surmised, taken hold with a firm hand, promptly relegating Henley and his immediate associates to secondary positions in both the share of the expedition and the loot.

It was Tuan Yuck that Addams feared. The wily Oriental's methods were not of the blundering sort that Henley would have employed. He would work out moves and counter moves rather as an expert chess player would handle a problem, content to wait until the last moment for the master stroke.

Addams realized the Chinaman's absolute disregard of life, and determined, with Peggy on board, to avoid all life-and-death issues, even at the hazard of losing the gold. In actual combat they would be outnumbered and outshot four to one, and he knew that Tuan Yuck would leave no traces, once he got the upper hand.

There was one hope—to reach the island far enough ahead to enter the reef, secure the gold and leave before the *Lei Lehua* arrived. But that hope was dwindling with the inconstant weather, though the latter showed signs of mending as the day wore on to afternoon. They could not expect, however, to reach the island at best before sundown, and, by the time the treasure was aboard, the *Lei Lehua* would more than likely have established a blockade.

Addams sat, planning strategy against possible strategy, praying for a breeze, while the rest practised with the firearms. At one o'clock the northeast trades evidently decided upon an attempt at mastery. The wind came charging over the watery hills, mustering the plumy crests beneath them. Once more sheets tautened and canvas bellied, and a creamy wake showed swift progress.

"Here's where we start to sail!" cried Addams with infectious enthusiasm. The foresail was winged out to port, the mainsail to starboard. Jib and flying jib ballooned ahead with the forestaysail set as a spinnaker.

The canvas was soaked down and all hands went aft as the schooner, light-breasted as a swan, surged onward. In half an hour the *Lei Lehua* was invisible, lost below the horizon.

Addams took the wheel, bending every energy to avoid lost motion. There were no sheets to tend with the fast-following, urgent breeze, and the little complement of seven—Peggy, the two white men, the Arab and the three Chinese—gathered about the wheel in silence, watching the full-bellied sails and listening to the hiss of the foam beneath the counter with mutual delight.

At eight bells Addams sent Selim, as the lightest, up to the main-spreaders. For fifteen minutes he perched there, scanning the horizon ahead for a sign of land, behind for a possible reappearance of the *Lei Lehua*. Suddenly he gave a hail, pointing beyond the starboard bow.

Addams, relinquishing the wheel to Foo Chin, ran forward with the deck-glasses, followed by Jim and Peggy. Ahead, low on the skyline, showed a tiny blue dot.

Addams handed the glasses to Peggy.

"It's the island," he said. "We ought to make it by sundown. We *must*. We've got to get inside that reef by nightfall. They'll hesitate to risk it after dark. If we've any luck with tides we'll have all night to work in."

"And find them waiting for us when we come out, like the big boy around the corner," suggested Winton.

"That depends on circumstances we'll have to wait for," said Addams. "But I've been taking a leaf from Tuan Yuck's book of tactics and we'll find a way to handle that possibility. The important thing is to get into that lagoon."

The land began to take shape before them. The sun had dropped among masses of clouds, sulfur-colored, enormous, against which the lift of the main crater showed in dull purple, with the promontory running to the cape, and beyond, the thimble-shaped islet, silhouetted against the yellow sky. The line of the reef showed snarlingly, and soon the thunder of its breakers sounded a warning.

"The opening's this side!" shouted Addams. "Take the wheel, Foo Chin, I'm going to the foretop to con in. Don't move a spoke till I tell you. Jim, you'll watch your jibs with Selim. Get in the foresheet now, all hands. Then stand by the main. Ah Sing, get forward there with the anchor!"

He volleyed his commands, then sprang to the foremast and climbed rapidly, holding to the halyards, using the rings as a ladder.

"Get in your sheets there!" he shouted, poised in the jaws of the gaff. "In with them! Stand by to go about. We'll make it on the port tack. Lively there! Now then, Foo Chin, hard alee!"

The schooner spun on her keel and sped, skirting the thundering reef.

Peggy looked up at the dominant figure, comparing him with the unsuccessful lawyer of less than a fortnight ago, and thrilled at the evidence of forceful manhood.

Great flocks of birds, disturbed by the advent of the schooner, wheeled dark against the sulfur sky, protesting at the rape of their privacy. As the schooner came under the lee of the main crater the wind failed.

"Ready about!" shouted Addams. "There she opens, straight ahead! Let her fall off a bit, Foo Chin. That's good. Steady she goes. Now—up with her.

Bring her up, man! We're through! Down jibs, Jim. Over with that anchor, Ah Sing!"

He came to the deck, hand over hand, and snapped his orders. Main and fore sail came down to be furled, the headsails were snugged, a second anchor dropped astern—for, though they were partially protected by the cape, the reef opening was in the weather side—and the *Wavecrest* swung to her moorings in the lagoon as the first stars broke through overhead among the cloud masses, now dark as the land which only showed as an indeterminate smudge of black.

"Well, we're here first," announced Addams. "They won't be able to make that passage tonight, if they dared, even in a small boat. They'll not be here for two hours. The moon's not up till midnight and the sky's thick with clouds. They won't be able to sight the island and they'll hate to venture too close to it. If they did they couldn't pick out the passage, and, on top of that, we got in on the middle of the flood. The ebb will be running well after daylight and that's as good as a solid reef to us. Selim, get dinner right away. We'll tackle those caves tonight, while we're safe from interruption."

"Going around by boat or climb over the ridge?" asked Winton. "The caves are on the other side, aren't they?"

"It's six of one and half a dozen of another, as far as time goes," answered Addams. "But it's too risky to tackle the row in the dark. We might get an upset or badly hung up. Help me get out those torches, Jim, with the spare batteries for them."

Peggy emerged from the galley.

"Dinner is served," she announced. "Am I to be allowed to go?"

Winton started to demur, but Addams checked him.

"We're safe as a church till morning," he said. "No reason why she shouldn't help us work out the secret, that I can see."

"Thank you," said Peggy. "After all it's my cave. Come on and eat, if you can. I'm far too excited for food."

XXII

THE HIDDEN HIEROGLYPHICS

THEY LEFT SELIM ABOARD the *Wavecrest*, with orders to climb to the ridge of the promontory as soon as it began to get light. From there he was to warn them of the approach of the *Lei Lehua*. It was difficult work making their way down to the little beach where the gold-schooner had been cast up sixty-five years before with Fellowes and the older Henley as the only survivors.

The moon was not due until long after midnight; the scanty stars, cloud-shrouded, gave little aid, and they picked their way with the light of electric torches. The three Chinamen carried iron rods for sounding the sand, also picks and shovels and crowbars. They seemed impassive as ever, but the rest of the little party was high-strung with excitement at the closing-in of their adventure. Addams felt Peggy's small hand trembling with eagerness as he helped her down the trails.

Once they paused for rest before they essayed the final clamber to the beach and sat together on the edge of the lava cliff. The sky overhead was purple velvet, spangled with golden stars; the sea beyond the reef seemed ebony. Ghostly waves rose against the barrier, and, robbed of their crests, hissed across the lagoon to break at last in phosphorescent, lacey foam. They were in the saddle of the promontory with the desolate crater peak splitting the sky like a great miter to their left, and the lower headland to their right.

"I feel as if I were part of an illustration to the *Arabian Nights*," declared Peggy, "the sister of Ali Baba, if he had one, about to enter the robbers' cave."

"I hope the *sesame* will work," said Addams.

"You haven't forgotten it, have you?" she asked. "A big fish, a canoe, five men and a ring. What are you so quiet about, Archer?"

"Thinking of magic words that open treasure-houses," he said. "There's one treasure-house I've wanted to enter for a long time, Peggy, and it begins to look as if I might have the right to try, at last."

He felt the girl's hand slip caressingly into his.

"I think you could always have found a way in, if you had tried," she said. "Even treasures don't want to be shut up all the time, you know."

"If we don't find the gold I think I'll stay behind on the island and turn hermit," he said jestingly.

"That would be very disagreeable, I should think," she answered. "What would we do when we quarreled with no one to be sympathetic but the shellfish?"

"Did you say 'we' Peggy?" he asked.

"Light-ho!" sung out Jim.

"Where away?" asked Addams, as he and Peggy rose and faced seaward.

"Right there, just below the Big Dipper," replied Winton. "I thought it was a star at first."

Addams picked up the light, rising and falling, lost now and then, to appear again close to the horizon.

"It's the *Lei Lehua*," he said. "She'll get close enough to hear the breakers pretty soon and stay off and on till daylight. Come on let's get busy!"

They clambered down the lava to the little beach. The flood-tide that had covered it was beginning to recede, leaving a narrow strip against the cliff in which they expected to find the caves. It was very dark still, a warm, almost tangible darkness, the ebony cliff on one hand and the dark sea on the other, out of which came the phosphorescent combers, seething to their feet. And it was very quiet, so that they talked involuntarily in whispers, secure from interruption or from being overheard as they were.

Addams had provided half a dozen electric torches with bull's-eye lenses and batteries of unusual strength. With these they sprayed the black face of the cliff with light, searching for the caves told of by Fellowes.

Peggy was the discoverer of the first of them, a low archway chocked by sand.

"There are six," she said, "all close together, with the gold in the third, counting seaward from the cape."

The rest of the openings were discovered, all level with the floor of the beach. Wet sand and shingle, with clumps of seaweeds still damp, made it evident that at high tide the floors were covered. Spiny crabs with long pipe-stemmed leg's scuttered away indignant under the electric rays and scraped across the shingle. The height of the archways varied, but, at the fourth, the third from seaward, there was room to enter without even Foo Chin having to bow his head, and ample space inside for them all to assemble.

The floor was covered with hard-packed sand, the lower walls festooned with weeds in streamers and pods that cracked under foot with reports like pistol shots.

Eagerly they swept the walls with the blue-white electric rays. The rock around and above them was covered with the rudely graven pictographs of men and animals, and symbols that might hold some hidden meaning, or represent the vagaries of some embryo Rodin of the South Seas.

Foot by foot they exploited the crude designs but nowhere could they find anything that the vividest imagination could twist into an interpretation of a fish. Addams had explained the signs they were looking for to the Chinamen and all feverishly searched the rock chamber for the totem that should show where the gold lay hidden.

The gold lust had possession of all of them, white and yellow, man and girl. They scraped off the shiny seaweed with flat stones and fingernails till the rock was bare, without success. The eyes of all shown unnaturally as they reflected the angled beams of the torches; all were breathing hard and dripping with perspiration in the muggy cave as they finally faced Addams in questioning despair.

"You're sure it was the third cave from the seaward, from the cape, that Fellowes said?" he asked Peggy. "Wasn't it the third from the crater?"

"I'm sure he said from the cape," she answered wearily, tears of vexation in her eyes.

"Let's take a look anyway," said Jim.

Outside, the air felt comparatively cool and refreshing. The lazy phosphorescent sea idly rolled the shingle back and forth as it had done through all the ages, sounding a lullaby to its own rocking of the world's great cradle, the sea. The sky had cleared somewhat and the stars glowed in the sky, reflected in the lagoon, serene above the adventurers who sought for the gold that meant so much of comfort and happiness, and even of love, so successful has man been in applying one currency for all things desirable.

The neighboring cave was smaller and easily covered. The carvings were scarcer and there was no sign of the group for which they were seeking. It looked as if their quest was to be fruitless after all. Addams looked at his watch. It was close to midnight. They had been searching for over two hours. The tide was well out now, rock pools rising here and there from the crescent beach.

As they came out of the smaller cave the moon looked over the ragged rim of the crater-bowl and threw ragged shadows clear-cut on the sand, its reflection shining in the pools. By one of these a dark spur was upthrust sharply. Addams walked over to it curiously.

"It's wood!" he cried. "Come over here, Jim and Peggy!"

A new note of hope rang in his voice as they joined him.

"It's the stem of a vessel about the size of the *Wavecrest*," he said, "deep-buried and left here long ago. See how smooth and sharp it's worn. That's Fellowes' schooner, or all that's left of it; enough for a sign-post to tell us he was here sixty odd years ago."

It looked as if his conjecture were a true one and their despondency lifted.

"You see," said Addams, "the beach has been piling up here for all those years. The keel is probably fifteen feet below us, covered with sand—so are the original floors of the caves. You remember what Fellowes said about there being carvings on the floors? All we've seen is sand. We've got to dig down!"

They raced back to the original cave, the third from seaward, and probed into the hard sand with the long iron rods. Some ten feet down they struck the hard rock.

"The gold was probably buried close to the wall," said Addams. "The question is, which? We'll have to trust to luck again; we haven't got too much time. Let's start a trench at the right. Peggy, will you repolish the glass of those torch batteries?"

They went at it with a will, pick and shovel, to expose the wall to bed-rock. It was hard work. The sand was firmly packed and beaten by the tides and they were soon soaked in perspiration. The displaced sand piled up behind them as they toiled, and they had to break shifts to take it out to the beach every now and then and make room for their efforts.

As they neared the rock Peggy got down into the trench and brushed

away the sand that still clung to the rough surface, searching with a torch
for the signs that marked the treasure. Carvings were disclosed as they dug,
grouping more thickly the nearer they got to the original floor of the cave.

"Here's my fish!" cried the girl triumphantly at last. "And here are the five
men! Archer! Jim! It's true! Oh, dig—dig—dig! Give me a spade, one of you!"

They swiftly uncovered the inscription, finding it complete, with the
canoe and the circle, and cleared on down to solid rock. Addams' pick broke
through an opening in the cave wall and he thrust an arm through the sand
and reached an inner chamber, back of an overhanging curtain of stone that
formed the false wall of the cave.

He groped about, full-length at the bottom of the trench, while the others,
sand-spattered and wet, anxiously watched him.

"I've found something," he said, withdrawing his hand and forearm.
"Give me that torch, Peggy."

He dug furiously at the hole with the blade of the sheath-knife he carried
in his belt, scooping out the sand. His full arm disappeared in the cavity.

"Here it is," he announced. "It's hard—yes, it's wood, and here's a hoop
about it. We've found it!"

He climbed out of the trench and slipped out to look at the tide while
Winton and the Chinamen dug furiously and Peggy, perched on a pile of
sand, a torch in either hand, illumined their efforts.

Outside, Addams found the moon sailing high, obscured now and then
by cloud-drift through which the stars peered, still bright; though he sensed
the vague trembling of the sky-curtain that, in the tropics, presages the swift
uprush of dawn.

The tide was still ebbing, guarding securely the entrance to the reef, as one
by one the stout wooden boxes, stained and rusty of iron bands, yet still resist-
ing damp and rot, were brought from the cave and set down on the beach.

Winton seated himself on one of them, mopping his forehead.

"Fellowes said they weighed two hundred pounds apiece, didn't he," he
asked. "I don't believe it! Don't believe they weigh a quarter of that, and half
an hour ago I thought I was just about fagged out. Funny how light gold is
when you own it."

"We don't own it yet, Jim," said Addams. "Here comes the dawn. We've
got to get back to the schooner."

The eastern sky was swiftly stained with red. The glittering star-points
turned to ash, then disappeared, and the wan moon faded to the semblance
of a lifeless gray wafer. Selim called from the ridge—

"Ship, he come now!"

"All right," said Addams, looking swiftly about him. "We've got an hour
to hide this stuff where they'll never think of it."

"Hide it?" said Peggy.

"We can't get clear with it now," answered Addams. "If that crowd saw us packing them over to the *Wavecrest* that would be the end of it. Anyhow we could never get them up that cliff until they were ashore. We'll have to bury them again, temporarily. I've got the place. We'll sink them in one of these pools under the seaweed. Take the big one by the stem of Fellowes' schooner. That'll serve as pointer. When the tide comes in they'll be safer than they ever were in the cave.

"Then we'll tackle our visitors. They'll never dream of looking for them under the water, and I've got a plan to put them off the scent altogether."

They carried the heavy boxes to the rock-rimmed pool and sunk them to the bottom, thrusting them beneath great beards of weed that effectually hid them from all view, save that of the startled and protesting rock-fish, and left the incoming tide to play guardian.

Then, suddenly conscious of exhaustion and the need of food, they climbed back to the ridge. Beyond the reef, the *Lei Lehua* was tacking up for the entrance.

They hurried with Selim to the shore of the lagoon and reached the *Wavecrest* before the other schooner had negotiated the passage.

"Down below with you, Peggy!" cried Addams. "Orders! You can help Selim get us something hot to eat and drink. They know you're aboard, of course, but there's no good showing yourself. They're a tough crowd, but I think we can handle them. You're all tired out. Better try and get some sleep."

"Sleep!" exclaimed the girl indignantly. "Sleep! While you're fighting off that crowd of pirates?"

"There isn't going to be any fighting, for the present, I think," said Addams. "I'm going to try a bluff on them. I'm going to tell them we couldn't find it. It may work. Help me get the rifles loaded, Jim; it's as well to be prepared, and we'll serve out the automatics."

The *Lei Lehua*, in somewhat lubberly fashion, made the lagoon in safety, and dropped anchor about a quarter of a mile away. There was a commotion of orders and men handling the sails, which were finally furled in bungling style.

A boat was launched and pulled toward the *Wavecrest*. In the stern were Tuan Yuck and Henley, with four Chinese effectively handling the oars.

XXIII
ADDAMS PLAYS AT CHESS WITH TUAN YUCK

ADDAMS WENT TO THE RAIL AS THE BOAT CAME ALONGSIDE.

"Keep your boathook clear there!" he shouted. "What do you want?"

"We want to come aboard and have a talk with you, Mr. Addams," said

Henley. "Me and Tuan Yuck here. You've been too smart for us this first trick, but the game ain't played out by a long shot. There's twenty men with us who ain't feelin' over an' above good-tempered. Might's right when it comes to hard cash. We're four to one. Better let us come aboard for a chat. Maybe we can come to terms."

Addams appeared to be reflecting.

"Who am I dealing with?" he demanded. "One's enough!"

Tuan Yuck looked up imperturbably.

"You'll deal with me," he said.

"Then you can come," returned Addams, "but you alone. Come 'round to the side ladder."

Henley started to bluster, but a look from Tuan Yuck quieted him. The boat came around to the starboard side, the Chinaman ascended the ladder, looking keenly about him and at Addams' orders the men rowed a short distance away and lay on their oars.

Tuan Yuck surveyed Ah Sing and his two compatriots with the hint of a smile. His eyes took in everything with a swift sweep, from deck to mast-trucks. Then he turned to Addams and Winton.

"Shall we talk on deck?" he asked.

Addams nodded.

"I have to congratulate you," he said. "I have a suspicion as to how you got out. Of course you had trailed that blundering fool Henley with his idiotic disguise he was so proud of. I am glad the young lady is no longer uncomfortable. But it seems to me a dangerous place for her aboard. It may have occurred to you the same way?"

Addams and Winton kept silent.

"We overlooked this schooner, too," went on the Chinaman. "I understood her owner was on the coast and she could not be obtained. That was more of Henley's asininity. I only came into the matter at the last moment. I regret that Henley should have fired at you. It was unnecessary. Bloodshed is unpleasant—unless as a last resort."

"Well," said Addams, as Tuan Yuck paused, "I don't yet see the object of the visit."

"I think you do," said the Oriental. "I think you do. Let us reason it out. Here is a treasure—three-quarters of a million dollars. You claim it, basing your claim principally upon the fact that you know where it is, gaining your information from a man who, in conjunction with Henley's father, buried it, after stealing it from some unfortunate miners.

"In a way, you condone the robbery by taking, or attempting to take, the treasure. But Henley's son, as a direct legatee, has a claim at least equal to yours. Both the elder Henley and Fellowes were rascals. In my philosophy, which applies merely to the span of my own existence, I see no reason why

I, learning of the treasure and being appealed to by Henley to finance and play executive to his expedition, should allow you to stand between me and my share of the money—particularly as I happen to have the *force majeure*. Through Henley's sister I have an accurate description of your armament and the personnel of your crew. I assure you it is in no way competent, compared with mine.

"You have a cook and a couple of hatchet-men aboard"—he looked contemptuously at Ah Sing and his fellows, who stood forward, watching the discussion—"while I have fourteen excellent gunmen—to say nothing of Henley's riff-raff, who will fight well enough when primed with whisky and the prospect of gold.

"We both have a woman aboard. They are of different fibers—"

"You can leave all mention of Miss Winton out of the talk," broke in Addams coldly.

"As you like. I merely wish to point out where you stand. As Henley said, it's four to one. I am willing to take a sporting chance. Turn over the gold and you go clear. If you think it worth while, you can inform the authorities of the—outrage. They will not find us."

"Do you think," retorted Winton, "after all you've done and tried to do to us, that we are going to stand by and calmly turn over the gold to that set of lawless ragamuffins you've brought with you?"

"Lawless hardly applies in this case, Mr. Winton," said the Chinaman blandly. "Law rarely applies to the possessors of sufficient wealth. Gold makes the law. And, as far as that law goes, I intend to administer it. If I thought my men would agree to giving you some share of the treasure as a recompense for your trouble and expense, I would agree to it. As it is—"

He spread his arms in the Oriental equivalent to a shrug.

"Is that what Henley meant by coming to terms?" asked Addams.

"I am making the terms!" answered Tuan Yuck. "Do you agree to them?"

"As far as the gold is concerned," said Addams, "you are welcome to it."

A questioning flare shot from Tuan Yuck's opening eyes.

"If you can find it," went on Addams. "I can't."

"What do you mean?" asked the Chinaman, his voice harsh with suspicion.

Addams shrugged his shoulders.

"You're welcome to look for it," he said. "I have—all last night. You'll see where we dug for it, according to Fellowes' instructions, in the cave on the other side of the ridge there. Perhaps the old man blabbed of it. Some one may have forestalled us, or Fellowes may have dreamed it. Henley will tell you he was half crazy."

He spoke carelessly, while Tuan Yuck watched him with narrow-lidded, calculating eyes.

"It naturally wouldn't be in the cave if you already had it aboard," said the Chinaman.

"I'll give you my word of honor it isn't," answered Addams. "You can look, if you want to. As for the caves—there are six of them. I searched the one it was supposed to be in. I've made up my mind it isn't there. If you want to, you can search the vessel. It's easily overhauled. There's no hold. You can satisfy yourself in ten minutes if you think it will save a row, though, to tell you the truth, I wouldn't mind one. The score's against me so far.

"One thing I'll promise you," he went on. "The first one of your outfit that touches this deck will do it lying down, and he'll not get up again. Also, he will have company. I'll leave you the island to scratch to pieces. We're going to leave on the next tide."

Tuan Yuck's imperturbability seemed to have been pierced by Addams' nonchalance. A film seemed lifted from eyes that looked venomous as a snake's.

"I don't think I'd try to leave, if I were you," he said. "I'm going to look for the gold. It will be better for your sake if we find it. I can not answer for my men. But don't try and leave the lagoon."

"I don't intend to, till the next tide," said Addams. "Do you want to look over the ship?"

"If you will not consider it an aspersion on your honor," said Tuan Yuck, "I think it would be advisable."

Addams conducted him below, where he bowed to Peggy, who watched him with indignant eyes. With Selim they raised the transoms and the bilge-boards, looked into staterooms, fore-peak and, by the aid of an electric torch, the lazarette, until the baffled Chinaman was convinced that the treasure was not on the schooner.

Apparently unmoved, he returned on deck and hailed the boat.

"Take my advice about leaving," he said, as he descended the side-ladder, and, with an imperative gesture to his men, ignoring Henley's questioning, was rowed swiftly back to the *Lei Lehua*.

"What's the idea?" asked Winton. "I don't quite get the hang of it."

"I was playing for a chance to get clear," Addams answered. "We can stand off and on for a week, or even two, come back when the coast is clear and dig up the money. They'll not dream of looking for it under tide-water. We can salve it any time inside of a month without trouble. I've put a strong suggestion in his mind that some one has been here beforehand. It's a doubt I've had in my own right along. They'll get tired of digging and may start quarreling among the crowd before long."

"How about not letting us get away?"

"We can stay here as long as they can. And we can keep them from boarding us. They're going to try and blockade us now, I fancy."

A boat was towing the *Lei Lehua* slowly nearer the reef entrance, evidently with a view to blocking the exit of the *Wavecrest*. Another boat was pulling for the shore. The schooner dropped anchor in her new position and a second boat left for the beach. Two men were left aboard, two more, rifle in hand, patrolled the edge of the lagoon. The rest, clambering up the rocks of the promontory, presently disappeared. Henley's sister apparently remained aboard.

"They intend to keep us where we are," said Addams. "I'll appoint watches and we can try and get some sleep. If that crowd gets drinking they may nerve themselves up to try and start something."

The day passed quietly. The men on the beach kept their patrol and the glint of a rifle barrel showed from the *Lei Lehua* as one of the men occasionally came to the side to survey the *Wavecrest*. Toward sunset the crowd came trooping back from the other side of the promontory, evidently tired and discouraged, talking and arguing in groups of two or three as they climbed down to the beach.

There they surrounded Henley and Tuan Yuck and an animated and apparently angry discussion took place. A boat rowed off to the ship and came back with provisions; while a big fire was lighted. The crowd settled around the blaze while the food was being cooked, drinking from bottles brought from the schooner. It was too far to distinguish more than a murmur that rose and fell, but the gesticulations showed plainly that the *Wavecrest* was the cause of discussion.

On board the latter they prepared for a possible invasion. The Chinamen took the situation calmly, taking the guns served out to them with smiles that bespoke only pleasant anticipation and assurance of handling any trouble that might break.

All stayed on deck after dark, watching the crowd about the fire. The discussion died down for a while after the men had eaten, and there were attempts at singing in broken choruses. Then Henley got upon his feet and spoke to the ring, and in a moment they were upon their feet, surging in upon him with angry gestures.

"It is like a scene played in pantomime," Peggy declared, "played for us as audience."

"But not necessarily for our benefit," said her brother. "Halloo! They're going off to the schooner."

"Look out for a visit," said Addams. "Peggy, you'd better get below."

"I can shoot as well as any of you," she demurred.

"Captain's orders!" said Addams, and she obeyed reluctantly.

But there was no occasion for alarm. Only one boat came near them to jeer across the water and then go to the schooner. The night passed without warning. Just at dawn, as the tide changed to flood, there was a stir aboard the *Lei Lehua*, the sound of a winch, the rattle of a chain and the bustle of hoisting sails. Tuan Yuck stood aft giving orders.

"I believe they've given it up," said Addams. "We can hardly hope for that, though it may be a bluff."

But the schooner hoisted her headsails and passed through the reef, standing away close-hauled on a long off-shore tack, apparently bound for Honolulu.

XXIV

TUAN YUCK MOVES

ADDAMS WAITED UNTIL the *Lei Lehua*, close-hauled to the north, was hull down.

"The wind's pretty light," he said. "They couldn't get back now inside of three hours. I wonder what's happened. It seems almost too good to be true. I suppose they've quarreled amongst themselves. Henley is likely to have a nasty trip back."

"You don't think they could have found the gold?" asked Peggy.

Addams smiled at her. It looked as if his strategy had succeeded, and he could afford to relax the strain that had lined his face and taxed strength and nerves to a limit the girl was far from suspecting.

"I don't think so," he said. "Anyway, we'll find out. This is our chance to get clear. We'll send a boat around to get the gold. They can set you and Jim and me ashore to cut across the ridge. It will take two trips to transport it. Let's get started. Once at sea, and the treasure below decks, we're through with trouble!"

The port boat was launched, putting the three ashore, while Ah Sing and his countrymen rowed around the cape. Selim was left on board. In case of the sudden return of the schooner or any signs of alarm he was to fire three shots from his rifle and, if possible, warn them from the ridge. All went armed. Even Peggy carried a spare automatic pistol. Addams was determined to carry out precaution to the finish, clear though the coast seemed to be.

The day was clear and cloudless, the sun brilliant. Flocks of birds wheeled crying in the blue, and the weather seemed a harbinger of ultimate success.

As the three neared the cliff, after watching the boat disappear behind a headland, a figure came hesitatingly from the rocks and advanced haltingly toward them, dragging one foot over the sand. It was Henley, woebegone, crestfallen, one hand raised in deprecation of expected hostilities.

He essayed a cringing smile as Addams, covering him with his automatic, ordered him to keep his distance.

"I can't do you any harm," whined Henley, holding his hands high above his head. "I was afraid to come out at first, knowing you held hard thoughts against me, but I'm down. I'm at your mercy. I had a right to a share of the gold, if any one did, but it's gone. Fellowes has played us all a dirty trick. He's laughing in his grave at all of us now, the canting hypocrite!"

"Why are you left behind?" asked Addams sternly.

"Why? Because I trusted to a slant-eyed, yeller-skinned cur who turned on me after all I've done for him. Why? Because I'm marooned. That's why. Marooned on an island where there ain't no food, nor no water! Left us to die of starvation and thirst, —— them! Without a drop or crum!"

He shook his clenched fists in imprecation.

"I didn't have you treated hard, miss," he appealed to Peggy. "I left my sister behind to see you wasn't left without food. You won't see me left here to die, will you?"

He threw himself on the sand, his hands clutching at the grit, a spectacle of despair.

"Who do you mean by 'us'?" asked Addams. "Is your sister here too?"

Henley, still groveling, raised his head.

"She's back there," he said. "You ain't going to be hard on a woman?"

From a niche in the cliff-wall came the woman, clad in sailor's clothes like a man, grimly defiant as she walked toward them.

"We can't leave them to die, Archer," pleaded Peggy.

Addams hesitated. It was no time to consider the ultimate disposition of the miserable pair, though thoughts of punishment for their treatment of Peggy in particular, were still paramount. At the sight of the girl's face he yielded, temporarily.

"We won't leave them here," he said. "Get up, man!" he told Henley. "We'll take you back to Honolulu. You," he added to the woman, "can stay here. We can use your brother."

Henley was profuse in his thanks and protestations of willingness and repentance. Addams cut him short, ordering him to lead the way across the promontory. The woman retreated to the shadow of the cliff, silent, uncompromising, as she had advanced.

The tide was falling when they gained the beach, the spur of the timber of Fellowes' schooner awash on the surf. Presently the boat with the Chinese came around the cape and made a landing on the sand, the Orientals hauling her up a little way on the beach, close to the remnant of the wreck and the pool where they had left the treasure, its rocks already showing above the retreating tide.

The men waded in to their knees, Henley helping with the rest, despite the handicap of his lame foot and a visible lack of strength in handling the heavy boxes as they retrieved them from the weedy pool and set them one by one beside the boat.

Peggy watched the work for a while, then wandered to the caves to see what evidence she could find of the disappointing search by the men from the *Lei Lehua*.

As the last box but one was set beside the rest and they halted for a brief respite, Henley sat limply on the thwart of the boat.

"A smart trick, Mr. Addams," he said. "I might have known you was too smart for me at the beginning. And you've fooled Tuan Yuck too. It galled him and I'm glad of it."

He put his hand to his side, breathing heavily.

"Might I rest a bit?" he asked. "I ain't as husky as I was a few years ago."

At Addams' nod he limped up the beach to the cliff and lay prone on the sand. Ah Sing and Foo Chin started to bring up the last box, Addams and Winton standing by the boat. Loo Chow, who had cut his bare foot on some coral, seated himself on a rock near Henley and examined his wound, binding it up in his neckerchief.

There was a sudden cry and Peggy came flying toward the boat from the caves, calling as she ran. A volley of shots sounded from behind her, the bullets sending up little spurts of sand. One thudded into a box, another hummed by Addams' ear as he snatched a rifle from where they had placed them in the bottom of the boat, and commenced firing from his hip at four men who came from the mouth of the caves, pumping their Winchesters as fast as they could work the mechanism.

One of them fell sprawling on the sand.

"Get behind the boxes, Peggy," cried Addams as he reached her. "I'll be with you right away."

He retreated slowly, firing at the men, who had halted before the fusillade that now came from Winton, Ah Sing and Foo Chin. A bullet flipped through the side of Addams' shirt, and another plowed through the sand at his foot, ripping part of the sole from his shoe as he gained the barricade of the treasure chests in safety, and dropped down beside Peggy.

"Henley's done for Loo Chow," said Winton. "He knifed him!"

Addams glanced over his shoulder to where Loo Chow sat huddled against his rock, the bright blood showing against his blouse. A bullet struck one of the iron hoops of a box with a *spang* and fell spent in the midst of them, coming from the direction of Henley, who had snatched Loo Chow's automatic from his belt and, hidden behind a boulder, was firing at them.

A growl came from Foo Chin. He pointed his rifle upward at the cliff and fired. Some one in the act of dropping down a rifle to Henley shrieked and spun about, falling, saving a drop to the beach by clutching at the edge of the precipice.

"It's Henley's sister," cried Peggy. "He's killed her."

"Ugh!" grunted the big Chinaman, refilling his magazine.

He spoke in rapid dialect to Ah Sing, who interpreted:

"He say he no know she woman. She dress all same man. Now she ghost."

Foo Chin sighted rapidly and fired once more at Henley who was creeping out from the shelter of his rock to gain the rifle. The bullet hit the weapon as Henley's hand was closing on the butt, and he swiftly sought cover again.

For a moment there was a lull. Henley appeared to have exhausted his ammunition. Peggy seized the pause to explain.

"I went into the cave," she said, "our cave, and walked right on to them. They hadn't heard me and they were all on the sand crawling toward the entrance. Then I ran and they started firing."

"You've probably saved the day," said Addams. "That's a return move of Tuan Yuck. He left them behind to take us by surprise, with Henley to talk us into thinking they had left for good. He didn't leave his own men, I notice, but put it up to Henley. We'll have to get out of this or we'll have the rest of them back.

A warning came from Winton. The sagging body of Loo Chow seemed to have taken on life, moving jerkily. It fell forward as Henley, whipping the belt from his victim, yelled in defiance while he secured the extra cartridges. Only his arm showed from the shelter of the rock, but Foo Chin sent the sand flying close to it, evincing his disappointment at the miss by chattering to Ah Sing.

"He say he get him bimeby, sure," said the latter. "He speak, Loo Chow all same his blotheh. Henley he kill Loo Chow, Foo Chin he kill Henley, sure."

"If we could only get him out from that rock," said Addams, "we could get the boat loaded and away. Those chaps in the cave are a lot of cowards. One of us can keep the three of them back. Henley's too close to be pleasant and he's making better shooting of it."

The rock behind which Henley was hidden was heavily fringed with seaweed and it was hard to tell from where the next shot would come. The body of Loo Chow lay in front and to one side of it, and they were repugnant at the thought of hitting it with their own bullets.

Meanwhile, as Addams said, Henley was getting the range. They moved two of the boxes to bulwark them, but the angle of fire was still acute enough for a well-aimed shot to do damage.

The three in the cave, who had left their comrade to struggle on the sand till he died, fired at desultory intervals, but they appeared afraid to expose themselves and the bullets went wild.

A shot rang out from the summit of the cliff. The figure of the woman still lay there but, close by, Selim, brought from the schooner by the firing, was making a target of Henley with his rifle. The Arab was not the best of shots, but the sand showed where he was finding the range.

Henley, finding the cross-fire too hot for safety, sprang from his shelter and ran in uneven leaps, with surprising swiftness for his lameness, under the protection of the cliff from Selim, dodging from loose boulder to boulder as they fired at the flying mark. They were out of range of his automatic now and Addams, anxious to get away before Tuan Yuck returned, issued new orders.

"Keep the cave-mouth covered, Jim," he said. "Peggy, see if you can find it. That's fine!" he cried, as a bullet from the rifle he had handed her clipped the rock at the entrance to the cavern and ricocheted inside. "Keep firing; don't aim too high. That's better! Any sign of the ship?" he shouted up at Selim.

The Arab, still taking ineffectual potshots at Henley, shook his head.

"Stay there and keep a lookout!" called Addams. "Now, Jim, let's get the boat into the water and some of these boxes into it. Keep firing, Peggy. Lend a hand, Ah Sing. Where are you going, Foo Chin?"

The giant Chinaman, who had been shooting steadily at Henley, dodging ever farther away among the boulders, threw down his rifle and, bent at the hips, glided cliffward. He reached the body of Loo Chow and lifting it easily brought it back and laid it on the sand by the boat. He spoke rapidly to Ah Sing, ignoring Addams' question, then, doubled at the waist, started after Henley.

"He say, we take Loo Chow to ship. He go kill. Bimeby he come back," said Ah Sing.

Foo Chin continued toward Henley in the face of a furious fire from the latter's automatic. Henley reached the last of the rocks, broke into the open and disappeared around a buttress of the rocks, Foo Chin in swift pursuit.

The three men got the boat into the water under cover of Peggy's rifle and carried half the cases aboard.

"Now, Peggy," said Addams, "you go in. Give me the rifle."

He took it, slipping in fresh cartridges.

"Aren't you coming?" she asked.

"Next trip," he said. "Jim and Ah Sing will row you to the schooner, and then Ah Sing will come back for me and the rest of the gold—and Loo Chow's body," he added in an aside to Ah Sing, who nodded understandingly.

"Please, Peggy," he asked as the girl hesitated. "Make her lie down, Jim. I'll hold these chaps back easily enough, but they are liable to take a shot at you as you pass them."

Winton picked up his sister in his arms and waded out with her to where Ah Sing held the boat on the tide. He set her in the stern with orders to crouch below the gunwale, which she mutinously disobeyed, and took his place on the forward thwart, his rifle across his knees, while Ah Sing took up the oars and put his sturdy back into the swing, keeping well out in the lagoon.

A spurt of fire came from the cave, answered by a shot from Winton. A man pitched headlong from the cave-mouth on to the sand and Winton's voice came triumphantly over the water—

"Got him!"

The two remaining, either miscalculating their numbers or in desperation, came from cover and, one kneeling, one standing, took deliberate aim at the boat. The bullet from one rifle struck the water ahead, the other gun was never fired. Addams hit the kneeling man squarely between the shoulders, so that he fell forward on the shingle and lay still. A shot from Selim on the cliff went wild. The lone survivor turned, his hands held high.

"I quit!" he called, throwing down his rifle. "I quit!"

"Walk up toward me till I tell you to stop," said Addams. "Keep your hands above your head!"

The man obeyed. It was the broken-nosed ex-pugilist who had met Henley at the wharf on the arrival of the steamer. Covering him with his automatic, Addams searched him for arms, relieving him of a knife.

"I'll work my way back," said the man, "if you'll take me."

"Not you," replied Addams. "You'll stay here till your own schooner comes back for you. Selim!"

The Arab came down from the cliff at his call and gathered up the rifles of the four men and the one that had been thrown down to Henley by his sister.

"What are you going to do with me?" asked the man.

"I told you," said Addams. "You wait here. Get into that cave and stay there!"

"Hold on, boss. That ain't right. You've got the goods. You're going to get away with it all. If they see you leaving they won't come after me at all. We didn't figure on the young lady finding us. We took that cave because you'd dug it up already. Tuan Yuck said you might be playin' a trick and he give Henley and us the chance to make good.

" 'If the treasure's there,' he said, 'you let 'em show you where it is an' ambush 'em.' He's a sly one, he is. He didn't take the chances. Waited, to let us do all the dirty work. You want to get out of it as quick as you can or he'll be back. But he won't take me. He's got no use for losers."

The boat was coming around the cape once more, Ah Sing rowing hard.

"You'll let me go along, guv'nor?" said the man.

Addams hesitated. His inclinations were to leave the wretch to die or live on the island, as chance might determine. But they needed a man to take the place of Loo Chow, dead at his feet.

"I won't promise what I'll do with you at Honolulu," he said.

"All right, sir. I'll do anything I'm told."

Ah Sing shouted over his shoulder as he came nearer.

"Ship he come back! Ship he come back!"

"How close, Ah Sing?" asked Addams, as they loaded the remainder of the gold and then laid Loo Chow's body on the bottom boards.

"He come from this-a-way!" Ah Sing pointed north. "I think he made plenty one big ring, come back all same behind mountain so we no can see. Now he sail along leef, plenty slow. No much wind."

Addams looked around for Foo Chin, loath to leave him. There was no one in sight and he had heard no sound of shots.

"Foo Chin, he come bimeby all li'," said Ah Sing. "He sabby come to schooneh. Suppose he no come I go get him. Tuan Yuck no get here one hour yet."

Selim and the survivor of Henley's ambuscade took the oars, with Addams and Ah Sing in the stern, the latter squatting on the bottom board, steadying the body of his dead comrade. They rowed swiftly, the renegade in particular needing no urging, evidently assured of a scant welcome from Tuan Yuck.

The breeze was light and changeable, though it seemed to be growing stronger and steadier from the north. As they rounded the cape, they could see the *Lei Lehua* close to the reef at the northern end of the island, making slow progress under the lee of the big crater.

On board the *Wavecrest*, Addams could see Peggy busy throwing the gaskets off the sails, and Winton working at the forward capstan, heaving short the anchor-cable in readiness for instant departure.

They shot alongside and the gold was taken up the side-ladder and deposited for the time on deck with the rest.

"Touch and go!" cried Winton. "We only sighted them as they rounded the crater. Selim couldn't see them from the ridge."

Ah Sing and Selim had carried the body of Loo Chow forward and now came aft again.

"Here's an extra hand," said Addams, indicating the renegade who stood by the rail. "I've promised to take him back. Keep your eyes on him, Jim."

"Where are you going?" asked Winton. "We haven't any time to lose, Archer. And where's Foo Chin?"

"That's what Ah Sing and I are going to find out," Addams answered, as the Chinaman followed him into the boat. "Get up your mainsail; I'll be back in time."

They swiftly covered the distance to the shore and raced across the sands to the ridge, up which they scrambled, following it north in the direction taken by Henley and Foo Chin. Along the reef the *Lei Lehua*, slowly crept toward the entrance to the lagoon.

XXV
CHECKMATE

ADDAMS AND AH SING RACED ALONG THE PROMONTORY RIDGE, bending low to avoid observation from the *Lei Lehua*. There was little time to spare in the search and every moment increased the risks to the maximum that Addams was willing to take on behalf of Foo Chin.

In the lagoon the *Wavecrest*, all sails set, her anchor ready to peak, was mirrored in the water, only casually flawed by the uncertain breeze. The *Lei Lehua* beyond the reef, close to the coral, yawed unevenly in the furtive spells, barely under steerageway.

They looked eagerly for signs of Henley and Foo Chin. The little beach along which the giant Chinaman had pursued the killer of his tong brother was deserted. At the crater end was a rubble of lava boulders, forming a rough stairway to the rim of the bowl, up which the chase must have progressed, unless both were lying somewhere among the rocky masses, dead at each other's hands.

They scrambled up the last rise, panting with their efforts, and looked down into the burned-out pit of Kalaulipelipe.

A bullet zipped between the two of them and a chink of *tufa* splintered at Addams' feet. A wisp of smoke showed from the rail of the *Lei Lehua* and the report of a rifle floated up to them.

"Saw us through the glasses," said Addams. "Get under cover, Ah Sing. They must realize their little plan to catch us napping failed. We haven't a minute to lose; they'll be firing at the *Wavecrest* as soon as they get in range. As long as they've seen us, Ah Sing, give Foo Chin a hail."

Ah Sing made a trumpet of his palms and shouted:

"*Hi-i-i-lo-ah!!*"

A flock of birds rose like spray from the farther side of the crater-bowl, as the echoes bandied the call back and forth. Beneath them the abrupt slope was hummocked with blocks of lava of all shapes and sizes. Ah Sing grasped Addams by the wrist and pointed downward, shouting once more.

Foo Chin was searching among the masses of lava as persistently as a hound that has run his fox to earth. He paid no attention to Ah Sing's signal, save by a dogged shake of his head as he continued his relentless pursuit.

"We can't wait for him much longer," said Addams, who had stayed at the rim, anxiously watching the *Lei Lehua's* slow but certain progress along the reef toward the channel entrance.

"I tell him to hully up," answered Ah Sing as casually as if Foo Chin's detention in the crater were a matter of little moment. "Eyah! He find Henley. Lookee!"

Foo Chin had stopped, alert, listening for the repetition of some sound that had caught the quick ear. They could see the whites of his eyes gleam as he turned his head from side to side. In one hand shone the long blade of his knife.

The crater-bowl was abrim with silence. The wheeling birds had settled down again. Addams fancied he could hear rather than feel the beating of his heart. Below, noiseless on his bare feet, Foo Chin padded toward two masses of fire-distorted rock, between which lay a narrow rift. As he reached the crack the sharp spit of an automatic sounded, then another, and from the other end of the crevice Henley sprang, mounting a cinder slope in uneven leaps, the ash rattling down behind him, one foot dragging, holding him with its fatal handicap.

Foo Chin bounded in pursuit as Henley toiled upward to the rim, wheeling every few steps to fire at the giant Chinaman who, disdainful of his own automatic, climbed, knife in hand, gaining at every stride.

Half way to the top of the bowl Henley turned like a cornered rat with a squeal of terror, firing his last shot point-blank at the Chinaman, who, unchecked, closed with his man.

It was over in a second. Henley twined desperately about the giant, who tore him free and literally dragged him by the collar of his coat and shirt at the full length of one powerful arm. Foo Chin's knife flashed once and came back for the second thrust, dull with crimson, ripping through the soft parts of Henley's body. The wretch dropped in a slack huddle, like a half-filled sack of sawdust, as the Chinaman released his hold, wiped his knife on the dead man's clothes and came striding up the slope toward Addams and Ah Sing, his moonlike face bland with content.

He spoke rapidly to Ah Sing without any show of excitement.

"He speak he want know about Loo Chow," translated the latter. "He ask, suppose you take along Loo Chow to Honolulu?"

"Of course," answered Addams, respecting the Oriental idea of burial. "You tell him Loo Chow's share goes to his family. We've got to hurry up if we expect to get away with any of it. Keep below the ridge, both of you."

They raced back along the slope at top speed, until they reached the place where they must descend from the ridge to the beach. Their appearance against the skyline was greeted by a scattering volley from the *Lei Lehua* that continued as they climbed down the face of the cliff and ran to the small boat; but the range was too great for any precision on the part of Tuan Yuck and any of his marksmen.

They reached the deck of the *Wavecrest* in safety, leaving the boat to trail. Winton had the entire armory on deck, and Selim was opening up cartridges.

The broken-nosed renegade stood apart by the rail.

"Did Foo Chin get Henley, Archer?" asked Winton.

Addams nodded.

"Break out the anchor, there," he ordered. "Get in that side ladder. There should be enough wind for steerageway, with the ebb to take us out. Where's Peggy?"

"I made her go below. We thought every shot they were going to get you and I figured they might try a spare bullet or so at us, so I made her watch you through a port-hole. Here's a bit of breeze, thank Heaven!"

The *Wavecrest's* stem hissed as the impulse of the wind urged the trim yacht toward the entrance. The *Lei Lehua* outside, slowly skirting the reef, and the *Wavecrest* inside the calm lagoon, were practically equi-distant from the channel entrance, which was about half a mile from either of them.

"I think we'll make it," said Addams. "If they can keep us inside, our chances are pretty slim. Once outside, we can beat them drifting or sailing. They'll do their best to shoot us down, of course, but there are two sides to that game. We'll keep under cover all we can and try and make every shot count."

The tide drew the yacht steadily toward the channel, Addams at the wheel. The *Lei Lehua* seemed practically becalmed.

"A good blind breaker will set them nicely on the reef if they're not careful," said Addams. "I don't see why they don't start trying to pick us off."

"They have," said Winton, as a stray bullet flipped through the luff of the mainsail, high up to the gaff.

"Get below the rail, all of you!" cried Addams. "Show as little as you can. Don't fire unless there's something to shoot at."

He stood by the wheel, exposed to the bullets that began to whip by them through the masts, the slant the yacht was making for the reef in a measure protecting him. Suddenly his face grew sterner as his gaze fell on Peggy at the head of the companionway.

"Get below!" he said harshly.

"I'm not exposed here," she protested. "I can sit at the top of the ladder and reload. You're in the open."

"They can shoot right through that scuttle," he said. "Get below."

She set her lips and thrust out her rounded face determinedly.

"I won't," she declared mutinously.

A call came from Selim forward and Winton came hurrying aft.

"They're putting off a boat, Archer!" he cried. "There's a dozen of them in it. They're going to board us!"

"Down you go, Peggy!" shouted Addams. "Foo Chin, take the wheel. As soon as we're clear, let her fall off."

He sprang to the companionway as the girl retreated to the cabin and closed the hatch doors, while Foo Chin took the wheel. The *Wavecrest* was in the jaws of the entrance. Fifty yards more on the ebb would see them free of the reef and enable them to make a running fight of it on a little better than even terms, with their superior speed. Beyond the reef the breeze was steadier, and seaward whitecaps proclaimed the ultimate arrival of the wind.

The *Lei Lehua* was still more than an eighth of a mile away, but between the two schooners a boat filled with Tuan Yuck's yellow cut-throat followers was speeding to intercept the *Wavecrest*. It was Tuan Yuck's last move for checkmate, realizing the impossibility of blocking off the lagoon channel to the swifter vessel.

The water surged at the bows of the whaleboat and the oars bent to the drive of the six who tugged at them. Two in the bows, four in the stern, yelled to the rowers, firing as they came on. All were naked to the waist, with cues coiled above their yellow faces, demoniacal with greed and hatred.

Tuan Yuck was not with them. The master chessman did not travel with his pawns. He stood in the waist of the *Lei Lehua*, directing the aim of the two men beside him, while the last of his crew handled the helm.

From the *Wavecrest* they fired at the boat. The bow oarsman dropped forward limply as a bullet struck home through his shoulder and one man in the stern sank to the bottom-boards.

"We'll jibe her," said Addams, as the schooner reached the angle in the channel still carried on the ebb. "Stand by to ease the sheets. We can't take chances. Now then, Foo Chin!"

"Give me a rifle," cried the renegade as Winton with Selim and Ah Sing sprang to the sheet-tackles. "Let me get a crack at the devils!"

There was no mistaking the earnestness of his purpose. Wherever safety lay for him it was not with Tuan Yuck's following. At Addams' nod he seized a Winchester and jumped to the rail. Before his finger could pull the trigger a red star showed in the center of his forehead and he fell smashing to the deck.

The booms swung amidship, then across to port, and the sails flapped in the half-hearted breeze as Foo Chin steered to the open sea. Now the schooner and the whaleboat filled with the shouting Chinese, were sailing on converging angles to meet at the opening of the reef-lane. Within a minute they would be in actual contact.

"They'll take us on the counter," said Addams. "Wait till they're alongside, then use your automatics. What is it, Ah Sing?"

"Foo Chin he speak some one else take wheel," said Ah Sing. "He speak betteh he fight. Too much plenty they got more peeple. Betteh he fight!"

"All right. Selim—you take the wheel. Keep it the way it is. Steady!"

The Arab took over the spokes as Foo Chin, jumping forward, seized an oaken bar that lay by the capstan and joined the rest at the starboard rail.

As the *Wavecrest* cleared the coral, slanting for the sea, the *Lei Lehua* trailing a hundred and fifty yards behind, the boat with its murderous load came alongside with a rush. Addams and Winton sprayed the onslaught with the contents of their automatics. Blood showed on the yellow skins, hands faltered as they clutched at the rail. The boat drifted astern, three dead men in it, one grasping impotently at the gunwale.

The rest, knives between their grinning lips, swarmed up the low freeboard and across the rail. Their rifles had been left in the boat. They were primitive pirates, intent upon hand-to-hand, cut-and-slash combat.

Addams crashed his empty automatic into the face of one of them, grasping at his knife-wrist and forcing him backward across the rail. Beside him he heard a yell from Foo Chin and dimly saw the giant swinging the club of his capstan-bar. Ah Sing was rolling on the deck with one assailant. Winton, hard pressed, seemed retreating. At close quarters the knife-men had at least the momentary advantage.

Addams rushed his man to the rail and bent him backward. The spine of the Chinaman thudded against the wood before the fury of the attack. His knife fell tinkling to the deck, the grasp of both hands loosened, the savagery died from his face as the shattered vertebrae tore loose the spinal cord.

Addams heaved the paralyzed body overboard and turned to meet a new enemy who closed with him, attacking with teeth and blade.

Winton, bleeding from a slash in the shoulder, had shot his man. Two more lay senseless on the deck from the mighty blows of Foo Chin's weapon. The odds were now equal, save that Selim was at the wheel. The fire from the *Lei Lehua* had ceased in the impossibility of distinguishing the opponents.

Addams, wrestling with a Chinaman who seemed a bundle of steel wires and a voice shrieking foul-breathed expletives, heard the thud of Foo Chin's capstan-bar as it crashed on the head of a victim. Then he stumbled across the dead body of the broken-nosed renegade and fell heavily, his head striking the deck, clutching his savage assailant as they rolled, while he strove to rally his clouding senses. Despite his struggles he felt himself suffocating, his arms pinioned, the weight of the pirate holding him down defenseless, the fall of the knife imminent.

Then a sharp report sounded, the grip of his antagonist relaxed and, as his brains cleared before the urgent summons of his will, he got to one knee, then his feet, supporting himself against the mainmast.

The attack was over. Six of Tuan Yuck's men lay on the deck, three of them were in the boat, now fallen astern, close to the *Lei Lehua*, from which Tuan Yuck was still directing futile bullets, and three had already gone to feed the sharks. Ah Sing and Foo Chin were already preparing to throw the dead men overboard. Winton, his face pale, was sitting on the skylight of the main cabin, nursing his wounded shoulder. Selim was at the wheel.

Addams looked down at the dead man at his feet, lying face downward, a puddle of blood flowing slowly from where a bullet had smashed through his skull.

"Whom do I thank for that?" he asked. "I thought I was gone when I tripped."

"Mees Peggy," said Selim. "She break open hatch and come on deck. Me, I fight with that one." He indicated one of the dead men sprawling on the deck. "Foo Chin, Ah Sing, Monsieur Winton, all fight. One man with you, he try to stab you. Mees Peggy, she break open door and come out wiz peestal. She look aroun'—she see you—she shoot! *Bismillah!* She shoot straight! Then she go below."

Addams glanced astern at the *Lei Lehua*. The wind had freshened during the fight. The whitecaps had worked shoreward and were fretting the sides of the *Wavecrest*.

"Ease off the sheets," he said. "Foo Chin, you take the wheel. Selim, we'll help clear the decks. Hello, what's the matter with Tuan Yuck?"

The *Lei Lehua* was in trouble. The rising wind had found her too close to the reef for safety, and, with an inadequate crew, the clumsy, wooden schooner had missed stays as she attempted to go about. Swept broadside to the trough, she had been smashed on the coral, striking hard and wedging herself fast.

"That's checkmate for Tuan Yuck," said Addams. "He'll not get clear of that in a hurry with the wind coming up."

He hurried down the steps into the cabin to find Peggy. She was lying on the transom cushions, the pistol with which she had saved her lover on the cabin floor. Her bravery had vanished with the accomplishment of its purpose. She had fainted.

That night the *Wavecrest* breasted the waves beneath the stars, her sails sheeted home, close-hauled for Honolulu. The decks had been cleared of all the stains of combat, the gold had been stowed in the lazarette, after one box had been broken open and the coarse, yellow dust and nuggets, panned from the rivers of California so many years ago, displayed and handled and admired.

While Winton ran the grains through his fingers, after dinner, rejoicing at the successful ending of his quest, proud of his wounded arm, which he fondly imagined would be considered by Miss Belmont as no mean trophy of adventure, Peggy and Archer slipped on deck.

Foo Chin was at the wheel, Selim and Ah Sing forward. The sky was a blaze of stars save where the big sails seemed trying to sweep them clear.

The two talked of future plans and reverted to Fellowes and the story of the burned gold. Addams tried to lead the talk to thoughts that were closer to his heart, but the girl, now that the quest was over, seemed strangely shy. Up the companionway came the scent of a cigar, followed by Winton's tenor, between the puffs:

> "Fifteen men on a dead man's chest,
> Yo-ho-ho! and a bottle of rum!"

"Jim gloating over the treasure-trove," laughed Addams.

"Just what is treasure-trove, Archer?" she asked.

He saw his opportunity, and the girl knew by the look in his eyes he was no longer to be denied.

"Treasure-trove?" he answered. "Gold to some people—Tuan Yuck, for instance, back there on the reef. To Jim, I fancy it means Miss Belmont, and for me—you!"

Peggy surrendered herself to his arms.

Adventure

July 1916
Vol.12
No.3

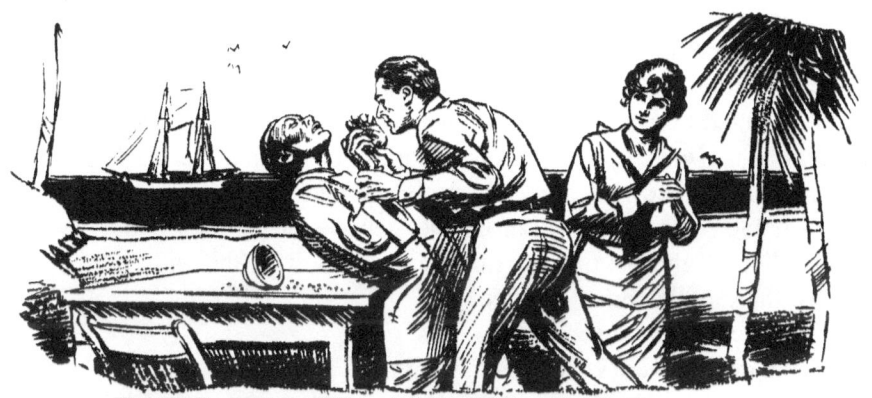

BEYOND THE RIM
A COMPLETE NOVEL *by*
J. Allan Dunn.

I

THE PINK PEARL

CHALMERS DID NOT GO UP to the *Times* office when the *Kinau* reached Honolulu. He was his own man for the time being and, being only in his middle twenties, vacations held for him too much of enjoyment to be spoiled by visiting the scene of his daily labors. The waterfront man of the afternoon paper met him with a grin.

"Come back for the shipwreck story?" the reporter asked. "It's a bunk. The only chap alive's a Solomon Islander who's half conscious and half *pupule* (crazy). Can't find out the ship's name or nationality, what she was or where she was bound. Tough luck to spoil your vacation."

"I'll have to cover it anyway," said Chalmers. "I'll take the rest of my holiday out yachting. Tell me, who's the Chinaman getting into the taxi with two others—the middle one. Tuan Yuck's his name, the purser told me. But what do you know about him? He's no ordinary Chink."

"I should say not. Tuan Yuck! He used to be the whole thing in Chinatown, kingpin of the gambling and dope ring, but he got in wrong with his *tong*, got them mixed up in a wild-goose chase after some buried treasure and he lost out all down the line and ducked for the 'big island.' He must have fixed things up to come back. That was all before your time, Chalmers. Anything stirring on the trip?"

"Not a thing. I'll see you later. Where's the chap that's still living from the wreck?"

"Sailors' Home. If he isn't *make* (dead) by now. The story's dead anyway."

Chalmers determined to cover the story, such as it was, at first hand, to get all there was out of it for his mainland correspondence columns. A wireless message had brought him hurrying back from a holiday trip to the volcano and he wanted to use his own judgment of its news value. He crossed the waterfront, passed through the Fish Market, unheeding the brilliant array of strangely shaped and more strangely colored fish strewn on the stalls like tangible rainbows, and ran up the steps of the Sailors' Home where the derelicts of the South Seas sunned themselves on the wide porch, and entered the superintendent's office.

The official nodded greetings.

"Thought you were on vacation, Chalmers. Have a good time?"

"So far, thanks. Have you got that chap picked up in the whaleboat by the *Lehua*. Can I see him?"

"Taroi? He's gone."

"Gone?"

"It wouldn't have done you much good to see him. He was in bad shape and we couldn't get much out of him. Half stupid from exposure. They were in the boat seventeen days from what we made out of his talk. He was a Solomon Islander from Malayta way, same place Sayers' *wahine* (woman) came from. She translated for us. He's up at Sayers' place now. They took him away yesterday."

Chalmers whistled under his breath. Sayers was a newspaper man of shady character who covered sports for the *Times*. He had lost all caste among his own people by marrying a native woman, one of the tribes alien to the islands that had been imported for labor in the early days of sugar planting. He was an Australian, clever at his work, not to be personally believed or trusted, suspected of too close acquaintanceship with native jockeys and turfmen of uneasy reputation. Chalmers knew him as a fellow-worker and had been in touch with him on yachting events, Chalmers' favorite recreation, and he knew that the list of Sayers' faults did not include an excess of hospitality.

The superintendent grinned understandingly.

"Chap's not expected to live," he said. "Sayers has taken the funeral off our hands. Going to look him up?"

Chalmers nodded.

"Do you know where he lives?" he asked.

The superintendent grinned again.

"Just where you'd expect him to," he said. "In Aloha Alley, back of Kawaiahao Church and opposite the brewery. Know it?"

"Yes. What about the wreck—on French Frigate Shoals. Any one gone out there for salvage?"

"No. She must have gone to pieces by this. There was a big *kona* blowing last week, you know. Nobody particularly interested, you see. There were no papers in the boat; only three dying Kanakas and one crazy one. Probably just a trading schooner. Might have been British or American or Dutch. None of the consuls have bothered their heads over it. They might be doing the other chap's work. Not much of a story in it, I imagine."

Chalmers left the place a little dispirited, though still bent on following up the story. It began to look as if there were nothing in it. Sayers' native wife might have taken the man in out of sympathy for a fellow tribesman, but Sayers was not the kind to encourage that sort of thing at his own expense. He decided there was something out of the ordinary back of the Australian's sudden generosity and as he determined to solve the problem his spirits rose again.

Aloha Alley consisted of a double row of primitive bungalows, facing each other across a tangled garden strip of bananas and motley-leaved crotons that skirted a dozen vine-clad royal palms.

The scroll-saw architecture was covered with purple bougainvilleas and orange hua-pala vines in a riot of violent tropical color. Sayers' dwelling was the second on the right, exactly like the rest, a dozen steps leading to the porch that ran all round the house. The main room extended across the entire front. The windows, like the door, were blinded with green slats, close-shut for coolness.

The whole of Aloha Alley seemed asleep in an afternoon languor. As Chalmers paused outside the door he heard the sound of groans that seemed to be emitted with every breath, a steady plaint for succor that made him open the blinds and step into the darkened room.

Against the farther wall beside a door stood the bed, and beneath the dingy mosquito curtain something writhed and tossed and moaned. As his pupils became adjusted to the dusk, Chalmers distinguished the figure of a native lying outside the sheets, clad only in a loin-cloth, throwing his head from side to side.

The man's naturally brown face was a grayish hue and twitched continually beneath a frizzly mop of hair, stiffened and dyed a rusty red by constant applications of lime. The place reeked of sickness.

Beyond the door Chalmers heard the loud murmur of two voices, one of which he recognized as Sayers'. The other, a woman's, he set down as his wife's. He was about to knock when his ear caught the monosyllable the fevered man repeated. Chalmers knew a few words of native and this was one universal through all the South Seas—*wai* (water).

There was a grimy pitcher on a chair beside the bed with a grimier glass beside it. The pitcher was half full of water with halved limes and a pebble of ice afloat in it.

Chalmers sat on the edge of the bed, poured some of the water into the glass, moistened his handkerchief with more, set aside the netting and slipped one arm about the shrunken shoulders of the man, raising him gently. The body was burning up with fever. As he dampened the flaked lips the native's eyes opened and rested on him with an expression half of dislike, half terror, that changed to animal gratitude as Chalmers wiped his lips and set the glass for him to drink. Chalmers mustered up his native, remembering the name he had heard.

"*Aloha, Taroi,*" he said.

"*Tarofa oe,*" the man responded huskily, as he made shift to gulp at the liquid. His figure relaxed and Chalmers let him down on the pillow he had reshaken.

It needed no medical expert to tell that the spark of life was at its faintest. A shudder ran through the gaunt figure, the jaw relaxed, then set again with an effort.

The sound of the voices beyond the door was suddenly raised, and a shadow of fear passed over Taroi's face. His claw-like fingers twisted upward to his mop of hair and burrowed in it gropingly. The right hand with something clutched in it reached out, found Chalmers and pressed something hard and round into the white man's palm.

Chalmers looked at it. Even in the dusk of the room he could tell the beauty and purity of the faintly iridescent globule, a pink pearl, perfectly round, the size of a marrow-fat pea. Even as he wondered, Taroi's eyes closed and his hands fell lax on the sheets.

"For Sayers?" asked Chalmers.

As the eyes opened he nodded toward the door. A look of protest widened the native's glance.

"*Aore!*" (no), he protested.

His right hand closed Chalmers' about the gem with feeble fingers of fire. The eyes rolled toward the door, the head shook in a final negation, then the body shuddered, the knees were drawn up, the hands clenched and the jaw fell.

Outside, the banana fronds tapped gently at the window. The voices in the inner room were quiet. A fly buzzed loudly.

Chalmers set down the pearl, straightened the limbs of the dead man, drew the sheet over him and replaced the mosquito netting. As he stood beside the bed, with the gem in the palm of his hand, the door opened, a shaft of sunshine pouring through the gap. Sayers stood on the threshold, his wife behind him, the two staring at Chalmers in an astonishment that held them spellbound.

II

THE STORY OF THE SOUTH SEA ISLANDER

SAYERS SPOKE FIRST, CHEWING HIS WORDS as if his mouth were half full, his eyes half closed in scrutiny of Chalmers.

"How long have you been here?" The tone was full of suspicion.

Chalmers put his finger to his lips and motioned with his head toward the bed.

"He's dead," he said.

The native woman brushed by Sayers with a loud wail of *Auwe!* The next instant she had thrust them both into the inner room, and shut the door upon them. Chalmers heard the outer door thrown open; another cry of *Auwe!* Then came the swift scurrying of curious feet upon the porch. In the confusion he slipped the pearl into his vest pocket.

"Let's get out of this," said Sayers. "She'll attend to it. The whole crowd of them will be howling all over the place in two minutes."

He led the way through the back door, down a flight of steps and through a gap in the ragged hibiscus hedge to the road. Aloha Alley was wide awake now with all the native excitement of hysteria over death.

"Where do you want to go?" asked Chalmers. "Make it somewhere close by." He was in no mood to walk far with Sayers at any time and his distaste of the man had heightened with the look of fear the dead man had shown at the sound of his voice. "Isn't there something we can do for him?"

"I'll 'phone the coroner," said Sayers callously. "She'll handle the rest of it. He came from the same place as she did. Let's go to the Art Saloon. I want to have a talk with you."

As they went, Sayers surveyed Chalmers with constant side looks of suspicion. Chalmers realized that this was bred of the doubt in Sayers' mind as to how much of his talk with his wife had penetrated the door. This advantage he determined to keep. There was no doubt in his mind now that there was a real story that tied up with Sayers' unusual hospitality to Taroi and the pearl the dying man had given him.

Arrived at the Art Saloon, they took one of the private snuggeries and Sayers called for drinks. At his request, the Chinese boy brought two bottles, gin for Sayers and beer for Chalmers.

Native fashion, Sayers drank his liquor neat, avidly, with a desire to get not so much the taste but the kick of the raw spirits. Excess had already trade-marked him. Powerful of build, still of some athletic prowess, his general condition was typified by the white duck suits he wore, constantly renewed by his wife's laundering, yet always limp and crumpled as if he slept in them.

His head, nearly bald, was frizzed with ginger-colored hair, his eyebrows showed faintly and the eyelids were scant in the red rims that framed shifty eyes the color of dishwater. Freckles and blotches covered the skin of face, neck and hands, the latter to the last joint of the stubby fingers. Broken veins showed purple along the lines of his jaw and flecked his nose, which had been battered in boxing contests. His teeth were yellow and distinctly apart behind full lips, half colored by a bristly sandy mustache. He walked and sat with a slouch.

Occasionally he showed flashes of good breeding. His articles, despite their sporting slang, had all the distinctions of an educated man. One quality that showed strangely amid his sordidness was a love of music coupled to an intimate knowledge of the art that had seen him detailed as critic to whatever musical affairs were given that were really worth while.

Chalmers, with the rest who gave any thought to the matter, set him down as the ne'er-do-well of a well-bred Australian family, who had developed the degenerate streak in his nature by self-indulgence, slumping year by year as he lost caste with his own race.

He was game. Chalmers knew that from yachting episodes. But his sporting instincts had deteriorated to shiftiness, though he kept up in talk and writing an appearance of playing square and, as a judge of sporting events, he was eminently an expert.

A love of fair play held Chalmers from a close analysis of the other's faults. There were fifteen years between them, and their thoughts and modes of living held little in common. At present he enjoyed the game he was playing, to outwit Sayers in craftiness and get the story he was convinced was in existence.

"You didn't tell me how long you were in the room," said Sayers, elbows on the table, his tumbler in his hand, a quarter full of raw gin, his colorless eyes covertly watching Chalmers' face.

"I hardly know. Several minutes. I heard you talking and was coming through when Taroi called for water. He was in a bad way, as you know, and died practically in my arms."

"I thought you were on your vacation. Funny I didn't hear you."

"You were talking pretty loudly."

Sayers grunted.

"I didn't suppose any one was in my front room, listening."

Chalmers ignored the suggestion. He took the pearl from his pocket and set it between them on the dark wood of the table. Under the electric lights it seemed to give off a shimmer of iridescence, as the down shows on a peach. Sayers' eyes glittered greedily and his fingers twitched as he reached to take up the gem. Chalmers forestalled him by putting it in his own palm.

"Taroi gave me this," he said.

"He meant it for me." Sayers put out his hand.

"He said it was *not* for you. He was afraid of you. What had you been doing to him, Sayers?"

"Doing! Didn't I take him in from those charity-mongers at the home and treat him like a white man? I got a doctor for him, my wife waited on him hand and foot and the ungrateful Kanaka dog held out on me. That pearl belongs to me by all rights, Chalmers. I want it."

He thrust his face across the table, his jaw stuck out, his fists clenched, his eyes narrowed, every inch the bully. Chalmers had no fear of him physically; mentally he felt himself the superior of the two.

"He didn't want you to have it, Sayers. I don't know why he gave it to me except that he knew I was friendly. You must have done something to make him dislike you."

"I did nothing, I tell you, but look out for him. The beggar didn't want to talk—I may have coaxed him a bit."

Chalmers mentally glimpsed Sayers urging his wife to bully all he knew out of the dying man, burning up with fever and desire for rest and quiet.

"Who's going to pay for his funeral, I'd like to know?" blurted Sayers. "Who's going to pay for the doctor and his medicine?"

"I fancy you got enough out of him to make it worth your while," said Chalmers. "But the pearl will pay for his funeral. I'll see to that—and a good one. It must be worth a hundred dollars or so."

Sayers snorted in disgust.

"A hundred. It's worth five if it's worth a cent. And—" He broke off short. "There's no need to waste expenses on him; it wasn't his pearl."

"How do you know it wasn't?"

Sayers sat back, emptied his glass, poured himself another measure, emptied that and once more leaned across the table confidentially.

"I don't know how much you know, Chalmers," he began, "or how much you've guessed. But I've had you in mind already over this affair—there's nothing crooked about it," he said hastily, as he noted Chalmers' face. "It's a clear open and shut proposition. I don't imagine you want to grind away for the *Times* all your life, do you?"

"What is it?" asked Chalmers.

"It's your big chance and mine," answered Sayers. "The chance of a lifetime."

"Go ahead," said Chalmers.

"You can navigate, can't you?" asked Sayers.

The question seemed irrelevant, but Chalmers answered it.

"You ought to know," he said. "I took the *Manuahi* up to the coast and sailed her down in the trans-Pacific race, trick and trick with Captain McParland. I passed the Board in San Francisco for the fun of the thing and I hold my ticket. Why?"

"That's where you come in. I've got to have some one who can navigate and one who's interested in the deal," answered Sayers. "You'll see why, in a minute."

Chalmers lit his pipe and sat back comfortably. His news sense had justified itself. Already he felt himself crossing the threshold of the commonplace, sure that the story held for him a personal element, subconsciously inclined already to listen favorably to the proposition that Sayers, his voice lowered and full of concentration, was unfolding.

"I was at the wharf when the *Lehua* came in, that trip," said Sayers. "Honamaku was on board, coming over for the swimming-races next week; but I passed up a talk with him for the story of the wreck. I knew enough of the Solomon dialect to talk to Taroi a bit.

"The others were too near being *make* to talk, but Taroi had chirped up with the soup and champagne they'd been feeding him. They took him up to the Sailors' Home and the others to the Queen's Hospital. One of 'em died that night and the two others next day. I volunteered to get Faleta—that's my wife—to interpret, and they were glad to let her.

"The *Lehua* people didn't know much outside of having picked them up, drifting in the Molokai Channel, Taroi trying to signal with an oar he was too weak to lift and the rest in the bottom of the boat, starved and nutty with thirst. No name on the whaleboat, no papers, nothing for identification."

Chalmers nodded as Sayers poured himself a drink.

"Seventeen days from French Frigate Shoals—four hundred miles," he commented. "They must have been blown down by the trades and then back again in the *kona*."

"Here's the part of the story you don't know," continued Sayers, "aside from what you may have overheard today. Taroi got delirious up at the home. By the time I had Faleta up there he was talking rot, but I got enough sense out of it to wise her up to listen and keep quiet herself. He was rolling his eyes and chucking himself over the bed with his temperature getting higher all the time, and the doc' told us to come back when he sent for us.

"That was in the evening. Taroi was quiet then and Faleta just translated answers to the questions they put. He wasn't much good at that. Didn't even know the skipper's name—just called him '*kapitani*.' Didn't know where the schooner was built or chartered; naturally enough, he didn't bother his head about it. He'd been hired as extra hand at the last minute to take the place of another Kanaka who got sick. What the hospital supe didn't ask for, we didn't tell; and that wasn't all that Taroi talked about by a long shot. He seemed a lot better and they gave us permission to take him to my place—glad to get rid of him. Early this morning he got worse again and—well, you saw him die."

"What about keeping back information from the authorities, Sayers?" asked Chalmers. "I thought you said there was nothing crooked about this."

"There isn't. What I found out wouldn't do them any good without what Faleta happened to know. I'm planning to do more than the authorities would. If I told them what Faleta knows they wouldn't thank me for it, even if they acted on it. I'll tell you the yarn in five minutes if you'll listen:

"The schooner was called the *Manu*. That's South Sea for bird and doesn't tip off where she comes from. There are fifty schooners named *Manu* in the trading line. I've a notion she was Australian, but I don't know for sure. Anyway, her captain owned her. He had got wind from some native he'd helped out of a hole of an island with a lagoon full of pearl-shell, way off by itself, not on the charts or in the directory. He started out to clean it up in a hurry. You know how that is. As I said, it isn't on the map and it hadn't been touched, but once let a hint of a find like that get out and you've got a government gunboat on top of you, claiming it. The Japs'll swipe anything and you can't argue with four-inch guns; or else it's the British or the Dutch.

"Anyway it's first come, first served with pearling; and this was a virgin lagoon and rich. They ran into the tail-end of a hurricane making the island, and the schooner got blown 'way out of her latitude and got pretty badly banged up. And they ran short of grub.

"Coming away in the rush they did, they were short on grub and equipment. They didn't dare buy any special stuff before starting. With a fortune lying in the open sea for the first one who grabs it, you can't be too careful not to tip it off. All they had with 'em was one diving outfit and not even a pop-gun on board to make a bluff with, in case they were trailed. And they were.

"A schooner followed 'em and they saw smoke on the horizon the day of the storm that might or might not have been a gunboat; they were 'way off the steamer routes. It threw a scare into the skipper, though he figured the gale would have covered them up.

"They tried out the lagoon. It was a big one—and rich. First day they found a dozen pearls, and Taroi either swiped one of them or found one of his own and tucked it away in that mop of his. It's an old trick. The skipper didn't want to leave the island open and he wanted to make a big clean-up—shell and all. So he decided to stay with his find and sent the schooner kiting up to Honolulu for more equipment, more grub and guns, and ammunition.

"I imagine the mate wasn't the greatest sailor in the world, and anyway he wasn't the first to run afoul of French Frigate Shoals in nasty weather. It must have been a bad smash. You know the rocks shape up at nightfall for all the world like a square-rigger under full sail.

"They went crashing on to the coral with the wind blowing half a gale, and a lee shore at that. The mate got his head crushed in by the gaff falling on it when they struck. Next morning the schooner was still there, what was left of it, and they got the boat that was still in the davits and seaworthy, and started off for nowhere.

"None of them knew where to go, none of 'em had sense enough to save any papers. Seventeen days afterward the *Lehua* picked 'em up.

"The point is"—Sayers' voice fell to a whisper—"there's the captain alone on the island with four kings' ransoms in pearls, and no chance of getting away—unless some one fetches him, and I'm the only one who knows where he is."

"The authorities would send after him from here," said Chalmers. "You don't suppose they'd leave the man to starve?"

Sayers looked at him with scornful amusement.

"No more would I. But they don't know where to go. Taroi couldn't tell 'em. He knew the name of the island, but that wouldn't do 'em any good without the latitude and longitude, for there's a dozen of the same name and I told you it wasn't on the chart. I *do* know where it is from what Faleta found out.

"If you were a man alone with a fortune in the middle of the sea and some one came along and offered to take you off after your own crowd had been wrecked and killed, wouldn't you be glad to see 'em? Wouldn't it be worth something to you?" He watched Chalmers' face narrowly. "Wouldn't you give anything in reason for expenses and a reward rather than sit there and rot on the chance of some one turning up?

"Mind you, I might take the trip without any thought of reward if I had a ship, but I haven't, and ships and crews cost money. It's only fair to be reimbursed, ain't it? You'd do it gladly, I'll bet!"

Chalmers, looking at Sayers, wondered how far his generosity would take him without hope of gain, but the main argument seemed fair enough. The man would be glad to recompense them. He would, in his place, he decided.

"We'll treat him fair and square," said Sayers. "There's enough for a dozen men according to what Taroi says, and if that pearl's any criterion of what the rest are, it's our chance to make a fortune and do a good turn."

"Where's your ship and your money?" asked Chalmers.

The sudden prospect of adventure appealed more to him than that of wealth. This would be getting beyond the rim with a vengeance.

Sayers sat up, relaxing, and poured himself more gin from the now half-empty bottle.

"I'll get the ship and the money. You can put in what's left of the value of that pearl after Taroi's buried. That'll help some. That's your share with your work as navigator," he said. "It'll take three of us. We don't want to noise this thing about or we'll all lose out. Some one'll suddenly discover the island belongs to the States or they'll just naturally grab it first. We'll keep it close. I've got the location of the island. That's my share. We don't need such a big schooner. A couple of Kanakas for crew should fix it. How much will it take?"

"We can't charter a schooner under five hundred a month for an unknown destination," said Chalmers. "We could buy one outright for a thousand, probably—one of the firewood fleet might do. But there's the grub and wages, chronometers and other things. Call it a couple of thousand."

"I've got the man who'll put up the balance of the money and go thirds in the deal. It's too bad Taroi didn't swipe a bigger pearl so we could do this on our own. But the man I've in mind is close-mouthed enough. What do you say?"

"We've got to give this captain a square deal, Sayers," said Chalmers.

"You're going to have your say in the matter, ain't you? I'm not going to take advantage of the man. We'll settle that matter before we start. Are you game?"

"Who's your third man. Do I know him?"

"He's a Chinaman," said Sayers; "a top-notcher. He's down and out in a way and he'll snatch at the chance. He'll keep it to himself and he can find the money. I don't suppose you know him."

"Maybe I do," Chalmers said quietly. "Is his name Tuan Yuck?"

Sayers looked at him in open, if grudging, astonishment.

"I don't know where you get your dope," he said. "But that's the man. You know more than I thought you did about the whole affair. But you don't know the whereabouts of the island. I do! Are you on?"

"Have you seen Tuan Yuck yet?"

"Not yet. He was expecting to be back this week from Hawaii."

"He came over on the *Kinau* with me. I had a talk with him. See him first and then I'll have time to think it over. You know where my place is?"

Sayers continued to look at Chalmers in wonderment. Hitherto, he told himself, he had underestimated the younger man. After this he would have to accord him a more prominent place in his plans. He got up, unaffected by the gin, save as to his breath and an extra cloudiness of the whites of his eyes.

"You're on," he said. "You'd be a fool not to come. As soon as we all three shake hands on it, I'll tell you the name and place of the island and we'll get busy. I'm off to hunt up Tuan Yuck. Good-by!"

"I don't like you overmuch," said Chalmers to himself, after Sayers left, "and I don't believe I'd trust you too far round a corner. But I can't stop you from going on the trip. And if I do go, I've a notion the captain will get a better bargain on account of being taken off. It's a real adventure. It's beyond the rim, all right."

His blood began to tingle with the excitement of the prospect. To sail the uncharted sea as the master of a stout little craft; to play the part of rescuer to a marooned mariner, to share in a well-earned reward!

Chalmers was twenty-five. Destiny seemed to be dropping gifts into his lap. He refilled his pipe, squared his shoulders unconsciously and smoked on, seeing in the smoke-drift the palms of an ocean oasis rising above the horizon in the morning haze.

III

The Pin-Prick on the Chart

The three men so widely apart in appearance and opinion, drawn together by the common interest of the venture, sat about a chart of the South Pacific in Chalmers' quarters. The French windows that led into the garden were closed and the blinds drawn.

Chalmers, flushed with excitement as much as the heat, fidgeted with a pair of dividers. Sayers' forehead was dewed with perspiration; he dabbed at it with his limp handkerchief; his scanty thatch of hair was wet on his scalp. Only Tuan Yuck was impassive to conditions.

"It's agreed then," said Chalmers, "that the three of us share equally in the net returns that may be made out of this undertaking from any share of pearls and pearling interest that the captain may make over to us for rescuing him."

"There'll be two sides to that bargain," said Sayers. "He's not going to give us just what he happens to feel like."

"Neither are we going to hold him up," rejoined Chalmers firmly. "It's fair to repay all our expenses and give us a reasonable share, but the man's got to be rescued. That's why I'm in on this. You can't leave a man marooned in mid-ocean on a question of bargaining, Sayers."

"The matter will surely be adjusted," intercepted Tuan Yuck in his silky voice. "I am sure we defer to Mr. Chalmers' philanthropic ideas. I suppose a fifth of what the find is estimated to be worth, to be divided between the three of us, would be called reasonable?"

He held Sayers' eyes with his own and the latter nodded.

"A fair show all round is what we want," said the latter. "Only I'm not in this for my health, Chalmers, nor for the captain's. It's my chance for a stake and I'm going to get all I can. But a fifth ought to make us all fat in the pocketbook. That suits me."

"And I, Mr. Chalmers," said Tuan Yuck, "am in the deal primarily for the money it offers. So that's understood. Frankly, while I admire your impulsiveness, from my standpoint it is quixotic. A man places himself in a false position. I see no reason why I should sacrifice the opportunity his bad move has opened up to me. Life is a good deal like a game of chess. Some of us may be born pawns and others outrank us in opportunity for action, but even a pawn can work its way across the board to supremacy if it is not too self-sacrificing."

"You talk as if we make our own moves, Tuan Yuck," said Sayers.

"We do," said the Chinaman. "That at least, is my philosophy, or part of it. What is yours, Mr. Chalmers?"

"Why, I don't know that I have one." Chalmers experienced a swift sense of extreme youth in the presence of Tuan Yuck. "To get all there is out of life without hurting anybody else, would about sum it up, I suppose."

"Change that to 'without getting hurt yourself' and you will find it more practical," said Tuan Yuck. "Eh, Sayers?"

"Grab it before the other fellow gets it. That's what I've had rubbed into me," said the Australian. "We'll play fair with the captain, Chalmers. It's only natural to get all we can out of him. So it's all hands round on the deal. Tuan Yuck puts up the money or most of it. Chalmers puts up the pink pearl, and acts as navigator, and I put up the idea and position of the island. No use for papers, I take it. This is a private venture and a gentleman's agreement."

He looked at Tuan Yuck and the ghost of a grin seemed to flicker across his face. If the Chinaman noticed it, he gave no sign.

"The interests are mutual. All of us need each other," he said. "Perhaps we need you most of all, Mr. Chalmers, not only to take us there, but to bring us back again."

"That's right!" exclaimed Sayers, almost with the air of having made a discovery. "So we'll all take a drink to success and call that our signatures. It's understood none of us talks outside?"

"Naturally," said Tuan Yuck. "We can't trust any one. They might get a faster vessel and get there first."

"That's fair," said Chalmers.

Sayers busied himself filling the glasses.

"What do you take, Tuan Yuck?" he asked. "Chalmers, yours is beer, I suppose?"

"Mine also," said Tuan Yuck. "The universal beverage."

"Beer for babes, and gin for grown-ups," answered Sayers, pouring himself a liberal tot of the spirits.

"You'll not find it pay in the long run," said Tuan Yuck, lifting his glass. "Good luck to all of us!"

They set down their tumblers and Chalmers once more took up his dividers.

"Now then," he said, "before we talk schooner and outfit, where is the island?"

The trio stood up, moved by a common impulse which even Tuan Yuck shared. The big hydrographic chart was held down flat by books placed about its edge and Sayers set the shaded oil-lamp so that a broad circle of light irradiated Micronesia and Melanesia.

Sayers took the dividers from Chalmers, and held one leg of the instrument poised above the map.

"Motutabu is the name of it," he said. "That means the forbidden or tabu'd island, and there are any amount of forbidden islands scattered over the map. Here's one in the New Hebrides, another in the Marshalls and in the Fijis, tabu'd usually on account of some misfortune overtaking the inhabitants or visiting natives. This Motutabu got its name from an epidemic brought on by eating fish, poisonous there, but not in other places. The place has been deserted ever since, though once a colony under an insurgent chief from Malayta lived there. My wife's father was one of them. So was Taroi's. That's how there's no doubt about it being the place."

"Many of the lagoon fish are poisonous during the breeding season," said Tuan Yuck. "It is a natural protection against being eaten by bigger fish."

"Here is Nameless Isle, close to the hundred and seventieth meridian and just under the equator, between the Solomons and the Gilberts," went on Sayers, "and, almost due south—about four hundred miles, I suppose, Chalmers, is Jesus Island. Motutabu is half-way between the two—just about here."

He speared the chart with the sharp point of the dividers while Chalmers and Tuan Yuck bent across the table to look at the mark made in the clear paper of the chart, a spot unknown to the hydrographers, far off the sea routes, a pin-prick that represented to Chalmers adventure, the surge of the sea, the opening up of things worth while; to Tuan Yuck and Sayers the indulgence in many things that neither shared with the other, but which meant ease and comfort to the latter and power to the Chinaman.

"You can take us there?" asked Tuan Yuck, his eyes glowing like polished bronze in firelight.

Chalmers took up his parallel rulers as Sayers gave him back the dividers.

"Easily," he said. "The latitude should be close to five degrees south. It's east of the hundred and seventieth, between the two islands charted. There should be no trouble about finding it. A straight run from Honolulu almost due southwest, a little longer than that from San Francisco to Honolulu. Call it twenty-three hundred miles."

"How long will it take?" asked Tuan Yuck. "Three weeks?"

"If we get the schooner I'm figuring on, the *Aku*—she's carrying algaroba wood from Molokai now, an old boat but in good shape and with good lines—we ought to average eight knots or better. That would mean three weeks. But the trades are uncertain and we've get to figure on spells of light weather. Call it a month."

Sayers' face lengthened ludicrously.

"A month!" he protested.

"And a week more for outfitting," added Chalmers. "The *Aku* is owned by Afong & Company. Tuan Yuck," he continued, "do you know any of the firm? We should buy her outright for somewhere about a thousand dollars."

"I can handle that part of it," said the Chinaman. "And if you will make out your list of stores I'll attend to the financial end of it. The pearl I can sell for at least six hundred dollars."

"A hundred of it goes for Taroi's funeral," said Chalmers.

Sayers shrugged his shoulders as Tuan Yuck replied:

"I'll give you that amount in cash now, Mr. Chalmers. How about crew?"

"Sayers can act as mate. We should have a good man to help steer, and at least one more—natives preferred. Do you know anything about sailing, Tuan Yuck."

"Not a great deal. But I can cook."

The idea of Tuan Yuck preparing meals struck both Americans as incongruous and they laughed.

"I do not mean it as a joke," said the Chinaman. "It is the means to an end. You handle the ship. I'll preserve our stomachs. You will not regret the suggestion, gentlemen, and I will give you something else besides Chop Suey and Chow Yuck! If you will honor me at dinner tomorrow night I will give you a specimen of my skill. I will have arranged for the schooner by then."

He counted out five twenty-dollar gold pieces to Chalmers, took the pink pearl and left with Sayers.

Chalmers remained gazing at the map till it changed to a heaving sea and the matting beneath his feet to a lifting deck. He set himself to marking off the course on the chart but paused before he finished. Visions still floated between him and the paper.

"I wouldn't have picked either of my partners on personal preference," he told himself. "Sayers will bear watching. Both of them, for that matter. I'd like to know more about the inside workings of Tuan Yuck. He is the original Mongolian Sphinx. He might be either a pirate or a philosopher—or both. His eyes are a thousand years old in experience. He made me feel like my first day at kindergarten."

He yawned, completed his work on the chart and went to dream that his head was a pink pearl and that Tuan Yuck and Sayers were throwing dice for the possession of it, a vision that was not altogether as remote from the truth as nightmares usually are.

IV

THE FORBIDDEN ISLAND

THREE WEEKS OF CLOSE CONTACT aboard an eight-ton schooner bring out characteristics and breed intimacies or aversions in swift and unerring fashion. To Chalmers, Tuan Yuck remained a mystery. The man lived absolutely within himself to his own complete satisfaction. He was not unwilling to talk, but his conversation was so preeminently born of experience, and so based on selfishness that Chalmers never felt he penetrated the other's screen of self-sufficiency. For Sayers, he felt a growing dislike. The Australian was both slovenly and lazy, and his especial brand of selfishness lacked, somehow, the quality of the Chinaman's.

Sometimes Sayers would show the better streaks of his cosmos. In discussing philosophies with Tuan Yuck, between the three of them, Sayers would show flashes of philosophic brilliancy, born of an education that Chalmers envied, while he wondered at the little permanent result it had against the man's coarser nature. And at times the Australian would bring a zither on deck and invest its strings with a quality that seemed utterly at variance with his character. They had shipped two Hawaiians as crew, a sturdy, good-natured Hercules named Hamaku, and a somewhat stupid, but willing younger man, known only as Tomi, who possessed a high tenor that held qualities many a famous singer would have envied for his higher register.

Some days the wind sulked beneath the horizon, and, after the heat of the day was over, Sayers would play such things as the barcarolle from the *Tales of Hoffmann*, or the sextette from *Lucia*, and then drift into accompaniments for Tomi, singing native *meles* full of plaintive melody born of coco-palms bending in the trades and surf, crooning lazily to coral reefs.

Then he would discuss the mathematics of harmony with Tuan Yuck, while Chalmers listened with quickening interest as the Chinaman infallibly discounted Occidental methods and accomplishments, and showed the Orient as the very matrix of philosophy and the birthplace of science.

An hour later, Sayers, a bottle of gin before him, would play solitaire until, soddened with liquor, he would stumble to his bunk to sleep away his trick at the wheel, and appear at noon the next day morose and red-eyed until twilight came and his fingers steadied enough to coax a melody from his zither.

With it all, Chalmers' view-point broadened. His vitality, the buoyancy of his youth, and his ardent belief in human impulse and action that were based on real friendliness toward one's fellow man, offset the cynicism of the Chinaman and the more brutal selfishness of the Australian. A sense of responsibility broadened his mental and spiritual shoulders. He was conscious of a link between Tuan Yuck and Sayers that was at variance with his own ideas of fair play, and, almost insensibly, he became the champion of the unknown captain, marooned by Fate, at the mercy of these mercenary rescuers.

His own dreams were those of youth crystallizing to manhood in the crucible of experience. The wide sea spaces, where the horizon seemed the veritable edge of the world, the vagrant clouds drifting across the sky, the starry infinitudes, the touch of the free-roving winds, strengthened the spirit within him.

Chalmers felt that behind the Chinaman's impassive exterior there dwelled absolutely human passions held in check until the owner willed to loose them. The shifting of the brilliant eyes behind the immobile eyelids constantly suggested the pacing of a beast within a cage that might open at any moment.

Meanwhile, as a cook, Tuan Yuck achieved wonders. From a scrawny, seasick chicken, with a handful of rice and a sprinkling of herbs, he could evolve a curry that, while it wholly satisfied the stomach, seemed, by the sheer savor of the dish, to evoke subtle suggestions of the Orient with all its hidden mysteries of dozing power and knowledge. And yet Chalmers could never lose the thought that, if it suited his purpose, Tuan Yuck would as callously poison the ship's company as he decapitated the chicken that formed the base of his culinary marvel.

He had shaken off the feeling of youth and ignorance with which the Chinaman had first inspired him. Something told him that Tuan Yuck missed the better part of life, had perhaps outlived it in the unknown years of his existence, and he rather pitied than resented him. At the beginning of the trip the Chinaman had produced a chessboard, and challenged both of them, proving them such amateurs before his brilliant, insoluble gambits that they had permanently retired.

Nights, when Sayers shuffled his cards at Canfield and Chalmers wrote up his log and checked his reckonings, Tuan Yuck worked out inscrutable problems on the squares, and at last retired to his cabin, whence the fumes of opium presently came pungently. Chalmers wondered if he sometimes smoked the poppy-seed to escape from his own philosophies.

Day in, day out, they sailed across the changing ocean without a trail of smoke or the gleam of a sail on the horizon, splitting the angle of the diverging

steamer trails that run from Honolulu to Guam, northward, and to the south
from Honolulu to Suva and to Apia. Fortune favored them for two weeks
with a steady following wind, and then they drifted, a squall sometimes a
few miles off, and lifeless, lumpy water all about them, in which dolphins
gamboled or chased great schools of flying-fish.

Their way lay through an ocean desert, set only with the scattered isles of
Johnston, Jane, San Pedro and Barber, too far off their route for sighting, until
they raised the Gilberts and sailed through the group, crossing the Equator
and the international date line almost simultaneously as they entered the last
quadrangle of their quest.

Chalmers grew daily more certain of some secret understanding between
Sayers and Tuan Yuck. The two never seemed to court privacy; there was
nothing on which to base his suspicions; but the consciousness deepened
that there was something between them in which he had no share. That it in
some way was aimed against his own interests or that of the captain, he felt
sure, and cautioned himself accordingly.

On the twenty-seventh day the crossing of his Sumner's lines by double
observation proved their position to be 171° 47' East, and 4° 30' South. He
had checked his nooning and dead reckoning by a stellar altitude record, and
was sure of his figures.

"Dawn tomorrow ought to show us Motutabu," he announced.

Tuan Yuck looked up more quickly than his wont from his chessmen, and
Sayers' nervous hands spoiled the stacks of his solitaire layout. Chalmers
thought a look passed between them.

"Dawn, eh?" said Sayers. "That's only five hours away. Five hours
from—"

He checked himself.

"Freedom," suggested Tuan Yuck. "We've made better time than we
hoped. My compliments to you, Mr. Chalmers, on your navigation."

Chalmers fancied a tinge of irony in the tone, but he accepted the
congratulations.

"Let's make a night of it," said Sayers. "Tuan, I'll match you drink for
drink to see who's the better man of the two. Come on, Chalmers, join the
tournament."

"I have to relieve Tomi," said Chalmers. "I'll be at the wheel till daylight.
Better turn in, Sayers. I'll call you if we sight anything."

"I'll take your wager if you'll match me pipe for pipe," said Tuan Yuck,
producing his silver-stemmed opium holder. "No? Then you to your vice, I
to mine. You'll call me, Mr. Chalmers?"

Chalmers went on deck and took the wheel. The wind filled the sails,
sheeted well out. Above the main gaff the Southern Cross hung suspended.
The slow hiss of the water, as it seethed from stem to stern and broadened

to the wake, the low croon of Tomi somewhere in the bows, produced a soothing hypnosis.

The hours seemed short until the sky shivered, turned from violet to gray, then flushed in radiant, tremulous pink to port. The western sky was pale green, and, above the sea-line, like an etching, showed the fronds of a cluster of palms, the land rise of Motutabu.

V

THE DEAD MAN OF MOTUTABU

THE ISLAND OF MOTUTABU was shaped like a broad-bladed sickle, the lagoon lying in the crook of the steel with low hills, thickly set with foliage, rising irregularly behind the emerald water patched with purple where the humps of coral came close to the surface. The handle of the sickle showed as a high, precipitous ridge, crowned with the clustering palms that Chalmers had first seen rise above the horizon.

Down the cliff fell a narrow white plume of water. From the tip of the crescent blade to the shoulder handle ran the line of the reef, accented here and there with creaming surf. Up to the barrier the free sea held the rich blue of a peacock's breast.

There was no sign of human life. A few birds wheeled above the hills, and once a flight of gulls scattered over the ridge like blossoms in a gale, and went soaring seaward bent on breakfast.

The dawn wind was fair from the sea, though light. Chalmers hauled in his sheets, dropped foresail and skirted the reef, looking for an opening.

Sayers and Tuan Yuck, the former in a high state of excitement, the latter impassive as ever, both scanned the shore line through binoculars, while Chalmers, setting his feet in the rings of the mainsail and grasping the halyards, mounted to the crotch of the main gaff, resigning the wheel to Hamaku, as he prepared to con the *Aku* in. His voice came clearly from aloft in the quiet morning air.

"Come up a bit, Hamaku. Little more. Steady. Tomi, come in on your main-sheet. Lend a hand there, Sayers, will you? Keep her up, Hamaku. There's a shore current. Stand by to let go the anchor. Down staysail, Sayers! Smartly. There's a back draft from the point."

The *Aku* glided through the reef passage into the broad lagoon, the chain rattled out and the anchor struck, holding bottom in eight fathoms.

"Give her three fathoms of slack, Tomi," called Chalmers, and slid down the halyards to the deck again.

"Chap must be asleep," said Sayers. "What the devil's that?"

His exclamation was echoed by cries from Tomi and Hamaku, who threw themselves face down on the deck, lamenting loudly—

"*Auwe, ke aitu!*" (Alas, the ghosts!)

Even Tuan Yuck had started at the sight, and Chalmers stared in bewilderment. From the shore all about them came blinding flashes of light in rapid succession, as if a battery had suddenly been unmasked.

There was no sound, no sign, only the silent hostility of unwinking flares. Despite himself, Chalmers felt imaginary hair-lifting along his spine. Then, one after the other, the glares were swiftly extinguished.

"What d'ye make of those?" asked Sayers. "Signals?"

Hamaku, still prostrate, broke into a torrent of Hawaiian. Sayers translated.

"He says there are spirits on the island lighting ghost fires."

The Australian himself seemed to half believe the superstition. A memory of Stevenson's stories of South Sea wizards burning fires that had no visible fuel flashed across Chalmers' recollection.

"Nonsense, Hamaku," he said. "No *pilikia* (trouble). *Aitu* no good along *haole* (white man)."

The natives raised their heads above the rail and looked fearfully shoreward. Perhaps the *Kapitani* was right. Maybe the *aitus* were afraid of the white man. It might be.

Suddenly they howled again. A secondary line of dazzling lights above the first, back in the hills, broke instantly out in brilliant flame. For two or three minutes they glared, too vivid for eyes to meet, then died away. Tuan Yuck set clown his glasses.

"Reflections of some sort, picking up the sun," he announced. "There were none in the shadow."

Sayers sighed with visible relief.

"My nerves are in rotten shape," he said, wiping off the sweat from his forehead.

"Obsidian cliffs, I fancy," said Tuan Yuck. "Volcanic glass. I've seen something like it before. Nothing like this though."

The two natives plucked up courage as they sensed the mood of their masters, and the minutes passed without any hostile demonstration from the ghosts or further display of the weird lights. But they absolutely refused to go ashore.

"We'll have to leave them aboard," said Chalmers. "I suppose we all three want to go. We'd better take our rifles and automatics."

Sayers came up from below, steadied by his universal stimulant, refusing the coffee that Tuan Yuck prepared and shared with Chalmers.

The two white men pulled ashore with the Chinaman sitting in the stern, a Winchester across his knees. Sayers tugged at his oar, setting a hard pace even for Chalmers, and the whaleboat made rapid progress over the quiet lagoon. They spoke little, and then in whispers as seemed to befit the occasion.

"Chap must be asleep, I fancy," said Sayers. "We'll be a surprise party. Funny he isn't on the lookout. He must be getting anxious by now over his own outfit."

"There's a pile of shell over there," announced Tuan Yuck. "They've done some rotting out. If the wind had been offshore we'd have noticed it before from the smell."

He leaned over the side of the boat as they neared the beach, a covetous look in his eyes, as he estimated the possible value of the shell that lay undisturbed on the floor of the lagoon, brilliant sea shrubbery waving about the patches, primary-colored fishes darting away as the boat passed over them.

Chalmers' mind was on the marooned captain, sleeping unconscious of his rescuers close at hand. Sayers and Tuan Yuck shared one thought—pearls. That betrayed itself in Sayers' nervous tugs at his oar, and a certain feverish glitter in the Oriental's eyes.

The keel slid softly over the white sand and they sprang out, hauling the boat up the slight incline out of tide reach, their rifles at the carry, hurried with long strides across the beach amid scuttling, rustling land-crabs toward the pandanus and palmetto scrub that shod the hills.

To their right mangroves apparently masked a swamp, and perhaps the exit of a stream. To their left the beach was strewn with irregular masses of coral. They had chosen the only practical landing-place.

With the exception of the faint screams of birds high in the hills, the place seemed invested with a strange silence, that infected them with a feeling of mystery. As they neared the scrub they insensibly slackened their pace.

The quiet was uncanny, utterly at variance with all preconceived ideas of a rescue party. The half-explained incident of the blinding flares still held them to caution. A shout to awaken the supposedly solitary inhabitant might bring a rush of savages or a shower of spears and arrows.

Chalmers, scouting to one side, stopped and beckoned to the Chinaman.

"Here's your volcanic glass," he said.

He had stopped at a mirror propped against a block of coral, a warped looking-glass, cheaply framed, of the type used for trading purposes. Its surface had caught the rising rays of the sun as they had dropped anchor in the lagoon.

"That's a clever idea," said Tuan Yuck. "The man knows his South Seas. You saw how it affected our boys. He's set these all about the place on exposed ledges to catch the sun and leave him undisturbed by the natives. They're not particularly friendly in these waters, and there may be other islands nearer than we imagine. I suppose he has them placed so as to catch the sun all the day round. The man has brains."

Tuan Yuck's masklike face never seemed to change, but a certain quality of hardness entered his glance that indicated his recognition of the brain quality of the captain of the shipwrecked *Manu* did not have his unqualified approval. It simply meant a harder bargain to drive.

Sayers came hurriedly toward them.

"There's a house back in the pandanus!" he cried excitedly. "And a tent behind it. No one in sight, though."

They turned and entered the scrub. The house stood in a little clearing beneath a clump of *hala* that had been left for shade. It was a cozy portable dwelling, that had evidently been shipped for the purpose in hand. Its original roof was supplemented by a thick thatch of dried palm-leaves for coolness. Just back of it showed a small tent with a fly roof against the heat.

The place looked eminently practical and comfortable, yet it, too, appeared invested with unnatural silence. There is a quality of humanity that links itself with man's habitation in lonely places that is unmistakable. Tent and house seemed alike deserted. Something of mystery the trio could not fathom emanated from the spot, intangible, illogical, but plainly making itself felt.

The natural impulse would have been to shout a welcome, but the three men almost tiptoed to the little veranda. Tuan Yuck noiselessly mounted the steps and knocked on the door softly, then with a vigorous tattoo of his knuckles. There was no answer.

If there had been, it would have startled them as unexpected. The window was draped with a *tapa* cloth of mulberry bark that did not quite cover it. The Chinaman stooped and looked through the opening. Chalmers and Sayers still stood on the level ground watching him.

"There's a man lying on the bed," he said, and kept on peering into the room.

Then he straightened up with determination, and the mystery of the occasion seemed to drop from his shoulders.

"Come on," he said abruptly, opening the unlocked door and leading the way into the house.

The room was one of two, a wooden partition dividing them. It was furnished with a pine bureau, a rough table, two wooden chairs, and a sea-chest under the window. An iron bedstead was in one corner. Clothes hung from hooks, here and there. On the chest a diving-suit was laid.

Tuan Yuck pulled down the *tapa* from the window and the rays of the early sun entered, irradiating the room, leveling their direct strength upon the bed where the figure of a bearded man lay in the rigidity that unmistakably revealed the hand of death.

VI

Leila

Chalmers stopped half way across the room. It was not his first encounter with death. His newspaper experience had divested it of much of its awe and dignity, but to him there seemed something peculiarly tragic about the sudden withdrawal of life from the man they had come so far to rescue. Possibly the dead captain had been alive when Chalmers had announced the schooner's position in *Aku's* cabin the night before, and had wondered in his last moments where his own schooner was, and if his men would come before the end.

Chalmers' main impulse was that of sympathy for the going-out of the man without a kindly word or friendly hand to minister to his last needs. He forgot the pearls. The long voyage had failed.

Sayers stood by the table, looking at some dishes that held the remnants of a meal. One platter was practically filled with small flat fish, like flounders, that had been fried in meal.

"He didn't die of starvation, that's a cinch," he announced.

Tuan Yuck wheeled, suddenly from the bed he had approached.

"Don't touch any of that food!" he cried sharply. "The man has been poisoned."

"Poisoned!"

Tuan Yuck nodded.

"By the same thing that killed off the natives," he said. "The fish in the lagoon. Probably ate them before, a dozen times, without their hurting him."

They grouped about the bed. A brief look was sufficient. The dead captain's face, where his beard left it uncovered, was blotched with livid purple. So were the hands, one on his breast, one hanging over the edge of the bed at the full length of the arm. The corpse was fully dressed.

"Must have got him right after he ate them," said Sayers. "I suppose it isn't catching?" he added suspiciously, drawing back a little.

The rare ejaculation that Tuan Yuck used for laughter escaped him.

"You needn't be afraid, Sayers," he said. "Unless you are scared of his ghost." Sayers shrugged his shoulders. "His capacity for good or evil will end with his burial."

"We've got no time to bother with that," said the Australian. "The Kanakas can bury him. The question is: where are the pearls?"

He commenced to pull the diving paraphernalia from the sea-chest. Chalmers caught his arm.

"The pearls can wait, Sayers," he said. "We're going to give this man burial, and find out what we can about who he is and where he comes from. Haven't you any sense of decency?"

Sayers turned upon him, his wide-set, yellow teeth showing between his drawn-back lips in a snarl.

"See here, Chalmers," he said. "You've been boss of this expedition aboard ship so far, but you're not running it from now on. What you need is to use some common sense of your own, and if you haven't got any I'll show you where to head in."

Chalmers turned to Tuan Yuck. The Chinaman's mouth was stretched in a mirthless grimace, his eyes gleamed in mockery.

"Dead men neither tell tales nor need pearls, my young friend," he said. "I see no reason for wasting any unnecessary time on this island. The man has made his second blunder, a frequent one, I grant you; he has died too soon."

Chalmers looked from one to the other. Sayers' snarl had changed to an open grin; Tuan Yuck stood suavely unemotional. The partnership had dissolved, the pretense of fairness was tossed aside. He was aware that they considered him as but one against two, a youngster incomparably their inferior, whose will was but a small matter to be set aside as if of no consequence compared to their own desires.

But he felt no sense of fear or weakness. His jaw set as his will hardened.

"The man is going to be justly treated, alive or dead. His family is to be considered. It is worse to cheat the dead than rob the living. You two promised me fair play when I went into this deal, and I'm going to see that you live up to the bargain."

His voice revealed the contempt in which he held them, and told of the action that lay behind the words. Sayers' right hand dropped casually toward his hip where the automatic pistol swung at his belt. At an almost imperceptible move of Tuan Yuck's head he arrested the action.

"Time enough to talk of division when we find the pearls," said the Chinaman. "If you are so desirous of ceremonial, Chalmers, why don't you superintend the funeral arrangements?"

It was the first time Tuan Yuck had dropped the prefix of "Mr." in addressing Chalmers, and it appeared to the latter as if the man's whole mask had fallen. A film seemed to have cleared from his eyes, and for a moment his soul looked out, sardonic, sinister, utterly selfish. He moved, giving Chalmers a clear view of the table.

Chalmers had paid no attention to the arrangement of the dishes. Now he saw something that first startled, then reassured him.

"There's one point you two seem to have overlooked," he said with a little ring of triumph in his voice. "This table is set for *two*. There is some one else on the island."

Sayers kneeling by the open sea-chest, tossing its contents on the floor, looked up.

"Why don't you go and find them?" he said.

"I am going to," answered Chalmers.

He swung out of the room, glad to escape from the sordid company it held. Tuan Yuck stood with his hands folded in his loose sleeves, his eyes still sneering. Sayers laughed as Chalmers went out. It was not until he was free of the house that he realized they had shown no surprise at his announcement. It looked as if the secret Sayers and Tuan Yuck had so evidently shared included knowledge of another besides the captain having been left on the island. If that were the case, they evidently held that person of little importance.

"As they do me," Chalmers finished the thought bitterly.

The resentment he had so often felt in the presence of the Chinaman's inscrutability changed to a determined hostility. He understood that caution was necessary. Until he could find the unknown, they were two against one. The native sailors were not to be counted on, save by the side apparently in power. It would not do to declare war too hastily, he decided.

As he approached the tent, the suggestion came suddenly, that whoever had sat at table with the dead captain was probably also poisoned. That would account for the apparent apathy of Tuan Yuck and Sayers.

He hesitated outside the tent. The canvas was in full sunshine. Any one sleeping there must surely have been aroused. Half reluctantly he raised the flap and looked in. There was a cot bed, empty, a camp-stool, a low bureau and a trunk. Chalmers halted as he took in a survey of the interior and drew a sudden breath. On the trunk was a hat of soft white duck, like a man-of-warsman's, but with a quill in it; something that was unmistakably a woman's skirt, and beside it a pair of shoes, workmanlike, but eminently feminine.

A whirl of emotions possessed him. Who was the woman? The captain's wife—if she was not dead? Sayers and the Chinaman would show scant respect for her sex and weakness.

He squared his shoulders with a fresh sense of responsibility. It was no longer merely a question of a dead man's burial and the rights of a dead man's heirs. The woman might be living, suffering.

There was no trace of any one about the clearing, and Chalmers followed a little trail that led across the open toward the hills.

Just within the brush a spring bubbled up in a little basin that had been built up artificially. The path passed it, leading up-hill through a grove of pandanus. Chalmers followed it, coming out on a plateau covered with long grasses. Beyond this the hills, clothed with denser shrubbery from which sandalwood and koa trees sprang thickly, mounted more abruptly.

As Chalmers gazed, a slender figure, clad in white, came out of the forest toward him, knee-high in the waving grasses. Her hair showed radiant in the sun, but her face was pale and the eyes unseeing as the girl came nearer.

Her arms were filled with great, white waxen blossoms and trailing vines. Chalmers caught the heavy, sickly scent of the flowers twenty feet away.

They reminded him of a mortuary and he knew they had been gathered for the dead.

At first he thought her blind, so vacant was the gaze of the eyes that were the deep blue of the open sea. Then, suddenly, she saw him standing there. The soul came back into her glance as if recalled from very far away. Her lips parted, the flowers fell to the ground.

One short-sleeved arm was raised toward him in appeal. Brief as the gesture was, Chalmers noticed the blue veins showing faintly beneath the satiny surface, tanned to pale gold.

"Who are you?" she asked.

Her voice held the quality of a linnet's song. The blue eyes were still a little vacant, the lids stained with grief. It seemed as if she were walking in her sleep.

Chalmers stammered a reply, trying to find phrases that would reassure her, all the chivalry of his nature aroused at the sight of her brave helplessness. But his words halted.

"I—why, I—we came to take you away," he said.

"To take us away? Why did you stay so long? You are a day too late—just a day too late. If you had only hurried—perhaps—"

The life in her eyes died out. Her hands groped toward him. She swayed uncertainly as Chalmers sprang forward and caught her in his arms.

He ran with her to the little spring and bathed her wrists and forehead in the cool water. Her head lay on his knees. In the checkered sunlight her hair was golden-brown and, despite the moisture that turned it to little tendrils on her brow, filled with the iridescence of splintered rainbows. The very ghost of a girl she seemed, Chalmers thought, as she lay slim and pale, her breast barely lifting beneath the white middy blouse she wore.

His manhood warmed at the sight of her utter helplessness. He wondered what relation she was to the dead captain. Probably his daughter, he decided, still working to bring her back to consciousness, already appointing himself her champion. As her protector he felt himself capable of handling a dozen Tuan Yucks, a score of Sayers!

He felt her body relax. A sigh parted her lips to which the color was beginning to return. The upper one drooped in a pendule over the pearly teeth. A faint rose tint came into her cheeks, and long lashes fluttered. A wave of tenderness came over him. He lifted the little hand he had been gently chafing, and raised it to his lips in token of fealty. She shivered a little at the contact and her eyes opened, looking questioningly into his.

There was a slight rustle in the thicket. Chalmers looked up to see Tuan Yuck regarding them, his face expressionless, his eyes inscrutable.

"You have found Miss Denman, I see," he said. "Our friend Sayers is still looking for—what he will not find in a hurry, I fancy. We are at your service, Miss Denman."

The girl shrank from him, closer to Chalmers.

"I do not know you," she faltered. "Where is Butler—and the crew? Did you come in the schooner with them?"

She was trembling violently. Chalmers gently took her arm.

"We'll tell you all about it presently, Miss Denman," he said. "We are here to help you. Perhaps we had better go down to the house."

"Yes," she assented, then started back. "Wait," she said. "Where are my flowers? I must get my flowers. They are for my father."

"They are just a little way back," said Chalmers. "Shall I get them?"

"No!" They went back along the trail together and gathered up the blooms.

"Thank you," she said. "My name is Leila Denman."

"And mine, Bruce Chalmers," he answered.

"I don't quite understand," she went on. "You say you came here to help me, and I should be very grateful—but"—her eyes filled with tears and she caught her under lip between her teeth—"I have tried to be brave," she went on, her voice tremulous, "but I could do nothing alone, I could not—even—bury him."

Chalmers longed to take her into his arms and comfort her as one would a child. Her broken phrases called up the horror of her situation, alone with her dead father, forced, in with her frail strength, to plan crude, helpless methods of disposing of the body. It was horrible. He marveled at the spirit that had kept her from madness.

"It will be all right now, Miss Denman," he said, conscious of the poverty of his phrase. "We will do all we can. We came to rescue your father. We—I—did not know you were here."

As he spoke the suspicion came to him that Tuan Yuck and Sayers had been aware of her presence from the first.

VII

CHALMERS HAS A CLOSE CALL

THE BURIAL OF THE DEAD SEA-CAPTAIN took place at night beneath a blaze of stars. Tuan Yuck cajoled Hamaku and Tomi ashore by explaining to them the mystery of the flashing mirrors, and a grave was dug in the deep soil of the first ridge of the hills.

The rude coffin was interred before Chalmers called the bereaved girl from the tent to which she had taken her sorrow after performing the last few personal offices for the dead that she had insisted on carrying out with her own hands. As they reached the grave beside which two great fires were leaping, sending out the incense of burning sandalwood, the Hawaiians tossed into the pit fragrant masses of wood orchids and *maile* vine, then stepped back into the shadows. Suddenly Tomi's sweet tenor chanted softly a native lament to the chords of Sayers' zither.

It was theatrical but somehow it did not seem bizarre. The night-wind waved the palm crests like funeral plumes and set the long grasses shivering on the ridge. The reef below them sighed faintly; beyond, the sea ran out in lonely leagues to where it blended with the starry sky. They seemed very remote from all the world and very close to the things that lie beyond it.

Chalmers stood beside the weeping girl in a silence full of sympathy but embarrassed for lack of words. Across the grave Tuan Yuck in his Oriental, priestlike robes was a mystic figure in the swift alternations of flame and shadow. It was he who had planned the obsequies and had persuaded Sayers into at least an outward show of sympathy. Yet Chalmers felt instinctively that all his deferential courtesy toward the girl covered some hidden purpose of his own to accomplish, which it was necessary to win her confidence.

As the music ended Tuan Yuck stepped to the other side of Leila Denman.

"Your philosophies and mine, Miss Denman," he said in his silken voice, "hold many minor differences, but in one main matter they agree—that there is no death. And I think your father, like Robert Louis Stevenson, would choose such a place as this for the last sleep. You remember:

> "Under the wide and starry sky,
> Dig the grave and let me lie."

The girl turned to him gratefully.

"Thank you," she said, "and thank you for him, too."

She took his arm and he led her down the ridge. Sayers came forward and joined Chalmers.

"The Chink's a wonder, isn't he?" he said. "You've got to hand it to him. A bit *too* smart for my way of thinking. We've got to keep our weather eyes open, Chalmers, or he'll get the best of us."

There was a quality in Sayers' voice that suggested that the Australian's admiration for Tuan Yuck was not unalloyed with envy. Chalmers determined to foster any spark of ill-will that existed. It might reduce the odds later on if any issue arose over his determination to protect the girl's interests.

"He likes to play the leader," he prompted.

"And he'd like to get a leader's share," said Sayers who had been drinking and whose voice was husky. "You and I have got to stick to each other, Chalmers," he went on. "White against yellow, you know. He's a sly one. A regular Mongolian Mephistopheles, he is."

They had been watching the natives pile a cairn of loose lava boulders above the dead and now they moved on down the hill.

"The girl's a wonder," said Sayers. "Did you notice her skin, Chalmers? Put pearls around that throat of hers and you couldn't see 'em, they'd match that close. And her figure!" His tongue clucked suddenly. "A man might do worse—eh? A beauty like that, fortune or no fortune!"

The reek of gin was on the Australian's breath and Chalmers turned away to conceal his disgust. They had crossed the clearing. Tuan Yuck and Leila Denman were standing by the veranda of the little house. The light of two lanterns showed her face wan and tired. But she held it proudly erect. As they came up she turned to them.

"I don't know what to say to you all," she said. "You've been—just wonderful."

She choked back a sob and stretched out her hand to each of them. Chalmers bit his lip in restraint as Sayers held it while he gazed at her appraisingly.

She turned to him.

"Good night, Mr. Chalmers," she said. "You have been very kind and thoughtful."

Chalmers, who had felt himself a blunderer all day as he tried to express his sympathy in ways that would not jar her sensitiveness, stammered something in reply. He fancied he felt a faint pressure return his handclasp. He watched her go into her tent, saw it faintly illumined through the trees and followed Tuan Yuck into the little house.

Sayers had already established himself at the little table with his deck of cards and a bottle of gin. He looked up from arranging his layout at Canfield as the others entered.

"Going to stay ashore tonight, Chalmers?" he asked. "I am. I've staked out the cot in the next room. I've no fancy for that. You're welcome to it." He jerked his head in the direction of the bed in which the captain had died.

"There's a hammock on the veranda," replied Chalmers. "I'll use that."

"Going to play sentinel over the lady, eh? All right, you watch me and I'll watch you. She's the best pearl on the island, and so far she's the only one in sight. Some figure, Chalmers. I envy you!"

He broke off, checked by the look in Chalmers' eyes.

"You needn't look at me as if you wanted to murder me, son," he said. "You needn't be jealous of me. I'm a married man. Hang it, I'll lend you my zither to serenade her if you think it'll help you any."

Tuan Yuck interrupted.

"I shall sleep on the schooner," he said silkily. "I prefer my own cabin. And let me recommend to you both the maxim that sex and business do not go together."

"You're a cold-blooded squid," said Sayers as the Chinaman went out.

For the first time the Australian showed the effects of liquor. His blotched face was crimsoned, the muddy whites of his eyes transfused with blood, and the veins on his temples stood out in painful relief.

"Listen, you young Puritan," he said, pouring some liquor into a cup and pushing it across the table to Chalmers, "have a drink for once. Drink to the lady, and no offense meant. An' good luck to you. 'Member what I said? A man might do worse. 'Member what else I said about that slit-eyed yellow devil that's just gone out. He don't pull any wool over my eyes with his smooth tricks."

He drained his own cup and took up his cards, shuffling them in nervous fingers, oblivious of the other's presence.

Chalmers left him, glad to breathe the outer air. He walked down to the edge of the water. The light in Leila's tent was out, he noticed. The lamp in Tuan Yuck's cabin showed like a baleful eye. Back in the dead man's room he heard Sayers singing in maudlin mood:

> "Drink to me only with thine eyes,
>   And I will pledge with mine;
> Or leave a kiss within the cup,
>   And I'll not ask for wine."

He strode the full length of the lagoon, responsibility heavy upon him and, taking advantage of the low tide, rounded a promontory that jutted out from the precipitous cliff that formed the handle of the island's sickle formation. He clambered over the scattered rocks at the end of the cape and jumped on to the wet beach.

Instantly he sank half-way to his knees, the sand holding him in a vise, while something tugged at him as if some buried monster was trying to pull him down. He had leaped into a quicksand. Instantly he flung himself forward, spreading his arms wide, flat on the surface as he felt himself buried almost to the hips.

The treacherous sand sucked at his finger-tips. Try as he would he could not free either of his legs. He battled ceaselessly, fighting off the panic that attacked him. As well as he could he raised his head and shouted. The cliff echoed it, a few startled seabirds rose screaming but, even as he called, he knew the uselessness of it. The schooner was too far away, almost half a mile from shore, and he had walked nearly two miles from the landing-place. His only help lay with himself and already he felt that he was weakening, the insidious steady pull of the sand winning its victory inch by inch.

Every effort only worked against him. At last he lay exhausted, his cheek against the sand. Above him the Southern Cross burned in a sky of velvet. The tide was at the slack. Presently it would turn, and long before morning, if the sand had not buried him, the water would act as his shroud. He could hear the ripples lapping as if they were chuckling at his predicament.

Leila would be left to the scant mercy of Tuan Yuck and Sayers. Tuan Yuck, who had said that "dead men neither told tales nor needed pearls," and Sayers, who had leered as he talked of the skin of her throat. And he would be as helpless as the dead captain lying in his grave on the ridge.

He lay quiet for a while, summoning all his energies. His body slowly sank into the treacherous surface. Once more he raised his head and shouted, only to hear the echo from the cliff and the cries of the protesting birds.

He turned his head shoreward. The rock he had jumped from was not very far away. Seaweed fringed its base. By a supreme effort he threw himself in its direction, twisting his body at the waist and struggling to free his legs from the steady suction of the sand. Cramped until rupture seemed imminent, his fingers just touched the fronds of the seaweed—and no more.

Fight as he might he could not gain a hand-grasp. And the pain of his position was paralyzing him below the waist.

His clawing fingers sank deep, his head dropped and the grit entered his lips. He had come to the end of his struggle. The sand clogged his nostrils and his hands twitched convulsively, burying themselves.

They struck something solid beneath the sand—the surface of a submerged rock. Hope marshaled the retreating remnants of his will and strength.

Groping while he raised his body, he found a crevice and wedged his fingers into it. The rock was only a few inches below the surface; his forearms rested on it. He gained an inch, two inches; at the expense of agony, three inches. One more and he clutched a stout stem of kelp weed. It was slippery but it held, and he got a second hand-grip.

In five minutes he had dragged himself clear, crawling to the top of the rock. He lay there exhausted for a while, then sat up to chafe his numbed legs. Far off, the tiny light in Tuan Yuck's cabin winked and went out.

Midway along the tall cliff the waterfall streamed down like a silken scarf in the wind. At the base of the precipice low feathery vegetation grew luxuriantly. The sand was dotted with clumps of lava. Close to shore it was probably firm, but Chalmers was in no mood for further adventure. At the cliff's end a high buttress of rock ran out into deep water. At flood tide the place was shut off from the rest of the island. At all but low tide the quicksand made it unapproachable.

As he rested, Chalmers reviewed the situation. He had cheated the quicksand, but the human odds were still against him. The death of Captain Denman had complicated matters.

He had anticipated Tuan Yuck and Sayers driving a hard bargain with the skipper, but at least it would have been two men against two for fair play. He felt certain that his own ideas of chivalry were not shared by either of his partners. The Chinaman had frankly said that sex and business were incompatible. Sayers regarded womanhood only from the coarser standpoint. The best thing would be, he decided, to wait until Tuan Yuck showed his hand, which he would undoubtedly when the pearls materialized.

The pearls! Chalmers chafed at his own stupidity. That was the reason of Tuan Yuck's kindliness to the girl and his persuasion of Sayers into a semblance of respect for the dead. They wanted to find out where the pearls were before they uncovered their real motives. And as soon as they did, he must be ready to act.

He freed himself from the useless labyrinth of conjecture. He would need all his wits about him on the morrow, and perhaps his strength. Every muscle in his body ached as he made his way back to the house. The lamp still burned above Sayers' head where he had fallen asleep amid the scattered cards.

There was a canvas hammock slung at one end of the veranda and Chalmers rolled into it. Almost instantly he was asleep, and for the first time a girl's face filled his dreams, the face of Leila Denman.

VIII

TUAN YUCK DROPS HIS MASK

CHALMERS AWOKE BEFORE SUNRISE, with stiffened limbs still aching from the struggle in the quicksand. He had turned in all standing and he now surveyed himself ruefully. Drying sand dripped from him like water, and his usually natty appearance was changed to that of a beachcomber sadly down on his luck.

A glance through the window showed Sayers still asprawl over the table. The flap of Leila Denman's tent was closed. He resolved to swim off to the schooner and secure fresh clothing, coming back in the whaleboat with Tuan Yuck.

He walked to the edge of the water, took off his belt and laid it with the automatic in its holster on a ledge of rocks. Then he stripped and swam out through the cool water with long, luxurious strokes, his tired muscles relaxing, and hauled himself up to the bows by the bobstay.

As he went toward the cabin, he saw Hamaku and Tomi by the taffrail busily plucking the last of the schooner's chickens. The natives responded to his greeting in a surly fashion they had developed of late.

Chalmers took no notice of it.

"Bimeby you bring chicken along shore for breakfast," he said.

Hamaku muttered something and Tomi laughed. Chalmers took the men up smartly.

"What was that?" he demanded.

"Big Boss speak you eat along schooner this morning," replied Hamaku, a spice of impudence in tone and look.

"What Big Boss? You sabe plenty I your boss?"

"Tuan Yuck he speak you boss along ship maybe. He boss along land. We along land now."

Chalmers looked at the man. The native's eyes shifted.

"Tuan Yuck he plenty big *kahuna* (wizard)," he said, half surly, half apologetic.

Chalmers forebore to press the point. It was evident that Tuan Yuck had impressed the natives with his own power through the most effective medium, their superstition. But he determined that Leila Denman, at least, should not come aboard the schooner until matters were satisfactorily arranged.

"You fetch me two, three pail fresh water," he said.

The natives obeyed and sluiced the brine from his skin. He went below to his own cabin, opposite the Chinaman's, and put on fresh underwear, clean duck trousers and a shirt. Then he fished out a pair of shoes, slipped them on and went into the main cabin.

Tuan Yuck's door opened and the Oriental came out, fully dressed. He expressed no surprise at Chalmers' appearance, beyond the slightest lift of his eyebrows at the latter's spruceness.

They rowed ashore in silence, and Chalmers retrieved his belt and pistol. As they walked up the beach, Leila Denman came toward them. Her face was pale, despite its golden weather-tan, but her eyes were clear and steady with only the faint trace of weeping about their long-lashed rims.

She greeted them cordially with perfect self-possession, with something almost boyish in her erectness and the way she gave to each her cool, slim hand.

"I don't know, Miss Denman," said Tuan Yuck, "whether Mr. Chalmers has told you that I am the *chef* of this expedition, but such is the case. And if you will breakfast with us aboard the schooner I can promise you broiled chicken and some excellent coffee. Perhaps you will give us some Motutabu *papayas* in exchange?"

Chalmers, standing beside him, caught the girl's glance and slightly shook his head.

"I am not so lacking in hospitality," she answered, accepting the cue without hesitation. "Though I must admit the chicken sounds tempting. I have almost forgotten what one looks like."

Chalmers, watching Tuan Yuck, thought he saw disappointment in the Oriental's eyes. But it did not show in his voice as he replied.

"That will be delightful. But you must let us provide the chickens." He turned and gave an order in Hawaiian to the natives, who started for the boat.

A hoarse shout stopped them. Sayers, sodden with liquor, unkempt and morose, slouched off the veranda and joined them. Leila bestowed an involuntary look upon his uncouth figure in the crumpled, dingy ducks, that made the Australian flush and mutter something about changing his clothes before he shambled down the beach and went off to the schooner.

The meal was served out-of-doors at a table placed under the *hala* trees. Leila Denman sat at one end, facing Tuan Yuck, with Chalmers at her right, opposite Sayers. The Australian gave evidence that his principal mission to the schooner had been to satisfy his appetite for liquor. He ate nothing, but sat with his hairy fingers beating a nervous tattoo on the table.

The Chinaman waited for the Hawaiians to clear away before he spoke. The quality of the Oriental's mood showed in his glances. His face was bland as ever, but his eyes held the hardness of orbs of polished metal. A sinister sternness seemed to emanate from the man as hidden flame or ice might make itself manifest.

To Chalmers the morning was rife with a prescience of malignancy that pressed on him even as the air. He sat with his mind alert, his nerves tense for action, waiting for the move that should determine what that action was to be.

"In the matter of leaving the island, Miss Denman," said Tuan Yuck at last. "Is there any particular place you want to go—Sydney, for example, or Honolulu?"

He spoke with grave courtesy, but to Chalmers, question and tone alike were tinged with mockery.

"I hardly know," she answered. "I have practically no relatives." Chalmers saw a swift glitter in Tuan Yuck's eyes. "I have no mother—we were quite alone, father and I."

Sayers' tongue clucked suddenly and his restless fingers pressed on the table till the tips whitened.

"You should consider that you are quite an heiress," went on the Chinaman, "that is, if the character of the shell already rotted out is any criterion, the lagoon should hold a fortune. The shells on the beach are typical pearl oysters. Aside, of course, from what your father found already?"

The inflection of the speech made it a question. Leila answered it readily.

"He found a great many," she said. "Some of them I believe are very valuable, though I am no judge."

Sayers' dull eyes sparkled. The glitter in Tuan Yuck's gaze intensified.

"Ah!" he said simply, but the ejaculation was far from colorless. "I should like to see them. I may be able to give you some idea of what they are really worth."

The girl got up from the table and went into her tent before Chalmers could prevent her. Sayers' glance followed her greedily, his jaw was thrust forward. The veins on his forehead seemed to writhe, and his big stumpy-fingered hands worked as if they already clutched the gems. Tuan Yuck sat immobile, his glittering eyes the only sign of life in the masklike face. Chalmers leaned forward speaking in a low voice.

"There is to be no bargaining," he said firmly. "Her heritage is all that is left her. You know our agreement?"

Tuan Yuck turned his baleful eyes toward the speaker. The shadow of a smile, or a sneer, flitted across his face.

"What agreement?" demanded Sayers hoarsely.

"You called it a gentlemen's agreement, Sayers," said Chalmers. "At all events I intend to see it carried out. We are not going to rob the dead or cheat the living while I can prevent it."

Sayers' retort was stopped by the reappearance of the girl, bearing a shallow wooden bowl. The Australian's tongue showed between his teeth like a panting dog's, his face was patched with purple, his eyes bloodshot, gazing on the calabash as if hypnotized.

Leila Denman set the polished bowl of native wood on the table before Tuan Yuck. It seemed to be nearly full of a milky opalescence. Sayers stood up and looked at it. He gave a bellow of disappointment.

"Those ain't all?" he demanded.

The girl looked up with surprise at the rudeness of his tone.

"These are only the seeds and *baroques*," she said. "I always carry the real pearls here to keep them in good condition."

She put her hand into the opening of her middy blouse and pulled up from her breast a bag of soft leather, untying the narrow silk ribbon that suspended it from her neck. About the collar of her blouse she wore a black silk handkerchief. This she unfastened and spread out on the table. On to it she poured out from the bag a number of shimmering globules that shone with satiny luster as they rolled a little way here and there and settled into groups.

Chalmers, who knew little of pearls, held his breath at the beauty of the nacreous mass of varying color, silver and rose and azure. The sunshine checkered the table-top with gold, and in it the pearls seemed to be alive, so vivid was the iridescence. A few were small, the majority larger than the pink pearl of Taroi. At least a dozen were the size of husked hazel-nuts and two, almost perfectly matched for size and shape, were as big as marbles, glorified, transcendent marbles, rosy-silver of hue with a bloom that seemed almost fuzzy in its refraction.

Tuan Yuck's eyes blazed. Sayers, his hands gripping the table, rocked gently to and fro as he stood licking his feverish lips with the tip of his tongue.

"There are fifty-nine of them," said Leila Denman. "They are beautiful, aren't they?"

Tuan Yuck, with fingers that trembled ever so slightly, drew the black square of silk with its precious contents slowly toward him. Sayers, breathing hard, followed every inch of the Chinaman's movements with fascinated avarice as Tuan Yuck delicately turned over the pearls with his pointed fingers.

"It is hard to fix values," he said. "All these are exceptionally well shaped and they are wonderfully alive, owing to your plan of keeping them close to your body, Miss Denman. These pearls"—he set apart six of the gems—"are easily worth twenty-five hundred apiece. There are ten at least worth much more than that. This matched pair I have never seen equaled. Their value is only to be estimated after they get in the market. I might miss the price they'll fetch by thousands. Roughly speaking I do not believe I am exaggerating by saying that the lot should represent between one hundred and fifty thousand and two hundred thousand dollars."

Leila Denman's face matched the palest of the pearls despite her tan. Chalmers gasped. Sayers moistened his dry lips with his tongue before he could speak in a voice that squeaked ludicrously.

"And the lagoon!" he ejaculated.

Tuan Yuck lifted his shoulders in a noncommittal shrug.

"These may have come from an exceptionally rich patch," he said. His voice had lost its silkiness and sounded sharply vibrant. "Pearl oysters are sick oysters and the sickness often runs in colonies or patches. The lagoon may yield as many more like these, or less. Or it may hold pearls to almost fabulous values, like the lagoon of Faleita where Nacre Williams harvested over four million dollars before he stripped it. Lagoons are lotteries."

He replaced the pearls gently, one by one, in the little bag and placed it on top of the seed pearls in the calabash in the center of the table.

"You are a very rich young woman, Miss Denman," he said.

The girl set a hand to her heart.

"It seems so unfair," she said. "Father risked his life for them. If it was not for them he would be alive. All that money, and none of it of use to help him."

"Pearls ain't much good on a desert island," said Sayers, looking hungrily at the bowl with its precious contents. "They ain't pills, you know."

Leila Denman looked at him but he seemed unconscious of his grossness. The man had coarsened rapidly in the last few hours. He laughed at what he esteemed a witticism.

"They wouldn't have been good for anything except to play marbles on the beach with, miss," he went on. "I'll warrant you'd be glad to trade 'em for a home trip."

Chalmers set his jaw, clenching his fists till the nails scored his palms. The pieces were being set on the board.

"Put your pearls away, Miss Denman," he said.

She reached for the bag but drew back her hand as Sayers clapped his big palm over the top of the calabash.

"Hold on a minute," he said. "There's no use beating about the bush. When your schooner got wrecked, miss, and all hands lost, I was the only one who found out where you and your father were stranded—lost in the middle of the ocean. You'd both of you have rotted if it hadn't been for me. I got up this expedition and Tuan Yuck there financed it. Young Galahad there"—he nodded at Chalmers—"was navigator. We were all in the deal. And it wasn't a pleasure trip. It cost money and we expect returns on the investment."

"That seems only fair," said the girl, trembling a little as she sensed the growing excitement. "How much do you want?"

"The expenses have been about two thousand dollars," broke in Chalmers. "The schooner can be resold for something. Give these men five thousand apiece for their investment returns, as they call them, and that will end it."

Sayers laughed loudly. Tuan Yuck's eyes danced behind their slitted lids like a mocking devil's. He said nothing, content while Sayers played his game.

"And you?" asked the girl, turning to Chalmers.

"I want nothing," he answered.

"To —— with you!" cried Sayers. "Because you are stuck on a pretty face do you think our brains are addled? This is a business proposition. It's all—or nothing!"

Chalmers' hand dropped to the grip of his automatic. Leila Denman looked at Tuan Yuck sitting opposite to her, bland, motionless, his cold glittering eyes the only signs of life or interest.

"You see," he answered her look, "our impulses are entirely mercenary. Chalmers has suffered a change of heart, quite natural at his age."

"You promised fair treatment and no bargaining!" cried Chalmers hotly.

Tuan Yuck emitted a derisive sound like a goat's bleat.

"You are still very young," he answered.

"We're wasting time," said Sayers. "I want to get at that lagoon. When we're through with that you two can get a free passage home, or you can stay behind and play Adam and Eve for all we care. Meanwhile I'll take care of these."

He lifted the bag in his left hand as Chalmers sprang to his feet, leveling his pistol at Sayers' head. The Australian drew simultaneously and fired as Chalmers pressed the trigger.

There was only one shot. The action of Chalmers' automatic had been choked by the quicksand. He heard the bark of Sayers' gun and felt the heat of the flame from the barrel as he vaulted across the table and crashed into the startled Australian. His swift leap had disconcerted Sayers' none-too-steady aim, and the bullet had gone wild.

Chalmers rushed his man who was still staggering from the impact. Sayers fired again wildly and in the same fraction of a second Chalmers' right smashed viciously up and landed on the Australian's jaw, straightening him for a second before he began to sag like a half-filled sack of meal and pitched forward senseless under the table.

The girl stood wide-eyed. The table was strewn with the scattered seed pearls and *baroques*, but the bag of pearls had vanished. Tuan Yuck stood at the other end of the table imperturbable, his arms folded. It was not his policy to interfere while others played his game, and the elimination of Chalmers or Sayers, or both of them, fitted in with the moves of his opening play.

"Have you got them?" asked Chalmers.

She shook her head, looking at Tuan Yuck.

Chalmers whirled. The Oriental's elbow twitched and Chalmers flung himself upon him, pinning his arms to his sides and grappling for the gun concealed in the long sleeves, twisting him round and bending him over the table until it seemed as if the Chinaman's back must break.

Tuan Yuck struggled fiercely but silently. Writhing, he snapped at Chalmers with his teeth like a mad dog, frothing at the lips, his eyes glaring, the mask of his face distorted with rage and pain. The pressure of his spine against the table-edge beneath Chalmers' weight paralyzed his nerve centers. His body collapsed beneath Chalmers' weight, his arms grew limp and the automatic fell to the ground.

"Give me that gun, Miss Denman," panted Chalmers.

The girl came swiftly to his side, knelt and picked it up. She was trembling, but she controlled her weakness and thrust the pistol into Chalmers' groping hand.

"I've got the pearls, too," she said. "They fell out of his sleeve."

Tuan Yuck, as his cracking spine got relief, suddenly shouted aloud in Hawaiian. Chalmers clamped his left hand over his mouth and rammed the automatic's muzzle viciously under the Chinaman's armpit.

"I'll kill you, cheerfully," he said, "if you don't keep quiet."

Tuan Yuck knew that he meant it. "Let me up," he whispered. "You've broken my back."

"Put up your hands!"

Tuan Yuck obeyed with a groan as Chalmers suffered him to stand up. His eyes gleamed as he straightened. Leila Denman cried out in swift alarm—

"The *Kanakas!*"

Chalmers, grinding the pistol-muzzle into Tuan Yuck's ribs, heard the soft pad of running feet on the firm sand behind him. It was Hamaku and Tomi coming to the rescue of the Big Boss.

"Tell them to stop," he said to Tuan Yuck. "In English! Quick!"

The Chinaman sullenly obeyed. The natives halted half-way down the beach.

"Tell them to go back—down to the water. Watch them, Miss Denman."

"They're going," she reported.

"All right. Now, do you think you can get me Sayers' gun? Take off his belt."

The girl was behind him and he did not see the strained look on her face nor the effort with which she pulled herself together. The loss of her father, the disclosure of the intentions of Tuan Yuck and Sayers, culminating with the swift turmoil of the last few minutes, had taxed her strength to the utmost. She did not trust herself to answer, but knelt beside Sayers, prostrate under the table, unfastened his belt and dragged it from beneath his body. He moaned a little, and she hurried back to where Chalmers still held the pistol against the Chinaman's body.

"He's coming to," she said.

"Quickly then," he answered, unconscious of everything but the need of haste. "Take the pistol out of the holster. Put down your arms," he commanded Tuan Yuck. "Now give me the belt, Miss Denman. Hold the gun against him. Arms close to your sides, Tuan Yuck. Now, Miss Denman, I'm going to strap him up. Remember he wouldn't hesitate to kill us. Fire if he makes a move. Can you do it?"

"Yes."

She bit her lips in the attempt to steady her voice. Chalmers cast a swift glance at her. Her face was deadly white, but her chin was uptilted and her eyes narrowed with determination. He swiftly ran Sayers' belt about the Chinaman's body, cinching it until the leather sank into the flesh.

"That holds him," he said triumphantly. "Now for the legs." He used his own belt to truss the other's ankles and leaned Tuan Yuck helplessly against a tree. "That's all over," said Chalmers. "Now for Sayers. Bravo for you, Miss Denman."

Even as he spoke the girl swayed, her eyes closed, the pistol dropped from her hand and she swooned. Chalmers caught her about the waist as she fell. Under the table Sayers was dragging himself up to his knees. Down the beach Hamaku and Tomi had jumped into the whaleboat and were pulling furiously for the schooner.

Chalmers thought rapidly. Hampered with the unconscious girl, the odds were against him. The rifles they had brought ashore the day before were still in the house, but there were more aboard the schooner. If Hamaku had gone for them they might be picked off at long range unless they sought cover.

He lowered the girl gently to the ground and picked up his own pistol from beside the table, as Sayers got waveringly to his feet and lunged toward him. Sidestepping, he brought the butt of the automatic down on the top of the Australian's head. Blood spurted and Sayers fell like a log.

Chalmers thrust all the guns into the bosom of his shirt and stooped to pick up the girl once more. Tuan Yuck still leaned helplessly against the tree, his eyes malignant as a shark's. The thought came into Chalmers' brain to kill both him and Sayers and make an end of it. For a second he hesitated.

A bullet came whining through the little grove high above his head. Hamaku had remembered the other rifles and was firing from the deck of the schooner. Another shot came lower but wide and to the right. With the girl in his arms Chalmers ran to the house, the bullets trailing him, sped up the veranda steps and into the house where he laid Leila on the bed.

The Winchesters were leaning against the bureau. He pumped a cartridge into the lever of one of them and knelt by the door to aim. Hamaku had jumped into the boat and was crouching in the bows while Tomi rowed for the shore.

Guessing at the range, Chalmers fired. The bullet hit the water and ricocheted, skipping over the surface close to the boat.

Hamaku replied and the shot smashed the window of the house, thudding into the wall above the girl and going on through the frail woodwork. Chalmers wondered at the native's skill, then remembered he had been a member of the Hawaiian National Guard. The flimsy house was only a protection in the way it might hide them from his aim.

He took the senseless girl from the bed and carried her into the next room and put her on the floor for safety. Back at the door again, he found the boat had landed under the cover of some rocks between which Hamaku and Tomi were now crawling toward the clearing.

IX

CHECK FOR TUAN YUCK

THE MINUTES PASSED IN A SILENCE THAT WAS OMINOUS. The trunks of the *hala* trees, though neither big nor thickly set, yet afforded a cover that made accurate shooting difficult. The beach itself, while fairly open from the front of the house to the water, was strewn with masses of lava and coral rock, behind which a whole company might advance in open order and never expose themselves.

Once the natives succeeded in getting in touch with Tuan Yuck and Sayers, the odds would be four to one; three to one actually, as far as firearms were concerned. They had brought six Winchesters on the trip besides the three automatics. These last, one out of commission until it could be cleaned of the sand, were in Chalmers' possession with three of the rifles. But his supply of cartridges was limited. And, if the others attacked simultaneously on three sides, they could riddle the house with every chance of at least crippling the girl and himself.

One hope lay in the smash over the head he had given the Australian with the pistol. He hoped he had put him seriously out of commission.

Either of them, he thought, would have had no compunction in killing him in cold blood. They had tried to. It would not have been murder if he had retaliated in kind. But the girl might not have so considered it. He wondered how much she thought him tarred with the same brush as the others. Their plan of getting money for the rescue, even on a compromise basis of reward, appeared to him now entirely too mercenary for him to have ever considered. That was the reason why Tuan Yuck and Sayers, reading him aright, had concealed their knowledge of the girl, fearing he would be overscrupulous.

They had used him as a cat's-paw. He burned with resentment at the thought. They had treated him as a youngster, but from now on they would find him a different person to deal with.

If only he could get on even terms! The Hawaiians were evidently under Tuan Yuck's control. That the Chinaman was absolutely treacherous was assured. He believed that the Oriental's crafty brain held a determination to ultimately take the entire treasure for himself after he had used, first Chalmers, and now Sayers to secure it.

Chalmers watched with every sense alert. He did not dare leave the doorway lest the natives should make a successful rush across the open to liberate Tuan Yuck. And all this time the girl lay unconscious. He was not afraid for her life, save from a stray bullet, understanding the exhaustion under which she had broken down, but it seemed heartless to make no attempt to revive her. Yet she was safer as she was, he concluded, listening for a sound from the other room.

It was oppressively hot. The perspiration ran off his forehead into his eyes. His palms were slippery on the rifle stock, and his thin clothes, saturated in spots with moisture, stuck to him unpleasantly. It was not yet noon, but a thermometer on the door-jamb registered 110°. There was a vague mistiness in the air that grayed the usually vivid shadows of the trees, and the sunshine seemed to have lost its brightness, though not its power for heat.

Two shots came together, wide-angled from his right. One plowed a furrow across the planking of the veranda in front of where he crouched. The other, doubtless fired by Tomi, had either hit a tree or gone wild.

He could see nothing, but the location of the firing bothered him. It meant that the two natives were working around to the back of the house. There was plenty of brush there to conceal them and no windows for outlook. It meant also that they were not going to risk themselves across the space in front.

There was a side window in the other room and he went swiftly to it, hoping for the chance of a lucky shot. His blood was up and he had no compunctions about firing to kill at the men who, from sheer lust of gain, were willing to shoot the girl and himself in cold blood. He was equally determined that they should not lay a finger on the girl's inheritance as long as he could prevent it. He wondered, grimly, what Tuan Yuck had promised Hamaku and Tomi.

Leila Denman stirred as he crossed the room, opened her eyes and looked dazedly about her. As she caught sight of Chalmers, kneeling beside the window, rifle in hand, terror joined the nausea that swept over her. For the moment all the events that had brought her to this pass were blotted out.

"Who are you?" she asked, staring at him. "Where is my father?"

She raised herself on one elbow as Chalmers turned toward her. A bullet suddenly sent the lower pane of glass shivering to the floor.

"Lie down flat!" he commanded. "It's all right, Miss Denman, please do as I tell you."

He caught sight of a brown figure bounding from a clump of coral to the undergrowth and fired hastily through the broken window. The bushes waved and rustled and he realized with a swift qualm of apprehension that he had missed and that Tuan Yuck would soon be released and their refuge made untenable.

While he hesitated, desperately seeking for some plan of action, the girl sat up, despite his protest, and then got to her feet.

"I'm all right now," she said. "I remember everything. They are firing at us. Give me a gun. I can shoot, too. The cowards!"

He looked at her in surprised admiration. The color had come back to her cheeks and lips and the sparkle to her eyes. Mouth and chin were set, every line of her lithe figure expressed determination.

"You must not expose yourself," he said.

She flashed him a look.

"I am not going to faint again," she answered. "I despise myself for it. And I am not going to let you do all the fighting. Give me the gun I took from that man."

A bullet came from the left, straight through outer wall and partition, humming between them where they stood.

"That's Tuan Yuck," said Chalmers.

The girl neither blanched nor wavered, even when a second missile came from the opposite direction and the upper half of the window tinkled on the floor. They were surrounded. The shell of the portable house was powerless to protect them. With three rifles pumping their contents, the place would soon be like a sieve. It seemed a miracle to Chalmers that neither of them had been hit. The situation was desperate, almost hopeless.

He swept the girl back into a corner.

"Listen," he said. "We're in hard case. But there's a way out. They are after the pearls. If we give them up—"

She stamped her foot.

"Give me something to help fight with!" she cried. "I wouldn't give them up if they were a handful of pebbles. What good would it do? I'd rather be dead than trust myself to them. They are brutes, both of them. Give me a gun."

The room darkened visibly. The daylight had given way to the gloom that precedes an eclipse. Through the door the sky back of the trees was a deep blue-black.

"Chalmers!"

It was Tuan Yuck's voice, speaking from the back of the house, clearly audible through the flimsy walls. It has a vibrant quality that was chilling in its utter lack of human attribute.

"It's no use, Chalmers," the voice went on. It was impossible to distinctly locate it and Chalmers, his finger on the trigger, cursed inarticulately at his impotence. "*Force majeure* rules, Chalmers. We'll give the girl and you passage to where you can get in touch with Honolulu or Sydney. But we want the pearls!"

"No!"

The girl's voice rang out shrilly before Chalmers could formulate an answer.

"As you like." Tuan Yuck's voice retained its even pitch. "Perhaps you'll think better of it presently. Bring up those dry palm-boughs, Tomi."

They were going to burn them out. The house would flame like a torch.

"No you won't!" The new voice was hard and rough. It was Sayers, recovered from the blow on his thick skull, furious at his defeat and eager for revenge. "You can fill that young fool's carcass full of lead if you like and I'll help you. But I want the girl."

"You heard," said Leila in a tense whisper. The room was dusky with the weird midday half-light. Chalmers could hardly distinguish her features. "Where are the pistols? I may need one—for myself."

Apparently powerless, Chalmers felt like an animal as the jaws of the trap clip home. The world seemed out of joint when chicanery and avarice held them at their mercy. It was not for himself he cared. He would have wished nothing better at the moment than to have rushed out and gone down fighting, content if he could win his way to hand grips.

But Leila! A picture flashed before him of her helpless in the power of Sayers. He slipped noiselessly into the other room and brought back the pistols. One was for the girl, one for himself when they came to close quarters at the last. And one of the three was the automatic that had failed him before.

It would not do to make a blunder now.

"I'll give you one minute to make up your minds," called Tuan Yuck.

"You can't hide behind a girl's skirts, Chalmers!"

That was Sayers. Leila snatched one of the pistols and fired through the wall in the direction of the sound. Chalmers tried one of the remaining guns. The action resisted his pull and he tossed the weapon aside, gripping the other. He contemplated a swift dash for the boat. They might successfully run the gantlet and perhaps gain the schooner.

"Hamaku! Tomi!"

"*Ai.*"

That hope faded as the native answered the Chinaman. Both Kanakas were posted close to the veranda.

"Have you got the pearls?" he whispered. "Perhaps we can make better terms."

"They are here," she answered. Chalmers could barely see the movement of her hand to her breast. "They would not keep any terms. They are no better than wild beasts."

He groaned as he acknowledged the truth of her reply. Resistance was useless. They were lost unless a miracle intervened in their favor.

"Time's up," called Tuan Yuck.

The twilight turned to dark as blackness rushed up from the sea and behind the hills, shutting out the sickly sun and enveloping the sky from horizon to zenith in a pall of ebony. A bolt of lightning fell athwart the sky and the rooms blazed blue. A terrific peal of thunder crashed immediately overhead with deafening oppression, there was a sudden rushing in the trees and the tropical torrent broke loose, the rain falling in sheets that battered down the foliage and pounded on the corrugated roof with increasing fury.

Tons of water descended. The earth was covered almost momentarily with a hissing torrent. The thunder seemed to peal incessantly and flash after flash ripped the ebony curtain of the saturated clouds. The lagoon was lashed into torment under the heavy drops and the shrubbery beaten down and stripped of its leaves.

The two stood awed before the rage of the elements as the artillery of the thunder roared, reechoing among the hills, while flash after flash wrapped the scene in a weird, sudden brilliance, then left it black as the pit. Between the peals, the rain fell with an uproar that forbade all attempts at speech. She had set her hand upon his arm and the little fingers clutched hard but did not tremble.

The fury of the storm increased until it seemed as if nothing could resist its violence, certainly nothing human could think of anything but shelter from the battery of the rain. The thought that the besiegers might attempt entrance sent Chalmers to the open door with ready rifle. Leila followed him.

In the blackness they could not see the rain, but they heard the battering smash of it above their heads and the hissing splash with which it fell into the ground that was unable to drain off the vehemence of the flood.

A streak of fire ran down the sky seaward and seemed to fuse into a coruscating mass that made them shield their eyes, but not before they had discerned four figures, drenched, half-drowned and bowed double, close to the waters edge. The downpour had driven them to the schooner for shelter. There was no danger to the ship in the lack of wind, and even the greed of Tuan Yuck and Sayers was not proof against that pitiless drenching.

Chalmers cupped his hand close to Leila's ear.

"They are trying to find the boat," he called. "We've won."

She shook her head.

"God won for us," she said as he bent to catch the words.

Chalmers smiled grimly. Not that he failed to respect either her reverence or the Power that had intervened in their favor, but Tuan Yuck's philosophies came into his mind.

He would call it "an unfortunate coincidence," he thought.

Coincidence or miracle, it had effectually called check to the crafty Oriental's game.

X

SAFETY HAVEN

IT RAINED ALL THE LONG AFTERNOON. The thunder and lightning died away after half an hour that seemed five times as long, but the steady downpour continued until night merged with the somber darkness of the day. Chalmers lit the lamp in one room while they remained in the other, but no shot came from the schooner.

He prepared an impromptu meal from canned goods that were stored in the inner room

He found some tins of salmon and sardines but Leila asked him to put them back.

"I shall never see fish again without a shudder," she said.

Chalmers set them aside, blaming himself for his lack of thought.

"You see I cooked that last meal," she said. "We had eaten those same fish many times before. Father"—her voice wavered—"was very fond of them but I had grown tired of them. He coaxed me to eat some but I refused, and then—"

She broke down and Chalmers sat dumbly awkward. Her head was on her arms as she sobbed and he reached over and put his hand on one of hers. She turned it palm upward and let it lie in his like a child seeking consolation.

"Let me cry," she said. "It will do me good. I don't mind crying before you."

Chalmers felt strangely warmed. The little speech showed how she appraised him.

"I am glad," he said softly, and her fingers closed about his.

Presently she sat up and smiled at him while she wiped her eyes.

"Thank you," she said. "It helped—lots. You won't think me a baby?"

All the protectiveness in Chalmers mingled with the admiration he had for her beauty and her bravery, a feeling that, had he had time or inclination for analysis, would have amazed him with the vigor of its far-reaching growth.

"A baby!" he exclaimed. "I think you are a—a wonder," he concluded somewhat lamely.

Leila Denman, being a woman, read the look in his eyes that he himself was unconscious of, even as she supplied the ardent nature of the word he had checked on his lips. She smiled at him again, not wistfully this time, but with the spirit that prompted it so blending with his own that for the moment he forgot time and place, the peril they were in, everything but the girl with her red lips parted, her blue eyes now violet between the long lashes with alight in them that challenged every element of his manhood, her hair beneath the lamp like peacock-copper matrix in the sun.

So, while the rain poured pitilessly down upon the sodden, protesting ground, they talked through the long afternoon—she with tales of her paldom with her father and their life together in the South Seas; he of his work as a newspaperman.

"I have always wanted to get out of it," said Chalmers. "My first job was in San Francisco on a daily. The city editor was my father's best friend until dad died—"

Leila slipped her hand into his in sympathy with the loss that seemed to bring them closer, and the touch sent the blood tingling to his finger-tips and he felt the pull at his heart from the swift flooding of his veins.

"He told me one day I would never make a newspaperman," he went on frankly. "Said I lacked the instinct and doubted if I would ever get the knack, and congratulated me on it. I didn't see it that way as it was the only thing I could do, but he said he wished he was out of it. Said if he was my age he'd quit it if he had to drive a hack.

"Get out of it son," he told me. "It's a rotten game. You have to stand by and see your best friend knifed one day, and a man you know is a blackguard, praised to the skies the next. We are like flies in a saucer we think is the world, half muddled, half intoxicated over some stale beer we think is news. Get out beyond the rim of the saucer while you're young and husky. Do things; don't write about what other people do."

"I think I should have liked him," said Leila softly, "and then?"

Chalmers gave a wary glance into the veil of driving rain.

"Then," he laughed, "he offered me the chance of a newspaper job in

Honolulu. I couldn't see how that shaped up with his argument, but he said it didn't call for a real, first class metropolitan reporter, but carried a good salary and that Honolulu was close to the rim of the saucer anyhow. So I went. The work was easy and, with the correspondence for mainland papers, the pay was good. I came back in the middle of my vacation to cover the story of a shipwrecked crew—"

"Our schooner?"

"Yes." And Chalmers told the story of Taroi and his partnership with Sayers and Tuan Yuck. "And so," he said, "that is how I came here."

"Beyond the rim," she concluded.

Chalmers looked at his watch. It was seven o'clock.

"It's time to get busy," he said. "I'm going to offset any interruptions.

"Can I help you?" she asked.

"Yes, by figuring out what we have to take. All that's most necessary. It's quite a walk and we won't be able to take many trips."

"But what are you going to do?"

"I'm going to take a little swim out to the schooner and put their ferry system out of commission."

"You mean you're going to steal their boat?"

"I don't know yet whether I can do that. It depends on conditions. But I'll promise to run no real risk."

He expected a protest, reluctant as he was himself to leaving her alone while he ran a hazard that he purposely made the least of. But she put an eager hand upon his arm.

"Let me go with you," she said. "I can swim like a fish. Really. And there's my bathing suit in my tent. Let me, please. I can help, I know, if it's only to keep my eyes open. There's no danger for me. I could swim all the way under water easily."

But Chalmers was adamant. His plan held dangers that he was not willing to have her share unnecessarily.

"You can be more help doing what I asked you to," he said.

"Truly?"

"Truly."

"Aye, aye, sir," she saluted in mock humility.

Chalmers was seized with a sudden desire to tell her how adorable she was, but there was serious work on hand and he merely registered the picture she made, adding to a gallery in his brain already better stocked with the same subject than he was aware of.

With the fatty part of some canned meat he carefully greased every inch of an automatic and slung it round his neck by a lanyard improvised from twine.

"It's a bit of a handicap," he said, "but it may come in handy. Now for a knife."

His own sheath-knife he had left behind when he stripped it with his pistol-holster from the belt before he bound Tuan Yuck. Leila took one down from a shelf and gave it to him.

"It was father's," she said. "Here's a belt. I wish you'd let me come along."

"I wish you'd have a list of what we need to take by the time I come back," he parried, as he greased the blade of the knife and tested its keenness. "I'm going to carry this in my teeth like a pirate," he said laughing. "*Au revoir.*"

Leila watched him as the rain and dark enveloped him and turned back into the room with a sigh that was not altogether unhappy. She took counsel with herself concerning the lightening of her grief and, reasoning, blushed; blamed herself for lack of loyalty to her father in forgetting her grief; blamed herself again for lack of loyalty to Chalmers and his sympathy and so, womanwise, set aside the argument by getting things together for the trip to the cliff.

Chalmers could hardly tell where the beach ended and the lagoon began. The ground was a foot deep with water racing from the hills and augmented by the rain. The latter was slackening perceptibly and he lost no time getting into deep water.

The surface of the lagoon was pitted with tiny spouting fountains beneath the fall of the heavy drops. They beat a tattoo on his head as he swam steadily out in the direction of the unseen schooner, nearly half a mile from shore.

The sky was black and starless. He seemed to be swimming in a black globe half filled with ink. There was no sign of the vessel and he began to wonder whether, in the dark, he was not swimming in a circle, when, close ahead, a dull light broke through the mist.

Paddling cautiously he made out the loom of the schooner, bows to the ebb tide. The whaleboat trailed alongside, its painter fast to the foremast stays, its hull directly beneath the port-hole from which came the light.

It was open. The vertical rain fell past it without entrance. Out of it came an acrid, pungent odor, beaten down toward the water by the rain. Chalmers recognized it as opium. He had already recognized the cabin as Tuan Yuck's. He wondered whether the Chinaman was under the influence of the drug. If he was, and Sayers drunk, he might board the schooner, overawe Hamaku and Tomi . . .

"Your methods are too crude, Sayers."

Tuan Yuck was awake and Sayers at least sober enough to be talked to. Chalmers clasped the stem of the whaleboat, drew up his knees, kicked vigorously downward and climbed like a cat into the boat.

"Yours are too —— slow to suit me," Sayers was saying as Chalmers crouched quietly down below the open port, straining to hear every word above the patter of the rain. Even as he listened he felt the downpour lessening. There was little time to waste, but the next sentence arrested him.

"You'll find them surer in the end, Sayers."

The silky tone seemed to hold a menace that the Australian missed or ignored.

"Well, my way is going to be your way, tonight," he answered truculently. D'ye think I'm going to stand being hammered over the head by that young cub without a comeback. And you, trussed up like a prize turkey for basting! A wise-looking bird you were." He broke into discordant laughter.

"The rain's slacking up now," he went on. "Listen to it on the deck. We ran off like a couple of drowning rats. But we're going to finish this affair before I sleep. We'll cut that young gamecock's comb and his throat into the bargain to stop his crowing. I'm not the one to be made a fool of by a half-baked man and a girl. If you're too yellow for the job—"

Some gesture or expression of Tuan Yuck's must have halted him, Chalmers fancied.

"Yes my friend, what then?" The Chinaman's voice almost purred.

"No offense, Tuan Yuck. But what's the use of shilly-shallying. There's four of us, ain't there? We can go ashore and settle the whole thing. You can handle the Kanakas. I'm going to sleep with my share of those pearls under my pillow tonight. And Chalmers'll sleep in the sand. There's a million or more in the lagoon, you say. We can clean that up and none the wiser. Dead men tell no tales. You said that yourself. We'll leave the mirrors on the island and it'll be Motutabu to the end of the time. As for the girl—"

He broke off again.

"As for the girl?" repeated Tuan Yuck quietly, with peculiar emphasis.

"Why—ha, ha! That's a good one. You don't mean to tell me you—" The sentence ended in the discordant laugh. "I'll tell you what we'll do about the girl," he said gaspingly. "We'll gamble for her!" But you'll have to roll your sleeves up when you deal the cards. Come on, the rain's quit. Let's turn out the Kanakas."

Chalmers glanced at the porthole above him in the wish that he could reach it and settle the matter with his greased automatic, there and then. But it was impossible. The rain had suddenly dwindled to a scanty sprinkle.

The cloud curtain was rolling up to the north like a great awning and the stars were showing through the frazzle of its rack. He had meant at first to row the boat ashore under cover of the rain and hide it in the mangroves. But with the passing of the storm he would undoubtedly be seen even if the noise of the oars passed notice. And under their fire he would infallibly be killed or desperately wounded before he half-way reached the shore.

He drew out the case-knife and swiftly severed the painter. Then with both hands he tugged at the plug. The bottom boards were already afloat with rainwater and, as the boat slowly drifted sternward with the ebb, the water from the lagoon gushed in. Chalmers slid over the side, tilting the gunwale before he let go and shipping water enough to make the boat commence to settle as it sluggishly followed the current.

He heard Sayers calling for Hamaku and Tomi and blessed the reason that still kept them in the forepeak. The Australian's curses died away as Chalmers filled his lungs and, with a glance to sight the lamp where Leila was working over the preparations for their exodus, swam hard under water shoreward.

When he came up he turned gently on his back, cautiously paddled till his head was toward the beach, dropped his legs and raised his head ever so slightly, still stroking against the ebb with his arms.

Sayers was on deck swearing at one of the natives who held a lantern aloft. Chalmers chuckled as he thought of the severed line that had been found. Against the white of the reef surf he could distinguish the rim of the whaleboat almost awash. It disappeared as a shout came from Sayers and some one dived from the stern of the schooner.

Chalmers turned on his chest again and once more swam under water, repeating the process until he felt the sand. He had swum to his left and crawled out on the beach close to the rocks at the side of the landing.

Half-way to cover he was discovered by the eyes watching for him. The *ping* of a bullet on the lava warned him, and he dived into a sand lane between the rocks, safe from the futile shots that followed him.

Bent double, he hurried up the beach, keeping well covered and shouting to Leila to put out the lamp that might be a target for a random shot. It was extinguished and the house was lost against the background of the hills.

Leila was waiting for him at the foot of the steps and he warmed to the anxiety in her voice.

"I was afraid they'd killed you," she said.

"Not this time, nor the next," he replied jauntily with a boyish ring to his voice. "But I've sunk their old whaleboat and they'll have a fine time getting it up again. Only I've left my shoes down there and those rocks cut like the devil."

She murmured her sympathy. Chalmers laughed.

"I can get you a pair of dad's," she said. "They'll be better than nothing."

"That's all right, Leila!"

She did not resent the name but caught at his hand as they crouched down by the steps.

"They'll stop firing soon," he said. "Tuan Yuck won't waste cartridges.

He knows we've won this trick."

"Won't they swim ashore?" she asked.

"Tuan Yuck can't. The main boom caught him one day and he nearly drowned before Hamaku got to him. Sayers always gets cramps. That's one thing we can bless his drinking for. The Kanakas won't tackle it alone. They think we had that storm made to order."

"It's a wonder they didn't hit you. I was terribly frightened."

"Were you?" He pressed the hand he still held. "They didn't see me till I landed. I swam under water. The only thing I worried about was a shark."

"A shark! They never come in the smaller lagoons. Dad said they are afraid of getting trapped by the tide."

"Don't they?"

There was something in the way Chalmers said it that made the girl look at him in the dim light the stars gave in the clearing.

"Was that the reason you didn't want me to go?" she asked.

"One of 'em," he answered, feeling rather foolish. "Did you get any things together? We must make a start. We'll keep in the brush and along the edge of the mangroves. Then there are rocks to the point that will cover us."

At three o'clock Leila Denman collapsed. She had been limping uncomplainingly for the last half hour.

Chalmers, packing double burdens, was almost played out. "There's a lot more I'd have liked to have brought," he said, "but I doubt if we could make another trip before dawn."

Leila, lying flat on the sand, her head pillowed on the crook of one arm, gave a weary little sigh. "I can hardly move," she confessed. We can get along with what we've got, can't we?"

"I think so," said Chalmers and went prospecting.

"Here's a cave for you with a nice smooth sandy floor," he said. And another for me right next door. That bedding from the house is dry. I'll fix it for you."

"Good night, Leila," he called presently after she had crept wearily into her cliff dwelling.

"There's no danger," he went on to assure her. "Sleep tight. The lagoon here is too shallow for the schooner. It'll take them all morning to get that boat up, if they're lucky. Tide's coming in and it's all hunky-dory. Everything's safe in our little haven. Let's name it 'Safety Haven.' That's the ticket."

There was no answer.

"Poor kidlets, she's tuckered out," he told himself remorsefully. "And I'm wide awake." Even as he formed the thought, he yawned. "Not so wide awake after all," he concluded. "Good night, Leila," he said aloud softly.

The repetition of her name roused her.

"Good night," she said.

"All comfy?"

"Yes, thank you. Good night, Bruce."

And, with that music to accompany his dreams, Chalmers too fell asleep.

XI

MONGOLIAN MAGIC

THE TRADITIONAL PAIR OF STRANGE BULLDOGS had little more in common than Tuan Yuck and Sayers aboard the schooner next morning. While the Chinaman showed no outward signs of irritation he was chagrined at the success of Chalmers in cutting off their shore communication.

Sayers openly growled and barked and vowed to get even. His head seemed split apart and the liquor he absorbed increased the aggravation until he vented his ill-temper upon everything in sight, glowering with bloodshot eyes and cursing the Kanakas as they hurried out of the way of his wrath, and finally spilling his spite against the armor of Tuan Yuck's impenetrability.

"A nice mess," he growled. "The only boat we've got gone to the bottom and hell and all ahead to get it up, if we can do it at all. It's all very well for you to sit there sneering at me like an ivory Buddha in a bazaar. It was no fault of mine! I'll tell you that to your face that I don't like your attitude, Tuan Yuck, with your 'wiser than thou' smile. I didn't sink the boat, did I? I wasn't to blame for it any more than you, was I? Then don't look so —— superior about it, because for two pins I'd change the look on your face and make the change permanent."

He had advanced his head with its undershot jaw and glaring eyes close to Tuan Yuck's across the cabin table, set with his own untasted breakfast and the Oriental's emptied dishes. Tuan Yuck did not move a muscle, the narrow eyelids were partly closed and behind them the dark eyes sparkled like a snake's, never moving from those of Sayers.

The Australian's bullying speech was mostly braggadocio, spoken not only to relieve his feelings but to reassure himself. He was conscious both of an increasing distrust of Tuan Yuck, and of a certain fear that was gradually growing within him and strengthening a conviction that before the trip was ended the two of them would come to open warfare. This belief was born of his own half-planned determination to possess himself of the Chinaman's share of the pearls—once they obtained them—and an instinctive, prophetic knowledge that Tuan Yuck held the same intent.

It was with a strong effort that he checked his outburst. His nerves were jumping with the reaction of the liquor and he knew that physically he would collapse after one fierce spurt of energy. How much strength there was in

Tuan Yuck's frame he did not know; it was the enigma of the man, bodily and mentally, that controlled while it enraged him. Besides there were yet the pearls to gain and the contents of the lagoon to reap. He could not handle the situation single-handed and he could not count upon the natives. How much they were under the Oriental's control he was presently to learn, but he already sensed that any act on his part would range them against him—unless he could catch Tuan Yuck unawares and single-handed—when the time was ripe.

The man's mind was like a stagnant gutter, never flushed, holding all the impurities that came to it and breeding more. The thought of being the possessor of unlimited wealth inflamed his selfishness with plans of debaucheries that included a circuit of the world and an orgy of wine, women and song, a vague mixture of intoxication that was a blend of the satisfaction of the vices one part of him wanted to wallow in, and a revel in the hearing of music and the operas that the remnant of his spiritual consciousness craved.

He reached out a trembling hand to refill his glass and knocked over the square-faced bottle of gin. Tuan Yuck caught it with a swift movement before it spilled and set it upright.

"That's your main trouble, Sayers," he said quietly, as he set it down. "If we are going to pull together in this thing we both of us need all our wits."

"What about your dope pills?" sneered Sayers.

"I use opium to quiet my nerves," said Tuan Yuck evenly, "not to set them on edge. Did you ever notice that it did me any harm?"

Sayers' half-muddled brain caught the logic of the retort. The Chinaman was right. He needed all his wits, not so much for joint action as to remain on even terms with his partner.

"You're right," he said, hesitating, with the bottle-neck clinking against his tumbler, "but I can't chuck it altogether—not right away." And he gulped down the liquor.

The hint of a smile passed over Tuan Yuck's countenance and faded.

"I didn't mean to do that," he said. "I only counseled moderation," he went on with eyes that mocked the Australian's endeavor to pull himself together. "When I said last night your methods were crude, I meant that you drink too much and forget to eat. You spilled the fat on the fire when you made a grab at those pearls—"

"While you were wasting time in words. The thing had to come to a head. What was the use in beating about the bush?"

"If we had promised everything and the girl had come on board, would it have been any harder to have eventually got what we wanted?" asked Tuan Yuck quietly. "Now, we have a fight on our hands and, so far, they have got a little the best of it."

Sayers looked at him in resentful appreciation.

So that had been Tuan Yuck's plan—to get the girl and the pearls aboard; to let Chalmers navigate until they were close enough to their destination to dispense with his services, and then . . .

"You're a better pirate than I am," he said grudgingly. "Why didn't you tip me off to your scheme?"

Tuan Yuck showed his teeth in a blank smile at the compliment.

"It seemed the obvious move," he answered. "I imagined you figured it out the same way."

Sayers pushed back the bottle and started to get up, holding his head in both hands as he did so.

"I've got to cut out the booze," he muttered.

Tuan Yuck, watching him, chuckled internally. The Oriental was a firm believer in the axiom that lookers-on see most of the game. His policy was to wait until the right moment, and then usurping the board, make the move that left him the ultimate conqueror.

"I can give you something for that headache," he said. "And presently you can eat something."

Sayers' bloodshot eyes viewed him suspiciously as he disappeared to his cabin, emerging with a lacquered box in his hand nearly full of greenish-gray tablets. Tuan Yuck placed two in the Australian's half-reluctant palm, and, with a quizzical look that showed how well he read the other's thoughts, put one into his own mouth.

"The Mongolian equivalent for hashish," he said. "Let it dissolve on your tongue."

Even as the pastils liquefied, Sayers felt their soothing effect. His head cleared as if by magic, his nerves steadied, and his pulses began to beat with a regularity that soon invigorated him.

"You're a wizard!" he exclaimed. "There's a fortune in those, Tuan Yuck! 'Morning After' tablets. Worth their weight in gold. And you could charge that much for 'em and get away with it."

"They cost more than that," Tuan Yuck answered dryly. "And as they are the most insidious of drug composites, they are likely to form a habit that is decidedly expensive and dangerous."

Sayers looked covetously at the little box.

"It's great stuff," he said. "I feel fit. Hanged if I haven't got the beginning of an appetite already. If I can get some food into my system presently I'll be in fine shape. Now the first thing to do is to get that boat up. That's going to be some job. I wish I had Chalmers by the neck and could make him do it. We'll have to make Hamaku dive and get a rope on to it. Then we can rig a line at the end of the main gaff and swing the spar out so as to get a fairly up-and-down haul, and snake her up with the capstan. We can do that as we lie without getting up anchor, and making sail on this flood-tide and trying to moor dead over the boat."

Tuan Yuck eyed him curiously.

"How good a sailor are you, Sayers?" he asked.

"Good enough to handle this schooner in everything outside of navigation," he boasted, feeling the increasing exhilaration of the drugs he had swallowed. "I can sail her as close as Chalmers any day in the week."

"Ah! You could make Nameless Isle at a pinch?"

"That's easy. Or to the Solomons for that matter. Just sail sou'west. You couldn't miss 'em. If the winds were steady I could come close to sailing all the way back, following up the course Chalmers laid out coming down. Yes—sir. Oh, Hamaku!" he called up the companionway. "You can handle him better than I can," he said to Tuan Yuck. "Tell him what we want."

Tuan Yuck explained, talking Hawaiian fluently, as did Sayers. Hamaku shook his head.

"I am no diver," he said. "I could not swim down to six fathoms with a rope and fasten it. My lungs are not big enough. And there is no height from which to dive."

"You can carry weights," said Sayers. "Put the line under your arms, Hamaku. You can take the chicken-coop or a grating for a raft, and paddle it out over the boat."

The Kanaka continued to protest. Both he and his fellow were still cowed by the storm, and the second win of Chalmers in sinking the boat. It was their disposition to always be with the victors.

"I am no diver," he repeated sullenly.

"Hamaku!" Tuan Yuck's voice held a vibrant note of command. Hamaku shifted on his feet, his head hanging.

"Look at me!" commanded the Chinaman sharply.

The silky tone sounded like the snap of a whiplash. The native lifted his eyes with evident reluctance, caught the challenge of the gaze that held his own and mastered it while the stronger spirit of the Oriental took possession of the Hawaiian's. For a moment Hamaku's will resisted, then his dwindling protests of "*Aole! Aole!*" (No! No!) stopped in midbreath, and he stood like a well trained servant waiting for orders, as impassive as his master.

It was the first time Sayers had witnessed a demonstration of Tuan Yuck's control of the natives. It was the first time he had ever seen hypnosis at close range, and he was inclined to be skeptical.

"Will he do anything you tell him to now?" he asked.

"Anything I will tell him to."

"Going to keep him in the trance while he dives?"

"No. He'll be a better judge of what should be done than I can be. But he thinks I can control him at any minute."

"Then it's bunkum?"

"Not at all. I'm going to speak aloud what I will him to do, so you can judge for yourself. Tuan Yuck tore a loose leaf from the end of Chalmers' carefully kept logbook and folded it into a narrow strip.

"Pick up this dagger, Hamaku," he said in a low voice. "You are afraid of Mr. Sayers. This will protect you. You can kill him with it if you hate him enough. See, he is asleep. Now you are not afraid of him any longer. Creep up on him. Be careful. Make no noise. Now! Strike!"

The Australian, with a fascination touched with awe, saw the emotions change on Hamaku's face from fear to convulsed hatred, then to cunning as, clutching the paper, he inched towards him. As the Hawaiian raised his arm for the blow, Sayers, despite himself, threw up his own arm in defense and clutched the descending wrist.

Tuan Yuck shouted a sharp command, and clapped his hands. Animation returned to Hamaku's eyes and confusion left him shamefaced, as Sayers, feeling almost as foolish, let go his wrist, and the mock weapon fluttered down.

"What have I done?" asked the native.

"Nothing. Go and get ready for the dive."

Hamaku left, cringing as he passed near Tuan Yuck.

"I thought you had to make passes or use something to *dazzle* them," said Sayers, trying to affect a nonchalance that he was far from feeling.

"Not always, with a good subject. The stronger will is sufficient. I might have to with you. Shall I try?"

Tuan Yuck's eyes mocked Sayers', as their glances met. The Australian doggedly endured the power that seemed to pour from the Chinaman's darkly glittering orbs until he felt a sudden desire to yield in answer to the imperative statement that rang in his brain in one repeated sentence:

"You are not so strong as I am. You are not so strong as I am."

He passed his hand across his forehead, summoning all his will to throw off its oppression, and his vision cleared. The room had been gradually filling with a mist out of which shone two points of light. Now he knew that these were Tuan Yuck's eyes, still mocking, and that the mist was the hallucination of his own brain.

"I'm going to rig up that tackle," he said shortly, rousing himself.

As he went on deck, still conscious of the Oriental's jeering gaze, he resolved to find some way of offsetting the latter's influence over Hamaku and Tomi. The prospect of having a knife stuck between his ribs at the will of Tuan Yuck was not a reassuring one.

"I've got to go slow on the booze," he told himself again, "and when I sleep it'll be behind a locked door or a long way from Mr. Yuck. I think I'll stay ashore nights after this, though I suppose I needn't worry till we've got our hands on something worth letting blood over; and then, my worthy Confucian, you'll find more than one can play that game."

XII
Sayers Finds a Weapon

Hamaku achieved a raft with a wooden grating. To this he attached a spare halyard, coiling the slack and making a loop of the loose end to slip over his neck and beneath one arm. He freighted the little craft with two pigs of cast-iron ballast, took one of the oars that had floated out of the boat when it sank, and which he had recovered with the bottom-boards the night before, and paddled off to where they had seen the whaleboat vanish. The schooner lay between him and the shore as a bulwark for possible bullets, but he worked quickly.

He soon located it in the clear lagoon, lying on a patch of sand between the live coral. Sitting on the edge of his raft, he adjusted the line for smooth uncoiling, weighted himself with a pig of iron in each hand, and, as the grating tilted, slid gently down to the bottom, the line snaking off the float above him.

It was well over two minutes before his head bobbed up with a triumphant grin of white teeth.

"*Hiki no!*" (All right!) he called, and swam back to the schooner, towing the grating with the halyard fastened to it. Climbing aboard, he spliced it to the spare line Sayers had reeved through a block at the end of the main gaff, running down the spar through the throat-halyard block to another at the foot of the mast and so forward.

The two natives set their strength to the bars of the little capstan, the line tautened at an obtuse angle, and the whaleboat came slowly to the surface, then above it, while Hamaku ran out on the main boom and, as the water spilled, handled the slackened line until the boat once more rode on the water, and communication with the shore was reestablished.

Tuan Yuck had been busy with the binoculars. He noticed the removal of the tent, and picked out its furniture still standing amid the trees. The mounting sun sucked up the moisture that the overladen earth had been unable to carry off. Leaves that had drooped beneath the downpour revived, and everywhere the wet surfaces reflected the light, so that the magic mirrors were hardly noticeable. A steamy mist hung over the mangrove swamp.

Nowhere could the Chinaman gain a hint of the whereabouts of Chalmers and the girl, though he was certain they had broken camp. Landing was dangerous until they were discovered. Tuan Yuck's policies called for the making of ambuscades, not attacking them.

At Sayers' suggestion, Tomi climbed to the main spreaders for a wider view. He had hardly reached his perch before he called down to them that he saw smoke at the foot of the cliff. From the deck it was not to be distinguished from the mist above the mangroves.

Sayers looked at the mast and grunted. With the sails furled there were no rings to serve for foothold. Tomi had gone up it like a cat, planting his bare feet against the mast and grasping the halyards.

"I can't make that," he said, "and I'm too heavy to haul. We could get you up easy enough, Tuan Yuck?"

"Why not?" assented the Chinaman. "I'll chance a stray shot."

The throat halyards were cast loose, a loop made in them for Tuan Yuck's foot, and, with Hamaku and Sayers hauling, Tuan Yuck, steadying himself by the peak halyard, was readily lifted to the side of Tomi, where he focused his glass on Safety Haven.

The height enabled him to look over the cape and see a portion of the beach, ending in the farther promontory. It was high tide, and he was quick to appreciate the value of the place as a base of defense. The glass revealed the steep, flinty sides of the nearer headland, impossible to climb, and the masses of rock on the beach beyond from behind which an attacking party could be driven off without exposure. There was no sign of an encampment save where, close to the foot of the waterfall, a thread of smoke proclaimed the presence of a fire, masked by boulders and the verdure at the foot of the cliff.

"Our friend, Chalmers, possesses more military strategy than I gave him credit for," he said to Sayers when he regained the deck. "He seems to have chosen a good place for defense. I'd like to get a closer look at it. I wonder how they are off for supplies. They've got plenty of water."

"They'd pot us if we took the boat," said Sayers. "Let Hamaku swim in. He may be able to sneak up between the rocks and get a look at them, and a line on how they are fixed for grub."

Hamaku took his instructions willingly enough, reassured of Tuan Yuck's power to compel ultimate obedience, and slipped quietly over the side for the long swim that meant nothing to his aquatic prowess. Sayers watched him start, then announced his intention of eating breakfast.

"I'm going to fill up on a square meal," he announced. "First time I've felt like touching food for three days, thanks to your pills."

Tuan Yuck looked at him curiously as he went below with more of vigor and purpose than he had shown for many days. The Oriental's shoulders lifted in the barest suggestion of a shrug as he went to the rail and trained his glasses on Hamaku's steady progress.

The sound of a shot and its echo from the cliff brought Sayers on deck.

"Did they get him?" he asked, hurrying to where Tuan Yuck stood gazing through the binoculars.

"I think not. I told him to look out and dive at the flash. I lost sight of him in the dazzle on the water just now. He's probably swimming underneath— there he is."

Sayers took the glasses and picked up Hamaku's head, like a seal's, close in by the cape, before the native dived again.

In half an hour Hamaku was aboard, unhurt but excited and eager for commendation.

"They saw me," he said. "Just a little way the other side of the point. I did not see them—only the flash of the gun. So I dived quick and swam under water. There is fresh water off the point," he went on, proud of his knowledge. "I felt it cooler as I swam through. Then I tasted, and I knew for sure. Plenty of fresh water coming up from the bottom, just off the point. That means a quicksand when the tide is low."

"They're in there. That's the main point," commented Tuan Yuck. "And if it's hard for us to get at them, it's just as hard for them to get out. You're a good boy, Hamaku."

The native beamed with pleasure.

"Yes, Hamaku, you're all right," seconded Sayers. "Well, we can work the lagoon for pearls and starve them out at the same time. Which reminds me I haven't finished my breakfast."

He went below, beckoning Hamaku to follow. In the cabin he poured out a generous measure of gin.

"That was a long swim, Hamaku," he said. "You did well. Take this."

The Hawaiian's eyes glistened as he took the glass.

"Thank you," he said in native, and tossed down the raw spirits with gusto.

"Have another?" asked Sayers, with the bottle ready tilted.

Hamaku beamed in gratitude at the unexpected access to the liquor he loved. It's warmth spread over his body, and he looked at the Australian as a starving dog might look at a man who tosses him a meaty bone, a glance that held readiness to serve, almost affection.

"This is just between you and me, Hamaku," warned Sayers, as the Kanaka set down the glass. "You understand?" He tossed his head upward meaningly.

Hamaku nodded.

"I tell my tongue not to speak," he said, and went on deck, carefully avoiding any proximity to Tuan Yuck.

Sayers smiled. He had found a weapon to offset Tuan Yuck's power over the natives.

"He can't keep 'em hypnotized all the time," he muttered. "Lucky I brought plenty of gin along. There's nothing they won't do for that." From force of habit he poured himself a drink, hesitated, then swallowed it. "Can't do any harm on a full stomach," he told himself. "But I mustn't let it get the better of me."

At which speech, Tuan Yuck, could he have heard it, would have smiled.

XIII

THE LAUNCH IN THE MANGROVES

THE SUN, STREAMING IN THROUGH THE BUSHES that fringed the mouth of Chalmers' cave, awakened him. His eyelids felt as if they were filled with a mixture of glue and sand, and each joint protested against coordinate action. He had packed every pound he could carry on the trips from the clearing, and he was still sore from the quicksand. But his mind, once roused, was speedily alert, and forced his sluggish limbs to action.

He picked up a rifle and, stepping cautiously, not to disturb the sleeping girl, made his way toward the headland that divided Safety Haven from the main beach and lagoon. The tide was washing the end of the cape, covering the quicksand and the scattered rocks as he sought for some place to climb the barrier, and get a glimpse of the enemy's operations.

The lava ridge was less steep on the side of Safety Haven, and he managed to pick a trail to the top. He had brought the glasses of the dead captain from the house, and with their aid he easily marked the cautious steps of Hamaku and Tomi, moving carefully on the schooner's decks, so as not to disturb their masters below.

"They haven't turned out yet," he commented. "That gives us an hour or so before they'll bother their heads about us."

He left his rifle in a shady crevice of the lava, where it would be handy when he returned for later observation and, unencumbered, swiftly climbed down to the beach again after one comprehensive view of their little dominion. There was driftwood among the rocks and he picked some of it up, still soaked with the rain, and set it to dry in the sun for a fire.

On his way back to the caves he made a hasty visit to certain rock-masses he had noted from the top of the ridge. Despite the almost boyish frankness of Leila Denman, he realized the delicacy of the situation, if they were forced to live in the intimate contact their quarters demanded; and he wanted to spare the girl's sensitiveness as much as possible. Presently he found what he wanted, a series of rocky rooms, high-walled, open to the sky, indeed—which meant nothing in that climate and season—all connecting, two of them floored with sand and shells, the largest of the latter broken, but many perfect and exquisitely tinted.

The third chamber was reached by natural rocky steps, leading to the rim of a lava bowl some ten feet in diameter, nearly filled with sea water, crystal clear and green as an emerald. A ledge of rock ran part way around the interior of the basin, an ideal platform for a bather.

Chalmers, smiling at his own folly, whimsically looked for the sea naiad who should, by rights, have inhabited the pool. All the rocks showed traces of wave action; the outer entrance to the rock chambers was an arch.

All signs pointed to the fact that Motutabu had once held a higher sea level. The beach of Safety Haven had undoubtedly long been exposed to the wash of ruder waves than the quiet ripples of the narrow lagoon that rimmed it now, though the sharp uneroded spine of the headland seemed of later origin.

Chalmers was in no mind for geological problems. He was delighted with his find of a complete suite of rooms which would insure absolute privacy for Leila Denman. The problem of their defense and existence, ever present as it was with him, was constantly disturbed by thoughts of the girl, remembrances of some turn of her head, the intonation of her voice, the color of her hair, her eyes, her lips, the piquant pendule in the upper one. He caught himself whistling softly, and thinking the words:

"And dark blue is her ee."

He checked himself with an embarrassed laugh.

"Anybody would think I was in love," he said aloud. A friendly gull, perched on a near-by rock, cocked a black eye at him, stretched its wings in a suggestive imitation of a yawn, and flapped away as if disgusted, with a throaty squawk of disdain that sounded exactly like—

"You are."

The resemblance was so startling that Chalmers called after the bird:

"What did you say? I wonder if I am," he asked himself.

The broaching of the subject, like the sounding of a dominant chord, seemed to set a hundred suggestions and instincts vibrating in harmony with the suggestion. The visions of her, mute in his arms, refusing to give up the pearls to Tuan Yuck, fighting with him pluckily against the odds, came to him in swift succession. He felt again the pull at his heart that had come at the touch of her fingers closing on his, and then flushed at his own foolishness.

"She's got no eyes for you, my boy," he muttered. "And if she had you've no right to think of her. If we get out of this muddle she'll be worth a quarter of a million, to say nothing of the pearls in the lagoon."

"I'll bet I'm a sight," he added, not altogether irrelevantly, as he passed his hand over his sprouting beard and looked ruefully at his besmeared ducks. "I'll have to make another trip to the schooner if it's only for a razor—not to mention other things."

All thoughts of Leila vanished from his mind as he confronted their necessities. Their supply of food was limited, aside from fish, which Leila would only touch as a last necessity, but his chief fear was lack of ammunition. He had only the cartridges that were left in the chambers of the rifles and the automatics. Tuan Yuck would be sure to think of that sooner or later, and, in the meantime, threatened attacks must be warded off.

"Good morning, Sir Sober Face."

He rounded a pile of rocks to meet Leila, her bright hair coiled, a flush in her cheeks, and her eyes alight with friendly greeting.

"I thought you were still asleep," she said gaily. "So I've gone about my duties on tiptoe. Look. Here's our kitchen, with a shelf just the right height for a pantry, and here's our dining-room. I've stocked the pantry, filled the kettle from the waterfall, and all I need is dry wood."

"That's easily supplied," said Chalmers, falling into her mood, "and if you go with me I'll show you a suite of rooms with boudoir, sun-parlor and private bath that I've taken an option on in your name. There was an impudent mermaid in possession, but I made faces at her, and she flapped her tail at me and ran—I mean swam."

So, talking nonsense, forgetting for the moment, with the privilege of golden youth, their present perils, Chalmers showed her what he called in jest, "Number One, Beach Avenue."

As Leila Denman finished looking delightedly about the place that Chalmers had found for her, she turned to him and held out her hand.

"I want to thank you, Mr. Chalmers," she said. "You've been more than kind. I—I can't tell you just what it means to me. When I think of how friendless, how defenseless I might have been, and all you have done for me—of your thoughtfulness—I wish I could reciprocate it. I *do* appreciate it."

Her eyes dewed with grateful tears, and Chalmers, stopping himself on the point of some such idiotic declaration that "one smile of hers was worth a lifetime of toil in her behalf," felt his own moisten and a lump come into his throat.

"I haven't done anything," he said as soon as speech was easy. "Nothing that I wouldn't have done for my own sister—or any one else's."

"Why, then I'll have to adopt you as my brother," she said.

His face fell involuntarily, and hers brightened, such being the way of a man with a maid, and *vice versa*. Then she laughed.

"Where's the firewood?" she asked.

Chalmers flushed guiltily. They were back to the caves already.

"Hurry up," she called gaily as he turned away. "Call at the grocery store and get some eggs—brother!"

There was a mocking emphasis on the "brother" that he did not altogether object to. It showed she was not altogether in earnest about the relation, he thought. Then Fortune favored him. Close to where he had set the driftwood in the sun he saw some telltale furrows in the sand. He had seen similar ones before on the quiet beaches beyond Pearl Harbor, on Oahu, and he swiftly utilized a piece of wood as a spade, and carefully upturned a dozen globular objects of a dingy white, covered with leathery skin—turtle's eggs, not to be despised as an auxiliary to an island menu, and an assurance of future sustenance.

Breakfast was a meal where happiness attended appetite, and it was not until the shrinking shadows warned Chalmers time was speeding, that he resumed his full measure of responsibility.

"I want you to keep in your rock-rooms or your cave," he said, "until I come back."

"Why can't I come with you?"

"I don't believe there will be anything interesting on hand," he answered. "Only a nasty climb which I have made before."

"Very well, ungallant one," she pouted, then changed, noting the gravity of his face. "You'll promise to let me know if it looks interesting or if I can help?" she asked.

"Surely."

He climbed the wall of the cape once more and watched the hauling aboard of the sunken whaleboat. He was tempted to try a shot, but the sun was in his eyes. Gazing against it he failed to see the approach of Hamaku until the native had actually passed the headland and was heading shoreward for the little beach. He cautiously leveled his Winchester and sighted until the bead on the muzzle of the rifle dropped into the notch of the hindsight and aligned with the black dot of the Kanaka's head. His finger instinctively pressed the trigger until the last ounce of resistance was reached.

Then mercy reasoned with the will to kill and he aimed ahead. The bullet splashed close enough to send Hamaku plunging down like a porpoise, and swimming beneath the surface back toward the schooner. From above, Chalmers could see the motion of his body, purple in the green shoal water, wriggling like an eel.

"He'll warn them that we're on the lookout," he told himself. "I can watch the rocks at low tide. There'll be a moon soon of nights by the time the ebb shifts 'round to daylight, and then I'll have to make a boom of palm-trunks. At present I'll sleep afternoons while Leila plays watchwoman, and keep sentry nights myself."

A call came to him, and he saw the running across the beach toward the cape. He waved at her in assurance of his safety, and climbed down to meet her.

"You're not hurt?" she asked breathlessly. "I heard the shot."

"Not I," he protested, and told her what he had seen. "They'll not trouble us for a while," he asserted. "We'll have to keep a smart lookout, that's all."

"I can do my share?"

He nodded. She was looking at him in a way that made him a little uncertain of what he was saying or doing.

"Steady, boy," he muttered. "Steady. You're on duty—on honor."

She saw his lips move, and her face blanched as she stretched out eager hands.

"You are hurt?" she declared. "What did you say? I couldn't hear you."

"I was talking to myself," he returned, vexed at his indiscretion. "Just foolishness."

"Oh!" she said, and her eyes lost their anxiety for another expression, less intimate, yet full of understanding.

"You are invited to my beach boudoir," she said, "to discuss the situation, and decide upon the division of watches."

"They'll try to take us unawares, I imagine," he told her when they had settled themselves. "Failing that, they'll probably go ahead and clean up the lagoon of pearls. Then they may try and navigate the schooner somewhere themselves—Sayers thinks he knows more than he really does about sailing—or they'll make some sort of an offer to us."

"Which we'll not accept."

"I don't know about that."

"We can't trust them. You know that."

"I wouldn't if there was any other way of getting you off the island. We can insist upon terms for our own protection."

"But there *is* another way," she said, while Chalmers stared open-eyed. "We brought two whaleboats on our schooner. One of them had an engine in it and a mast and sail, and father kept it for our use. After the natives landed here the first time Dad hid it in the mangroves near where we came when we moved to Safety Haven. It's there now, with several cans of gasoline!"

"That's fine," said Chalmers. "I'm sorry it's in their territory. I hope they don't take it into their heads to go nosing in the mangroves and find it."

"I don't think they could," she answered. "Dad dragged it up the creek and off to one side. It's covered with vines, and a lot of those have sprouted. I could hardly see it when he pointed it out to me."

XIV

SAYERS GOES PEARLING

CHALMERS AND THE GIRL SAT SNUGLY ENSCONCED in a niche on the edge of the ridge, watching the whaleboat put out for shore, all four of the schooner's occupants aboard. Save for some broken branches unnoticed in the general wealth of foliage, there was no trace of the storm, except that perhaps the air held more of coolness and the atmosphere more of clarity, so that the whole island appeared to have had its face washed, and to be basking in the sunshine.

Peaceful as the scene was, it held all the elements of tragedy. Death, under the long grasses on the hill, love in the pocket of the lava ridge, greed and murder and lust in the boat on the lagoon.

"It would be easy enough to pick them off from here," said Chalmers half in earnest, cuddling the stock of the rifle that lay beside him.

Leila shrank away from him a trifle, doubt and consternation in her eyes.

"You wouldn't murder them?" she asked.

"No, I suppose I wouldn't," he answered. "That's the worst of it. They'd pot us without a scruple. Fighting fair with men of their caliber is handicapping yourself pretty heavily. I wonder what they're up to now?"

Sayers and Tuan Yuck, each carrying a rifle, were walking up the beach towards the clearing; Hamaku, also armed, remaining at the boat with Tomi. Leila focused the glasses upon them as they disappeared in the house for a few moments, and came out again bearing what looked like clothes.

"It's father's diving suit," she said.

"Then they are going to let us alone for a while and go after the pearls in the lagoon," said Chalmers. "I wanted to bring that suit along the worst way last night, but I left it to the last on account of its bulk. If I was either Sayers or Tuan Yuck I'd hate to have to be dependent on the other's hand on the air supply."

"It is a patent suit," said Leila. "It has a compressed-air cylinder you fill with that rotary pump Sayers is carrying. It supplies air for thirty minutes after it's charged up to capacity. It's a bit complicated. I fancy they'll have some trouble with it."

"It looks as if they are having it now," he said, watching the two figures in consultation, presently joined by the natives. "They seem to be scrapping as to who's going to put it on. It'll have to be one of them. They'll never get the natives to trust themselves inside that gear. Sayers loses the toss," he announced. "Wonder if he's going to waste time and air wading in from shallow water."

"Dad used to go in by the rocks where the shell is. They go down like steps. When the natives landed here he was under water. I was in the house working, and I didn't see them till the big double canoe sailed into the lagoon. I didn't know what to do. There were fifty of them, at least, armed with spears and bows, big men, smeared with paint, horrible looking savages. And there was Dad, unconscious of it all, liable to come up any minute in the middle of them.

"While I was looking some of them jumped out on to the beach and suddenly they shouted. The crowd broke, and I could see Dad coming slowly out of the water all wet and shiny, the metal gleaming on the helmet, and the two great eyes goggling, like a sea monster. It was weird. To the savages it must have been terrible. Dad kept on rising, walking up the rocks, and, just as he left the water and started toward them they could stand it no longer. Some of them were on their knees, but they jumped up with the rest, scurried into the canoe, and paddled off in terror.

"Dad told me afterwards he saw they were frightened from the first. He said they probably took him for Maui, their great god, who lived in the sea and built their islands. He was afraid that I would show up somewhere and dispel the idea that he was superhuman, or they'd see the boat. After that he kept the launch hidden and arranged the mirrors. They never came near the island after that, though we used to see them sometimes far out at sea. Dear old Dad!"

She set her chin in the hollow of one hand and gazed pensively toward the ridge that held her father's grave. Chalmers, not wishing to intrude upon her grief, sat silently watching the investment of Sayers with the diving equipment, over the handling of which there still seemed to be considerable discussion.

Finally, Hamaku left the rest and ran along the rocks at the edge of the lagoon, looking searchingly into the water. He shouted, and the little group joined him, Sayers lumbering along in the center. At the rocks the Australian sat down, his feet swinging over the water, adjusted the necessary weights, and put on the lead-soled shoes. Then he knelt and lowered himself awkwardly backwards, disappearing gradually below the surface. Tuan Yuck and the two natives got into the boat and paddled slowly toward the place where Sayers had submerged, the Chinaman peering over the side.

"Directing him and keeping tab on him at the same time," thought Chalmers. "That's some scheme for supervising pearl fishing. I wonder what their luck is going to be?"

Leila touched him on his arm. "Look!" she said tensely, pressing the binoculars into his hands. "There—far out where the clouds end."

Where a pearly mass of trade-wind cumulus showed its sharply defined curves against the blue, Chalmers saw a sail that gleamed for a moment like gold in the sunlight. In the field of the powerful glasses it showed as a double canoe, joined by a high platform, outrigged on either side and driven by a great square sail of fine matting.

The canoes were filled with paddlers, and dark forms lounged on the deck. As he watched, the war-craft grew larger and came swiftly on before the wind. Then it swung around, the canoemen churning the sea into foam as they paddled and backed water to assist the maneuver. The big sail was lowered and quickly raised again and the great canoe raced off on the opposite tack, gradually disappearing until it was only a speck on the water.

"It's lucky they didn't come in close enough to sight the schooner's masts," he said, "or they might have been tempted to investigate. A crowd like that would be a nasty lot to tackle. I suppose they saw the reflections of the higher mirrors and it scared them off. There comes Sayers out of the water. Tuan Yuck doesn't seem to fancy the shell he's brought up."

The boat had been beached as Sayers emerged and emptied from a net bag on the sand the oysters he had found. Tuan Yuck kicked them with an emphasis that was contemptuous even at that distance. He picked up a shell and showed it to the Australian, apparently giving him a lecture on the subject of pearl oysters.

"He's picked out the wrong kind," said Leila. "It's always a distorted, crumpled shell that holds a pearl. The smooth, symmetrical ones never hold anything larger than seeds. He is going to try again."

Sayers picked up the bag and the air-cylinder was recharged. This time he sat astride of the boat's bow and let himself drop to the bottom on a signal from Tuan Yuck.

"Perhaps there are no more rich patches in the lagoon," said Leila. "It often happens that way. It would serve them right."

"It wouldn't suit us best just now," said Chalmers. "We've got a fine position, but—"

"But what? Won't you tell me exactly what you think of the situation? Please."

He looked at her calm face, the unwavering eyes and steady hands.

"All right," he said. "That's only fair. Let's thrash it out together.

"We've got to look at it from both sides. As they figure it, it's a question of us having the pearls and they the schooner. The lagoon is a side issue. They've seen what you carry in that bag." He nodded toward the black ribbon about her neck, nearly concealed by her blouse. "They think sooner or later we'll capitulate and give up the pearls for a passage. Or they may starve us out. Or they may try and rush us. They want the pearls first and last, hook or crook. And they care very little what happens to us.

"We've got the launch, unknown to them as long as they don't find it. That's to our advantage. It's good for a long voyage, barring storms. So we can eliminate the schooner. We don't want it. If we had it we could hardly handle it without help. But they are going to watch us as closely as we keep tab on them. It's a good deal of a deadlock. My best hope is to take them by surprise or that they start a quarrel between the two of them. The most serious thing is lack of ammunition. I've got to get hold of that somehow—and soon. But we'll manage somehow, don't you worry?"

Leila Denman smiled back at him. She was beginning to appraise him, and ranked him far higher than he dreamed. Through all the whirl of events since his arrival she had been inclined to look upon him as frank, impetuous, generous, courageous, but, after all, a good deal of a boy. Now as she noted the set of his lean jaw, the gray of his eyes, like hardened steel, while he calculated their chances and faced them, she felt an absolute sense of protection, and recognized him not as merely manly, but a man, in every stalwart seventy-two inches of him.

His unshaven beard furred his sunburned face, his duck clothes were rumpled, torn and grimed, but they did not hide the well-muscled strength of his broad shoulders nor the litheness of the waist above the narrow hips. Altogether Leila found him very good to look upon. She made a permanent decision in favor of aquiline noses and straight hair, dark brown and closely trimmed to the well-shaped skull.

"That's the way he must always wear it," she told herself, then, noting his steady glance, blushed, afraid he might have read her thoughts.

Suddenly the lava ridge upon which they were perched vibrated and swung beneath them. The crests of the hills seemed to waver. The still water of the lagoon flowed like a splintered mirror. A rasping, grinding sound as of thunder came from the interior of the island. A myriad birds rose and wheeled, screaming.

The boat below them made frantically for the schooner, looking, with its outspread moving oars, like some frightened water-bug. The schooner plunged at its cable like a startled horse at the halter-rope and brought up rocking in the troubled water. The whole place seemed to move as the clear sky above them pitched, and for a second the sea-line tilted as one sees it through a ship's porthole. Then came the grinding noise again with a rasping jar as if the island had been adrift and suddenly had run aground.

Leila had naturally stretched out both arms to Chalmers in her terror, and he, as instinctively, had enfolded her in his own.

"It's all over now," he said, holding her for a moment longer while she still trembled.

Her head was on his breast and the fragrance of her hair filled his nostrils and left them spoiled for all other perfumes.

"It's silly of me, isn't it," she said as he released her. "But that was my very first earthquake and one seems so utterly helpless. Thank you!"

She blushed again while her eyes pleaded with him to ignore her confusion.

"Look there, Leila," he said pointing to the lagoon.

A strange figure, gleaming with the water that ran from the harness it wore, the sun making bursts of radiance on the metal of his helmet, Sayers broke from the water, stumbling clumsily to the sand where, anchored by his weighted boots, he stood swaying, shaking his fists at the boat and raving impotently while he strove to unfasten his helmet.

It was a ludicrous sight and Chalmers guffawed outright, the girl joining in the laugh and forgetting her own fright.

"It must have given him a rare scare under the water," said Chalmers at last.

"He'll not want to go pearling again in a hurry," suggested the girl.

Chalmers' face lost all traces of laughter. The tremor was likely to force matters to an issue all around. The natives would believe this a fresh proof that Motutabu was bewitched, and that might lead to a decision to leave the island, which would infallibly be prefaced by a determined attempt to get the pearls.

Ammunition was a prime necessity. He must devise some means of securing it. He was not greatly alarmed about the earthquake, unless it should be repeated. The island was evidently of volcanic origin and might have been affected by a main disturbance a thousand miles or more away.

Nor was he discouraged at the odds against him. Chalmers was essentially human. He had enough of the true gambler in him to enjoy the game the more as his stake diminished. Any fool could ride a winning horse, he believed, and he possessed another attribute that stood him in good stead, an increasing desire to fight back harder and harder as the contest grew more difficult.

On the beach, Sayers was showing that he was made of sterner stuff than Chalmers had credited him with. As the boat came back for him, he succeeded in freeing himself of his helmet and at the same time his opinion of Tuan Yuck's desertion of him.

"So you *are* a yellow cur after all," he shouted, "a sneaking, cowardly Mongolian mongrel. Thought I was dead and hoped it too, I suppose. You low-lived, Oriental hound!"

His language grew more livid at Tuan Yuck's imperturbability.

"The water was safer than the land, my friend," said the Oriental suavely. "If we had tried to jump out on the beach we should likely have broken our legs. Anyway, we could not help you until we saw you. Also the boys were frightened at first, but I have convinced them that this is nothing more than happens in Hawaii every month. If you do not want to go down again I will put on the suit, though, as I warned you, I can not go very deep on account of my heart."

The logic of the speech was good, but Sayers, convinced that Tuan Yuck had meant to desert him, could not recognize it. The incident renewed the determination he had made to stay ashore nights and let Tuan Yuck go off to the schooner. But he said nothing of that thought for the moment.

"I didn't say I was going to quit, did I?" he growled. "I didn't forget to bring up my haul, either. Look at those. Are they any better?"

Tuan Yuck toed over the oysters and shook his head.

"Not worth opening, Sayers. A *baroque* or two, perhaps. Even that is doubtful. Good for shell only. We'll have to try another patch."

Later in the afternoon Chalmers saw the boat take Tuan Yuck off to the schooner, leaving Sayers, now freed from his diving-garb, on the beach. The boat returned in a little while and the two natives carried up some stores and set them down on the sand, The Kanakas started to leave, but Sayers detained them and they went up to the clearing, coming back with material from which they started a fire blazing in the dusk.

A case was broached and a bottle passed round. Tomi's voice was lifted up in song and the others joined in. The Australian took up his zither that had been brought in the boat and soon native songs of questionable delicacy were being roared out.

Here was Chalmers' opportunity. Sayers and the natives, between the attractions of the gin and the singing, were evidently ashore for a night of it. Tuan Yuck would be on the schooner alone, and sooner or later must succumb to the seduction of his opium pipe.

A voice called to him out of the darkness below him:

"Dinner is served, Sir Sentinel. Look out you don't fall coming down."

"What is the program for tonight?" she asked presently. "Why so serious and silent? Who takes the dog-watch? And, if I do, am I supposed to bark at all intruders?"

"I'm going to swim off to the schooner tonight," he said. "Sayers and the boys are ashore and Tuan Yuck will be in poppy-land. I'm going to build a raft after dinner and I'm going to bring back some ammunition and a lot of other things, including a razor."

"All right," she said. "What time do you start?"

"I'll have to go just before the end of the ebb and come back on the flood."

"And that means?"

"About midnight."

"I'll be ready."

"There's no need for you to stay up."

"Indeed there is. I'm going with you."

XV

LOVE LEAVEN

CHALMERS' PROTESTS WERE UNAVAILING. Leila Denman's arguments were both convincing and numerous.

"I am not going to be left alone on this beach imagining all sorts of dreadful things happening to you," she said. "If there should, I want to be there. They can't be more dreadful than what would happen to me if you didn't come back. I can swim as well as you can. Wait till you see me. I've got my bathing-suit, and I can really help you."

"There seems to be a mutiny in full progress," Chalmers answered, "but I've got to quell it. Some one's got to stay on watch here."

"Pouf!" She dismissed the reason with a charming moue, like the puff of an imaginary cigarette. "We can watch them ever so much better from the lagoon. You are afraid I'm going to be a hindrance—I'm not. You are going to make a little raft, you said, for the things you are going to bring back?"

"Yes, ammunition, some clothes, my charts, the chronometer, and, if I can get away with it, the schooner's compass."

"You are going to climb aboard and get them?"

"Naturally."

"And how are you going to load up your raft without help?"

Chalmers laughed.

"Fairly won," he said. "It would take me ever so much longer by myself. I'll give in—as long as we know there are no sharks. But you must promise to stay in the water."

"Aye, aye, sir! The mutineers return to duty," she said gaily.

"Having achieved their point," he countered.

He marveled at the buoyancy of her spirit, at the sheer pluck of her. That she was not in the least disillusioned concerning the dangers that hourly surrounded them he was assured. Yet, in the face of them all, in the prospect of being left to the vicious whims of Tuan Yuck and Sayers, should he fail her, she was the gay comrade, the gallant "pal" who insisted upon her full share of the perils.

And she trusted him. The thought was an elixir. To its inspiration the subtle alchemy of his body responded, charging the blood with energies that gave new strength to his muscles, invigorating every nerve and sinew till the whole coordinated like the parts of a perfect machine.

Both were heart free, both ripe for the friendly virus with which Cupid tips his arrows, and that ubiquitous godling chuckled at Chalmers' attempts to regulate his passion as the two built their little raft by the light of their fire, the blazing stars and a sinking moon.

The setting could not have been completer for romance. Each was conscious of the proximity of the other and felt little rippling thrills of delight as they came into casual contact over their work. But to Chalmers, the pearls that nestled in her bosom, gaining fresh luster from the magnetism of her young body, seemed as insuperable a barrier between them as if they had been the actual boulders of an impassable wall.

Without conceit, he recognized that both of them were seeped in an exaltation of spirit that made life seem very sweet and free from care, despite their dangers. He was not blind to the fact that Leila shared the emotions that possessed him as their hands met, or that a certain adorable shyness that was both a lure and a promise shone sometimes in her eyes; but he hugged the thought that he would be dishonorable to take any advantage of a mood that might pass, hugged it as the Spartan boy held the fox that gnawed his breast.

She was an heiress; he had nothing ahead but the earnings of a profession to which he was not accredited by nature. So he controlled himself as best he could and checked the growing impulse to tell her how sweet and brave and altogether desirable she was. Once, when the mischievous wind whipped a perfumed strand of her hair across his face, he deliberately went away from her on the idle pretense of looking for more driftwood, though the raft was then complete, and stood dizzily facing the lagoon to fight it out.

"You came pretty close to being a cad," he told himself. "Another second and you would have kissed her. A fine protector you are for a lonely girl."

A tiny voice—it was Cupid's—whispered, "She would not have minded." And he thrust it from him as unworthy. Whereat Cupid, counting his remaining arrows, laughed, knowing well the power of that beneficent venom on their tips, composed of elements allied to hope and youth and health that would crystallize to happiness.

Leila recognized his restraint, guessed partly at its reasons, admired it and was piqued at it at the same moment. At times she devoutly wished the pearls were still at the bottom of the sea, though her father's spirit, strong within her, fiercely resented the giving of them up to their would-be possessors, and, womanlike, she loved them as gems and for what they would bring, and could not see why such a dower should make her less desirable.

So Cupid, well satisfied, left them there beneath the stars, and winged his way to other targets.

It was close to midnight before their task was ended and the little float of driftwood and boughs, compactly lashed together, carried to the water's edge ready for launching. The rays of Sayers' fire flickered beyond the cape and the sound of ribald voices came to them now and then in the quiet night. The scattered rocks at the foot of the headland were clear and the ebb was nearly at its limit.

"We'll pile it up with seaweed," said Chalmers, "and let it drift down on the current. It runs nearly as fast as we can swim. All we have to do is to guide it. We'll keep low in the water, and if any one should be on the lookout they'll take it for a loose mass of weed. It's about time to start."

"I'll be ready in five minutes," said Leila, disappearing into her cave with one of the lanterns they had brought from the clearing.

Chalmers took off his shoes and with his case-knife hacked off the legs of his grimy trousers well above the knee for freedom in swimming, promising himself a new outfit from the schooner. Tuan Yuck by this time would be well under the influence of opium, he imagined, and there would be little trouble or danger about securing what he wanted. He discarded his shirt, tightened his belt and stood up stalwart and ready for action.

While he waited he examined the clip of cartridges in the automatic handle, regreased the weapons and the blade of the knife and replaced the latter in his belt. The pistol was on a lanyard ready to put round his neck at the end of the swim. For the trip it would ride on the raft.

Leila came to her cave-mouth, trim in her bathing-suit, and looked at him admiringly as he stood by the light of their fire, gazing seaward. He looked very capable, very handsome, in a manly way, she thought.

"I'm ready," she said.

He looked at her approvingly.

"I'd slip off that skirt when we get into deep water," he suggested.

"I will," she answered. "I'm not going to be handicapped."

They waded quietly into the water, impressed with the necessity for caution, and pushed the raft before them into the swing of the current. Seaweed was piled upon it, trailing in the water. The moon had sunk, the dim mass of the platform was hardly distinguishable as it floated down the star-sown lagoon toward the cape.

They made as little motion as possible, fearing the phosphorescence they disturbed might betray them by its regular flashes. Leila slipped off her skirt and they swam in water that was as warm as midday and luminously alive. Green fire swirled from them as they paddled easily along, their hands resting on the raft. Bubbles and streaks of liquid flame the color of burning alcohol broke along the sides and in the wake of the float.

The blaze where Sayers and the two natives caroused burned brightly. The three still chanted in snatches, and boisterous laughter punctuated the songs. The voices were obviously those of drunken men whose debauch was soon likely to end in heavy sleep. Reefward, the masts of the schooner showed faintly against the sky. As they drew near to the hull they looked in vain for a light in Tuan Yuck's cabin. Everything seemed set for the success of their undertaking.

Chalmers guided the raft to the bows and, clinging to the bowsprit stays with one hand, fastened the raft by a line already attached to it.

"Hang on here," he whispered. "I'll lower the things down to you. I'll be as quick as I can."

"All right," she answered softly, and he deftly swung himself up and clambered over the bowsprit.

The tide was on the turn and Leila prepared to keep the raft from bumping at the schooner's side. Presently the influence of the flood swung it clear as the schooner slowly responded to the shifting current. She let go of the stays, resting her folded arms on the raft, her body in the warm water, and waited for Chalmers' reappearance. Farther aft, the open porthole of Tuan Yuck's cabin remained dark, like the socket of a blind eye.

On deck, Chalmers, treading lightly as a cat, stepped to the open companionway and stealthily descended into the cabin. He had no light, but he knew the familiar position of everything, and there had been no changes.

He listened at the door of Tuan Yuck's cabin. Inside, he could hear the Chinaman breathing heavily. The door was light proof.

He tiptoed into his own cabin and found an electric torch, safe where he had left it. He touched the contacts and the ray shone out brightly.

XVI

The Raid on the Schooner

The raft was laden to its full capacity as Chalmers descended into the cabin for his last trip. He had built it so that the deck rode high above the water, and he blessed its buoyancy as he lowered the things he selected, slung in a bag improvised from his oilskin coat, to Leila, who stowed them deftly on the float.

The cartridges he had found in their original stowage under a locker seat and these he took first. Then followed canned goods from another locker, the bulk of his personal belongings—including the razor—the schooner's log, the case of charts, the chronometer, his sextant, and, last of all, the compass, which he unscrewed from the binnacle post.

It was not his intention to leave the schooner destitute of steerage implements. Now that he knew of the launch in the mangroves, it was his first desire that Sayers would muster up enough cocksureness to take the schooner under his command, providing they could be persuaded to give up the pearls as too difficult to procure, content perhaps with what they found in the lagoon.

But there was a spare compass in the cabin and he wanted the more reliable instrument. He took the automatic on its lanyard from his neck and lowered it to Leila, together with the electric torch. As he prepared to slip over the side and rejoin her, elated at the success of the raid, he remembered Tuan Yuck's rule. To secure it would be to reduce the enemy's efficiency by one third. He had taken all the spare loads for the Winchesters save what might be carried in their belts.

"Just a minute," he called down to the waiting girl, hardly discernible beneath the curve of the bows, her face a dim gray oval looking up at him with eyes that held the sparkle of the reflected stars that spangled the water all about her. "Never mind the torch!"

He remembered where the rifle stood when he had first noticed it and determined to take it. As he reached carefully for it in the velvety blackness, he fancied he heard a faint hissing, sputtering sound, like a noisy fuse.

He stopped, every movement arrested, intent upon the strange sound. Suddenly his spine tingled and he knew that he was not alone in the cabin. His senses, almost supernaturally alert, telegraphed to his brain that a door had been opened, ever so softly, behind him—the door of Tuan Yuck's cabin.

He crouched rapidly, circling about in the same motion. He heard the swift intake of a breath, the swish of an arm in a silken covering above his head and, grappling for his foe, found only vacancy.

Which side of him the Oriental stood he could not tell. The cabin was in pitchy darkness through which his sight strained helplessly. How Tuan Yuck was armed he could only guess. The rifle was useless in this kind of *mêlée* and he reached for his knife. Instantly two hands that seemed made of steel clutched at his wrist and twisted skin and flesh in opposite directions. In the swift agony of the attack his tortured tendons were momentarily paralyzed and the knife fell tinkling to the floor.

He heard the scuff of Tuan Yuck's foot as the weapon was kicked away at the same instant that he managed to tear himself free, and groped for his opponent's arms. They writhed from his grasp with a vigor that astounded him. In his first struggle with the Oriental, in the clearing, he had been surprised at the other's wiry strength where he had expected flaccidity. But then he had held him pinioned and now the Chinaman was taking the offensive. He pursued Tuan Yuck, bumping against the fixed table in the center of the cabin, unable to obtain more than the briefest grip on the arms that warded him off so effectually.

The uncanny presentiment came to him that the Oriental's eyes possessed the faculty of seeing in the dark. The next second he was sure of it. The steely hands caught him again, one at the right wrist, the other high up, pressing a nerve that left the arm numb and helpless. A swiftly thrown-up knee was applied to his elbow, an instant more and his arm would have been broken, but Chalmers kicked out viciously in a wide circle and swept Tuan Yuck's legs from under him.

Both crashed to the ground together. Chalmers was amazed at the tiger-like ferocity with which Tuan Yuck strained against his hold and the claw-like grip that tore at his muscles, fighting always to reach his throat. The thought flashed that this fury must be born of opium and would diminish.

He held his own as they writhed on the floor of the cabin, waiting for the right time to exert all his strength in one explosive impulse. The moment came and he rolled uppermost, his fingers feeling for the other's throat. As they twisted, Tuan Yuck's head struck the post of the table with a thud, his form suddenly grew limp and his struggling arms fell outstretched on the floor.

As Chalmers instinctively relaxed his hold, Tuan Yuck's chest heaved upward and his whole body came to sudden life. The crafty Oriental had seized upon the sounding but comparatively harmless blow as a ruse. His right arm eluded Chalmers' swift pounce and twisted upward like a snake. Chalmers brought his left knee down hard upon the other's right biceps, striving to keep his poise upon the writhing form, but the action was too late.

Tuan Yuck had found the knife, perhaps his cat-like eyes had seen it!

The blade slashed Chalmers' shoulder. He could hear the squeak of the steel against his collar-bone. By some miracle of luck the plunging point was diverted in the scuffle and the blow was only a glancing one.

With the shock of the wound Chalmers' fury outmatched that of Tuan Yuck.

"You yellow devil!" he exploded pantingly as he held the other's wrists in his clutch at last, squatting upon his chest, each knee in the hollow between the Chinaman's upper and forearms. The warm blood that ran down his left arm angered him. He held but one desire—to gain possession of the knife and drive it home, the primal instinct of a man fighting for his life.

Tuan Yuck's teeth gritted and the reek of his opium-tainted breath came upward as he spat in Chalmers' face. He flinched at the nastiness of it and the Chinaman with one mighty effort set his foot against a locker and, so braced, upset Chalmers' balance, smashing the latter's head against a locker.

Now their positions were reversed though Chalmers still held the other's wrists in a vise-like grip, dizzy as he was from the blow and the loss of blood. Already he felt a faintness growing upon him as Tuan Yuck pressed his advantage. His grasp was almost automatic now, and it was the hand of the arm that was wounded that resisted the tug of the Chinaman's right wrist to be free and deal the fatal blow.

Hitherto he had thought of nothing but the fight. It had taken only a minute or two of swift, strenuous struggle in the dark and there had been no time to consider other matters. Now, as he lay prone, his strength ebbing, the thought of Leila waiting in the water outside, only a few feet away, maddened him to fresh effort. Tuan Yuck met it with a cackling laugh.

"Yellow devil, am I?" he said. "I'll send you to a white man's hell, you young fool."

Chalmers' fingers seemed nerveless. He could no longer fill his lungs beneath his opponent's weight.

There was a swift pattering on deck, a rush of feet down the companionway, a circle of brilliant light that searched the gloom and caught the blade of Tuan Yuck's knife as the Oriental plucked his wrist free at last and started the lunge that would end the fight.

The sudden glare from behind startled him but did not halt the blow. Swiftly as it descended, the girl was quicker and the tube of the lamp came down clubwise, the heavy bull's-eye of the lens striking the base of Tuan Yuck's skull with all the force her strong young arm could muster.

Tuan Yuck pitched forward, his head striking the floor beyond Chalmers' shoulder, the knife driven into the floor of the cabin, where it snapped off short. The ray of the lamp went out with the blow and Leila's efforts failed to relight it.

Chalmers, roused from his swooning condition by the torch ray and his recognition of Leila, struggled to free himself from the incubus of Tuan Yuck's weight. Leila, kneeling on the floor, assisted him to rise.

"Quick!" she said. "Tuan Yuck has signaled ashore. They are coming in the boat!"

She gave her strength to him as his will fought its way back to full consciousness and supported him with her shoulder as he staggered up the companionway and across the deck to the rail. A confused shouting came over the water. The fresh air helped to revive Chalmers and the emergency rallied his forces, though his head ached furiously.

"Are you badly hurt?" Leila asked anxiously.

His forearm rested on her shoulder, one of her slender arms was about his waist. He braced himself to stand without her aid.

"I'm all right," he said. "Come on, we've got to be getting out of this. We might hold them off, I suppose; but we don't want their old schooner."

He essayed a laugh and hurried forward, reeling a little as he went.

"You're bleeding." she said with a half-checked sob.

The revelation of her tenderness did more for him than any surgery.

"It's only a surface slash," he said. "The salt water will help, and we can patch it up when we get back. There's nothing serious. I got a whack on the head that did the most damage."

He proved it by straddling the rail and, hanging to it by his uninjured arm, slipping into the water. Leila was there before him, ready to aid. The salt water smarted, but it acted both as a tonic and as an astringent and he reached the raft easily enough.

"You'll have to cast it adrift," he said. "Pull the loose end."

She tugged at the slipknot, the rope fell with a little splash and the raft began to fall away from the schooner, the flood-tide bearing it back toward the cape and Safety Haven.

Inshore, there was splashing and confusion, the shouting of orders by Sayers and the drunken babble of the two natives. Spurts of pale flame flashed up as their oars beat the phosphorescent water in an effort to get the whaleboat straightened out for the schooner.

Chalmers floated full length, his right hand on the raft for support. Beside him Leila, with a steady scissors stroke of her legs, drove the raft onward, aided by the tide.

All their attention centered on their own craft, the Australian and his Kanaka aids failed to see the raft, succeeding at last clumsily in getting the whaleboat in line for the schooner, Sayers cursing loudly at every inefficient stroke and the natives answering him in the coarse familiarity of mutual drunkenness.

The flood was strengthening and the raft was soon beyond the headland

and in the home waters of Safety Haven. They found bottom off their starting point and stood upright. An indistinct murmur from the schooner barely reached them.

"How do you feel?" asked Leila. "Can you walk up to the caves?"

"I'm not even wobbly any more," he answered, not with absolute truth. "I've stopped bleeding. But I'd better stay down here to repel boarders in case they try to start something. You might fetch down a rifle. We'll want to stop them at long range."

"I'll bring two," she answered, "and something to dress that wound."

Grateful for the chance to more completely pull himself together, Chalmers sat on the beach, his back against a rock. Aside from a little light-headedness he felt fairly fit. The slash from Tuan Yuck had evidently severed no important veins nor arteries and, though his shoulder was stiffening, he felt no severe pain.

"Flesh wound, I guess," he soliloquized. "Pretty lucky for our side. The darling!" He closed his eyes and saw again the ray of the torch, the flare of it on Leila's face as she raised her arm for the blow. "The darling!" he said again, more loudly.

Leila, coming quietly and swiftly down the beach, lantern in hand, heard it. Her heart bounded and she kissed her hand to him in the darkness.

"Did you call?" she asked.

"Me? Why, no," he answered.

Her lips silently formed two syllables that by daylight might have been recognized as "stu-pid" though coupled with a smile that robbed them of any sting.

"Here are the rifles," she said. "And now, if you'll sit still, I'll dress your wound."

She set the lantern on a rock and cut his sleeveless vest away with the scissors she had brought. The blood had not stiffened owing to the soaking of the return swim, and the wound showed clean-lipped and pale. With strips of plaster she dexterously strapped the edges together and applied a cooling salve, above which she laid a pad of cotton and bound the shoulder up with a broad bandage.

"I brought our surgical kit along last night," she said. "The salve is wonderful. It's made from native herbs. If you don't have to use your arm any more tonight that cut will be healing up by tomorrow. Really, it's not very deep."

"I thought it wasn't," he said. "I used my arm after it happened and I knew there was nothing very much the matter outside of the loss of a little blood. And that won't hurt me. Tell me, how did you arrive on time to give our Oriental friend that most prodigious swat in exactly the right place?"

"I didn't know where I hit him," she said. "I struck blindly. You had just left me. I had the torch still in one hand when something made me look along the ship's side and I saw Tuan Yuck's head stuck out of his porthole looking forward toward me. It disappeared and I pushed the raft under the bows, hoping he had not seen me. Then his arm was thrust out. There was some sort of a torch in his hand that broke out into a crimson flame."

"A Coston signal," said Chalmers. "That's what I heard sputtering. He must have taken them in his cabin for emergencies. Go on!"

"As soon as it started to flare I slipped my finger through the ring on the torch, reached up for the stay with that hand and drew myself up out of sight. They were shouting on the beach and I knew they'd be on board in a few moments, so I managed to scramble over the bows somehow, with the torch still in my hand, and started to warn you.

"I heard you scuffling in the cabin. I didn't know what else to do—I'd left the pistol on the raft, like a ninny—so I went down into the cabin and flashed the light on, and when I saw you underneath and covered with blood I—I struck at the back of his head. I wish I'd killed him!" she ended passionately, her eyes blazing in the lantern light; then she bowed her head on her knees and sobbed.

Chalmers looked at her helplessly. He wanted to gather her into his arms and comfort her, but reached over and patted her shoulder instead.

"Don't cry," he said.

She lifted her head and looked at him as if he had struck her. Then she bounded to her feet.

"Perhaps I did kill him," she cried. "I hope so. I hate him. I hate all men!"

Astounded into silence and inaction Chalmers saw her disappear up the beach.

"I wonder what I've done?" he asked himself, not knowing that his sin was one of omission, not commission.

He sat there a little wearily, his rifle across his knees, watching the point. There was no sound from the schooner, the night seemed very quiet after the excitement of the fight and he was very lonely.

There was a light step at his side, felt rather than heard, and he turned his head to see Leila. She had discarded her bathing-suit and wore her linen skirt and middy blouse, with her hair braided in long plaits that hung over her shoulders and bosom. In her hands she carried two mugs of steaming liquid.

"I left the soup kettle on the ashes when we started," she said demurely. "This will do you a world of good. I brought one for myself, so we can drink it together."

The aroma of the thick soup was supremely grateful. The draught heartened him. He marveled at the swift change in the girl's demeanor and wondered how many Leilas there were in the one dainty body. But, acquiring wisdom, however tardily, he said nothing.

"That soup has made me drowsy instead of waking me up," he said. "I've got to keep awake, you know. And we've got to haul up that raft."

He yawned prodigiously.

"I'll pull up the raft," she said. "You've got to rest your arm. It will be easy on the rising tide."

When she came back he was asleep under the influence of the veronal she had mixed with his soup. She smiled, lifted his head gently and pillowed it on her lap, then, with the rifles handy, leaned back against the rock and kept watch until long after dawn.

XVII

Sayers Makes a Proposition

Chalmers was furious with himself when he awoke and saw Leila's tired face and the eyes that had purple shadows beneath them, and he was even disposed to be indignant with her when she confessed that she had drugged him.

"Suppose they had tackled us?" he asked.

"I only gave you five grains," she said. "I could have awakened you easily enough. You simply *had* to get some rest. You are the mainstay of the camp, you know." She smiled at him wearily as he helped her with his sound arm stiffly to get up. "How are you feeling?"

"Bully! And I've got the appetite of a shark. If you'll help me pack some of these canned things up to the caves, we'll get breakfast and then you'll turn in and get some sleep. That salve is wonderful. I can use my arm, and my shoulder only feels a bit stiff."

"You'll wear that arm in a sling, sir," she said with a pretty show of authority. "I'll fix one for you as soon as I've dressed your wound."

"That isn't a wound," he protested. "That's only a scratch. I'll bet it isn't a circumstance to the way Tuan Yuck's head feels this morning. Mine's stopped buzzing, thank Heaven. I wonder what their next move will be? Did you see any signs of them?"

"Neither sight nor sound."

"Well, we've got all the spare ammunition. That shoe that pinched is on their foot now.

"What did you do with your pearls last night?" he asked later, as they ate their breakfast.

"I buried them in the cave. I've got them on now." She pointed to the ribbon about her neck. "If dad hadn't worked so hard to get them and planned what they were going to mean for me, I'd give them up if they'd only go away and give us a chance to follow later. I'm a little afraid of this island after that earthquake."

"No use worrying about that," he said. "What did your father plan for you with the pearls?"

"Oh—we were going to travel lots. And then he wanted me to have clothes, I suppose, and all the things a girl wants."

"Humph!"

Chalmers set down his mug of coffee and gazed gloomily in front of him. Leila looked at him for a moment, her eyes tender.

"Don't be silly," she said softly.

As he looked up she blushed scarlet, jumped up and ran to her cave. She paused at the entrance and spoke over her shoulder.

"I'm going to sleep for a while," she said. "Take care of yourself."

Chalmers' shoulder hurt more than he had acknowledged to Leila but the native ointment really possessed great curative qualities and the slash when it was dressed showed every sign of healing by first intention. But he managed to sprawl his way up to the lookout.

The beach was deserted. So, to all appearances, was the schooner. The whaleboat trailed alongside, the oars sticking up from between the thwarts as they had been left by the natives overnight. Through the glasses he made out the ashes of Sayers' beach fire, with empty gin bottles scattered here and there in the sand.

"Headache of more than one sort aboard the schooner this morning, I fancy," he told himself. "They are not likely to disturb us for a while, at least."

He clambered down again and busied himself removing the cartridges and the rest of the load on the raft up to his cave, where he stored them with satisfaction, burying the shells in the sand. Working with only one hand, the morning was well gone by the time he had finished the task.

Leila came out from her cave soon after noon, refreshed from her sleep, smiled at him and passed to her rock apartments, returning presently fresh from a dip in the mermaid's pool, her golden-brown hair streaming down to her waist, full of rainbow iridescence.

She perched on a rock beside him.

"You don't mind if I let it hang down while it dries?" she asked him.

"No, I don't mind," answered Chalmers dryly.

She looked at him quickly, as if trying to read his mood.

"You look all fagged out," she declared. "And I'm feeling fresh and rested. Nothing's happened?"

"Not yet. I think they are all glad to layoff for a while. You must have given our friend Tuan Yuck a pretty hard smash. He's not the sort to put off trying to get even. Sayers and the crew will probably sleep all day. We're tolerably safe as long as we keep a good lookout. We may run a little shy on the menu, but we won't starve. All we have to do is to watch the front door. And that reminds me, did you notice the alarm-clock I lowered down to you in the first load for the raft?"

"I did. And I was afraid the thing would go off. I could just imagine it ringing away and I turned the alarm switch off, though the clock wasn't going. What's it for?"

"For our watches. It won't do for either of us to watch all night and be sleepy all day. We can split the night up into tricks. It isn't dark until seven and the days are getting longer. We'll make the first watch from dark until midnight, then midnight to four in the morning, and a short trick from four until daylight. We can make up lost sleep in the afternoons."

"You'll let me do my share, as you promised?"

"Surely. We'll alternate. I'll take the first and last tricks tonight and tomorrow morning—and tomorrow it's your turn. The alarm-clock is for the one who's sleeping. One of us must be on the beach or up on the headland all the time. Daytimes there's little danger of surprise."

"Then you'll turn in for a nap now, while I keep a lookout?"

"I will," he consented. "I am tired. You're the best kind of a partner, Leila. Fire, if anything shows up. We can afford the cartridges now, thank Heaven."

She flushed with pleasure, picked up a rifle and went down to the lagoon.

Chalmers was roused out of a sound sleep by the signal, sounding like an explosion to his sleepy ears. He jumped up, wincing as he forgot to favor his damaged shoulder, and raced down the sand between the rocks, pistol in hand. At first he could not see Leila, and his heart sank within him at the thought that she had been surprised or surrounded. Then he heard her calling to him from the aerie on the headland.

"There's a boat putting off from the schooner and heading this way," she called down to him. "The natives are rowing and Sayers is steering. He's got a white flag on a pole. They stopped when I fired in the air, but they are coming on slowly."

Chalmers considered rapidly.

"It can't do any harm to see what they are up to," he said. "Better come down, Leila. We'll wait for them on the beach."

She climbed down lightly and stood by his side. In a few minutes the whaleboat showed, rowing slowly past the cape. The lagoon between there and the reef was barely fifty yards across. Chalmers challenged them.

"Way enough there," he cried. "Keep your oars in the water. Don't come in too close. Sayers, put your hands up! Cover him, Leila."

She lifted her rifle obediently. The natives, backing water, held the boat almost motionless as Sayers held up his arms.

"Don't shoot, miss," he grinned. "This is a peace mission. Flag of truce, you know."

"You keep your hands up, just the same, Sayers," commanded Chalmers. "You boys row in till you touch bottom. You'll have to wade ashore, Sayers. I'm taking no chances. Don't put down your hands till I tell you, and the first one who takes his hands off those oars gets a hole through him."

The Kanakas rowed carefully into the shallows and the Australian got out awkwardly into the water, his hands above his head.

"I'm not armed, Chalmers," he said. "I'm trusting you."

"I'm not trusting you," retorted Chalmers sternly. "Come on up on the beach. That's close enough. You boys back off and row up and down slowly till we call for you. No monkey business."

A look at his face convinced Hamaku and Tomi that strict obedience was a very urgent necessity and they followed out his instructions, rowing gingerly up and down a short distance from shore, the whites of their eyes showing ludicrously as they watched the rifle that the girl handled with grim precision.

"Turn around, Sayers."

As the Australian showed his shoulders, Chalmers walked up to him, placed the muzzle of his pistol in the small of his back with a convincing firmness and, taking his left arm from the sling, felt for any weapons the other might carry.

"Honor bright," said Sayers. "I'm playing fair. Glad your arm isn't entirely out of commission. You put Tuan Yuck properly on the shelf. Walloped him with that light-stick of yours, didn't you? I found it smashed after we got there and got a lamp going. Can I put these down now? Thanks. If you don't mind, I'll take a seat."

He settled himself comfortably on a rock.

"Don't mind if I smoke a cigarette, do you? I've got the makings." He started to roll one, but the tobacco shook out of the paper in his nerveless hands. "I don't suppose you've got a drink, have you? There's a bottle in the boat."

"It can stay there," said Chalmers shortly. "What's the idea, Sayers?"

The Australian leered evilly, and there was a malicious gleam in his bloodshot eyes.

"Visitors not welcome, eh?" he said. "I don't know that I blame you any."

Chalmers took a step toward him.

"No offense!" Sayers hastened to say deprecatingly. "You mistake my meaning. Now this is what I've come for."

He had bunglingly achieved a cigarette at last and now lit it, crossing his legs, blowing out a cloud of smoke, and looking keenly at Chalmers.

"You don't like Tuan Yuck and you don't like me. That's granted," he commenced. "You don't think we've got anything in common, but there's one thing we both agree upon—neither of us have any use for Tuan Yuck."

He paused to notice the effect of his words. Leila called a crisp word of warning to the natives who had slowed up in their rowing, evidently trying to listen.

"You work well together, you two," went on Sayers. "I'll say that for your side. We don't. If I'd known you were so close to murdering that Chink last night I'm —— if I'd have tried to help him. I suppose, though, the two of you would have stolen the schooner if we hadn't come off. I see you took most everything you could lay your hands on as it was." His eyes roved to the raft on the beach close by.

"I've got to hand it to you, Chalmers," he said half grudgingly. "You're smarter than I gave you credit for. That's where I was a fool. I ought to have tied up with you instead of with Tuan Yuck long ago. That's all right," he deprecated as he caught the look in Chalmers' eyes. "We may get together yet.

"Tuan Yuck's a crook," he went on. "He'd double-cross the devil and come close to getting away with it. He's for Tuan Yuck first, last and all the time. He's tried to turn the Kanakas against me. As it is I daren't let 'em out of my sight or he'll hypnotize 'em. And I wouldn't trust myself on that schooner with him for sour apples.

"Now see here, Chalmers." He leaned forward, trying to speak convincingly. "You've got Tuan Yuck sized up. You couldn't believe anything he promised. You've made a fool of him into the bargain. He's crazy mad to get even. His head is so stiff from that wallop he can't move it. And those eyes of his ain't pleasant company at the best of times. Now you can trust me because I've got to trust you. I'll give you the best of it.

"I don't believe there's any more rich shell in that lagoon. I brought up a dozen samples from different patches yesterday and they were all blanks. I don't give a solitary whoop if there's a million in there. I want to get shut of Tuan Yuck, and off this island. If you want to come back to the lagoon later, well and good. The girl's got plenty to pay all expenses and set us all three up.

"Now here's my proposition. Split the pearls into three shares. That means one for me and two for you if you play your cards right. Hold on! No offense, I tell you. I'm just using my eyes. A blind man could see she's in love with you—and ought to be after all you've done for her."

"Go on," said Chalmers grimly.

"Now don't go to getting huffy, Chalmers. I'm talking sense. I deserve something. I started the trip. The girl would have died here if we hadn't come. I supplied the information, didn't I?"

"What do you propose to do with Tuan Yuck?"

"Do with him? Do what you like with him. Feed him to the sharks. Leave him here to make faces at himself in the mirrors if you're tender-hearted about hurting him. You take up my proposition and I'll attend to Tuan Yuck. I know what he'd do to me if he got the chance.

"I could sail the schooner back to the Gilberts at a pinch," he went on, his face smoothing from the convulsed snarl it had worn when he was speaking of Tuan Yuck. "But you've got the pearls and you've fixed yourself properly to keep 'em. I don't want to go empty-handed. Tuan Yuck'll do both of us dirt. You know that. Now you and me and the girl can fix it up nicely. You can't leave here without the schooner. Now what do you say?"

Chalmers said nothing but motioned toward the boat.

"I'm too high, am I?" asked Sayers. "Then cut my share in half. You can land me anywhere you want to where I can get in touch with the outside and go on. Don't be a fool. Say the word and I'll agree to turn over Tuan Yuck. He's doped with opium now in his cabin."

"Call the boat in, Leila," said Chalmers.

"Hold on, now. The girl's got some say in the matter. Do the fair thing, miss," said Sayers as the girl came within easy earshot. "Make it your own terms. I leave it to you."

"I wouldn't give you one of those pearls if I never left the island alive," said Leila, looking at him with utter contempt in her eyes.

"You see, Sayers," said Chalmers. "There's your boat."

"I see all right," said the Australian, his face vicious with the sudden hate that flared into it. "It'd please both of you better to stay here honeymooning, I suppose."

Leila shrank back.

"One more word like that, Sayers, and I'll put a bullet through your head as you stand." Chalmers' finger was on the trigger as he spoke.

"All right, then. I'll go. Remember, I gave you a fair chance on your own terms." He waded out to the waiting boat and stepped in.

"You'll keep your hands up until you've passed the cape," said Chalmers.

Sayers spat venomously into the water.

"I'll come back," he said. "I give you warning. And you won't see me coming till I've got the drop on you."

Chalmers laughed.

"Pull away, boys," he said. "Smartly now. Don't drop your oars by any mistake."

The whaleboat swiftly surged down the lagoon, the oars bending under the tug of the demoralized Kanakas, anxious to get clear of the trouble. As it passed out of sight Chalmers turned to Leila. She was leaning on the rifle, shivering as if cold.

"Don't let anything that blackguard said affect you, Leila," he said.

She looked at him with eyes that were cold with rage.

"Why didn't you kill the beast?" she asked, and ran swiftly from him up the beach.

Chalmers followed slowly, perplexed and unhappy, wondering a little why he had not done as she suggested. The man was not fit to live. If he had only been armed!

Ahead of him Leila turned into the archway of her rock house and flung herself face down on the sand. He hesitated, then went on slowly to the caves.

He dismissed the threat of Sayers' last words as idle, but the Australian had brought up more clearly than ever the delicacy of the situation of Leila and himself. Now, he thought, there would be another barrier between them, and he made up his mind to be more circumspect than ever in word and deed.

"Something will have to break soon," he told himself, "with Sayers and Tuan Yuck at odds. I suppose the next thing will be overtures from Tuan Yuck."

XVIII

THE COUNTER CHECK

AN HOUR FROM MIDNIGHT CHALMERS heard the sound of oars and saw from his station on the lava ridge the blur of the whaleboat crossing the lagoon, its progress punctuated by the little spatters of phosphorescence where the oars dipped. The moon was down and it was hard to distinguish figures even through the night-glasses, but he counted four that landed the boat and went up the beach toward the house.

A light appeared in the window. In about fifteen minutes the two natives returned to the boat, lit a fire and disposed themselves to sleep.

Sayers and Tuan Yuck remained in the house. Evidently there was to be no recurrence of last night's debauch. Before long the window was darkened. The enemy was disposed of for the night.

Presently he heard the distant tinkle of the alarm-clock in Leila's cave and hastened down to meet her. He would gladly have eliminated her from the night watching, but he knew that she was happier in doing it, and his own chance to secure a fair measure of sleep increased the element of safety.

He saw the lantern dancing over the sand and between the rocks like a will-o'-the-wisp, though to himself he called it a love-light. She met him with her eyes wide open and sparkling with excitement.

"Twelve o'clock and all's well," he chanted.

"Including your shoulder?" she asked.

"Nearly. It's just sore from hurrying up to heal. I can use my arm well enough. They are asleep, or at least they've turned in for the night. Take the glasses and watch our front door. No need to climb the cliff. Where's the clock?"

"In your cave entrance, set for four o'clock. You are not to be late, sir. I still have my beauty sleep coming to me."

"I think you've had it," he said involuntarily.

Leila applauded with softly clapping palms.

"You're improving," she called after him in a low voice as he strode off, vexed with himself at having crossed the line of neutrality he had set.

The faithful clock awakened him and he sent her back to bed. The stars were still bright, but the mysterious stir of dawn, so prescient in even the loneliest of deserts, was in the air. Imperceptibly the constellations paled and the deep purple of the sky faded. He clambered to the lookout once again. This day, he felt sure, would see some crisis in their affairs, and he wanted to be forehanded.

A light shone in the house. About the dull embers of the fire he could make out the prostrate figures of the Kanakas. They stirred as the man who sleeps in the open always does with the coming of dawn, still half-conscious, then sat up, stretching and rubbing their eyes as a call sounded from the house.

It was Tuan Yuck's voice. He came out, followed by Sayers. In the still morning Chalmers could hear the latter grumbling. The horizon to the east was turning olive-green, with the suggestion of orange beginning to tinge it below the rim of the sea. The golden stars were now white points of light that trembled and disappeared in rapid succession.

The four men busied themselves about the boat and Chalmers picked up his rifle, alert for any advance. The orange turned to salmon color. Little clouds, high up, suddenly flamed to rose. Birds awoke, chirping in the hills. The sun was due.

Sayers was putting on the diving-suit and Chalmers, reassured, set down his rifle. They were going pearling before breakfast. Apparently they had determined to make a thorough prospect of the lagoon. That might mean that they were inclined to give up the attempt for the pearls that Leila held, if they found anything worth while in the fresh shell.

Chalmers had doubted whether Sayers' overtures had been made in good faith, inclined to suspect that it had been a ruse of Tuan Yuck's to get them away from their base. Now the pearling maneuvers puzzled him. It was not like Tuan Yuck to forego a speedy revenge, he thought, and yet the Oriental's infinite capacity for biding his time was hard to estimate.

The boat put off; Sayers, equipped for diving, astride the bows, Tuan Yuck steering, the natives rowing. They proceeded obliquely toward the outer reef, reaching it at a point nearly opposite the lagoon. Tuan Yuck appeared to be giving final directions for Sayers' guidance.

Tomi, at bow oar, handed the Australian an implement that Chalmers guessed was for the purpose of loosening the oysters from their bed. He took it and slipped into the water, hung for a moment by his hands, and disappeared just as the sun showed an arc of red gold above the sea-line and then shot up as if propelled, a dazzling disk of brightness. The bird-chorus swelled. Early gulls wheeled out to sea. It was day.

The boat came back to the beach and landed Tuan Yuck, then returned to the lagoon and drifted, as the Kanakas began to eat. Tuan Yuck walked up the beach to the house. They were breakfasting after all. Sayers, Chalmers reasoned, had probably taken his usual morning's meal out of a glass and bottle. There would be no attack on Safety Haven that morning.

Chalmers went noiselessly up to the caves, intent upon lighting the fire and preparing breakfast while the girl slept. He went to the waterfall and let the cool water cascade upon his head, then filled the kettle.

Fearing that the crackle of the burning twigs might disturb Leila, he made the fire away from the usual place, choosing a spot close to the cliff wall between some fallen boulders. Above him the precipice lifted sheer. Seaward, the lagoon was hidden by rocks, but with Sayers exploring the bottom for oysters and Tuan Yuck doubtless busy emulating his own example of getting breakfast, he had no present fear of interruption. He piled the twigs, struck a match and soon the preliminary smoke of his fire went streaming up the face of the cliff.

If he had followed its ascent he might have marked a yellow face with eyes cruelly intent upon him shining in it like candles through the eyeholes of a mask. Tuan Yuck was lying prone upon a slope that edged the cliff, sprawling at the peril of his life, his feet hooked into a crevice of the rock, his hands taloned about some scrubby growths, straining his neck like a venomous snake about to strike.

Chalmers opened a jar of sliced bacon that he had commandeered from the schooner on their raid, humming a tune below his breath.

Turtle eggs and bacon, coffee and ship's biscuit, a jar of marmalade to follow! He smiled as he thought of Leila's delight at the unexpected tribute to her frankly keen appetite.

On the cliff, Tuan Yuck edged back from the verge and looked at his rifle regretfully. The angle of fire made it useless unless Chalmers ventured away from the face of the precipice. Tuan Yuck's clothing was torn. The climb had been a hard one.

Sayers would not have attempted it, but the Chinaman had believed it feasible and chose it as his part of the attack which was to raise the siege. The excitement of trying the lagoon bed for pearls had put off his attempting it so far, though he had carefully sized up the possibilities of the climb from the deck of the schooner through binoculars.

Now he was here, and for the present, impotent. His eye caught a boulder lying almost loose in its bed near the beginning of the slope. He tested it with his arms, then his shoulders, cautiously. It resisted. Using the butt of his rifle he pried at it again. It shifted a trifle and he smiled evilly. Then his eyes roved seaward. Something was disturbing the water in the narrow lagoon of Safety Haven.

Tuan Yuck squatted on his haunches complacently, as a yellow toad watching for flies. Some one else, as usual, was going to play his game.

The still surface of the lagoon broke silently as a gleaming object appeared, the diving helmet of Sayers. The Australian's shoulders showed, then his body as he advanced, bent from the waist, wading out of the water. In one hand he held the implement which Chalmers had noticed.

He had walked unseen along the bed of the lagoon from the point where he had slid from the boat near the outer reef, perhaps a quarter of a mile of submarine progress, safely hidden beneath an average of eight fathoms. Now he was masked by the maze of boulders from any casual gaze of Chalmers or the girl.

Sayers sat on a low ledge by the water's edge and took off his rubber gauntlets, then his helmet, taking deep breaths. His face was scarlet. It was slow work over the uneven bottom and he had nearly exhausted his supply of air in his endeavor to get as far up the lagoon as possible. He looked cliffward and saw Tuan Yuck, who waved his arms and motioned downward to where the unconscious Chalmers tended his fire.

Sayers wagged one hand in reply and divested himself of the rest of his suit and his heavy shoes. Then he severed the tightly bound cords that wrapped an oilskin coat about the object he had brought ashore and disclosed a rifle. He worked the lever, opening the slide gently to make sure of a cartridge ready for action.

Barefooted and bareheaded, clad in a singlet and trousers, he sprawled full length on the sand and writhed up between the rocks like the reptile he was, carrying the rifle clear of the sand, lifting his head cautiously now and then to take his directions from Tuan Yuck, who stood far enough back to avoid any risk of Chalmers catching sight of him, semaphoring a signal for murder to the Australian.

Chalmers poured the superfluous grease from the frying-pan and set the bacon on some hot ashes. Breakfast was ready.

He stood up to call Leila, looking toward the mouth of her cave, and found her already standing in the entrance, her face frozen into an expression of fear and horror, the rising sun full in her eyes that stared through the blinding rays at something behind Chalmers—a cruel face, blotched with debauchery, the cheek cuddling to a gunstock, an arm stretched across the top of a rock to steady the aim, the rest of the body hidden behind the lava barrier.

"Toss up your hands, —— you! Up with 'em. Don't you stir out of that cave, missy, or I'll spatter his brains against the cliff."

Chalmers turned his head, raising his arms. The tone of the Australian's voice warned him that the threat was not an empty one. Raging inwardly, but impotent, he faced Sayers' taunting face.

"I told you, you wouldn't see me when I came," sneered Sayers with a derisive chuckle. "I suppose you thought you had all the brains, as well as all the virtue, eh! Well, now I've got you where I want you. Too good to associate with me, are you, you and your innocent-faced charmer? Keep your eyes up, too!" he snarled as Chalmers' glance shifted to the rifle slanted against the cliff. "So! Well, I'm going to send you where, if you're as holy as you pretend, you'll be twanging a harp inside of the next minute. Say your prayers, you —— hypocrite, for I've got the drop on you. Don't you move, missy—ah!"

The girl had raised her arm. She held a hand-mirror and the level sun-rays concentrated in its field. The quicksilver flung them back into the bloodshot eyes of Sayers. Dazzled, he flung a hand up in protection.

"Quick, Bruce, the rifle!" shrilled the girl.

Chalmers stooped swiftly. Above, Tuan Yuck, hearing the outcry, pried at the boulder with his riflestock. It left its bed sluggishly, slid down the first slope, braked by the crumbling tufa, and fell, striking Chalmers high upon the shoulders. He crumbled beneath the blow, dropped, the earth whirling, a fiery rush of comets before his eyes, and lay prone, the boulder beside his senseless, prostrate form.

Chalmers came slowly to his senses, his mind, groping through a fog of pain, slowly connecting with the sluggish nerve-centers. He was lying in the sand, his lips gritty with it, salty with his own blood.

Memory asserted itself and he strove to rise. His body from the waist up seemed rigid. His neck when he tried to raise his head burned with agony. But Leila's last cry communicated itself to his rousing faculties, and he persisted, lifting himself on his forearms and looking about him with eyes that gradually regained their function.

The long shadows of the rocks had retreated half their length as he grasped at the rough surface of the lava and dragged himself to his feet. The realization of what had happened came back in a rush while he stood swaying, his dull glance searching for the girl and then for his enemy.

Somewhere in his brain-cells lurked the registration of a shot. He looked for his rifle. It was gone, and his fumbling glance could not find the handle of his automatic in his belt. His wound had reopened and his shirt was drenched with blood. He tried to call to Leila, but his parched throat failed him and there was an intolerable pain where his neck set into his spine.

With his teeth set into his lower lip to prevent his jaw from sagging, he tottered like a drunken man among the rocks, supporting himself by their friendly sides, pistol in hand.

The beach was vacant. A huddled heap of white lay at the water's edge, a burnished mass spread out beside, it like seaweed—or hair. With an inarticulate cry he staggered toward it and fell on his knees beside the unconscious form of Leila.

There were dull marks about her neck, upcurved between the dimpled chin and the huddled bundle of her body. There was a crimson ring about it where the neck ribbon that had held the bag of pearls had been rudely torn away.

With a hoarse cry of rage strangely blended with tenderness, Chalmers gathered her up in his arms, strong for the moment in his fury at the brute who had mishandled her.

Her head fell back, the eyes closed, the long masses of golden-brown hair trailing to the sand. With the last remnants of his strength he bore her to the caves, stumbling at every step, and set her down upon the sand, falling over her on his hands and knees. He chafed her wrists and beat upon her palms, hoarsely, calling her name. Then the sky descended upon him like a pall and he fainted.

XIX

LEILA LOSES HER PEARLS

WHEN HE OPENED HIS EYES AGAIN it was to find Leila bending over him, his head raised in her arms, the pungent smell of brandy assailing his nostrils. He suffered a few burning drops to pass between his lips and swallowed them with difficulty.

It was cool and dark with a light shining somewhere on Leila's face. As she raised his head on her arm and begged him to drink again, he saw bright specks against a field of ebony and realized they were stars. The sting of the brandy in his throat reached his stomach and a delicious warmth spread through him.

"Where am I?" he asked, knowing it was his own voice that spoke, but not recognizing its feeble, faraway tone.

"Thank God," she said, and something warm fell on his upturned face, followed by another drop—Leila's tears.

"Don't cry," he muttered. "I'm all right." The shrill clarion of the alarm-clock sounded. "It's my watch," he said. "I must get up, Leila. They may be coming any minute now."

He took the cup from her in trembling hands and drained it, memory and strength returning.

"Have they gone?" he asked, sitting up with a violent effort. "Get me a rifle."

"Oh, lie down," she said. "Lie down and rest. They've gone. Everything's all right now—now you've come back again."

Her voice quavered and dissolved in tears. He slipped a feeble arm about her.

"Come, Leila, dearest girl," he said. "I'm not hurt. See! Don't cry! Don't cry. I'm fine—just a bit wobbly." He forced a laugh. "Have they really gone? What's happened?"

She got to her knees beside him.

"You must rest," she said. "Wait."

She brought a roll of something soft and placed it under his head.

"It's rotten to be a girl," she said. "To cry like a fool."

"I'm glad you are," he whispered.

She set a cool palm on his lips and he kissed it. She withdrew it, not very quickly.

"You mustn't talk," she said. "I'm going to get you some soup."

But her face glowed as though the lantern-light had been suddenly quadrupled.

"Did they get the pearls?" he asked.

"Yes. Hush!"

She was back in a moment, blowing on a cup of soup, tasting it with puckered lips to test the heat while he lay quiescent, looking at her contentedly. The pearls were gone! In spite of everything, the loss soothed him and brought new vigor to his veins. The barrier was down! Then came the revulsion.

"It was my fault," he said.

"It was not," she protested fiercely. "Tuan Yuck threw down a rock from the cliff. It struck you as you stooped for a rifle. But you must not talk. Take this."

He suffered himself to be fed, spoonful by spoonful, satisfied to have her minister to him. When the cup was ended, he sat up despite her remonstrance.

"I'm fine now," he said. "I'll take some more of that if you have any. My shoulders and neck are stiff, but there's a whole lot of life in me yet."

"Don't sit up, please," she said, slipping her arm about him. "Oh, are you sure you are strong enough? Here's some more broth."

He watched her as she flitted out of the cave and back again.

"Now then," he said, as he finished the second cup, "tell me."

There were hollows under her eyes; he saw faint shadows of them in her cheeks.

"Tell me," he repeated. "Are you sure they're gone?"

"Sure," she answered. "In the schooner. I saw it sailing away."

"They've gone!"

He sat up of his own accord, invigorated at the news.

She brought a box and set it back of him, wadding it with the improvised pillow.

"You drink some of that soup," he ordered; "with some brandy in it. Now!"

She smiled at the assertion in his tone.

"Aye, aye, sir," she answered.

"When the rock hit you," she said presently, "I forgot Sayers and ran toward you. He—Sayers—jumped over the rock and rushed at me. I dodged, thinking perhaps I could get at the rifle, but I was half stupid, thinking you were dead, and he cut me off. His face was horrible. I ran the only way I could, toward the beach, with him after me. If you're going to grit your teeth and get excited," she interrupted herself, "I'll stop talking."

Chalmers relaxed and reached out his hand to grasp hers as she extended it.

"I don't remember what he said," she went on, and Chalmers, seeing by her averted eyes that she lied, reregistered the vow he had already sworn; "but he caught up with me at the water's edge and spun me around with his hand on my shoulder. He put his arms about me and lifted me. I beat at his face and scratched it, but he laughed and crushed me against him. Then I bit him—ugh!" She brushed her free hand across her lips. "He swore at me and started to carry me out into the water. The boat with the natives in it was coming toward us.

"Some one shouted from the cliff—Tuan Yuck. I couldn't hear what he said, but Sayers stopped and turned round. Then Tuan Yuck called again— something about 'leave the girl.' Sayers shouted back. His face was bloody where I had scored it and all asnarl with rage. He swore at Tuan Yuck, and the Chinaman stood up on the edge of the cliff pointing one arm at us, and his voice sounded like a trumpet."

"I wonder why he interfered?" said Chalmers. "What did he say the last time?"

"It wasn't complimentary." Leila smiled at Chalmers, who sat with both fists clenched, the bone of his jaw showing white through the flesh. "But it saved me, or what followed did, though I don't know why he did it. Sayers hesitated for a moment, and a shot plunged into the water beside us. Tuan Yuck stood with his rifle to his shoulder. Sayers cursed again and tore the ribbon from my throat. I hit up at him, and he struck at me—"

"—— him!" said Chalmers. "When I catch up with him I'll kill him with my bare hands."

Leila looked at him with a little thrill of primeval ecstasy. Here was a man who had fought for her, who would kill for her. An ancient strain of savagery surged up within her, the glory of the pristine woman for the protecting male. Then civilization conquered.

"I hope we never see him again," she said with a shudder. "That was all I knew," she went on presently, "till I came to, outside the caves with you by me. The pearls were gone."

It was Chalmers' turn to tell what he knew. He made short work of it.

"And then?" he asked.

"I tried to revive you, but I couldn't. And I was afraid. I was afraid you were going to die. I didn't know how badly you were hurt. I was afraid they would come back. I went to the fall for fresh water after a while, and I saw the schooner standing out to sea, close to the reef, with the natives hauling on the foresail.

"I fell on my knees and thanked God for our deliverance and"—she lowered her voice to a tremulous whisper, dulcet to his ears with its tenderness—"I prayed you might be spared. When I came back you moaned, and presently you went to sleep. Then I knew my prayer was answered."

Chalmers' eyes softened. His hand sought hers. "God bless you, dear," he said.

They sat for a little while in silence.

"Last night," she said after a pause, "I was most afraid of all. There was a terrible earthquake. It kept on, shock after shock, for a long time. The clock stopped. I was afraid the cave would fall in on us. And when it was light, this morning, I saw that part of the big cape—not the one we watched from—had fallen into the sea. And there's a big split in the cliff behind us. The waterfall has almost stopped flowing and I believe the whole island has sunk. The waves came almost up to my rock chambers at high tide and the pool you found for me is full right to the brim."

"A tidal wave," said Chalmers.

"I looked at the pool again this afternoon when you were quietly asleep, and it hadn't gone down."

"Poor Leila! You must have been terribly afraid."

"I was," she smiled rather wanly. "But I'm not now. Only it's so terribly hot I'm afraid it isn't all over."

Chalmers pressed her hand.

"It is hot," he said. "But I'm feverish. You must be, too. What time is it?"

She looked at the clock.

"Half-past three," she announced. "It will soon be morning."

"Why did you set the alarm?"

"I was so sleepy," she confessed shamefacedly, "and I wanted to wake every little while, so I set it."

She swayed wearily and he put his sound arm about her.

"You darling!" he whispered.

She murmured something in return and put up her head to his. Her mouth drooped pitifully, appealingly. Her eyes were wistful, her glance seemed to melt into his, and their lips met.

With a little sigh of absolute comfort she nestled close to him and closed her eyes. He held her tightly, with a savage desire to shield her from all perils, and in a little while her soft breathing told him she was asleep.

Chalmers gradually shifted his position and presently she lay with her body relaxed, her head on his breast, content to know that he had taken up once more the role of protector.

He felt ineffably tender to her, weary as he was. The moments passed, marked by the comfortable ticking of the clock, and soon he himself was asleep beside her. In his dreams, made more real by her presence, he passed with her—always with her—far beyond the rim of ordinary things into a fairyland of perpetual youth and happiness.

It was dark when he opened his eyes again. The air was oppressive on his lungs. The dream had turned to a nightmare of them alone on a turbulent ocean, tossed by the waves.

The nightmare was a reality. The solid earth rocked beneath them. Leila was wide awake, clinging to him in terror. He sat up in the blackness and his hand struck the upset lantern. The glass burnt him. It had only just gone out. Leila's arms were about him.

"An earthquake," she gasped. "I can't breathe. I'm stifling."

"Matches?" he asked.

"By the lantern."

His groping hand found the box. He struck a match that seemed to burn dimly, and relit the lantern. The clock was still going. It was six o'clock—daylight.

Filled with swift dread he arose and held the light above his head. The front of the cave was filled with debris. The cliff had fallen in upon them and blocked their exit. Another tremor threw him headlong, close to where Leila crouched in terror, crying:

"Bruce! Bruce! Where are you? I am so afraid!"

XX
THE LAST OF MOTUTABU

CHALMERS STOOD UP, HOLDING THE LANTERN AT ARM'S LENGTH.

"Why, this is my cave!" he said, surprise in his voice.

"Yes," she answered. "It was the nearer to where you fell. I couldn't lift you. I had hard work getting you here, out of the sun."

"Why, then we can get out of this yet," he said, "unless—"

He began to dig with his hands at the sand.

"Ah!" he cried in a relieved tone, "here they are. I buried them in case they might raid us sometime."

He brought up the extra cartridges for the rifles and automatics.

"I suppose they took the Winchesters while you were senseless," he said. "Sayers wouldn't leave them lying around. He knew we had them, and the automatics. But he didn't find these shells. And there's the rifle I left on top of the ridge. He probably overlooked that."

While he spoke he worked at the smaller calibered cartridges for the pistols, wrenching at the bullets with his back teeth and twisting feverishly to get them free with his fingers, emptying out the powder on to his neckerchief.

"I can do that," said Leila, reaching for a shell.

"No, you can't," he answered. "I'm not going to open all of them. There isn't time. My knife's on the schooner, confound it. It broke off, anyway. Give me that saucepan."

She handed him the pot in which she had brought his broth. He smashed it against the rocky side of the cave and wrenched off the handle.

"Dig a hole with this where you can find loose earth," he said. "Near the bottom of the opening, if you can. You can clear it out with that spoon. Make it as deep as possible. I'm going to try and blast a way out! There isn't air enough in here to waste time."

She set to work diligently, scraping and rasping at the fallen debris. Presently she exclaimed. Her crude tool had broken through into a cavity. She enlarged the hole with the iron spoon and thrust in her arm.

"There's quite a big space here," she said, "but it's all hard rock beyond."

"Never mind. That's more than I hoped for," he replied.

He had moistened half of the powder he had obtained with the soup that remained in the pot and smeared the thick paste heavily upon a long strip torn from the handkerchief. Then he half filled the pot with rifle cartridges and packed sand tightly about them.

"The handle," he said.

Leila passed it to him. It was hollow. He straightened out as best he could the end flattened by the girl's digging, ran his fuse through it, made a space between the cartridges and set into it the stiff cardboard case that had contained the bullets for the pistols. Into this he poured the rest of his powder, carefully placed the end of the fuse into it, ran the tube of the handle down to the top of the case, repiled cartridges closely about it and filled the pot to the brim with sand, ramming it down hard so that the handle projected from it with the other end of the fuse showing loose.

He attacked the opening she had made until it was large enough to pass the pot through to the space she had found, and packed that as tightly as he could with sand and small fragments of rock. The extreme end of the handle he left clear and trailed the remainder of the fuse through a little trench he scraped and bridged over with the thin wood from the boxes which had held the Winchester shells.

With the sweat streaming from him in the close atmosphere of the cave, he filled in the tunnel compactly. Only the extreme end of the fuse now showed dangling from the opening of the groove, the rest leading back to the pot holding the larger shells.

"It's a poor bomb at the best," he said, "but it *is* the best we can do. Come back here, Leila!"

She followed him to the rear of the cave where it turned sharply to the right and ended.

"We'll stand here," he said. "I don't know which way those bullets may fly. I don't know, Leila, exactly what is going to happen. It may bring down more rock and bury us absolutely, but it's the only chance. I hope the fuse works. I haven't made a spit-devil like that since I was a kid."

He tried to speak lightly, but his tone carried the tension he felt.

"Stay here," he told her. "Don't move till I join you. There's no danger."

She had caught at his arm. He gently but firmly released it and hurried back to the fuse, lighting it with a match.

It sputtered, almost died out, then spat sparks bravely. He bounded back to the cave end and stood in front of her, pressing her back against the rock.

He could feel her quick breath on his neck, her heart pounding against him. He reached back both hands and found hers. She gripped them hard.

So they stood silently for what seemed an hour of tense waiting. Chalmers groaned.

"It's gone out," he said. "I'll have to try it again."

The air was hot as well as scant and their lungs burned as they labored. Leila's grasp loosened and her body grew limp against Chalmers.

There was a roar, a concussion of the air that hurled them flat to the back of their rocky alcove and a sound of falling fragments thudding on the sand and against the sides of the cave. The place was full of the salty tang of exploded powder.

Chalmers leaped out into the main cave. Light poured through a jagged hole at the mouth and fresh air stirred the vapor of the powder-smoke. He tore at the opening, eagerly yet carefully, lest he disturb some key-rock of the pile and close the way to liberty once more. The bomb had done its work well and he was soon able to enlarge the aperture enough for exit.

He crawled through, found another pot and raced to the fall for water. There was only a thread left of the cascade, but he half filled the vessel and hurried back with it to where Leila lay at the end of the cave. The dash of it in her face revived her, and his assurance of the success of their mine roused her to her feet to follow him out to the free world once more.

Even on the beach the air was overwarm. The sky was the color of a tarnished copper bowl, the sun fogged to a tawny blue, ray-less and dull. As they stood leaning against the face of the cliff, weak with effort and the foul air of the cave, the ground rocked beneath their feet. A harsh rasping thunder sounded from the hills, the farther headland wavered in its outline and a great mass of it tore apart and fell into the sea.

Leila gasped in terror.

"Come on!" cried Chalmers. "We've got to get out of this!"

He caught her hand and started to run toward the water when a second shock threw them on their faces. It lasted longer than the first, with a recurrence of the grinding thunder in the hills.

He got to his knees. The seas were mounting beyond the reef, high crestless waves of oily brown that rolled across the coral barrier and sent the lagoon water surging far up the sand. Behind them the cliff had split apart showing a raw wedge where protruding rocks quivered and crashed down upon each other in a cloud of red dust.

Then the tremor ended. Thousands of birds wheeled shrieking and squawking above them. The sullen sea slid greasily over the reef and claimed another fathom of beach.

"Come, Leila," he called.

She crouched on the sand with her face buried in her hands. He shook her roughly by the shoulder.

"Come on. I can't carry you. We've got to swim round and get to that launch."

His intentional rudeness roused her. She raised a face blanched with terror, reproach in her eyes.

"The island is sinking," she said. "We can't escape."

"Nonsense," he answered, though his own secret fear matched hers. "Don't be a coward, Leila."

The words stung her like the blow of a whip and she sprang to her feet.

"What am I to do?" she asked, her eyes resolute.

"Swim round the point. Get the boat back here, load it with what we most need, and make for the open sea."

She nodded comprehension and splashed into the lagoon ahead of him, loosening her outer skirt as she went. The back of Chalmers' neck was stiff, but his shoulder had ceased to trouble him and the danger called out all his reserves of strength. Leila reached shore first, racing into the mangroves.

"Here it is," she called, tearing at a thick growth of vines and disclosing the outlines of a twenty-foot whaleboat, staunchly built, covered with canvas. Chalmers, joining her, stripped off the covering.

"Gasoline?" he questioned.

"In drums," she said. "Four of them, back of you."

He freed them from the tangled growth and rolled them away from the boat. The keel was set in the sand and he rocked at it until it loosened.

They slid and dragged the boat over the sand to where a stream ran sluggishly among the mangroves, launching it at last. Then they returned for the gasoline, rolling down the drums and tipping the boat to get them inboard.

There was a water breaker in the stern and Chalmers submerged it in the creek to fill it, first scooping up the water to be sure it was fresh. The creek was shallow and they waded beside their craft, dragging it over the little bar where the stream entered the lagoon and tumbling into the boat as they reached the deeper water.

"Can you row? There's no time to fuss with the engine."

Leila nodded and seized an oar, keeping time to Chalmers' stroke. Well out in the lagoon, rowing furiously back to their own beach, the boat shuddered the length of its keel as if it had struck a shoal, yet kept its momentum. The roar came once more from the interior. The side of a hill wavered, the dense forest glided downward and vanished in a valley, leaving a scar of brown earth where once it had waved in tropical luxuriance. A blind breaker lifted them shoreward, while they tugged to bring the boat bow on, and rolled high up the beach. A second followed and they rode it. The shock was over.

They ran the boat well up the beach, sprang out and hauled it higher for safety from the threatening waves. Already the water was far above the regular boundary of high tide and this should have been the ebb.

They raced up to the caves and swiftly gathered up stores and a few clothes, stowing them away in the boat with frantic speed. Three trips they made, fearful every second of the return of the earthquake.

"That's all," said Chalmers. "I'll get the chronometer and compass. They are in my cave. Stay by the boat."

In the cavern the sight of the unused cartridges reminded him of the Winchester in the lookout. He did not know what perils might be ahead of them and determined to secure it. He gathered up the shells and took them along with the instruments.

"I'm going to get the rifle," he said.

"I'll get it!" cried Leila.

She started to run for the cliff, determinedly forgetful of her fear, bent upon proving to him that she was not a coward.

"Come back!"

As Chalmers called, a wave advanced far beyond its predecessors, clutched at the boat and threatened to set it adrift. He jumped to steady it and Leila was already clambering up the headland before he had it under control. A minute more and she was down again, climbing with the grace and freedom of a young chamois.

"Here it is," she said breathlessly, "and the glasses."

They rowed hard for the reef-opening across the troubled lagoon, indistinguishable now from the outside sea save where the great waves suddenly reared themselves as they reached the wall of the reef. There was nothing to mark the passage, but Chalmers knew the bearings that the earthquake had mercifully spared, and, keeping a tall palm on the first ridge in line with a notch in the farthest hills, they cleared the lagoon and fought their way to the open sea.

A steady wind blew from the land and Chalmers determined to take advantage of it. The engine, installed beneath a roughly built-in but practical and weather-proof hood, needed more time to connect than they had then to spare, so he resolved to set up the mast that lay in the open cockpit by the exposed shaft of the screw, a lug-sail rolled about it.

"Can you take both oars and keep our head to the sea?" he asked Leila.

"Easily," she answered and he passed her his oar, going forward with the mast where he stepped it through the forward thwart and stayed it to the gunwales and hoisted the leg-o'-mutton sail, first reefing it as the wind was appreciably strengthening.

His back was to the girl as he worked, her face, while she tugged at the heavy oars, toward the island.

The breeze caught the sail and filled it. The boat leaped to its impulse and Chalmers prepared to go aft and steer. They were free at last, in a well-built boat that, with careful handling, was well fitted for open sea-work, barring a gale.

Leila uttered a cry and he turned. Above Motutabu a cloud of birds still circled, loath to leave, afraid to stay. Beneath them, as he gazed, the outline of the island changed, the hills crumbled and fell in, the sea seemed to be dashing upon the lower ridges. He sprang aft.

"Ship your oars!" he cried, and as the girl obeyed he seized one of them with which to steer.

The rudder was still unshipped but he knew their danger. Motutabu was sinking into the sea and its disappearance would be inevitably followed by a local storm. Leila covered her eyes.

"It's gone!" she said.

Chalmers knew that her terror was augmented by the memory of her father's grave, once on the hilltop, now beneath the waves. But their peril was too imminent for words.

The waves rose all about them in sudden confusion, tumbling angrily at cross purposes and gradually assuming the circular motion of a whirlpool. A furious wind blew out of where the island had gone down. He blessed the forethought that had made him reef the little sail, striving to prevent the steering oar from being torn from his grasp, and to keep the boat from being drawn into the vortex. They were on the verge of the circle and, aided by the great gusts of wind the little craft fought gallantly up the oily crests, tipped with greasy spume, and down the shifting hollows, where the wind failed for the moment.

At length the mad turmoil of the sea gave place to a regular succession of waves, running strong and high but holding little menace to the buoyant whaleboat. The breeze that had blown them due east from the island gave way to a steady northeast trade and Chalmers hauled their course, sailing as close to the wind as the boat would point.

Giving over the steering oar to Leila for a while, with instructions how to keep it set against the seas, he shipped the rudder and tiller. He had belayed the sail forward; now he ran its sheet aft over the engine housing to where he could handle it from the stern.

"Now we are shipshape," he announced. "If the sea goes down presently we'll overhaul the engine. I'm afraid I'm not much of an expert at it. Are you, Leila?"

"I know something about it. I've run it," she answered apathetically.

Her eyes were darkly circled, but she smiled pluckily back at him.

"Thank you for calling me names, when I funked things on the beach," she said. "I am a coward, you know."

Chalmers flushed.

"I apologize," he said. "And I think you are far braver than I am."

"Then we're even. Where are we going?"

"I think we'd better make the Gilberts. Byron Island, perhaps. That's British. What speed can we make?"

"A little over ten knots."

"Bully! We'll get there in a little over two days, after we get the engine going, if the gasoline holds out. Meanwhile if you'll take the tiller, I'll stow our grub and stuff."

He put away the things in shipshape order and arranged the boat canvas covering so as to turn the engine housing into a cabin. There was plenty of space in the double-ended craft, open save for wooden hood built before and above the engine and the voyage of five hundred miles did not seem so formidable. He set up his compass, arranged his sextant chronometer and then unrolled a chart upon the engine hood to confirm their position before dark.

"We've no log but we can get along without that," he said, as he resumed the tiller. "The Ellice Group is nearer than the Gilberts, perhaps, but I think we'd better tackle the latter. Look at the sunset, Leila. It's like the flare from a volcano. Perhaps it is. There must have been some great disturbance somewhere. Motutabu didn't sink of its own weight."

He talked lightly, hoping to divert her. She smiled faintly at him as she sat drooping on a thwart. It was a frightful position for her, he realized, orphaned, absolutely alone, save for a friend of a few days, racked by her sorrows and the trials they had gone through, dependent upon him for safety and comfort. It was not the moment for love-making nor did he think of it, feeling himself powerless to console her.

"I've fixed up a sort of cabin for you," he said. "Don't you think you'd better lie down for a while. We'll get something to eat presently."

She started to obey listlessly.

"You'll call me for my turn at the rudder," she asked.

"As soon as the sea goes down enough," he said. "It's tricky work in the dark. Try and sleep a little."

She disappeared behind the canvas curtain. Chalmers sat at the tiller, nodding for sleep and shaking his head fiercely to keep awake, tired in every ounce of him. But he remembered the night that she had put the veronal in his broth and watched for him and shook off his drowsiness.

The flaming sky in the west, metallic in its radiance as fire reflected from copper, died down, the seas lessened and a star or two came out. Behind the canvas he could hear Leila sobbing softly.

In a little while weariness had conquered her grief and Chalmers sat alone by the tiller holding the whaleboat to her course away from sunken Motutabu with its pearl lagoon and the grave of the man who discovered it, his eyelids weighted with sleep but his heart stout within him as becomes one who has faced perils and mastered them, not merely for his own sake, but another's.

XXI

Engine Trouble

Leila came aft a little after midnight.

"I'm a pig," she said, "sleeping all this time. But it's done me a world of good aside from making me thoroughly ashamed of myself. How it's cleared up! The stars are wonderful, and I can read the compass by the moon. What's my course, Captain Chalmers?"

The few hours rest had given her a grip on her courage once again and she was her old audacious self.

"Turn in, skipper," she said. "I'll call you at eight bells. You'll have to trust me. We left the poor old alarm-clock behind in the hurry."

He found some clothes arranged to pad the bottom boards and with his head on the same pillow she had used, still fragrant with her hair, floated off into restful unconsciousness.

They had breakfast when she called him and then started to overhaul their engine. Finally adjusted and oiled from a supply they discovered in one of the drums, they filled the gasoline tank, primed it, and Chalmers, practically his own man again, heaved on the fly-wheel. There was a spatter and a buzz and then—inaction. They tried again and again, applying all their mutual knowledge without results, while the boat rocked gently on a breezeless sea.

At last, spattered and smeared with grease, they looked at each other in sympathetic disgust. Leila wrinkled her brows.

"The batteries are all right, we've got a good spark, the cylinders are clean, carburetor's in shape, gasoline I know was strained before it went in the drums. It's just sheer perverseness. It was always like that. It would run like a clock for days and then when you most wanted it, sulk till it got to feeling better."

Chalmers laughed.

"Don't make faces at it," he said. "You look demoniacal with those smuts on your cheeks and chin. Give it a rest."

"You have a large one on your nose," she answered. "I'm not going to give in to the beast."

He straightened up, cramped from stooping over the engine. Then he reached quietly for the binoculars. The field showed him a double canoe, its mat sail flapping above the platform deck that swarmed with men, paddles flashing as the men in the canoes forced the craft along toward them.

"I wonder if they got blown out of their island," he asked himself, "or if it sunk under them like ours. They don't seem particularly friendly. Let's hope it's curiosity, though I don't like the armory. And not wind enough to fill a fan. We're still in the woods."

The canoe was coming up rapidly, the natives brandishing their spears. Chalmers picked up his Winchester, filled the chamber and spilled a lot of cartridges where they would be handy. Leila turned at the rattle they made.

"Your friends, the savages," he said. "It seems we are not out of our troubles. But I'll handle them. I'm not going to let them get within arrow range if I can help it. You've got your hands full with that engine. Coax it. If you can get it to running we can laugh at them. At present we look over-easy."

He sighted, resting the barrel on the gunwale, crouching well down, and fired. The bullet went high through the sail but he depressed his muzzle and the next sang true. One of the savages on the platform tossed up his arms and fell into the sea, while the others yelled and brandished their weapons. A score of arrows whizzed toward the whaleboat but fell short half-way.

Three men were down now but the canoe came on. Fire as he might, they would reach them, with overwhelming numbers, within a minute or two. He began trying to pick off the paddlers, but every time he paused to refill the magazine the gap between them closed ominously.

The barrel burned his fingers. Behind him he sensed Leila throwing over the wheel, repriming the stubborn cylinders, while she talked to the engine as if it were a refractory child. Twice she got a response that failed as soon as it had raised hope.

The arrows were coming thick now, feathering the sides of the boat, singing over him as he crouched.

"Lucky they haven't sense enough to try a dropping shot," he muttered. "Wonder if they're poisoned. Ah! I got you."

A tall Micronesian, bushy-haired, tinkling with brass armlets, who appeared to be the leader, spun about and fell from the deck into one of the canoes. There was instant confusion and the craft halted while Chalmers pumped shot after shot into the mass of them. Then they came on again, only fifty yards away. The air filled with their imprecations.

Just then the engine coughed, snorted, coughed again, and settled down into a steady *puttera-pattera* that was music to Chalmers' ears. The screw churned the water and the whaleboat lurched ahead.

"Keep back there!" he called to Leila. "We'll be out of it in a minute."

He cautiously crawled aft and tossed the loop of a sheet about the tiller to steady it. A howl of rage came from the Micronesians. They plied their paddles at double speed and for a few seconds held their own while the bowmen sped their arrows. But the relenting engine warmed to its work and the whaleboat was soon out of range.

Chalmers gave them a few parting shots.

"Want to try your hand?" he asked Leila jestingly. "Careful with those arrows, they may be poisoned. There's the start of a nice collection for a museum. I'm sorry I ever abused you," he apologized to the engine with a mock bow. "You're all your sales-agent ever claimed for you. Listen to that ragtime purr, Leila. *Puttera-pattera*, my name's Pat. Catch it? Go ahead Pat, and patter along to Byron Island."

Leila laughed at his nonsense as he wanted her to.

"You're much too ridiculous for dignity," she said.

"Do you prefer me dignified?"

"Sometimes. I was quite afraid of you on the island at times, when you ordered me about like a cabin-boy."

"I was afraid of you, too," he confessed.

"Not now?"

"Not now. You're not an heiress any longer."

"Oh!"

"I shouldn't joke about your losing the pearls, Leila, though I'm afraid the chances are slim of ever seeing them again. Do you feel very badly about losing them?"

She looked him squarely in the eyes. Her own held a twinkle, almost an invitation.

"No," she answered. "I'm really rather glad."

Looking at him while she slowly and adorably reddened, she saw his eyes change to a stare of incredulity.

"What is it?" she asked.

"It seems incredible," he said, "but it's the schooner. And she's headed this way, as much as the wind will let her. She's hardly got steerageway. There's something wrong aboard of her. The sheets are hauled in and there's no one at the wheel, apparently. Give me the glasses.

"There's some one now in the bows. It's Hamaku. He's waving a cloth. There's Tomi, beside him. They don't know who we are."

"You'll not go near them?"

"I'll go near enough to find out what's up. They wouldn't be coming back for nothing. There must be something that's upset your calculations. I've got a score to even with Sayers. Your pearls are aboard."

"I told you I didn't want them. Don't go near them."

"You lost the pearls through my fault, Leila. I should have thought of that diving-suit. It's not going to be my fault if you don't get them back again."

He spoke with decision. It was his duty, as he considered it, to recover Leila's fortune, and he tingled at the hope of getting his eyes on Sayers. Leila sat silent as he steered the launch toward the schooner. As they neared it he called out to Hamaku.

The native started as he heard his name, spoke to Tomi, peered at the launch from under his hand and sprang into the water from the bowsprit, swimming swiftly toward them.

"Eh, Kapitani," he said as his fingers clutched the gunwale. "Eyah, Kapitani, plenty pilikea aboard."

"Climb in," ordered Chalmers.

The dripping Hamaker came lithely overside and sat on the thwart his skipper indicated. His face was drawn and gray instead of its usual healthy brown, and his body twitched.

"Now then," said Chalmers. "Out with it."

"*Sayasi* (Sayers), he *make* (dead). Tuan Yuck he nearly *make*, too. One, two night ago they play cards together for pearl. Last night Tuan Yuck he win—everything. Sayasi he laugh and call for gin. I bring. Sayasi he say, 'All right, you too smart for me.' Then very quick he pull out gun and shoot Tuan Yuck. Big Boss he fall on floor and not move. Sayasi he got up and laugh some more. Then he take big drink of gin. Me, I keep back where he not see me. So then Sayasi he kneel along Tuan Yuck on floor and he say, 'Last man he laugh more loud.' Tuan Yuck open his eyes and say, 'Yes, —— you.' He strike at Sayasi with knife quick like that, all same cat. Knife he cut Sayasi all through stomach. He *make*, right away. Too much blood he lose.

"Tuan Yuck he no can move his legs. He make me pick him up and put him in cabin. He no eat. All the time smoke *lele* pipe. Very soon I think he die. So I frighten. I try make boat go along back Motutabu."

Chalmers looked at the native searchingly. It was evident he was telling the truth. He restarted the engine and ran alongside the schooner. Tomi came to the side, his eyes bulging with terror.

"God bless it, you come Kapitani," he said. "Too much *pilikea*."

"Up you swarm, Hamaku," commanded Chalmers, "and get out the side-ladder. You'll stay here for a few minutes, won't you please?" he asked Leila.

"Yes," she answered, pale at the mental picture of Sayers lying in his own blood on the cabin floor, much as she hated him.

The two natives under Chalmers' orders rolled the stiffened form into canvas and sewed it into a rude sacking. This they weighed with ballast and carried it up the companionway, where they slid it quietly into the sea from the opposite rail to which the launch lay. Then they cleared up the cabin while Chalmers went for Leila. The door of Tuan Yuck's room was closed.

When he came down with the girl, Chalmers, armed with the automatic that he had picked up on the cabin floor close to the dead body, opened Tuan Yuck's door.

The Chinaman lay in his bunk, smoking. His skin had the look of dirty wax; his glittering eyes seemed to have lost their luster.

"Ah!" he said as Chalmers entered. "So you have the last trick after all. Our Australian friend got me with his pistol, the same one you hold, I fancy. I'm done for, Chalmers. You couldn't do anything for me if you would. The spine's injured. I'm partly paralyzed. More every hour. I can just raise my arms to smoke. It's a good vice. It helps."

"Where are the pearls?" asked Chalmers.

"So mercenary! Where are they? Ask me after I'm dead, Chalmers. I won't tell you while I'm alive."

His eyes held a mocking light.

"Are you there, Miss Denman," he called. "I did you a good turn once when I made Sayers leave you behind. I did it selfishly. I didn't want to be bothered with a woman. You see I figured on winning out from Sayers. It was clumsy of me to lose. Now do me a favor in return. Leave me alone until the end. It won't be long."

"We will, if you tell us where the pearls are," said Chalmers.

A smile that was half sneer broke the mask of Tuan Yuck's face. His voice had grown feebler.

"I've hidden them, Chalmers. They're aboard. But I don't think you'll find them, even though you search me after I am dead. But if you look in the right place you'll find them."

His eyes held an impenetrable enigma as he puffed at his metal pipe with its bamboo stem and jade mouthpiece. His eyes closed. Only the movement of his chest and the curl of the acrid smoke that issued from his lips showed life was still in his body.

Chalmers hesitated. He could not torture a dying man. Leila set a hand on his arm.

"Come away," she said. "We do not care about the pearls."

Half an hour later Hamaku came hurriedly on deck.

"Kapitani, you come quick," he said.

Tuan Yuck was dead in his bunk, his jaw fallen. A lacquered box lay on the counterpane between his nerveless fingers.

"I hear noise," said Hamaker. "I come in quick. He try to swallow pearl. I think he choke. Look!"

He put his fingers into the dead man's mouth and drew out half a dozen of the pearls. The rest were in the box and spilled upon the covering of the bunk. Tuan Yuck's last trick had failed him.

The wind was fair and the schooner sailed as if eager to leave latitudes that had held so much of danger and distress. Leila, in reaction from the terrific strain to which she had been subjected, kept closely to the cabin Chalmers overhauled for her.

He himself was glad of long lazy hours in the sunshine, drowsing off the consequences of his own ordeal. His shoulder had healed almost completely, thanks to the magic of Leila's ointment, and the stiffness and pain at the base of his neck disappeared as the great bruise made by the falling boulder took on all the colors of a dying dolphin.

On the afternoon of the third day, Leila, a little languid, but smiling, faced him on deck. In her hand she held the little lacquered box.

"I want you to take half these pearls," she said and frowned as Chalmers shook his head.

"I insist. You've saved them time and time again. If you don't, I swear, I'll toss them overboard this minute."

He temporized but the girl was determined. She walked to the rail and held her hand with the box in its palm above the water.

"Promise," she said.

Her eyes looked at him tenderly, invitingly, wistfully. They held a hundred variants of the one theme in their liquid depths. And in those depths Chalmers' last remnants of pride dissolved.

"I'll take them," he said, "but I'll give them back to you again."

She stepped backward, her face changing.

"Why?" she faltered.

"As a wedding-present, sweetheart," he whispered.

OFF-TRAIL PUBLICATIONS
Specializing in the era of American pulp fiction

THE WEIRD DETECTIVE ADVENTURES OF WADE HAMMOND
By Paul Chadwick
Volume 1: 10 stories, 180 pages, $18
Volume 2: 10 stories, 172 pages, $18
Volume 3: 10 stories, 202 pages, $18
Volume 4: 9 stories, 232 pages, $18

> *The Wade Hammond stories complete in four volumes. In these chilling adventures, all from the classic 1930's pulps,* Detective-Dragnet *and* Ten Detective Aces, *freelance investigator Wade Hammond battles a series of weird enemies. Some of the best of '30s pulp fiction.*

DOCTOR COFFIN: The Living Dead Man
By Perley Poore Sheehan • Introduction by John Wooley
8 novelettes, 178 pages, $16

> *Weird stories from* Thrilling Detective, *1932-33. A former character actor who faked his own death, Doctor Coffin runs a string of mortuaries by night and fights crime at night. One of the strangest detective series.*

SUPER-DETECTIVE FLIP BOOK: Two Complete Novels
From the pulp *Super-Detective*:
"Legion of Robots" (November 1940) by Victor Rousseau • Introduction by John McMahan •• "Murder's Migrants" (March 1943) by Robert Leslie Bellem and W.T. Ballard • Introduction by John Wooley
2 short novels, 174 pages, $18

> Super-Detective *started as a Doc Savage-like adventure pulp, then changed format to hardboiled detective. The* Flip Book *features a novel from each of the two phases with intros exploring the historical background. Exciting!*

AMAZON STORIES
Volume 1: Pedro & Lourenço
Volume 2: Pedro & Lourenço
By Arthur O. Friel • Introductions by John Locke
Vol 1: 10 stories, 222 pages, $18 • **Vol 2**: 10 stories, 286 pages, $20

Collects Friel's first twenty stories from Adventure *(1919-21), following the strange experiences of two Amazon Basin rubber workers as they explore the jungle. The best of pulp adventure fiction.*

GROTTOS OF CHINATOWN: The Dorus Noel Stories
By Arthur J. Burks • Introduction by John Locke
11 stories, 194 pages, $16

The complete adventures of Dorus Noel from All Detective Magazine *(1933-34). Burks' Manhattan Chinatown is a place of dark mystery, riddled with secret passageways, menaced by hatchetmen. Introduction discusses the history of* All Detective *and the career of the Speed-King of the Pulps, Arthur J. Burks.*

THE GOLDEN ANACONDA: And Other Strange Tales of Adventure
By Elmer Brown Mason • Introduction by John Locke
10 stories, 260 pages, $20

Fantastic and horror-laden stories set in the exotic corners of the world known to their globe-trotting entomologist author. Includes all five Wandering Smith stories from The Popular Magazine; *and five tales from* All-Story Weekly. *All published, 1915-16.*

CITY OF NUMBERED MEN: The Best of Prison Stories
Introduction by John Locke
12 stories, 278 pages, $20

During Prohibition, famed publisher Harold Hersey turned America's disintegrating prison system into the hardboiled Prison Stories *(1930-31). Included are stories from all issues of this rare pulp, the startling history of* Prison Stories, *cover gallery, and the first comprehensive biography of pulp publishing's most colorful character, Harold Hersey.*

THE MAGICIAN DETECTIVE: And Other Weird Mysteries
By Fulton Oursler
Introduction by John Locke
7 stories, 210 pages, $18

> *Fulton Oursler was one of the great editors of his time, ruling over the Macfadden publishing empire for two decades. But stage magic was his first love. In this collection of early fiction, Oursler's bewitching imagination takes flight in tales of magic, murder and mystery. Featured is an exploration of the astonishing career of Fulton Oursler.*

GHOST STORIES: The Magazine and Its Makers
Edited by John Locke
Vol 1: 19 stories, 256 pages, $24 • **Vol 2**: 15 stories, 272 pages, $24

> *Macfadden's* Ghost Stories *(1926-31) presented haunted tales in every exciting arena: the Western Front, gangland, aviation, the Klondike, the circus, etc. The personnel behind* Ghost Stories *were a fascinating group: poets and scholars, war heroes and war correspondents, adventurers and Bohemians; a few became prolific pulpsters; a few became bestselling authors. And a few led haunted lives. Vol 1 includes the history of* Ghost Stories, *bios of every editor, and every Vol 1 author. Vol 2 includes bios of every Vol 2 author, every cover artist, and a gallery of all 64* Ghost Stories *covers.*

HOBO STORIES
By Patrick & Terence Casey • Introduction by John Locke
6 stories, 332 pages, $20

> *The Caseys were two brothers from San Francisco who broke into the pulps while still teenagers. Within a few years, they had conned their way into the prestigious pages of* Adventure. Hobo Stories *reprints their series of exploits of a teenage hobo and his dog from* The Saturday Evening Post *(1914) and* Adventure *(1916-21). Included is their story of a teenage pulp writer from* Romance *(1920); and a lengthy introduction which explores the lives of the Caseys and the origins of their hobo stories.*

OUTDOOR STORIES
By J. Allan Dunn • Introduction by John Locke
3 stories, 190 pages, $16

Presented are all three of Dunn's tales from the ultra-rare Outdoor Stories *(1927-28). These gripping adventures, set in the exotic places of another day, rank with Dunn's best. The featured story, "New Guinea Gold," is an epic tale of friendship, survival and revenge. Included is a history of* Outdoor Stories, *a biography of editor Edmund C. Richards, and an examination of Dunn's role in the magazine.*

THE PERIL OF THE PACIFIC
By J. Allan Dunn • Introduction by John Locke
Complete 5-part serial, 168 pages, $14

Dunn's Japanese invasion epic is future history, published as a five-part serial in People's *in 1916, but set in 1920.* Peril *pits a force of American irregulars armed with futuristic technology against a relentless naval empire bent on conquest. Dunn uses San Francisco and California's Central Coast as his main settings, drawing upon his well-traveled past more than in any other story he ever published.*

IF SHE ONLY HAD A MACHINE GUN: Crime Stories by Richard Credicott
Introductions by Dave Credicott & John Locke
Edited by John Locke & Rob Preston
18 stories, 360 pages, $20

The complete stories of one of the best gang-pulp authors. Includes gang stories from Racketeer Stories, Mobs, *etc., wildly entertaining tales of mob intrigue and mayhem, and the violent whims of molls; and detective stories from* The Dragnet, Dime Detective, *and others. All from 1929-33. A complete biographical profile offers rare insights into the pulps during the early years of the Depression. As a special feature, Dave Credicott provides reminiscences of his father's life.*

QUEEN OF THE GANGSTERS: Volume 1: Broadwalk Empire
Introductions by David Bischoff & John Locke
8 stories, 234 pages, $18

Tough, rough, remorseless stories from the first woman hardboiled crime fiction writer; from gang pulps like Gangland Stories, Racketeer Stories *and* Mobs. *Margie Harris slammed her typewriter like a machine gun, mowing down good guys and bad guys alike; shooting them, knifing them, blowing them up—lacing her prose with metaphysical commentary on the destinations of their damned souls. This is the first time her work has been collected. Introduction from bestselling author David Bischoff.*

THE OCEAN: 100th Anniversary Collection
Edited by John Locke
20 stories, 234 pages, $18

Munsey's The Ocean *(1907-08) was one of the first specialized pulps, a sea-story magazine. The best adventure stories are included here, along with 30+ pages of nonfiction material: a history of the pulp, and extensive author profiles.*